More praise for
DEFEND AND BETRAY

"In this wonderful novel, master storyteller Anne Perry moves closer to Dickens as she lifts the lace curtain from Victorian society to reveal its shocking secrets."
—SHARYN MCCRUMB

"[A] richly textured re-creation of a bygone age. . . Culminat[es] in an explosive courtroom confrontation in which a shameful secret is finally revealed."
—*The San Diego Union-Tribune*

"A richly detailed period atmosphere . . . revealing social and moral nuances in the grand tradition of the Victorian novel."
—*Publishers Weekly*

"Wonderful . . . Rich period detailing, masterful characterizations, subtle romantic subplots, disturbing flashbacks, and powerful courtroom drama recommend this."
—*Library Journal*

"Marvelous . . . A totally absorbing novel that completely hooks the reader. The storyline is a heartbreaker, and only the most hardened reader will have a dry eye at the end of this tale."
—*Rave Reviews*

Also by Anne Perry
Published by Ivy Books:

Featuring Inspector William Monk
THE FACE OF A STRANGER
A DANGEROUS MOURNING

Published by Fawcett Books:

Featuring Thomas and Charlotte Pitt
THE CATER STREET HANGMAN
CALLANDER SQUARE
PARAGON WALK
RESURRECTION ROW
BLUEGATE FIELDS
RUTLAND PLACE
DEATH IN THE DEVIL'S ACRE
CARDINGTON CRESCENT
SILENCE IN HANOVER CLOSE
BETHLEHEM ROAD
HIGHGATE RISE
BELGRAVE SQUARE

DEFEND AND BETRAY

A Victorian Mystery featuring Inspector Monk

Anne Perry

IVY BOOKS • NEW YORK

Ivy Books
Published by Ballantine Books
Copyright © 1992 by Anne Perry

All rights reserved under International and Pan-American Copyright Conventions. Published in the United States by Ballantine Books, a division of Random House, Inc., New York, and simultaneously in Canada by Random House of Canada Limited, Toronto.

Library of Congress Catalog Card Number: 92-52665

ISBN 0-8041-1188-X

Manufactured in the United States of America

First Hardcover Edition: October 1992
First Mass Market Edition: October 1993

To my father

With thanks to Jonathan Manning,
B.A. (Cantab.), for advice on points of law
regarding manslaughter, perverse
verdicts, etc. in 1857.

1

HESTER LATTERLY ALIGHTED from the hansom cab. A two-seater vehicle for hire by the trip, it was a recent and most useful invention enabling one to travel much more cheaply than having to hire a large carriage for the day. Fishing in her reticule, she found the appropriate coin and paid the driver, then turned and walked briskly along Brunswick Place towards Regent's Park, where the daffodils were in full bloom in gold swaths against the dark earth. So they should be; this was April the twenty-first, a full month into the spring of 1857.

She looked ahead to see if she could discern the tall, rather angular figure of Edith Sobell, whom she had come to meet, but she was not yet visible among the courting couples walking side by side, the women's wide crinoline skirts almost touching the gravel of the paths, the men elegant and swaggering very slightly. Somewhere in the distance a band was playing something brisk and martial, the notes of the brass carrying in the slight breeze.

She hoped Edith was not going to be late. It was she who had requested this meeting, and said that a walk in the open would be so much pleasanter than sitting inside in a chocolate shop, or strolling around a museum or a gallery where Edith at least might run into acquaintances and be obliged to interrupt her conversation with Hester to exchange polite nonsense.

Edith had all day in which to do more or less as she pleased; indeed, she had said time hung heavily on her hands. But Hester was obliged to earn her living. She was presently employed as a nurse to a retired military gentleman who had fallen and broken his thigh. Since being dismissed from the hospital where she had first found a position on returning from the Crimea—for taking matters into her own hands and treating a patient in the absence of the doctor—Hester had been fortunate to find private positions. It was only her experience in Scutari with Florence Nightingale, ended barely a year since, which had made any further employment possible at all.

The gentleman, Major Tiplady, was recovering well, and had been quite amenable to her taking an afternoon off. But she was loth to spend it waiting in Regent's Park for a companion who did not keep her appointments, even on so pleasant a day. Hester had seen so much incompetence and confusion during the war, deaths that could have been avoided had pride and inefficiency been set aside, that she had a short temper where she judged such failings to exist, and a rather hasty tongue. Her mind was quick, her tastes often unbecomingly intellectual for a woman; such qualities were not admired, and her views, whether right or wrong, were held with too much conviction. Edith would need a very fine reason indeed if she were to be excused her tardiness.

Hester waited a further fifteen minutes, pacing back and forth on the path beside the daffodils, growing more and more irritated and impatient. It was most inconsiderate behavior, particularly since this spot had been chosen for Edith's convenience; she lived in Clarence Gardens, a mere half mile away. Perhaps Hester was angry out of proportion to the offense, and even as her temper rose she was aware of it, and still unable to stop her gloved fists from clenching or her step from getting more rapid and her heels from clicking sharply on the ground.

She was about to abandon the meeting altogether when at

2

last she saw the gawky, oddly pleasing figure of Edith. She was still dressed predominantly in black, still in mourning for her husband, although he had been dead nearly two years. She was hurrying along the path, her skirts swinging alarmingly and her bonnet so far on the back of her head as to be in danger of falling off altogether.

Hester started towards her, relieved that she had come at last, but still preparing in her mind a suitable reproach for the wasted time and the inconsideration. Then she saw Edith's countenance and realized something was wrong.

"What is it?" she said as soon as they met. Edith's intelligent, eccentric face, with its soft mouth and crooked, aquiline nose, was very pale. Her fair hair was poking out untidily from under her bonnet even more than would be accounted for by the breeze and her extremely hasty progress along the path. "What has happened?" Hester demanded anxiously. "Are you ill?"

"No . . ." Edith was breathless and she took Hester's arm impulsively and continued walking, pulling Hester around with her. "I think I am quite well, although I feel as if my stomach were full of little birds and I cannot collect my thoughts."

Hester stopped without disengaging her arm. "Why? Tell me, what is it?" All her irritation vanished. "Can I help?"

A rueful smile crossed Edith's mouth and disappeared.

"No—except by being a friend."

"You know I am that," Hester assured her. "What has happened?"

"My brother Thaddeus—General Carlyon—met with an accident yesterday evening, at a dinner party at the Furnivals'."

"Oh dear, I am sorry. I hope it was not serious. Is he badly hurt?"

Incredulity and confusion fought in Edith's expression. She had a remarkable face, not in any imagination beautiful, yet there was humor in the hazel eyes and sensuality in the mouth, and its lack of symmetry was more than made up for by the quickness of intelligence.

3

"He is dead," she said as if the word surprised even herself.

Hester had been about to begin walking again, but now she stood rooted to the spot. "Oh my dear! How appalling. I am so sorry. However did it happen?"

Edith frowned. "He fell down the stairs," she said slowly. "Or to be more accurate, he fell over the banister at the top and landed across a decorative suit of armor, and I gather the halberd it was holding stabbed him through the chest. . . ."

There was nothing for Hester to say except to repeat her sympathy.

In silence Edith took her arm and they turned and continued again along the path between the flower beds.

"He died immediately, they say," Edith resumed. "It was an extraordinary chance that he should fall precisely upon the wretched thing." She shook her head a little. "One would think it would be possible to fall a hundred times and simply knock it all over and be badly bruised, perhaps break a few bones, but not be speared by the halberd."

They were passed by a gentleman in military uniform, red coat, brilliant gold braid and buttons gleaming in the sun. He bowed to them and they smiled perfunctorily.

"Of course I have never been to the Furnivals' house," Edith went on. "I have no idea how high the balcony is above the hallway. I suppose it may be fifteen or twenty feet."

"People do have most fearful accidents on stairs," Hester agreed, hoping the remark was helpful and not sententious. "They can so easily be fatal. Were you very close?" She thought of her own brothers: James, the younger, the more spirited, killed in the Crimea; and Charles, now head of the family, serious, quiet and a trifle pompous.

"Not very," Edith replied with a pucker between her brows. "He was fifteen years older than I, so he had left home, as a junior cadet in the army, before I was born. I was only eight when he married. Damaris knew him better."

"Your elder sister?"

"Yes—she is only six years younger than he is." She stopped. "Was," she corrected.

Hester did a quick mental calculation. That would have made Thaddeus Carlyon forty-eight years old now, long before the beginning of old age, and yet still far in excess of the average span of life.

She held Edith's arm a little closer. "It was good of you to come this afternoon. If you had sent a footman with a message I would have understood completely."

"I would rather come myself," Edith answered with a slight shrug. "There is very little I can do to help, and I admit I was glad of an excuse to be out of the house. Mama is naturally terribly distressed. She shows her feelings very little. You don't know her, but I sometimes think she would have been a better soldier than either Papa or Thaddeus." She smiled to show the remark was only half meant, and even then obliquely and as an illustration of something she did not know how else to express. "She is very strong. One can only guess what emotions there are behind her dignity and her command of herself."

"And your father?" Hester asked. "Surely he will be a comfort to her."

The sun was warm and bright, and hardly a breeze stirred the dazzling flower heads. A small dog scampered between them, yapping with excitement, and chased along the path, grabbing a gentleman's cane in its teeth, much to his annoyance.

Edith drew breath to make the obvious answer to Hester's remark, then changed her mind.

"Not a lot, I should think," she said ruefully. "He is angry that the whole thing has such an element of the ridiculous. It is not exactly like falling in battle, is it?" Her mouth tightened in a sad little smile. "It lacks the heroic."

Hester had not thought of it before. She had been too aware of the reality of death and loss, having experienced the sudden and tragic deaths of her younger brother and both her parents within a year of each other. Now she visualized General Carlyon's accident and realized precisely what Edith meant. To fall over the banister at a dinner party and spear yourself on the halberd of an empty suit of armor was hardly a glorious military death. It might take a better man than his father, Colonel Carlyon, not to feel a certain resentment and sting to family pride. She said nothing of it, but she could not keep from her mind the thought that perhaps the general had been a great deal less than sober at the time.

"I imagine his wife is very shocked," she said aloud. "Had they family?"

"Oh yes, two daughters and a son. Actually, both daughters are older and married, and the younger was present at the party, which makes it so much worse." Edith sniffed sharply, and Hester could not tell if it was a sign of grief, anger, or merely the wind, which was decidedly cooler across the grass now they were out of the shelter of the trees.

"They had quarreled," Edith went on. "According to Peverell, Damaris's husband. In fact, he said it was a perfectly ghastly party. Everyone seemed to be in a fearful temper and at each other's throats half the evening. Both Alexandra, Thaddeus's wife, and Sabella, his daughter, quarreled with him both before dinner and over the table. And with Louisa Furnival, the hostess."

"It sounds very grim," Hester agreed. "But sometimes family differences can seem a great deal more serious than they really are. I know, it can make the grief afterwards much sharper, because quite naturally it is added to by guilt. Although I am sure the dead know perfectly well that we do not mean many of the things we say, and that under the surface there is a love far deeper than any momentary temper."

Edith tightened her grip in gratitude.

"I know what you are trying to say, my dear, and it is not unappreciated. One of these days I must have you meet Alexandra. I believe you would like her, and she you. She married young and had children straightaway, so she has not experienced being single, nor had any of the adventures you have. But she is of as independent a mind as her circumstances allow, and certainly not without courage or imagination.''

"When it is suitable I shall be delighted,'' Hester agreed, although she was not in truth looking forward to spending any of her very precious free time in the company of a recent widow, however courageous. She saw more than sufficient pain and grief in the course of her profession. But it would be gratuitously unkind to say so now, and she was genuinely fond of Edith and would have done much to please her.

"Thank you.'' Edith looked sideways at her. "Would you think me unforgivably callous if I spoke of other things?''

"Of course not! Had you something special in mind?''

"My reason for making an appointment to meet you where we could speak without interruption, and instead of inviting you to my home,'' Edith explained, "is that you are the only person I can think of who will understand, and who might even be able to help. Of course in a little while I will be needed at home for the present, now this terrible thing has happened. But afterwards . . .''

"Yes?''

"Hester, Oswald has been dead for close to two years now. I have no children.'' A flicker of pain crossed her features, showing her vulnerable in the hard spring light, and younger than her thirty-three years. Then it was gone again, and resolve replaced it. "I am bored to distraction,'' she said with a firm voice, unconsciously increasing her pace as they turned on the path that led down to a small bridge over ornamental water and on towards the Royal Botanical Society Gardens. A small girl was throwing bread to the ducks.

"And I have very little money of my own,'' Edith went on. "Oswald left me too little to live on, in anything like the way I am accustomed, and I am dependent upon my parents—which is the only reason I still live at Carlyon House.''

"I assume you have no particular thoughts on marrying again?''

Edith shot her a look of black humor, not without self-mockery.

"I think it is unlikely,'' she said frankly. "The marriage

7

market is drenched with girls far younger and prettier than I, and with respectable dowries. My parents are quite content that I should remain at home, a companion for my mother. They have done their duty by me in finding one suitable husband. That he was killed in the Crimea is my misfortune, and it is not incumbent upon them to find me another—for which I do not hold them in the least to blame. I think it would be an extremely difficult task, and in all probability a thankless one. I would not wish to be married again, unless I formed a profound affection for someone.''

They were side by side on the bridge. The water lay cool and cloudy green below them.

''You mean fell in love?'' Hester said.

Edith laughed. ''What a romantic you are! I would never have suspected it of you.''

Hester ignored the personal reference. ''I am relieved. For a fearful moment I thought you were going to ask me if I could introduce you to anyone.''

''Hardly! I imagine if you knew anyone you could whole-heartedly recommend, you would marry him yourself.''

''Do you indeed?'' Hester said a trifle sharply.

Edith smiled. ''And why not? If he were good enough for me, would he not also be good enough for you?''

Hester relaxed, realizing she was being very gently teased.

''If I find two such gentlemen, I shall tell you,'' she conceded generously.

''I am delighted.''

''Then what is it I may do for you?''

They started up the gentle incline of the farther bank.

''I should like to find an occupation that would keep my interest and provide a small income so that I may have some financial independence. I realize,'' Edith put in quickly, ''that I may not be able to earn sufficient to support myself, but even an increment to my present allowance would give me a great deal more freedom. But the main thing is, I cannot bear sitting at home stitching embroidery no one needs, painting pictures I have neither room nor inclination to hang,

8

and making endless idiotic conversation with Mama's callers. It is a waste of my life.''

Hester did not reply straightaway. She understood the emotion and the situation profoundly. She had gone to the Crimea because she wanted to contribute to the effort towards the war, and to relieve the appalling conditions of the men freezing, starving, and dying of wounds and disease in Sebastopol. She had returned home in haste on hearing of the deaths of both her parents in the most tragic circumstances. Very soon after, she had learned that there was no money, and although she had accepted the hospitality of her surviving brother and his wife for a short time, it could not be a permanent arrangement. They would have agreed, but Hester would have found it intolerable. She must find her own way and not be an added burden upon their strained circumstances.

She had come home on fire to reform nursing in England, as Miss Nightingale had in the Crimea. Indeed most of the women who had served with her had espoused the same cause, and with similar fervor.

However, Hester's first and only hospital appointment had ended in dismissal. The medical establishment was not eager to be reformed, least of all by opinionated young women, or indeed by women at all. And considering that no women had ever studied medicine, and such an idea was unthinkable, that was not to be wondered at. Nurses were largely unskilled, employed to wind bandages, fetch and carry, dust, sweep, stoke fires, empty slops and keep spirits high and morality above question.

"Well?" Edith interrupted. "Surely it is not a hopeless cause." There was a lightness in her voice but her eyes were earnest, full of both hope and fear, and Hester could see she cared deeply.

"Of course not," she said soberly. "But it is not easy. Too many occupations, of the forms that are open to women, are of a nature where you would be subject to a kind of discipline and condescension which would be intolerable to you."

"You managed," Edith pointed out.

"Not indefinitely," Hester corrected. "And the fact that you are not dependent upon it to survive will take a certain curb from your tongue which was on mine."

"Then what is left?"

They were standing on the gravel path between the flowers, a child with a hoop a dozen yards to the left, two little girls in white pinafores to the right.

"I am not sure, but I shall endeavor to find out," Hester promised. She stopped and turned to look at Edith's pale face and troubled eyes. "There will be something. You have a good hand, and you said you speak French. Yes, I remember that. I will search and enquire and let you know in a few days' time. Say a week or so. No, better make it a little longer, I would like to have as complete an answer as I can."

"A week on Saturday?" Edith suggested. "That will be May the second. Come to tea."

"Are you sure?"

"Yes of course. We shall not be entertaining socially, but you are coming as a friend. It will be quite acceptable."

"Then I shall. Thank you."

Edith's eyes widened for a moment, giving her face a brightness, then she clasped Hester's hand quickly and let it go, turning on her heel and striding along the path between the daffodils and down towards the lodge without looking back.

Hester walked for another half hour, enjoying the air before returning to the street and finding another hansom to take her back to Major Tiplady and her duties.

The major was sitting on a chaise longue, which he did under protest, considering it an effeminate piece of furniture, but he enjoyed being able to stare out of the window at passersby, and at the same time keep his injured leg supported.

"Well?" he asked as soon as she was in. "Did you have a pleasant walk? How was your friend?"

Automatically she straightened the blanket around him.

"Don't fuss!" he said sharply. "You didn't answer me.

How was your friend? You did go out to meet a friend, didn't you?"

"Yes I did." She gave the cushion an extra punch to plump it up, in spite of his catching her eye deliberately. It was a gentle banter they had with each other, and both enjoyed it. Provoking her had been his best entertainment since he had been restricted to either his bed or a chair, and he had developed a considerable liking for her. He was normally somewhat nervous of women, having spent most of his life in the company of men and having been taught that the gentle sex was different in every respect, requiring treatment incomprehensible to any but the most sensitive of men. He was delighted to find Hester intelligent, not given to fainting or taking offense where it was not intended, not seeking compliments at every fit and turn, never giggling, and best of all, quite interested in military tactics, a blessing he could still hardly believe.

"And how is she?" he demanded, glaring at her out of brilliant pale blue eyes, his white mustache bristling.

"In some shock," Hester replied. "Would you like tea?"

"Why?"

"Because it is teatime. And crumpets?"

"Yes I would. Why was she shocked? What did you say to her?"

"That I was very sorry," Hester smiled with her back to him, as she was about to ring the bell. It was not part of her duty to cook—fortunately, because she had little skill at it.

"Don't prevaricate with me!" he said hotly.

Hester rang the bell, then turned back to him and changed her expression to one of sobriety. "Her brother met with a fatal accident last evening," she told him. "He fell over the banister and died immediately."

"Good gracious! Are you sure?" His face was instantly grave, his pink-and-white skin as usual looking freshly scrubbed and innocent.

"Perfectly, I am afraid."

"Was he a drinking man?"

"I don't believe so. At least not to that extent."

11

The maid answered the summons and Hester requested tea and hot crumpets with butter. When the girl had gone, she continued with the story. "He fell onto a suit of armor, and tragically the halberd struck his chest."

Tiplady stared at her, still not totally sure whether she was exercising some bizarre female sense of humor at his expense. Then he realized the gravity in her face was quite real.

"Oh dear. I am very sorry." He frowned. "But you cannot blame me for not being sure you were entirely serious. It is a preposterous accident!" He hitched himself a little higher on the chaise longue. "Have you any idea how difficult it is to spear a man with a halberd? He must have fallen with tremendous force. Was he a very large man?"

"I have no idea." She had not thought about it, but now that she did, she appreciated his view. To have fallen so hard and so accurately upon the point of a halberd held by an inanimate suit of armor, in such a way that it penetrated through clothes into the flesh, and between the ribs into the body, was an extraordinary chance. The angle must have been absolutely precise, the halberd wedged very firmly in the gauntlet, and as Major Tiplady said, the force very great indeed. "Perhaps he was. I had never met him, but his sister is tall, although she is very slight. Maybe he was of a bigger build. He was a soldier."

Major Tiplady's eyebrows shot up. "Was he?"

"Yes. A general, I believe."

The major's face twitched with an amusement he found extreme difficulty in concealing, although he was perfectly aware of its unsuitability. He had recently developed a sense of the absurd which alarmed him. He thought it was a result of lying in bed with little to do but read, and too much company of a woman.

"How very unfortunate," he said, staring at the ceiling. "I hope they do not put on his epitaph that he was finally killed by impaling himself upon a weapon held by an empty suit of armor. It does seem an anticlimax to an outstanding military career, and to smack of the ridiculous. And a general too!"

"Seems not at all unlikely for a general to me," Hester said tartly, remembering some of the fiascoes of the Crimean War, such as the Battle of the Alma, where men were ordered first one way and then the other, and were finally caught in the river, hundreds dying unnecessarily; not to mention Balaclava, where the Light Brigade, the flower of the English cavalry, had charged into the mouths of the Russian guns and been mown down like grass. That was a nightmare of blood and slaughter she would never forget, nor the succeeding days and nights of sleepless labor, helplessness and pain.

Suddenly Thaddeus Carlyon's death seemed sadder, more real, and at the same time far less important.

She turned back to Major Tiplady and began straightening the blanket over his legs. He was about to protest, then he recognized the quite different quality in her expression and submitted wordlessly. She had changed from a pleasant and efficient young woman, whom he liked, into the army nurse she used to be such a short time since, seeing death every day and hideously aware of the magnitude and the futility of it.

"You said he was a general." He watched her with a pucker between his brows. "What was his name?"

"Carlyon," she replied, tucking in the ends of the blanket firmly. "Thaddeus Carlyon."

"Indian Army?" he asked, then before she could reply, "Heard of a Carlyon out there, stiff sort of fellow, but very much admired by his men. Fine reputation, never backed down in the face of the enemy. Not all that fond of generals myself, but pity he should die like that."

"It was quick," she said with a grimace. Then for several moments she busied herself around the room, doing largely unnecessary things, but the movement was automatic, as if remaining still would have been an imprisonment.

Finally the tea and crumpets came. Biting into the crisp, hot dough and trying to stop the butter from running down her chin, she relaxed and returned to the present.

She smiled at him.

"Would you like a game of chess?" she offered. She was

exactly skilled enough to give him a good game without beating him.

"Oh I would," he said happily. "Indeed I would."

Hester spent her free time for the next several days in pursuing possible opportunities for Edith Sobell, as she had promised. She did not think nursing offered any openings Edith would find either satisfying or indeed available to her. It was regarded as a trade rather than a profession, and most of the men and women employed in it were of a social class and an education, or lack of it, which resulted in their being regarded with scant respect, and paid accordingly. Those who had been with Miss Nightingale, now a national heroine only a little less admired than the Queen, were viewed differently, but it was too late for Edith to qualify for that distinction. And even though Hester herself most definitely did qualify, she was finding employment hard enough, and her opinions little valued.

But there were other fields, especially for someone like Edith, who was intelligent and well-read, not only in English literature but also in French. There might well be some gentleman who required a librarian or an assistant to research for him whatever subject held his interest. People were always writing treatises or monographs, and many needed an assistant who would perform the labor necessary to translate their ideas into a literary form.

Most women who wished a lady companion were intolerably difficult and really only wanted a dependent whom they could order around—and who could not afford to disagree with them. However, there were exceptions, people who liked to travel but did not find it pleasurable to do so alone. Some of these redoubtable women would be excellent employers, full of interest and character.

There was also the possibility of teaching; if the pupils were eager and intelligent enough it might be highly rewarding.

Hester explored all these areas, at least sufficiently to have something definite to tell Edith when she accepted the invitation to go to Carlyon House for afternoon tea on May the second.

Major Tiplady's apartments were at the southern end of Great Titchfield Street, and therefore some distance from Clarence Gardens, where Carlyon House was situated. Although she could have walked, it would have taken her the better part of half an hour, and she would have arrived tired and overheated and untidy for such an engagement. And she admitted with a wry humor that the thought of afternoon tea with the elder Mrs. Carlyon made her more than a little nervous. She would have cared less had Edith not been her friend; then she could have been free to succeed or fail without emotional damage. As it was, she would rather have faced a night in military camp above Sebastopol than this engagement.

However there was no help for it now, so she dressed in her best muslin afternoon gown. It was not a very glamorous affair, but well cut with pointed waist and softly pleated bodice, a little out of date, though only a lady of fashion would have known it. The faults lay all in the trimmings. Nursing did not allow for luxuries. When she went to bid Major Tiplady good-bye, he regarded her with approval. He had not the least idea of fashion and very pretty women terrified him. He found Hester's face with its strong features very agreeable, and her figure, both too tall and a little too thin, to be not at all displeasing. She did not threaten him with aggressive femininity, and her intellect was closer to that of a man, which he rather liked. He had never imagined that a woman could become a friend, but he was being proved wrong, and it was not in any way an experience he disliked.

"You look very . . . tidy," he said with slightly pink cheeks.

From anyone else it would have infuriated her. She did not wish to look tidy; tidiness was for housemaids, and junior ones at that. Even parlormaids were allowed to be handsome; indeed, they were required to be. But she knew he meant it well, and it would be gratuitously cruel to take exception,

15

however much *distinguished* or *appealing* would have been preferred. *Beautiful* was too much to hope for. Her sister-in-law, Imogen, was beautiful—and appealing. Hester had discovered that very forcefully when that disastrous policeman Monk had been so haunted by her last year during the affair in Mecklenburg Square. But Monk was an entirely different matter, and nothing to do with this afternoon.

"Thank you, Major Tiplady," she accepted with as much grace as she could. "And please be careful while I am away. If you wish for anything, I have put the bell well within your reach. Do not try to get up without calling Molly to assist you. If you should"—she looked very severe—"and you fall again, you could find yourself in bed for another six weeks!" That was a far more potent threat than the pain of another injury, and she knew it.

He winced. "Certainly not," he said with affronted dignity.

"Good!" And with that she turned and left, assured that he would remain where he was.

She hailed a hansom and rode along the length of Great Titchfield Street, turned into Bolsover Street and went along Osnaburgh Street right into Clarence Gardens—a distance of approximately a mile—and alighted a little before four o'clock. She felt ridiculously as if she were about to make the first charge in a battle. It was absurd. She must pull herself together. The very worst that could happen would be embarrassment. She ought to be able to cope with that. After all, what was it—an acute discomfort of the mind, no more. It was immeasurably better than guilt, or grief.

She sniffed hard, straightened her shoulders and marched up the front steps, reaching for the bell pull and yanking it rather too hard. She stepped back so as not to be on the very verge when the door was opened.

It happened almost immediately and a smart maid looked at her enquiringly, her pretty face otherwise suitably expressionless.

"Yes ma'am?"

16

"Miss Hester Latterly, to see Mrs. Sobell," Hester replied. "I believe she is expecting me."

"Yes of course, Miss Latterly. Please come in." The door opened all the way and the maid stepped aside to allow her past. She took Hester's bonnet and cloak.

The hallway was as impressive as she had expected it to be, paneled with oak to a height of nearly eight feet, hung with dark portraits framed in gilt with acanthus leaves and curlicues. It was gleaming in the light from the chandelier, lit so early because the oak made it dim in spite of the daylight outside.

"If you please to come this way," the maid requested, going ahead of her across the parquet. "Miss Edith is in the boudoir. Tea will be served in thirty minutes." And so saying she led Hester up the broad stairs and across the first landing to the upper sitting room, reserved solely for the use of the ladies of the house, and hence known as the boudoir. She opened the door and announced Hester.

Edith was inside staring out of the window that faced the square. She turned as soon as Hester was announced, her face lighting with pleasure. Today she was wearing a gown of purplish plum color, trimmed with black. The crinoline was very small, almost too insignificant to be termed a crinoline at all, and Hester thought instantly how much more becoming it was—and also how much more practical than having to swing around so much fabric and so many stiff hoops. She had little time to notice much of the room, except that it was predominantly pink and gold, and there was a very handsome rosewood escritoire against the far wall.

"I'm so glad you came!" Edith said quickly. "Apart from any news you might have, I desperately need to talk of normal things to someone outside the family."

"Why? Whatever has happened?" Hester could see without asking that something had occurred. Edith looked even more tense than on their previous meeting. Her body was stiff and her movements jerky, with a greater awkwardness than usual, and she was not a graceful woman at the best of

17

times. But more telling was the weariness in her and the total absence of her usual humor.

Edith closed her eyes and then opened them wide.

"Thaddeus's death is immeasurably worse than we first supposed," she said quietly.

"Oh?" Hester was confused. How could it be worse than death?

"You don't understand." Edith was very still. "Of course you don't. I was not explaining myself at all." She took a sudden sharp breath. "They are saying it was not an accident."

"They?" Hester was stunned. "Who is saying it?"

"The police, of course." Edith blinked, her face white. "They say Thaddeus was murdered!"

Hester felt momentarily a little dizzy, as though the room with its gentle comfort had receded very far away and her vision was foggy at the edges, Edith's face sharp in the center and indelible in her mind.

"Oh my dear—how terrible! Have they any idea who it was?"

"That is the worst part," Edith confessed, for the first time moving away and sitting down on the fat pink settee.

Hester sat opposite her in the armchair.

"There were only a very few people there, and no one broke in," Edith explained. "It had to have been one of them. Apart from Mr. and Mrs. Furnival, who gave the party, the only ones there who were not my family were Dr. Hargrave and his wife." She swallowed hard and attempted to smile. It was ghastly. "Otherwise it was Thaddeus and Alexandra; their daughter Sabella and her husband, Fenton Pole; and my sister, Damaris, and my brother-in-law, Peverell Erskine. There was no one else there."

"What about the servants?" Hester said desperately. "I suppose there is no chance it could have been one of them."

"What for? Why on earth would one of the servants kill Thaddeus?"

Hester's mind raced. "Perhaps he caught them stealing?"

"Stealing what—on the first landing? He fell off the balcony of the first landing. The servants would all be downstairs at that time in the evening, except maybe a ladies' maid."

"Jewelry?"

"How would he know they had been stealing? If they were in a bedroom he wouldn't know it. And if he saw them coming out, he would only presume they were about their duties."

That was totally logical. Hester had no argument. She searched her mind and could think of nothing comforting to say.

"What about the doctor?" she tried.

Edith flashed a weak smile at her, appreciating what she was attempting.

"Dr. Hargrave? I don't know if it's possible. Damaris did tell me what happened that evening, but she didn't seem very clear. In fact she was pretty devastated, and hardly coherent at all."

"Well, where were they?" Hester had already been involved in two murders, the first because of the deaths of her own parents, the second through her acquaintance with the policeman William Monk, who was now working privately for anyone who required relatives traced, thefts solved discreetly, and other such matters dealt with in a private capacity, where they preferred not to engage the law or where no crime had been committed. Surely if she used her intelligence and a little logic she ought to be of some assistance.

"Since they assumed at first that it was an accident," she said aloud, "surely he must have been alone. Where was everyone else? At a dinner party people are not wandering around the house individually."

"That's just it," Edith said with increasing unhappiness. "Damaris made hardly any sense. I've never seen her so . . . so completely . . . out of control. Even Peverell couldn't calm or comfort her—she would scarcely speak to him."

"Perhaps they had a . . ." Hester sought for some polite way of phrasing it. "Some difference of opinion? A misunderstanding?"

19

Edith's mouth twitched with amusement. "How euphemistic of you. You mean a quarrel? I doubt it. Peverell really isn't that kind of person. He is rather sweet, and very fond of her." She swallowed, and smiled with a sudden edge of sadness, as of other things briefly remembered, perhaps other people. "He isn't weak at all," she went on. "I used to think he was. But he just has a way of dealing with her, and she usually comes 'round—in the end. Really much more satisfactory than ordering people. I admit he may not be an instant great passion, but I like him. In fact, the longer I know him the more I like him. And I rather think she feels the same." She shook her head minutely. "No, I remember the way she was when she came home that evening. I don't think Peverell had anything to do with it."

"What did she say about where people were? Thaddeus— I beg your pardon, General Carlyon—fell, or was pushed, over the banister from the first landing. Where was everyone else at the time?"

"Coming and going," Edith said hopelessly. "I haven't managed to make any sense of it. Perhaps you can. I asked Damaris to come and join us, if she remembers. But she doesn't seem to know what she's doing since that evening."

Hester had not met Edith's sister, but she had heard frequent reference to her, and it seemed that either she was emotionally volatile and somewhat undisciplined or she had been judged unkindly.

At that moment, as if to prove her a liar, the door opened and one of the most striking women Hester had ever seen stood framed by the lintel. For that first moment she seemed heroically beautiful, tall, even taller than Hester or Edith, and very lean. Her hair was dark and soft with natural curl, unlike the present severe style in which a woman's hair was worn scraped back from the face with ringlets over the ears, and she seemed to have no regard for fashion. Indeed her skirt was serviceable, designed for work, without the crinoline hoops, and yet her blouse was gorgeously embroidered and woven with white ribbon. She had a boyish air about her, neither coquettish nor demure, simply blazingly candid. Her face was long, her features so mobile and sensitive they reflected her every thought.

She came in and closed the door, leaning against it for a moment with both hands behind her and regarding Hester with a frankly interested stare.

"You are Hester Latterly?" she asked, although the question was obviously rhetorical. "Edith said you were coming this afternoon. I'm so glad. Ever since she told me you went to the Crimea with Miss Nightingale, I have been longing to meet you. You must come again, when we are more ourselves, and tell us about it." She flashed a sudden illuminating smile. "Or tell me, anyway. I'm not at all sure Papa would approve, and I'm quite certain Mama would not. Far too independent. Rocks the foundations of society when women don't know their proper place—which, of course, is at home, keeping civilization safe for the rest of us."

She walked over to a neo-rococo love seat and threw herself on it utterly casually. "Seeing we learn to clean our teeth every day," she went on. "Eat our rice pudding, speak correctly, never split infinitives, wear our gloves at all the appropriate times, keep a stiff upper lip whatever vicissitudes we may find ourselves placed in, and generally set a good example to the lower classes—who depend upon us for precisely this." She was sitting sideways over the seat. For anyone else it would have been awkward, but for her it had a kind of grace because it was so wholehearted. She did not care greatly what others thought of her. Yet even in this careless attitude there was an ill-concealed tension in her, and Hester could easily imagine the frenzied distress Edith had spoken of.

Now Damaris's face darkened again as she looked at Hester.

"I suppose Edith has told you about our tragedy—Thaddeus's death—and that they are now saying it was murder?" Her brow furrowed even more deeply. "Although I can't imagine why anyone should want to kill Thaddeus." She turned to Edith. "Can you? I mean, he was a terrible bore at times, but most men are. They think all the wrong

21

things are important. Oh—I'm sorry—I do mean most men, not all!" Suddenly she had realized she might have offended Hester and her contrition was real.

"That is quite all right." Hester smiled. "I agree with you. And I daresay they feel the same about us."

Damaris winced. "Touché. Did Edith tell you about it?"

"The dinner party? No—she said it would be better if you did, since you were there." She hoped she sounded concerned and not unbecomingly inquisitive.

Damaris closed her eyes and slid a little farther down on her unorthodox seat.

"It was ghastly. A fiasco almost from the beginning." She opened her eyes again and stared at Hester. "Do you really want to know about it?"

"Unless you find it too painful." That was not the truth. She wanted to know about it regardless, but decency, and compassion, prevented her from pressing too hard.

Damaris shrugged, but she did not meet Hester's eyes. "I don't mind talking about it—it is all going on inside my head anyway, repeating over and over again. Some parts of it don't even seem real anymore."

"Begin at the beginning," Edith prompted, curling her feet up under her. "That is the only way we have a hope of making any sense of it. Apparently someone did kill Thaddeus, and it is going to be extremely unpleasant until we find out who."

Damaris shivered and shot her a sour glance, then addressed Hester.

"Peverell and I were the first to arrive. You haven't met him, but you will like him when you do." She said it unselfconsciously and without desire for effect, simply as a comment of fact. "At that time we were both in good spirits and looking forward to the evening." She lifted her eyes to the ceiling. "Can you imagine that? Do you know Maxim and Louisa Furnival? No, I don't suppose you do. Edith says you don't waste time in Society."

Hester smiled and looked down at her hands in her lap to avoid meeting Edith's eyes. That was a charmingly euphemistic way of putting it. Hester was too old to be strictly marriageable, well over twenty-five, and even twenty-five was optimistic. And since her father had lost his money before his death, she had no dowry, nor any social background worth anyone's while to pursue. Also she was of an unbecomingly direct character and both held and expressed too many opinions.

"I have no time I can afford to waste," she answered aloud.

"And I have too much," Edith added.

Hester brought them back to the subject. "Please tell me something of the Furnivals."

Damaris's face lost its momentary look of ease.

"Maxim is really quite agreeable, in a brooding, dark sort of way. He's fearfully decent, and he manages to do it without being stuffy. I often felt if I knew him better he might be quite interesting. I could easily imagine falling madly in love with him—just to know what lies underneath—if I didn't already know Peverell. But whether it would stand a close acquaintance I have no idea." She glanced at Hester to make sure she understood, then continued, staring up at the molded and painted ceiling. "Louisa is another matter altogether. She is very beautiful, in an unconventional way, like a large cat—of the jungle sort, not the domestic. She is no one's tabby. I used to envy her." She smiled ruefully. "She is very small. She can be feminine and look up at any man at all—where I look down on far more than I wish. And she is all curves in the most flattering places, which I am not. She has very high, wide cheekbones, but when I stopped being envious, and looked a little more closely, I did not care for her mouth."

"You are not saying much of what she is like, Ris," Edith prompted.

"She is like a cat," Damaris said reasonably. "Sensuous, predatory, and taking great care of her own, but utterly charming when she wishes to be."

Edith looked across at Hester. "Which tells you at least

that Damaris doesn't like her very much. Or that she is more than a trifle envious.''

"You are interrupting," Damaris said with an aloof air. "The next to arrive were Thaddeus and Alexandra. He was just as usual, polite, pompous and rather preoccupied, but Alex looked pale and not so much preoccupied as distracted. I thought then that they must have had a disagreement over something, and of course Alex had lost.''

Hester nearly asked why "of course," then realized the question was foolish. A wife would always lose, particularly in public.

"Then Sabella and Fenton came," Damaris continued. "That's Thaddeus's younger daughter and her husband," she explained to Hester. "Almost immediately Sabella was rude to Thaddeus. We all pretended we hadn't noticed, which is about all you can do when you are forced to witness a family quarrel. It was rather embarrassing, and Alex looked very . . ." she searched for the word she wanted. ". . . very brittle, as though her self-control might snap if she were pressed too hard." Her face changed swiftly, and a shadow passed over it. "The last ones to arrive were Dr. Hargrave and his wife." She altered her position slightly in the chair, with the result that she was no longer facing Hester. "It was all very polite, and trivial, and totally artificial.''

"You said it was ghastly." Edith's eyebrows rose. "You don't mean you sat around through the entire evening being icily civil to each other. You told me Thaddeus and Sabella quarreled and Sabella behaved terribly, and Alex was white as a sheet, which Thaddeus either did not even notice—or else pretended not to. And that Maxim was hovering over Alex, and Louisa obviously resented it.''

Damaris frowned, her shoulders tightening. "I thought so. But of course it may simply have been that it was Maxim's house and he felt responsible, so he was trying to be kind to Alex and make her feel better, and Louisa misunderstood.'' She glanced at Hester. "She likes to be the center of attention and wouldn't appreciate anyone being so absorbed in someone else. She was very scratchy with Alex all evening.''

"You all went in to dinner?" Hester prompted, still searching for the factual elements of the crime, if the police were correct and there had been one.

"What?" Damaris knitted her brows, staring at the window. "Oh—yes, all on each other's arms as we had been directed, according to the best etiquette. Do you know, I can't even remember what we ate." She lifted her shoulders a little under the gorgeous blouse. "It could have been bread pudding for all I tasted. After the desserts we went to the withdrawing room and talked nonsense while the men passed the port, or whatever men do in the dining room when the women have gone. I've often wondered if they say anything at all worth listening to." She looked up at Hester quickly. "Haven't you?"

Hester smiled briefly. "Yes I have. But I think it may be one of those cases where the truth would be disappointing. The mystery is far better. Did the men rejoin you?"

Damaris grimaced in a strange half smile, rueful and ironic. "You mean was Thaddeus still alive then? Yes he was. Sabella went upstairs to be alone, or I think more accurately to sulk, but I can't remember when. It was before the men came in, because I thought she was avoiding Thaddeus."

"So you were all in the withdrawing room, apart from Sabella?"

"Yes. The conversation was very artificial. I mean more so than usual. It's always pretty futile. Louisa was making vicious little asides about Alex, all with a smooth smile on her face, of course. Then Louisa rose and invited Thaddeus to go up and visit Valentine—" She gave a quick little gasp as if she had choked on something, and then changed it into a cough. "Alex was furious. I can picture the look on her face as if I had only just seen it."

Hester knew Damaris was speaking of a subject about which she felt some deep emotion, but she had no idea why, or quite what emotion it was. But there was little point in pressing the matter at all if she stopped now.

"Who is Valentine?"

Damaris's voice was husky as she answered. "He is the Furnivals' son. He is thirteen—nearly fourteen."

"And Thaddeus was fond of him?" Hester said quietly.

"Yes—yes he was." Her tone had a kind of finality and her face a bleakness that stopped Hester from asking any more. She knew from Edith that Damaris had no children of her own, and she had enough sensitivity to imagine the feelings that might lie behind those words. She changed the subject and brought it back to the immediate.

"How long was he gone?"

Damaris smiled with a strange, wounded humor.

"Forever."

"Oh." Hester was more disconcerted than she was prepared for. She felt dismay, and for a moment she was robbed of words.

"I'm sorry," Damaris said quickly, looking at Hester with wide, dark eyes. "Actually I don't know. I was absorbed in my own thoughts. Some time. People were coming and going." She smiled as if there were some punishing humor in that thought. "Maxim went off for something, and Louisa came back alone. Alex went off too, I suppose after Thaddeus, and she came back. Then Maxim went off again, this time into the front hall—I should have said they went up the back stairs to the wing where Valentine has his room, on the third floor. It is quicker that way."

"You've been up?"

Damaris looked away. "Yes."

"Maxim went into the front hall?" Hester prompted.

"Oh—yes. And he came back looking awful and saying there had been an accident. Thaddeus had fallen over the banister and been seriously hurt—he was unconscious. Of course we know now he was dead." She was still looking at Hester, watching her face. Now she looked away again. "Charles Hargrave got up immediately and went to see. We all sat there in silence. Alex was as white as a ghost, but she had been most of the evening. Louisa was very quiet; she turned and went, saying she was fetching Sabella down, she ought to know her father had been hurt. I can't really remember what else happened till Charles—Dr. Hargrave—came back to say Thaddeus was dead, and of course we would have to report it. No one should touch anything."

"Just leave him there?" Edith said indignantly. "Lying on the floor in the hallway, tangled up with the suit of armor?"

"Yes . . ."

"They would have to." Hester looked from one to the other of them. "And if he was dead it wouldn't cause him any distress. It is only what we think . . ."

Edith pulled a face, but said nothing more, curling her legs up a little higher.

"It's rather absurd, isn't it?" Damaris said very quietly. "A cavalry general who fought all over the place being killed eventually by falling over the stairs onto a halberd held by an empty suit of armor. Poor Thaddeus—he never had any sense of humor. I doubt he would have seen the funny side of it."

"I'm sure he wouldn't." Edith's voice broke for a moment, and she took a deep breath. "And neither would Papa. I wouldn't mention it again, if I were you."

"For heaven's sake!" Damaris snapped. "I'm not a complete fool. Of course I won't. But if I don't laugh I think I shall not be able to stop crying. Death is often absurd. People are absurd. I am!" She sat up properly and swiveled around straight in the seat, facing Hester.

"Someone murdered Thaddeus, and it had to be one of us who were there that evening. That's the awful thing about it all. The police say he couldn't have fallen onto the point of the halberd like that. It would never have penetrated his body—it would just have gone over. He could have broken his neck, or his back, and died. But that was not what happened. He didn't break any bones in the fall. He did knock his head, and almost certainly concuss himself, but it was the halberd through the chest that killed him—and that was driven in after he was lying on the ground."

She shivered. "Which is pretty horrible—and has not the remotest sort of humor about any part of it. Isn't it silly how we have this quite offensive desire to laugh at all the worst

27

and most tragic things? The police have already been around asking all sorts of questions. It was dreadful—sort of unreal, like being inside a magic lantern show, except that of course they don't have stories like that.''

"And they haven't come to any conclusions?" Hester went on relentlessly, but how else could she be of any help? They did not need pity; anyone could give them that.

"No." Damaris looked grim. "It seems several of us would have had the opportunity, and both Sabella and Alex had obviously quarreled with him recently. Others might have. I don't know." Then suddenly she stood up and smiled with forced gaiety.

"Let us go in to tea. Mama will be angry if we are late, and that would spoil it all."

Hester obeyed willingly. Apart from the fact that she thought they had exhausted the subject of the dinner party, at least for the time being, she was most interested in meeting Edith's parents, and indeed she was also ready for tea.

Edith uncurled herself, straightening her skirts, and followed them downstairs, through the big hall and into the main withdrawing room, where tea was to be served. It was a magnificent room. Hester had only a moment in which to appreciate it, since her interest, as well as her manners, required she give her attention to the occupants. She saw brocaded walls with gilt-framed pictures, an ornate ceiling, exquisitely draped curtains in claret-colored velvet with gold sashes, and a darker patterned carpet. She caught sight of two tall bronzes in highly ornate Renaissance style, and had a dim idea of terra-cotta ornaments near the mantel.

Colonel Randolf Carlyon was sitting totally relaxed, almost like a man asleep, in one of the great armchairs. He was a big man gone slack with age, his ruddy-skinned face partially concealed by white mustache and side whiskers, his pale blue eyes tired. He made an attempt to stand as they came in, but the gesture died before he was on his feet, a half bow sufficing to satisfy etiquette.

Felicia Carlyon was as different as was imaginable. She was perhaps ten years younger than her husband, no more than her mid-sixties, and although her face showed a certain strain, a tightness about the mouth and shadows around the large, deep-set eyes, there was nothing in the least passive or defeated about her. She stood in front of the walnut table on which tea was laid, her body still slender and rigidly upright with a deportment many a younger woman would have envied. Naturally she was wearing black in mourning for her son, but it was handsome, vivid black, well decorated with jet beading and trimmed with black velvet braid. Her black lace cap was similarly fashionable.

She did not move when they came in, but her glance went straight to Hester, and Hester was intensely aware of the force of her character.

"Good afternoon, Miss Latterly," Felicia said graciously, but without warmth. She reserved her judgment of people; her regard had to be earned. "How pleasant of you to come. Edith has spoken most kindly of you."

"Good afternoon, Mrs. Carlyon," Hester replied equally formally. "It is gracious of you to receive me. May I offer you my deepest sympathies for your loss."

"Thank you." Felicia's complete composure and the brevity with which she accepted made it tactless to add anything further. Obviously she did not wish to discuss the subject; it was deeply personal, and she did not share her emotions with anyone. "I am pleased you will take tea with us. Please be comfortable." She did not move her body, but the invitation was implicit.

Hester thanked her again and sat, not in the least comfortably, on the dark red sofa farthest from the fire. Edith and Damaris both seated themselves and introductions were completed, Randolf Carlyon contributing only what was required of him for civility.

They spoke of the merest trivialities until the maid came with the last of the dishes required for tea, paper-thin sandwiches of cucumber, watercress and cream cheese, and finely chopped egg. There were also French pastries and cake with cream and jam. Hester looked at it with great appreciation, and wished it were an occasion on which it would be acceptable to eat heartily, but knew unquestionably that it was not.

When tea had been poured and passed Felicia looked at her with polite enquiry.

"Edith tells me you have traveled considerably, Miss Latterly. Have you been to Italy? It is a country I should have liked to visit. Unfortunately at the time when it would have been suitable for me, we were at war, and such things were impossible. Did you enjoy it?"

Hester wondered for a frantic moment what on earth Edith could have said, but she dared not look at her now, and there was no evading an answer to Felicia Carlyon. But she must protect Edith from having appeared to speak untruthfully.

"Perhaps I was not clear enough in my conversation with Edith." She forced a slight smile. She felt like adding "ma'am," as if she were speaking to a duchess, which was absurd. This woman was socially no better than herself—or at least than her parents. "I regret my traveling was in the course of war, and anything but educational in the great arts of Italy. Although I did put in to port there briefly."

"Indeed?" Felicia's arched eyebrows rose, but it would be immeasurably beneath her to allow her good manners to be diverted. "Did war oblige you to leave your home, Miss Latterly? Regrettably we seem to have trouble in so many parts of the Empire at the moment. And they speak of unrest in India as well, although I have no idea whether that is serious or not."

Hester hesitated between equivocation and the truth, and decided truth would be safer, in the long run. Felicia Carlyon was not a woman to overlook an inconsistency or minor contradiction.

"No, I was in the Crimea, with Miss Nightingale." That magic name was sufficient to impress most people, and it was the best reference she had both as to character and worth.

"Good gracious," Felicia said, sipping her tea delicately.

"Extraordinary!" Randolf blew out through his whiskers.

"I think it is fascinating." Edith spoke for the first time

30

since coming into the withdrawing room. "A most worth-while thing to do with one's life."

"Traveling with Miss Nightingale is hardly a lifetime occupation, Edith," Felicia said coolly. "An adventure, per-haps, but of short duration."

"Inspired by noble motives, no doubt," Randolf added. "But extraordinary, and not entirely suitable for a—a—" He stopped.

Hester knew what he had been going to say; she had met the attitude many times before, especially in older soldiers. It was not suitable for gentlewomen. Females who followed the army were either enlisted men's wives, laundresses, ser-vants, or whores. Except the most senior officers' ladies, of course, but that was quite different. They knew Hester was not married.

"Nursing has improved immensely in the last few years," she said with a smile. "It is now a profession."

"Not for women," Felicia said flatly. "Although I am sure your work was very noble, and all England admires it. What are you doing now you are home again?"

Hester heard Edith's indrawn breath and saw Damaris swiftly lower her eyes to her plate.

"I am caring for a retired military gentleman who has broken his leg quite severely," Hester answered, forcing her-self to see the humor of the situation rather than the offense. "He requires someone more skilled in caring for the injured than a housemaid."

"Very commendable," Felicia said with a slight nod, sip-ping at her tea again.

Hester knew implicitly that what she did not add was that it was excellent only for women who were obliged to support themselves and were beyond a certain age when they might reasonably hope for marriage. She would never countenance her own daughters descending to such a pass, as long as there was a roof over their heads and a single garment to put on their backs.

Hester made her smile even sweeter.

"Thank you, Mrs. Carlyon. It is most gratifying to be of

31

use to someone, and Major Tiplady is a gentleman of good family and high reputation.''

''Tiplady . . .'' Randolf frowned. ''Tiplady? Can't say I ever heard of him. Where'd he serve, eh?''

''India.''

''Funny! Thaddeus, my son, you know, served in India for years. Outstanding man—a general, you know. Sikh Wars—'45 to '46, then again in '49. Was in the Opium Wars in China in '39 as well. Very fine man! Everyone says so. Very fine indeed, if I do say so. Son any man would be proud of. Never heard him mention anyone called Tiplady.''

''Actually I believe Major Tiplady was sent to Afghanistan—the Afghan Wars of '39 and '42. He talks about it sometimes. It is most interesting.''

Randolf looked at her with mild reproof, as one would a precocious child.

''Nonsense, my dear Miss Latterly. There is no need to affect interest in military matters in order to be polite. My son has very recently died''—his face clouded—''most tragically. As no doubt you are aware from Edith, but we are used to bearing our loss with fortitude. You do not need to consider our feelings in such a way.''

Hester drew breath to say her interest had nothing to do with Thaddeus Carlyon and long predated her even having heard of him, then decided it would not be understood or believed, and would appear merely offensive.

She compromised.

''Stories of courage and endeavor are always interesting, Colonel Carlyon,'' she said with a very direct stare at him. ''I am extremely sorry for your loss, but I never for a moment considered affecting an interest or a respect I did not feel.''

He seemed caught off balance for a moment. His cheeks grew pinker and he blew out his breath sharply, but glancing sideways at Felicia, Hester saw a flicker of appreciation and something which might have been a dark, painful humor, but it was too brief for her to do more than wonder at it.

Before any reply was required, the door opened and a man came in. His manner seemed on the surface almost deferential, until one observed that actually he did not wait for any approval or acknowledgment; it was simply that there was no arrogance in him. Hester judged he was barely an inch taller than Damaris, but still a good height for a man, of very average build if a little round-shouldered. His face was unremarkable, dark eyed, lips hidden by his mustache, features regular, except that there was an aura of good humor about him as though he held no inner anger and optimism were a part of his life.

Damaris looked up at him quickly, her expression lightening.

"Hallo, Pev. You look cold—have some tea."

He touched her gently on the shoulder as he passed and sat down in the chair next to hers.

"Thank you," he accepted, smiling across at Hester, waiting to be introduced.

"My husband," Damaris said quickly. "Peverell Erskine. Pev, this is Hester Latterly, Edith's friend, who nursed in the Crimea with Florence Nightingale."

"How do you do, Miss Latterly." He inclined his head, his face full of interest. "I hope you are not bored by endless people asking you to tell us about your experiences. We should still be obliged if you would do it for us."

Felicia poured his tea and passed it. "Later, perhaps, if Miss Latterly should call again. Did you have a satisfactory day, Peverell?"

He took her rebuff without the least irritation, almost as if he had not noticed it. Hester would have felt patronized and retaliated. That would have been far less satisfying, and watching Peverell Erskine, she realized it with a little stab of surprise.

He took a cucumber sandwich and ate it with relish before replying.

"Yes thank you, Mama-in-law. I met a most interesting man who fought in the Maori Wars ten years ago." He looked at Hester. "That is in New Zealand, you know? Yes, of course you do. They have the most marvelous birds there. Quite unique, and so beautiful." His agreeable face was full of enthusiasm. "I love birds, Miss Latterly. Such a variety. Everything from a hummingbird no bigger than my little finger, which hovers in the air to suck the nectar from a flower, right up to an albatross, which flies the oceans of the earth, with a wingspan twice the height of a man." His face was bright with the marvels he perceived, and in that instant Hester knew precisely why Damaris had remained in love with him.

She smiled back. "I will trade with you, Mr. Erskine," she offered. "I will tell you everything I know about the Crimea and Miss Nightingale if you will tell me about what you know of birds."

He laughed cheerfully. "What an excellent idea. But I assure you, I am simply an amateur."

"By far the best. I should wish to listen for love of it, not in order to become learned."

"Mr. Erskine is a lawyer, Miss Latterly," Felicia said with distinct chill. Then she turned to her son-in-law. "Did you see Alexandra?"

His expression did not alter, and Hester wondered briefly if he had avoided telling her this immediately because she had been so curt in cutting him off. It would be a good-natured and yet effective way of asserting himself so she did not overrule him completely.

"Yes I did." He addressed no one in particular, and continued sipping his tea. "I saw her this morning. She is very distressed of course, but bearing it with courage and dignity."

"I would expect that of any Carlyon," Felicia said rather sharply. "You do not need to tell me that. I beg your pardon, Miss Latterly, but this is a family matter which cannot interest you. I wish to know her affairs, Peverell. Is everything in order? Does she have what she requires? I imagine Thaddeus left everything tidy and well arranged?"

"Well enough . . ."

Her eyebrows rose. "Well enough? What on earth do you mean?"

"I mean that I have taken care of the preliminaries, and

34

so far there is nothing that cannot be satisfactorily dealt with, Mama-in-law.''

''I shall require to know more than that, at a suitable time.''

''Then you will have to ask Alexandra, because I cannot tell you,'' he said with a bland and totally uncommunicative smile.

''Don't be absurd! Of course you can.'' Her large blue eyes were hard. ''You are her solicitor; you must be aware of everything there is.''

''Certainly I am aware of it.'' Peverell set down his cup and looked at her more directly. ''But for precisely that reason I cannot discuss her affairs with anyone else.''

''He was my son, Peverell. Have you forgotten that?''

''Every man is someone's son, Mama-in-law,'' he said gently. ''That does not invalidate his right to privacy, nor his widow's.''

Felicia's face was white. Randolf retreated farther back into his chair, as if he had not heard. Damaris sat motionless. Edith watched them all.

But Peverell was not disconcerted. He had obviously foreseen both the question and his answer to it. Her reaction could not have surprised him.

''I am sure Alexandra will discuss with you everything that is of family concern,'' he went on as if nothing had happened.

''It is all of family concern, Peverell!'' Felicia said with a tight, hard voice. ''The police are involved. Ridiculous as that seems, someone in that wretched house killed Thaddeus. I assume it was Maxim Furnival. I never cared for him. I always thought he lacked self-control, in a finer sense. He paid far too much attention to Alexandra, and she had not the sense to discourage him! I sometimes thought he imagined himself in love with her—whatever that may mean to such a man.''

''I never saw him do anything undignified or hasty,'' Damaris said quickly. ''He was merely fond of her.''

''Be quiet, Damaris,'' her mother ordered. ''You do not

35

know what you are talking about. I am referring to his nature, not his acts—until now, of course.''

''We don't know that he has done anything now,'' Edith joined in reasonably.

''He married that Warburton woman; that was a lapse of taste and judgment if ever I saw one,'' Felicia snapped. ''Emotional, uncontrolled.''

''Louisa?'' Edith asked, looking at Damaris, who nodded.

''Well?'' Felicia turned to Peverell. ''What are the police doing? When are they going to arrest him?''

''I have no idea.''

Before she could respond the door opened and the butler came in looking extremely grave and not a little embarrassed, and carrying a note on a silver tray. He presented it not to Randolf but to Felicia. Possibly Randolf's eyesight was no longer good.

''Miss Alexandra's footman brought it, ma'am,'' he said very quietly.

''Indeed.'' She picked it up without speaking and read it through. The very last trace of color fled from her skin, leaving her rigid and waxy pale.

''There will be no reply,'' she said huskily. ''You may go.''

''Yes ma'am.'' He departed obediently, closing the door behind him.

''The police have arrested Alexandra for the murder of Thaddeus,'' Felicia said with a level, icily controlled voice, as soon as he was gone. ''Apparently she has confessed.''

Damaris started to say something and choked on her words. Immediately Peverell put his hand over hers and held it hard.

Randolf stared uncomprehendingly, his eyes wide.

''No!'' Edith protested. ''That's—that's impossible! Not Alex!''

Felicia rose to her feet. ''There is no purpose in denying it, Edith. Apparently it is so. She has admitted it.'' She squared her shoulders. ''Peverell, we would be obliged if

36

you would take care of the matter. It seems she has taken leave of her senses, and in a fit of madness become homicidal. Perhaps it can be dealt with privately, since she does not contest the issue.''

Her voice gained confidence. ''She can be put away in a suitable asylum. We shall have Cassian here, naturally, poor child. I shall fetch him myself. I imagine that will have to be done tonight. He cannot remain in that house without family.'' She reached for the bell, then turned to Hester. ''Miss Latterly, you have been privy to our family tragedy. You will surely appreciate that we are no longer in a position to entertain even the closest friends and sympathisers. Thank you for calling. Edith will show you to the door and bid you goodbye.''

Hester stood up. ''Of course. I am most extremely sorry.''

Felicia acknowledged her words with a look but no more. There was nothing to add. All that was possible now was to excuse herself to Randolf, Peverell and Damaris, and leave.

As soon as they were in the hall Edith clasped her arm.

''Dear God, this is terrible! We have to do something!''

Hester stopped and faced her. ''What? I think your mother's answer may be the best. If she has lost her mind and become violent—''

''Rubbish!'' Edith exploded fiercely. ''Alex is not mad. If anyone in the family killed him, it will be their daughter Sabella. She really is . . . very strange. After the birth of her child she threatened to take her own life. Oh—there isn't time to tell you now, but believe me there is a long story about Sabella.'' She was holding Hester so hard there was little choice but to stay. ''She hated Thaddeus,'' Edith went on urgently. ''She didn't want to marry; she wanted to become a nun, of all things. But Thaddeus would not hear of it. She hated him for making her marry, and still does. Poor Alex will have confessed to save her. We've got to do something to help. Can't you think of anything?''

''Well . . .'' Hester's mind raced. ''Well, I do know a private sort of policeman who works for people—but if she has confessed, she will be tried, you know. I know a brilliant lawyer. But Peverell . . ."

"No," Edith said quickly. "He is a solicitor, not a barrister—he doesn't appear in court. He won't mind, I swear. He would want the best for Alex. Sometimes he appears to do whatever Mama says, but he doesn't really. He just smiles and goes his own way. Please, Hester, if there is anything you can do . . . ?"

"I will," Hester promised, clasping Edith's hand. "I will try!"

"Thank you. Now you must go before anyone else comes out and finds us here—please!"

"Of course. Keep heart."

"I will—and thank you again."

Quickly Hester turned and accepted her cloak from the waiting maid and went to the door, her mind racing, her thoughts in turmoil, and the face of Oliver Rathbone sharp in her mind.

2

As soon as Hester returned, Major Tiplady, who had had little to do but stare out of the window, observed from her face that something distressing had happened, and since it would soon be public knowledge in the newspapers, she did not feel she was betraying any trust by telling him. He was very aware that she had experienced something extraordinary, and to keep it secret would close him out to no purpose. It would also make it far harder to explain why she wished for yet further time away from the house.

"Oh dear," he said as soon as she told him. He sat very upright on the chaise longue. "This is quite dreadful! Do you believe that something has turned the poor woman's mind?"

"Which woman?" She tidied away his tea tray, which the maid had not yet collected, setting it on the small table to the side. "The widow or the daughter?"

"Why—" Then he realized the pertinence of the question. "I don't know. Either of them, I suppose—or even both. Poor creatures." He looked at her anxiously. "What do you propose to do? I cannot see anything to be done, but you seem to have something in mind."

She flashed him a quick, uncertain smile. "I am not sure." She closed the book he had been reading and put it on the table next to him. "I can at least do my best to find her the very best lawyer—which she will be able to afford." She tucked his shoes neatly under the chaise.

"Will her family not do that anyway?" he asked. "Oh, for heaven's sake sit down, woman! How can anyone concentrate their thoughts when you keep moving around and fussing?"

She stopped abruptly and turned to look at him.

With unusual perception he frowned at her. "You do not need to be endlessly doing something in order to justify your position. If you humor me, that will be quite sufficient. Now I require you to stand still and answer me sensibly—if you please."

"Her family would like her put away with as little fuss as possible," she replied, standing in front of him with her hands folded. "It will cause the least scandal that may be achieved after a murder."

"I imagine they would have blamed someone else if they could," he said thoughtfully. "But she has rather spoiled that by confessing. But I still do not see what you can do, my dear."

"I know a lawyer who can do the miraculous with causes which seem beyond hope."

"Indeed?" He was dubious, sitting upright and looking a little uncomfortable. "And you believe he will take this case?"

"I don't know—but I shall ask him and do my best." She stopped, a slight flush in her face. "That is—if you will permit me the time in which to see him?"

"Of course I will. But . . ." He looked vaguely self-conscious. "I would be obliged if you would allow me to know how it proceeds."

She smiled dazzlingly at him.

"Naturally. We shall be in it together."

"Indeed," he said with surprise and increasing satisfaction. "Indeed we shall."

* * *

Accordingly, she had no difficulty in being permitted to leave her duties once more the following day and take a hansom cab to the legal offices of Mr. Oliver Rathbone, whose acquaintance she had made at the conclusion of the Grey murder, and then resumed during the Moidore case a few months later. She had sent a letter by hand (or to be more accurate, Major Tiplady had, since he had paid the messenger), requesting that Mr. Rathbone see her on a most urgent matter, and had received an answer by return that he would be in his chambers at eleven o'clock the following day, and would see her at that hour if she wished.

Now at quarter to eleven she was traveling inside the cab with her heart racing and every jolt in the road making her gasp, trying to swallow down the nervousness rising inside her. It really was the most appalling liberty she was taking, not only on behalf of Alexandra Carlyon, whom she had never met, and who presumably had not even heard of her, but also towards Oliver Rathbone. Their relationship had been an odd one, professional in that she had twice been a witness in cases he had defended. William Monk had investigated the second one after the police force officially closed it. In both cases they had drawn Oliver Rathbone in before the conclusion.

At times the understanding between Rathbone and herself had seemed very deep, a collaboration in a cause in which they both fiercely believed. At others it had been more awkward, aware that they were a man and a woman engaged in pursuits quite outside any rules society had laid down for behavior, not lawyer and client, not employer and employee, not social friends or equals, and most certainly not a man courting a woman.

And yet their friendship was of a deeper sort than those she had shared with other men, even army surgeons in the field during the long nights in Scutari, except perhaps with Monk in the moments between their quarrels. And also there had been that one extraordinary, startling and sweet kiss, which she could still recall with a shiver of both pleasure and loneliness.

The cab was stopping and starting in the heavy traffic along High Holborn—hansoms, drays, every kind of carriage.

Please heaven Rathbone would understand this was a call most purely on business. It would be unbearable if he were to think she was pursuing him. Trying to force an acquaintance. Imagining into that moment something which they both knew he did not intend. Her face burned at the humiliation. She must be impersonal and not endeavor to exercise even the slightest undue influence, still less appear to flirt. Not that that would be difficult; she would have no idea how to flirt if her life depended upon it. Her sister-in-law had told her that countless times. If only she could be like Imogen and appeal with sweet helplessness to people, simply by her manner, so men instinctively would desire to help her. It was very nice to be efficient, but it could also be a disadvantage to be obviously so. It was also not especially attractive—either to men or to women. Men thought it unbecoming, and women found it vaguely insulting to them.

Her thoughts were interrupted by the hansom's arrival at Vere Street and Oliver Rathbone's offices, and she was obliged to descend and pay the driver. Since it was already five minutes before her appointment, she mounted the steps and presented herself to the clerk.

A few minutes later the inner door opened and Rathbone came out. He was precisely as she had remembered him; indeed she was taken aback by the vividness of her recall. He was little above average height, with fair hair graying a trifle at the temples, and dark eyes that were acutely aware of all laughter and absurdity, and yet liable to change expression to anger or pity with an instant's warning.

"How agreeable to see you again, Miss Latterly," he said with a smile. "Won't you please come into my office, where you may tell me what business it is that brings you here?" He stood back a little to allow her to pass, then followed her in and closed the door behind him. He invited her to sit in one of the large, comfortable chairs. The office was as it had been last time she was there, spacious, surprisingly free from the oppressive feeling of too many books, and with bright light from the windows as if it were a place from which to observe the world, not one in which to hide from it.

"Thank you," she accepted, arranging her skirts only minimally. She would not give the impression of a social call.

He sat down behind his desk and regarded her with interest.

"Another desperate case of injustice?" he asked, his eyes bright.

Instantly she felt defensive, and had to guard herself from allowing him to dictate the conversation. She remembered quickly that this was his profession, questioning people in such a way that they betrayed themselves in their answers.

"I would be foolish to prejudge it, Mr. Rathbone," she replied with an equally charming smile. "If you were ill, I should be irritated if you consulted me and then prescribed your own treatment."

Now his amusement was unmistakable.

"If some time I consult you, Miss Latterly, I shall keep that in mind. Although I doubt I should be so rash as ever to think of preempting your judgment. When I am ill, I am quite a pitiful object, I assure you."

"People are also frightened and vulnerable, even pitiful, when they are accused of crime and face the law without anyone to defend them—or at least anyone adequate to the occasion," she answered.

"And you think I might be adequate to this particular occasion?" he asked. "I am complimented, if not exactly flattered."

"You might be, if you understood the occasion," she said a trifle tartly.

His smile was wide and quite without guile. He had beautiful teeth.

"Bravo, Miss Latterly. I see you have not changed. Please tell me, what is this occasion?"

"Have you read of the recent death of General Thaddeus Carlyon?" She asked so as to avoid telling him that with which he was already familiar.

"I saw the obituary. I believe he met with an accident, did he not? A fall when he was out visiting someone. Was it not accidental?" He looked curious.

"No. It seems he could not have fallen in precisely that way, at least not so as to kill himself."

"The obituary did not describe the injury."

Memory of Damaris's words came back to her, and a wry, bitter humor. "No—they wouldn't. It has an element of the absurd. He fell over the banister from the first landing onto a suit of armor."

"And broke his neck?"

"No. Please do not keep interrupting me, Mr. Rathbone—it is not something you might reasonably guess." She ignored his look of slight surprise at her presumption. "It is too ridiculous. He fell onto the suit of armor and was apparently speared to death by the halberd it was holding. Only the police said it could not have happened by chance. He was speared deliberately after he had fallen and was lying senseless on the floor."

"I see." He was outwardly contrite. "So it was murder; that, I presume, I may safely deduce?"

"You may. The police enquired into the matter for several days, in fact two weeks. It occurred on the evening of April twentieth. Now the widow, Mrs. Alexandra Carlyon, has confessed to the crime."

"That I might reasonably have guessed, Miss Latterly. It is regrettably not an unusual circumstance, and not absurd, except as all human relationships have an element of humor or ridiculousness in them." He did not go on to guess for what reason she had come to see him, but he remained sitting very upright in his chair, giving her his total attention.

With an effort she refrained from smiling, although a certain amusement had touched her, albeit laced with tragedy.

"She may well be guilty," she said instead. "But my interest in the matter is that Edith Sobell, the sister of General Carlyon, feels most strongly that she is not. Edith is convinced that Alexandra has confessed in order to protect her daughter, Sabella Pole, who is very lightly balanced, and hated her father."

"And was present on the occasion?"

"Yes—and according to what I can learn of the affair from Damaris Erskine, the general's other sister, who was also at the ill-fated dinner party, there were several people who had the opportunity to have pushed him over the banister."

"I cannot act for Mrs. Carlyon unless she wishes it," he pointed out. "No doubt the Carlyon family will have their own legal counsel."

"Peverell Erskine, Damaris's husband, is their solicitor, and Edith assures me he would not be averse to engaging the best barrister available."

His fine mouth twitched in the ghost of a smile.

"Thank you for the implied compliment."

She ignored it, because she did not know what to say.

"Will you please see Alexandra Carlyon and at least consider the matter?" she asked him earnestly, self-consciousness overridden by the urgency of the matter. "I fear she may otherwise be shuffled away into an asylum for the criminally insane, to protect the family name, and remain there until she dies." She leaned towards him. "Such places are the nearest we have to hell in this life—and for someone who is quite sane, simply trying to defend a daughter, it would be immeasurably worse than death."

All the humor and light vanished from his face as if washed away. Knowledge of appalling pain filled his eyes, and there was no hesitation in him.

"I will certainly keep my mind open in the matter," he promised. "If you ask Mr. Erskine to instruct me, and engage my services so that I may apply to speak with Mrs. Carlyon, then I will give you my word that I will do so. Although of course whether I can persuade her to tell me the truth is another thing entirely."

"Perhaps you could engage Mr. Monk to carry out investigations, should you—" She stopped.

"I shall certainly consider it. You have not told me what

45

was her motive in murdering her husband. Did she give one?"

She was caught off guard. She had not thought to ask.

"I have no idea," she answered, wide-eyed in amazement at her own omission.

"It can hardly have been self-defense." He pursed his lips. "And we would find it most difficult to argue a crime of passion, not that that is considered an excuse—for a woman, and a jury would find it most . . . unbecoming." Again the black humor flickered across his face, as if he were conscious of the irony of it. It was a quality unusual in a man, and one of the many reasons she liked him.

"I believe the whole evening was disastrous," she continued, watching his face. "Apparently Alexandra was upset, even before she arrived, as though she and the general had quarreled over something. And I gather from Damaris that Mrs. Furnival, the hostess, flirted with him quite openly. But that is something which I have observed quite often, and very few people are foolish enough to take exception to it. It is one of the things one simply has to endure." She saw the faint curl of amusement at the corners of his lips, and ignored it.

"I had better wait until Mr. Erskine contacts me," he said with returning gravity. "I will be able to speak to Mrs. Carlyon herself. I promise you I will do so."

"Thank you. I am most obliged." She rose to her feet, and automatically he rose also. Now it suddenly occurred to her that she owed him for his time. He had spared her almost half an hour, and she had not come prepared to pay. His fee would be a considerable amount of money from her very slender resources. It was an idiotic and embarrassing error.

"I shall send you my account when the matter is closed," he said, apparently without having noticed her confusion. "You will understand that if Mrs. Carlyon engages me, and I accept the case, what she tells me will have to remain confidential between us, but I shall of course inform you whether I am able to defend her or not." He came around from behind the desk and moved towards the door.

"Of course," she said a little stiffly, overwhelmed with relief. She had been saved from making a complete fool of herself. "I shall be happy if you are able to help. I shall now go and tell Mrs. Sobell—and of course Mr. Erskine." She did not mention that so far as she was aware, Peverell Erskine knew nothing about the enquiry. "Good day, Mr. Rathbone—and thank you."

"It was a pleasure to see you again, Miss Latterly." He opened the door for her and held it while she passed through, then stood for several moments watching her leave.

Hester went immediately to Carlyon House and asked the parlormaid who answered the door if Mrs. Sobell were in.

"Yes, Miss Latterly," the girl answered quickly, and from her expression, Hester judged that Edith had forewarned her she was expected. "If you please to come to Mrs. Sobell's sitting room, ma'am," the maid went on, glancing around the hallway, then lifting her chin defiantly and walking smartly across the parquet and up the stairs, trusting Hester was behind her.

Across the first landing and in the east wing she opened the door to a small sunlit room with floral covered armchairs and sofa and soft watercolor paintings on the walls.

"Miss Latterly, ma'am," the maid said quietly, then withdrew.

Edith rose to her feet, her face eager.

"Hester! Did you see him? What did he say? Will he do it?"

Hester found herself smiling briefly, although there was little enough humor in what she had to report.

"Yes I saw him, but of course he cannot accept any case until he is requested by the solicitor of the person in question. Are you sure Peverell will be agreeable to Mr. Rathbone acting for Alexandra?"

"Oh yes—but it won't be easy, at least I fear not. Peverell may be the only one who is willing to fight on Alex's behalf. But if Peverell asks Mr. Rathbone, will he take the case? You did tell him she had confessed, didn't you?"

"Of course I did."

"Thank heaven. Hester, I really am most grateful to you for this, you know. Come and sit down." She moved back to the chairs and curled up in one and waved to the other, where Hester sat down and tucked her skirts comfortably. "Then what happens? He will go and see Alex, of course, but what if she just goes on saying she did it?"

"He will employ an investigator to enquire into it," Hester replied, trying to sound more certain than she felt.

"What can he do, if she won't tell him?"

"I don't know—but he's better than most police. Why did she do it, Edith? I mean, what does she say?"

Edith bit her lip. "That's the worst part of it. Apparently she said it was out of jealousy over Thaddeus and Louisa."

"Oh—I . . ." Hester was momentarily thrown into confusion.

"I know." Edith looked wretched. "It is very sordid, isn't it? And unpleasantly believable, if you know Alex. She is unconventional enough for something so wild and so foolish to enter her mind. Except that I really don't believe she ever loved Thaddeus with that sort of intensity, and I am quite sure she did not lately."

For a moment she looked embarrassed at such candor, then her emotions at the urgency and tragedy of it took over again. "Please, Hester, do not allow your natural repugnance for such behavior to prevent you from doing what you can to help her. I don't believe she killed him at all. I think it was far more probably Sabella—God forgive her—or perhaps I should say God help her. I think she may honestly be out of her mind." Her face tightened into a somber unhappiness. "And Alex taking the guilt for her will not help anyone. They will hang an innocent person, and Sabella in her lucid hours will suffer even more—don't you see that?"

"Yes of course I see it," Hester agreed, although in honesty she thought it not at all improbable that Alexandra Carlyon might well have killed her husband exactly as she had confessed. But it would be cruel, and serve no purpose, to say so to Edith now, when she was convinced of Alexandra's

48

innocence, or passionately wished to be. "Have you any idea why Alexandra would feel there was some cause for jealousy over the general and Mrs. Furnival?"

Edith's eyes were bright with mockery and pain.

"You have not yet met Louisa Furnival, or you would not bother to ask. She is the sort of woman anyone might be jealous of." Her expressive face was filled with dislike, mockery, and something which could almost have been a kind of admiration. "She has a way of walking, an air to her, a smile that makes you think she has something that you have not. Even if she had done nothing whatsoever, and your husband found no interest in her at all, it would be easy to imagine he had, simply because of her manner."

"That does not sound very hopeful."

"Except that I would be amazed if Thaddeus ever gave her more than a passing glance. He really was not in the least a flirt, even with Louisa. He was . . ." She lifted her shoulders very slightly in a gesture of helplessness. "He was very much the soldier, a man's man. He was always polite to women, of course, but I don't think he was ever fearfully comfortable with us. He didn't really know what to talk about. Naturally he had learned, as any well-bred man does, but it was learned, if you know what I mean." She looked at Hester questioningly. "He was brilliant at action, brave, decisive, and nearly always right in his judgment; and he knew how to express himself to his men, and to new young men interested in the army. He used to come alight then; I've watched his eyes and seen how much he cared."

She sighed. "He always assumed women weren't interested, and that's not true. I would have been—but it hardly matters now, I suppose. What I'm trying to say is that one doesn't flirt with conversation about military strategy and the relative merits of one gun over another, least of all with someone like Louisa. And even if he did, one does not commit murder over such a thing, it is . . ." Her face puckered, and for a moment Hester wondered with sudden hurt what Oswald Sobell had been like, and what pain Edith might have suffered in their brief marriage, what wounds of jealousy she

49

herself had known. Then the urgency of the present reasserted itself and she returned to the subject of Alexandra.

"I imagine it is probably better that the truth should be learned, whatever it is," she said aloud to Edith. "And I suppose it is possible the murderer is not either Alexandra or Sabella, but someone else. Perhaps if Louisa Furnival is a flirt, and was casting eyes at Thaddeus, her own husband might have imagined there was more to it than there was, and might finally have succumbed to jealousy himself."

Edith put her hands up and covered her face, leaning forward across her knees.

"I hate this!" she said fiercely. "Everyone involved is either family or a friend of sorts. And it has to have been one of them."

"It is wretched," Hester agreed. "That is one of the things I learned in the other crimes I have seen investigated: you come to know the people, their dreams and their griefs, their wounds—and whoever it is, it hurts you. You cannot island yourself from it and make it 'them,' and not 'us.' "

Edith removed her hands and looked up, surprise in her face, her mouth open to argue; then slowly the emotion subsided and she accepted that Hester meant exactly what she said.

"How very hard." She let her breath out slowly. "Somehow I always took it for granted there would be a barrier between me and whoever did such a thing—I mean usually. There would be a whole class of people whose hurt I could exclude . . ."

"Only with a sort of dishonesty." Hester rose to her feet and walked over to the high window above the garden. It was a sash window open at top and bottom, and the perfume of wallflowers in the sun drifted up. "I forgot to tell you last time, with all the news of the tragedy, but I have been enquiring into what sort of occupation you might find, and I think the most interesting and agreeable thing you could do would be as a librarian." She watched a gardener walk across the grass with a tray of seedlings. "Or researcher for someone who wishes to write a treatise, or a monograph or some such thing. It would pay you a small amount insufficient to support you, but it would take you away from Carlyon House during the days.''

''Not nursing?'' There was a note of disappointment in Edith's voice, in spite of her effort to conceal it, and a painful self-consciousness. Hester realized with a sudden stab of embarrassment that Edith admired her and that what she really sought was to do the same thing Hester did, but had been reluctant to say so.

With her face suddenly hot she struggled for a reply that would be honest and not clumsy. It would not be kind to equivocate.

''No. It is very hard to find a private position, even if you have the training for it. It is far better to use the skills you have.'' She did not face her; it was better Edith did not see her sudden understanding. ''There are some really very interesting people who need librarians or researchers, or someone to write up their work for them. You could find someone who writes on a subject in which you might become most interested yourself.''

''Such as what?'' There was no lightness in Edith's voice.

''Anything?'' Hester turned to face her and forced a cheerfulness into her expression. ''Archaeology . . . history . . . exploration.'' She stopped as she saw a sudden spark of real excitement in Edith's eyes. She smiled with overwhelming relief and a surge of unreasonable happiness. ''Why not? Women have begun to think of going to most marvelous places—Egypt, the Magreb, Africa even.''

''Africa! Yes . . .'' Edith said almost under her breath, her confidence returned, the wound vanished in hope. ''Yes. After all this is over I will. Thank you, Hester—thank you so much!''

She got no further because the sitting room door opened and Damaris came in. Today she looked utterly different. Gone was the contradictory but distinctly feminine air of the previous occasion. This time she was in riding habit and looked vigorous and boyish, like a handsome youth, faintly Mediterranean, and Hester knew the instant their eyes met

51

that the effect was wholly intentional, and that Damaris enjoyed it.

Hester smiled. She had dared in reality far further than Damaris into such forbidden masculine fields, seen real violence, warfare and chivalry, the honest friendship where there was no barrier between men and women, where speech was not forever dictated by social ritual rather than true thoughts and feelings, where people worked side by side for a desperate common cause and only courage and skill mattered. Very little of such social rebellion could shake her, let alone offend.

"Good afternoon, Mrs. Erskine," she said cheerfully. "I am delighted to see you looking so well, in such trying circumstances."

Damaris's face broke into a wide grin. She closed the door behind her and leaned against the handle.

"Edith said you were going to see a lawyer friend of yours who is totally brilliant—is that true?"

This time Hester was caught off guard. She had not thought Damaris was aware of Edith's request.

"Ah—yes." There was no point in prevarication. "Do you think Mr. Erskine will mind?"

"Oh no, not at all. But I cannot answer for Mama. You had better come in to luncheon and tell us about it."

Hester looked desperately at Edith, hoping she would rescue her from having to go. She had expected simply to tell Edith about Rathbone and then leave her to inform Peverell Erskine; the rest of the family would find out from him. Now it seemed she was going to have to face them all over the luncheon table.

But Edith was apparently unaware of her feelings. She stood up quickly and moved towards the door.

"Yes of course. Is Pev here?"

"Yes—now would be a perfect time." Damaris turned around and pulled the door open. "We need to act as soon as we can." She smiled brilliantly at Hester. "It really is most kind of you."

The dining room was heavily and ornately furnished, and

with a full dinner service in the new, fashionable turquoise, heavily patterned and gilded. Felicia was already seated and Randolf occupied his place at the head of the table. He looked larger and more imposing than he had lounging in the armchair at afternoon tea. His face was heavy, and set in lines of stubborn, weary immobility. Hester tried to imagine him as a young man, and what it might have been like to be in love with him. Was he dashing in uniform? Might there have been a trace of humor or wit in his face then? The years change people; there were disappointments, dreams that crumbled. And she was seeing him at the worst possible time. His only son had just been murdered, and almost certainly by a member of his own family.

"Good afternoon, Mrs. Carlyon, Colonel Carlyon," she said, swallowing hard, and trying at least temporarily to put out of her mind the confrontation which must come when Oliver Rathbone was mentioned.

"Good afternoon, Miss Latterly," Felicia said with her eyebrows arched in as much surprise as was possible with civility. "How agreeable of you to join us. To what occasion do we owe the pleasure of a second visit in so short a time?"

Randolf muttered something inaudible. He seemed to have forgotten her name, and had nothing to say beyond an acknowledgment of her presence.

Peverell looked as benign and agreeable as before, but he smiled at her without speaking.

Felicia was very obviously waiting. Apparently it was not merely a rhetorical question; she wished an answer.

Damaris strode over to her place at the table and sat down with something of a swagger, ignoring the frown which shadowed her mother's face.

"She came to see Peverell," she answered with a slight smile.

Felicia's irritation deepened.

"At luncheon?" Her voice held a chill incredulity. "Surely if it were Peverell she wished to see she would have made an appointment with him in his offices, like anyone else. She would hardly wish to conduct her private business in our

53

company, and over a meal. You must be mistaken, Damaris. Or is this your idea of humor? If it is, it is most misplaced, and I must require you to apologize, and not do such a thing again.''

"Not humorous at all, Mama," she said with instant sobriety. "It is in order to help Alex, so it is entirely appropriate that it should be discussed here, with us present. After all, it does concern the whole family, in a way."

"Indeed?" Felicia kept her eyes on Damaris's face. "And what can Miss Latterly possibly do to help Alexandra? It is our tragedy that Alexandra would seem to have lost her sanity." The skin across her cheekbones tightened as if she were expecting a blow. "Even the best doctors have no cure for such things—and not even God can undo what has already happened."

"But we don't know what has happened, Mama," Damaris pointed out.

"We know that Alexandra confessed that she murdered Thaddeus," Felicia said icily, concealing from them all whatever wells of pain lay beneath the bare words. "You should not have asked Miss Latterly for her help; there is nothing whatsoever that she, or anyone else, can do about the tragedy. We are quite able to find our own doctors who will take care of her disposition to a suitable place of confinement, for her own good, and that of society." She turned to Hester for the first time since the subject had been raised. "Do you care to take soup, Miss Latterly?"

"Thank you." Hester could think of nothing else to say, no excuse or explanation to offer for herself. The whole affair was even worse than she had foreseen. She should have declined the invitation and excused herself. She could have told Edith all she needed to know quite simply and left the rest to Peverell. But it was too late now.

Felicia nodded to the maid and the tureen was brought in and the soup served in silence.

After taking several sips Randolf turned to Hester.

"Well—if it is not a doctor you are counseling us about, Miss Latterly, perhaps we had better know what it is."

54

Felicia looked at him sharply, but he chose to ignore her.

Hester would like to have told him it was between her and Peverell, but she did not dare. No words came to her that could have been even remotely civil. She looked back at his rather baleful stare and felt acutely uncomfortable.

There was silence around the table. No one came to her rescue, as if their courage had suddenly deserted them also.

"I—" She took a deep breath and began again. "I have the acquaintance of a most excellent barrister who has previously fought and won seemingly impossible cases. I thought—I thought Mr. Erskine might wish to consider his services for Mrs. Carlyon."

Felicia's nostrils flared and a spark of cold anger lit her face.

"Thank you, Miss Latterly, but as I think I have already pointed out, a barrister is not required. My daughter-in-law has already confessed to the crime; there is no case to be argued. It is only a matter of arranging for her to be put away as discreetly as possible in the place best suited to care for her in her state."

"She may not be guilty, Mama," Edith said tentatively, the force and enthusiasm gone out of her voice.

"Then why would she admit to it, Edith?" Felicia asked without bothering to look at her.

Edith's face tightened. "To protect Sabella. Alex isn't insane, we all know that. But Sabella may well be . . ."

"Nonsense!" Felicia said sharply. "She was a trifle emotional after her child was born. It happens from time to time. It passes." She broke a little brown bread on the plate to her left, her fingers powerful. "Women have been known to kill their children sometimes, in such fits of melancholia, but not their fathers. You should not offer opinions in matters you know nothing about."

"She hated Thaddeus!" Edith persisted, two spots of color in her cheeks, and it came to Hester sharply that the reference to Edith's ignorance of childbirth had been a deliberate cruelty.

"Don't be ridiculous!" Felicia said to her sharply. "She

was unruly and very self-willed. Alexandra should have been much firmer with her. But that is hardly the same thing as being homicidal.''

Peverell smiled charmingly. ''It really doesn't matter, Mama-in-law, because Alexandra will give me whatever instructions she wishes, and I shall be obliged to act accordingly. After she has thought about it awhile, and realized that it will not simply be a matter of being shut away in some agreeable nursing establishment, but of being hanged . . .'' He ignored Felicia's indrawn breath and wince of distaste at the grossness of his choice of words. ''. . . then she may change her plea and wish to be defended.'' He took another sip from his spoon. ''And of course I shall have to put all the alternatives before her.''

Felicia's face darkened. ''For goodness sake, Peverell, are you not competent to get the matter taken care of decently and with some discretion?'' she said with exasperated contempt. ''Poor Alexandra's mind has snapped. She has taken leave of her wits and allowed her jealous fancies to provoke her into a moment of insane rage. It can help no one to expose her to public ridicule and hatred. It is the most absurd of crimes. What would happen if every woman who imagined her husband paid more attention to another woman than he should—which must be half London!—were to resort to murder? Society would fall apart, and everything that goes with it.'' She took a deep breath and began again, more gently, as if explaining to a child. ''Can you not put it to her, when you see her, that even if she has no feeling left for herself, or for us, that she must consider her family, especially her son, who is a child? Think what the scandal will do to him! If she makes public this jealousy of hers, and goodness knows there was no ground for it except in her poor mad brain, then she will ruin Cassian's future and at the very least be a source of embarrassment to her daughters.''

Peverell seemed unmoved, except by politeness and a certain outward sympathy for Felicia.

''I will point out all the possible courses to her, Mama-in-law, and the results, as I believe them, of any action she might make." He dabbed his lips with his napkin and his face retained so smooth an expression he might have been discussing the transfer of a few acres of farmland, with no real perception of the passions and tragedies of which they were speaking.

Damaris watched him with wide eyes. Edith was silent. Randolf continued with his soup.

Felicia was so angry with him she had great difficulty in controlling her expression, and on the edge of the table her fingers were knotted around her napkin. But she would not permit him to see that he had beaten her.

Randolf put his spoon down. "I suppose you know what you are doing," he said with a scowl. "But it sounds very unsatisfactory to me."

"Well the army is rather different from the law." Peverell's expression was still one of interest and unbroken patience. "It's still war, of course; conflict, adversarial system. But weapons are different and rules have to be obeyed. All in the brain." He smiled as if inwardly pleased with something the rest of them could not see, not a secret pleasure so much as a private one. "We also deal in life and death, and the taking of property and land—but the weapons are words and the arena is in the mind."

Randolf muttered something inaudible, but there was acute dislike in his heavy face.

"Sometimes you make yourself sound overly important, Peverell," Felicia said acidly.

"Yes." Peverell was not put out of countenance in the least. He smiled at the ceiling. "Damaris says I am pompous." He turned to look at Hester. "Who is your barrister, Miss Latterly?"

"Oliver Rathbone, of Vere Street, just off Lincoln's Inn Fields," Hester replied immediately.

"Really?" His eyes were wide. "He is quite brilliant. I remember him in the Grey case. What an extraordinary verdict! And do you really think he would be prepared to act for Alexandra?"

"If she wishes him to." Hester felt a surge of self-consciousness that took her by surprise. She found herself unable to meet anyone's eyes, even Peverell's, not because he was critical but because he was so remarkably perceptive.

"How excellent," he said quietly. "How absolutely excellent. It is very good of you, Miss Latterly. I am sufficiently aware of Mr. Rathbone's reputation to be most obliged. I shall inform Mrs. Carlyon."

"But you will not allow her to entertain any false notions as to her choices in the matter," Felicia said grimly. "No matter how brilliant"—she said the word with a peculiar curl of her lip as though it were a quality to be held in contempt—"this Mr. Rathbone may be, he cannot twist or defy the law, nor would it be desirable that he should." She took a deep breath and let it out in an inaudible sigh, her mouth suddenly tight with pain. "Thaddeus is dead, and the law will require that someone answer for it."

"Everyone is entitled to defend themselves in their own way, whatever they believe is in their interest, Mama-in-law," Peverell said clearly.

"Possibly, but society also has rights, surely—it must!" She stared at him defiantly. "Alexandra's ideas will not be allowed to override those of the rest of us. I will not permit it." She turned to Hester. "Perhaps now you will tell us something of your experiences with Miss Nightingale, Miss Latterly. It would be most inspiring. She is truly a remarkable woman."

Hester was speechless with amazement for a moment, then a reluctant admiration for Felicia's sheer command overtook her.

"Yes—by—by all means . . ." And she began with the tales she felt would be most acceptable to them and least likely to provoke any further dissension: the long nights in the hospital at Scutari, the weariness, the patience, the endless work of cleaning to be done, the courage. She forbore from speaking of the filth, the rats, the sheer blinding incompetence, or the horrifying figures of the casualties that could have been avoided by foresight, adequate provisions, transport and sanitation.

That afternoon Peverell went first to see Alexandra Carlyon, then to Vere Street to speak to Oliver Rathbone. The day after, May 6, Rathbone presented himself at the prison gates and requested, as Mrs. Carlyon's solicitor, if he might speak with her. He knew he would not be refused.

It was foolish to create in one's mind a picture of what a client would be like, her appearance, or even her personality, and yet as he followed the turnkey along the gray passages he already had a picture formed of Alexandra Carlyon. He saw her as dark-haired, lush of figure and dramatic and emotional of temperament. After all, she had apparently killed her husband in a rage of jealousy—or if Edith Sobell were correct, had confessed it falsely in order to shield her daughter.

But when the turnkey, a big woman with iron-gray hair screwed into a knot at the back of her head, finally unlocked the door and swung it open, he stepped into the cell and saw a woman of little more than average height. She was very slender—too slender for fashion—her fair hair had a heavy natural curl, and her face was highly individual, full of wit and imagination. Her cheekbones were broad, her nose short and aquiline, her mouth beautiful but far too wide, and at once passionate and humorous. She was not lovely in any traditional sense, and yet she was startlingly attractive, even exhausted and frightened as she was, and dressed in plainest white and gray.

She looked up at him without interest, because she had no hope. She was defeated and he knew it even before she spoke.

"How do you do, Mrs. Carlyon," he said formally. "I am Oliver Rathbone. I believe your brother-in-law, Mr. Erskine, has told you that I am willing to represent you, should you wish it?"

She smiled, but it was a ghost of a gesture, an effort dragged up out of an attempt at good manners rather than anything she felt.

"How do you do, Mr. Rathbone. Yes, Peverell did tell

me, but I am afraid you have wasted a journey. You cannot help me.''

Rathbone looked at the turnkey.

''Thank you—you may leave us. I will call when I want to be let out again.''

''Very well,'' said the woman, and she retreated, locking the door behind her with a loud click as the lever turned and fell into place.

Alexandra remained sitting on the cot and Rathbone lowered himself to sit on the far end of it. To continue standing would be to give the impression he was about to leave, and he would not surrender without a fight.

''Possibly not, Mrs. Carlyon, but please do not dismiss me before permitting me to try. I shall not prejudge you.'' He smiled, knowing his own charm because it was part of his trade. ''Please do not prejudge me either.''

This time her answering smile was in her eyes only, and there was sadness in it, and mockery.

''Of course I will listen to you, Mr. Rathbone; for Peverell's sake as well as in good manners. But the truth remains that you cannot help me.'' Her hesitation was so minute as to be almost indiscernible. ''I killed my husband. The law will require payment for that.''

He noticed that she did not use the word *hang*, and he knew in that moment that she was too afraid of it yet to say it aloud. Perhaps she had not even said it to herself in her own mind. Already his pity was engaged. He thrust it away. It was no basis on which to defend a case. His brain was what was needed.

''Tell me what happened, Mrs. Carlyon; everything that you feel to be relevant to your husband's death, starting wherever you wish.''

She looked away from him. Her voice was flat.

''There is very little to tell. My husband had paid a great deal of attention to Louisa Furnival for some time. She is very beautiful, and has a kind of manner about her which men admire a great deal. She flirted with him. I think she flirted with most men. I was jealous. That's all . . .''

"Your husband flirted with Mrs. Furnival at a dinner party, so you left the room and followed him upstairs, pushed him over the banister," he said expressionlessly, "and when he fell you went down the stairs after him, and as he lay senseless on the floor you picked up the halberd and drove it through his chest? I assume this was the first time in your twenty-three years of marriage that he had so offended you?"

She swung around and looked at him with anger. Phrased like that and repeated blindly it sounded preposterous. It was the first spark of real emotion he had seen in her, and as such the very beginning of hope.

"No of course not," she said coldly. "He was more than merely flirting with her. He had been having an affair with her and they were flaunting it in my face—and in front of my own daughter and her husband. It would have been enough to anger any woman."

He watched her face closely, the remarkable features, the sleeplessness, the shock and the fear. He did see anger there also, but it was on the surface, a flare of temper, shallow and without heat, the flame of a match, not the searing heat of a furnace. Was that because she was lying about the flirting, the affair, or because she was too exhausted, too spent to feel any passion now? The object of her rage was dead and she was in the shadow of the noose herself.

"And yet many women must have endured it," he replied, still watching her.

She lifted her shoulders very slightly and he realized again how thin she was. The white blouse and gray unhooped skirt made her look almost waiflike, except for the power in her face. She was not a childlike woman at all; that broad brow and short, round jaw were too willful to be demure, except by deliberate artifice, and it would be a deception short-lived.

"Tell me how it happened, Mrs. Carlyon," he tried again. "Start that evening. Of course the affair with Mrs. Furnival had been continuing for some time. By the way, when did you first realize they were enamored of each other?"

"I don't remember." Still she did not look at him. There was no urgency in her at all. It was quite obvious she did not care whether he believed her or not. The emotion was gone again. She shrugged very faintly. "A few weeks, I suppose. One doesn't know what one doesn't want to." Now suddenly there was real passion in her, harsh and desperately painful. Something hurt her so deeply it was tangible in the small room.

He was confused. One moment she felt so profoundly he could almost sense the pulse of it himself; the next she was numb, as if she were speaking of total trivialities that mattered to no one.

"And this particular evening brought it to a climax?" he said gently.

"Yes . . ." Her voice was husky anyway, with a pleasing depth to it unusual in a woman. Now it was little above a whisper.

"You must tell me what happened, event by event as you recall it, Mrs. Carlyon, if I am to . . . understand." He had nearly said *to help*, when he remembered the hopelessness in her face and in her bearing, and knew that she had no belief in help. The promise would be without meaning to her, and she would reject him again for using it.

As it was she still kept her face turned away and her voice was tight with emotion.

"Understanding will not achieve anything, Mr. Rathbone. I killed him. That is all the law will know or care about. And that is unarguable."

He smiled wryly. "Nothing is ever unarguable in law, Mrs. Carlyon. That is how I make my living, and believe me I am good at it. I don't always win, but I do far more often than I lose."

She swung around to face him and for the first time there was real humor in her face, lighting it and showing a trace of the delightful woman she might be in other circumstances.

"A true lawyer's reply," she said quietly. "But I am afraid I would be one of those few."

"Oh please. Don't defeat me before I begin!" He allowed an answering trace of lightness into his tone also. "I prefer to be beaten than to surrender."

"It is not your battle, Mr. Rathbone. It is mine."

"I would like to make it mine. And you do need a barrister of some kind to plead your case. You cannot do it yourself."

"All you can do is repeat my confession," she said again.

"Mrs. Carlyon, I dislike intensely any form of cruelty, especially that which is unnecessary, but I have to tell you the truth. If you are found guilty, without any mitigating circumstances, then you will hang."

She closed her eyes very slowly and took a long, deep breath, her skin ashen white. As he had thought earlier, she had already touched this in her mind, but some defense, some hope had kept it just beyond her grasp. Now it was there in words and she could no longer pretend. He felt brutal watching her, and yet to have allowed her to cling to a delusion would have been far worse, immeasurably dangerous.

He must judge exactly, precisely all the intangible measures of fear and strength, honesty and love or hate which made her emotional balance at this moment if he were to guide her through this morass which he himself could only guess at. Public opinion would have no pity for a woman who murdered out of jealousy. In fact there would be little pity for a woman who murdered her husband whatever the reason. Anything short of life-threatening physical brutality was expected to be endured. Obscene or unnatural demands, of course, would be abhorred, but so would anyone crass enough to mention such things. What hell anyone endured in the bedroom was something people preferred not to speak of, like fatal diseases and death itself. It was not decent.

"Mrs. Carlyon . . ."

"I know," she whispered. "They will . . ." She still could not bring herself to say the words, and he did not force her. He knew they were there in her mind.

"I can do a great deal more than simply repeat your confession, if you will tell me the truth," he went on. "You did not simply push your husband over the banister and then stab him with the halberd because he was overfamiliar with Mrs. Furnival. Did you speak to him about it? Did you quarrel?"

"No."

"Why not?"

She turned to look at him, her blue eyes uncomprehending.

"What?"

"Why did you not speak to him?" he repeated patiently. "Surely at some time you must have told him his behavior was distressing you?"

"Oh . . . I—yes." She looked surprised. "Of course . . . I asked him to be—discreet . . ."

"Is that all? You loved him so much you were prepared to stab him to death rather than allow another woman to have him—and yet all you did was to ask—" He stopped. He could see in her face that she had not even thought of that sort of love. The very idea of a consuming sexual passion which culminated in murder was something that had not occurred to her with regard to herself and the general. She seemed to have been speaking of something else.

Their eyes met, and she realized that to continue with that pretense would be useless.

"No." She looked away and her voice changed again. "It was the betrayal. I did not love him in that way." The very faintest smile tugged at the corners of her wide mouth. "We had been married twenty-three years, Mr. Rathbone. Such a long-lived passion is not impossible, I suppose, but it would be rare."

"Then what, Mrs. Carlyon?" he demanded. "Why did you kill him as he lay there in front of you, senseless? And do not tell me you were afraid he would attack you for having pushed him, either physically or in words. The last thing he would have done was allow the rest of the dinner party to know that his wife had pushed him downstairs. It has far too much of the ridiculous."

She drew breath, and let it out again without speaking.

"Had he ever beaten you?" he asked. "Seriously?"

She did not look at him. "No," she said very quietly. "It would help if he had, wouldn't it? I should have said yes."

"Not if it is untrue. Your word alone would not be greatly helpful anyway. Many husbands beat their wives. It is not a

64

legal offense unless you feared for your life. And for such a profound charge you would need a great deal of corroborative evidence.''

''He didn't beat me. He was a—a very civilized man—a hero.'' Her lips curled in a harsh, wounding humor as she said it, as if there were some dark joke behind the words.

He knew she was not yet prepared to share it, and he avoided rebuff by not asking.

''So why did you kill him, Mrs. Carlyon? You were not passionately jealous. He had not threatened you. What then?''

''He was having an affair with Louisa Furnival—publicly—in front of my friends and family,'' she repeated flatly.

He was back to the beginning. He did not believe her; at least he did not believe that was all. There was something raw and deep that she was concealing. All this was surface, and laced with lies and evasions. ''What about your daughter?'' he asked.

She turned back to him, frowning. ''My daughter?''

''Your daughter, Sabella. Had she a good relationship with her father?''

Again the shadow of a smile curled her mouth.

''You have heard she quarreled with him. Yes she did, very unpleasantly. She did not get on well with him. She had wished to take the veil, and he thought it was not in her best interest. Instead he arranged for her to marry Fenton Pole, a very agreeable young man who has treated her well.''

''But she has still not forgiven her father, even after this time?''

''No.''

''Why not? Such a grudge seems excessive.''

''She—she was very ill,'' she said defensively. ''Very disturbed—after the birth of her child. It sometimes happens.'' She stared at him, her head high. ''That was when she began to be angry again. It has largely passed.''

''Mrs. Carlyon—was it your daughter, and not you, who killed your husband?''

She swung around to him, her eyes wide, very blue. She

really did have a most unusual face. Now it was full of anger and fear, ready to fight in an instant.

"No—Sabella had nothing to do with it! I have already told you, Mr. Rathbone, it was I who killed him. I absolutely forbid you to bring her into it, do you understand me? She is totally innocent. I shall discharge you if you suggest for a moment anything else!"

And that was all he could achieve. She would say nothing more. He rose to his feet.

"I will see you again, Mrs. Carlyon. In the meantime speak of this to no one, except with my authority. Do you understand?" He did not know why he bothered to say this. All his instincts told him to decline the case. He could do very little to help a woman who deliberately killed her husband without acceptable reason, and a flirtation at a dinner party was not an acceptable reason to anyone at all. Had she found him in bed with another woman it might be mitigating, especially if it were in her own house, and with a close friend. But even that was not much. Many a woman had found her husband in bed with a maid and been obliged to accept in silence, indeed to keep a smile on her face. Society would be more likely to criticize her for being clumsy enough to find them, when with a little discretion she could have avoided placing herself—and him—in such a situation.

"If that is what you wish," she said without interest. "Thank you for coming, Mr. Rathbone." She did not even ask who had sent him.

"It is what I wish," he answered. "Good day, Mrs. Carlyon." What an absurd parting. How could she possibly have a good anything?

Rathbone left the prison in a turmoil of mind. Every judgment of intelligence decreed that he decline the case. And yet when he hailed a hansom he gave the driver instructions to go to Grafton Street, where William Monk had his rooms, and not to High Holborn and Peverell Erskine's offices, where he could tell him politely that he felt unable to be of any real assistance to Alexandra Carlyon.

All the way riding along in the cab at a steady trot his mind was finding ways of refusing the case, and the most excellent reasons why he should. Any competent barrister could go through the motions of pleading for her, and for half the sum. There was really nothing to say. It might well be more merciful not to offer her hope, or to drag out the proceedings, which would only prolong the pain of what was in the end inevitable.

And yet he did not reach forward and tap on the window to redirect the cabby. He did not even move in his seat until they stopped at Grafton Street and he climbed down and paid the man. He even watched him move away along towards the Tottenham Court Road and turn the corner without calling him back.

A running patterer came along the footpath, a long lean man with fair hair flopping over his brow, his singsong voice reciting in easy rhymes some domestic drama ending in betrayal and murder. He stopped a few yards from Rathbone, and immediately a couple of idle passersby hesitated to hear the end of his tale. One threw him a threepenny piece.

A costermonger walked up the middle of the street with his barrow, crying his wares, and a cripple with a tray of matches hobbled up from Whitfield Street.

There was no purpose in standing on the paving stones. Rathbone went up and knocked on the door. It was a lodging house, quite respectable and spacious, very suitable for a single man of business or a minor profession. Monk would have no need of a house. From what he could remember of him, and he remembered him very vividly, Monk preferred to spend his money on expensive and very well-cut clothes. Apparently he had been a vain and highly ambitious man, professionally and socially. At least he had been, before the accident which had robbed him of his memory, at first so totally that even his name and his face were strange to him. All his life had had to be detected little by little, pieced together from fragments of evidence, letters, records of his police cases when he was still one of the most brilliant detectives London had seen, and from the reactions of others and their emotions towards him.

Then had come his resignation over the Moidore case, both on principle and in fury, because he would not be ordered against his judgment. Now he struggled to make a living by doing private work for those who, for one reason or another, found the police unsuitable or unavailable to them.

The buxom landlady opened the door and then, seeing Rathbone's immaculate figure, her eyes widened with surprise. Some deep instinct told her the difference between the air of a superior tradesman, or a man of the commercial classes, and this almost indefinably different lawyer with his slightly more discreet gray coat and silver-topped cane.

"Yes sir?" she enquired.

"Is Mr. Monk at home?"

"Yes sir. May I tell 'im 'o's calling?"

"Oliver Rathbone."

"Yes sir, Mr. Rathbone. Will you come in, sir, an' I'll fetch 'im down for yer."

"Thank you." Obediently he followed her into the chilly morning room, with its dark colors, clean antimacassars and arrangement of dried flowers, presumably set aside for such purposes.

She left him, and a few minutes later the door opened again and Monk came in. Immediately he saw Monk, all the old emotions returned in Rathbone: the instinctive mixture of liking and dislike; the conviction in his mind that a man with such a face was ruthless, unpredictable, clever, wildly humorous and quick tongued, and yet also vindictive, fiercely emotional, honest regardless of whom it hurt, himself included, and moved by the oddest of pity. It was not a handsome face; the bones were strong and finely proportioned, the nose aquiline and yet broad, the eyes startling, but the mouth was too wide and thin and there was a scar on the lower lip.

"Morning Monk," Rathbone said dryly. "I have a thankless case which needs some investigation."

Monk's eyebrows rose sharply. "So naturally you came to

me? Should I be obliged?'' Humor flashed across his face and vanished. ''I presume it is not also moneyless? You certainly do not work for the love of it.'' His voice was excellent. He had trained himself to lose his original lilting provincial Northumbrian accent, and had replaced it with perfectly modulated Queen's English.

''No.'' Rathbone kept his temper without difficulty. Monk might irritate him, but he was damned if he would allow him to dictate the interview or its tone. ''The family has money, which naturally I shall use in what I deem to be the client's best interest. That may be to employ you to investigate the case—but I fear there will be little to find that will be of use to her.''

''You are quite right,'' Monk agreed. ''It does sound thankless. But since you are here, I presume you want me to do it anyway.'' It was not a question but a conclusion. ''You had better tell me about it.''

With difficulty Rathbone kept his equanimity. He would not permit Monk to maneuver him into defensiveness. He smiled deliberately.

''Have you read of the recent death of General Thaddeus Carlyon?''

''Naturally.''

''His wife has confessed to killing him.''

Monk's eyebrows rose and there was sarcasm in his face, but he said nothing.

''There has to be more than she has told me,'' Rathbone went on levelly, with some effort. ''I need to know what it is before I go into court.''

''Why does she say she did it?'' Monk sat down astride one of the two wooden chairs, facing Rathbone over the back of it. ''Does she accuse him of anything as a provocation?''

''Having an affair with the hostess of the dinner party at which it happened.'' This time it was Rathbone who smiled bleakly.

Monk saw it and the light flickered in his eyes. ''A crime of passion,'' he observed.

''I think not,'' Rathbone answered. ''But I don't know

why. She seems to have a depth of feeling in inappropriate places for that.''

"Could she have a lover herself?'' Monk asked. "There would be a great deal less latitude for that than for anything he might do in such a field.''

"Possibly.'' Rathbone found the thought distasteful, but he could not reason it away. "I shall need to know.''

"Did she do it?''

Rathbone thought for several moments before answering.

"I don't know. Apparently her sister-in-law believes it was the younger daughter, who is seemingly very lightly balanced and has been emotionally ill after the birth of her child. She quarreled with her father both before the night of his death and at the dinner party that evening.''

"And the mother confessed to protect her?'' Monk suggested.

"That is what the sister-in-law says she believes.''

"And what do you believe?''

"Me? I don't know.''

There was a moment's silence while Monk hesitated.

"You will be remunerated by the day,'' Rathbone remarked almost casually, surprised by his own generosity. "At double police pay, since it is temporary work.'' He did not need to add that if results were poor, or hours artificially extended, Monk would not be used again.

Monk's smile was thin but wide.

"Then you had better tell me the rest of the details, so I can begin, thankless or not. Can I see Mrs. Carlyon? I imagine she is in prison?''

"Yes. I will arrange permission for you, as my associate.''

"You said it happened at a dinner party . . .''

"At the house of Maxim and Louisa Furnival, in Albany Street, off Regent's Park. The other guests were Fenton and Sabella Pole, Sabella being the daughter; Peverell and Damaris Erskine, the victim's sister and brother-in-law; and a Dr. Charles Hargrave and his wife—and of course General and Mrs. Carlyon.''

"And the medical evidence? Was that provided by this Dr. Hargrave or someone else?"

"Hargrave."

A look of bitter amusement flickered in Monk's eyes.

"And the police? Who is on the case?"

Rathbone understood, and for once felt entirely with Monk. A pompous fool who was prepared to allow others to suffer to save his pride infuriated him more than almost anything else.

"I imagine it will fall under Runcorn's command," he said, meeting Monk's eyes with understanding.

"Then there is no time to be wasted," Monk said, straightening up and rising from his seat. He squared his shoulders. "The poor devils haven't a chance without us. God knows who else they will arrest—and hang!" he added bitterly.

Rathbone made no answer, but he was aware of the quick stab of memory, and he felt Monk's anger and pain as if it were his own.

"I'm going to see them now," he said instead. "Tell me what you learn." He rose to his feet as well and took his leave, passing the landlady on the way out and thanking her.

At the police station Rathbone was greeted with civility and some concern. The desk sergeant knew his reputation, and remembered him as being associated with Monk, whose name still called forth both respect and fear not only in the station but throughout the force.

"Good afternoon, sir," the sergeant said carefully. "And what can I do for you?"

"I should like to see the officer in charge of the Carlyon case, if you please."

"That'll be Mr. Evan, sir. Or will you be wanting to see Mr. Runcorn?" His blue eyes were wide and almost innocent.

"No thank you," Rathbone said tartly. "Not at this stage, I think. It is merely a matter of certain physical details I should like to clarify."

"Right sir. I'll see if 'e's in. If 'e in't, will you call again, sir, or will you see Mr. Runcorn anyway?"

"I suppose I had better see Mr. Runcorn."

"Yes sir." And the desk sergeant turned and disappeared up the stairs. Three minutes later he came back and told Rathbone that if he went up Mr. Runcorn would give him five minutes.

Reluctantly Rathbone obeyed. He would much rather have seen Sergeant Evan, whose imagination and loyalty to Monk had been so evident in the Moidore case, and in the Grey case before that.

Instead he knocked on the door and went in to see Superintendent Runcorn sitting behind his large, leather-inlaid desk, his long, ruddy-skinned face expectant and suspicious.

"Yes, Mr. Rathbone? The desk sergeant says you want to know about the Carlyon case. Very sad." He shook his head and pursed his lips. "Very sad indeed. Poor woman took leave of her senses and killed her husband. Confessed to it." He looked at Rathbone with narrowed eyes.

"So I heard," Rathbone agreed. "But I assume you did look into the possibility of the daughter having killed him and Mrs. Carlyon confessing in order to protect her?"

Runcorn's face tightened. "Of course."

Rathbone thought he was lying, but he kept the contempt from his face.

"And it could not be so?"

"It could be," Runcorn said carefully. "But there is nothing to suggest that it is. Mrs. Carlyon has confessed, and everything we have found supports that." He leaned back a little in his chair, sniffing. "And before you ask, there is no way that it could possibly have been an accident. He might have fallen over by accident, but he could not possibly have speared himself on the halberd. Someone either followed him down or found him there, and picked up the halberd and drove it into his chest." He shook his head. "You'll not defend her, Mr. Rathbone, not from the law. I know you're a very clever man, but no one can deny this. A jury is ordinary men, sensible men, and they'll hang her—whatever you say."

"Possibly," Rathbone agreed with a feeling of defeat. "But this is only the beginning. We have a long way to go yet. Thank you, Mr. Runcorn. May I see the medical report?"

"If you like. It will do you no good."

"I'll see it anyway."

Runcorn smiled. "As you wish, Mr. Rathbone. As you wish."

3

Monk accepted the case of Alexandra Carlyon initially because it was Rathbone who brought it to him, and he would never allow Rathbone to think any case daunted him too much even to try. He did not dislike Rathbone; indeed there was much in him he both admired and felt instinctively drawn towards. His wit always appealed to Monk no matter how cutting, or against whom it was directed, and Rathbone was not cruel. He also admired the lawyer's brain. Monk had a swift and easy intelligence himself, and had always felt success enough in his own powers not to resent brilliance in others—or to fear it, as Runcorn did.

Before the accident he had felt himself equal to any man, and superior to most. All the evidence he had uncovered since, both of his actual achievements and of the attitudes of others towards him, indicated his opinion was not merely arrogance but a reasonably well-founded judgment.

Then one night of torrential rain, less than a year ago, the carriage in which he was riding had overturned, killing the cabby and knocking Monk senseless. When he awoke in hospital he knew nothing, not even his name. Over the succeeding months he had learned his own nature slowly, often unpleasantly, seeing himself from the outside, not understanding his reasons, only his acts. The picture was of a ruthless man, ambitious, dedicated to the pursuit of justice greater than merely the law, but a man without friendships or family ties. His only sister he had seemed to write seldom and not to have visited for years, in spite of her regular, gentle letters to him.

His subordinates admired and feared him. His seniors resented him and were frightened of his footsteps on their heels—most especially Runcorn. What injuries he had done any of them he still could only guess.

There was also the fleeting memory of some gentleness, but he could put no face to it, and certainly no name. Hester Latterly's sister-in-law, Imogen, had first woken in him such a sweetness it was momentarily almost numbing, robbing him of the present and tantalizing him with some indefinable comfort and hope. And then before he could force anything into clarity, it was gone again.

And there were also memories of an older man, a man who had taught him much, and around whom there was a sense of loss, a failure to protect at a time when his mentor desperately needed it. But this picture too was incomplete. Only fragments came into his mind, a face imperfectly, an older woman sitting by a dining room table, her face filled with grief, a woman who could weep without distorting her features. And he knew he had cared for her.

Then he had left the force in a rage over the Moidore case, without even thinking what he could do to survive without his profession. It had been hard. Private cases were few. He had only begun a couple of months ago, and the support of Lady Callandra Daviot had been necessary to avoid being put out of his rooms onto the street. All that remarkable woman had asked in return for being a financial backer in his new venture was that she be included in any story that was of interest. He had been delighted to agree to such terms, although so far he had dealt only with three missing people, two of whom he had found successfully; half a dozen minor thefts; and one debt collection, which he would not have taken had he not known the defaulter was well able to pay. As far as Monk was concerned, debtors in poverty were welcome to escape. He certainly was not going to hunt them down.

But he was very glad indeed of a well-paying job now funded by a lawyer's office, and possibly offering interest for Callandra Daviot as well, insofar as it contained more passion and need for help than anything he had worked on since leaving his position.

It was too late that afternoon to accomplish anything; already the shadows were lengthening and the evening traffic was filling the streets. But the following morning he set out early for Albany Street and the house of Maxim and Louisa Furnival, where the death had occurred. He would see the scene of the crime for himself, and hear their account of the evening. As Rathbone had said, it appeared on the surface a thankless task, since Alexandra Carlyon had confessed; but then the sister-in-law might be right, and she had done so only to protect her daughter. What they did with the truth was Alexandra Carlyon's decision, or Rathbone's, but the first thing was to find it. And he certainly did not trust Runcorn to have done so.

It was not very far from Grafton Street to Albany Street, and since it was a brisk, sunny morning he walked. It gave him time to order in his mind what he would look for, what questions to ask. He turned up Whitfield Street, along Warren Street and into the Euston Road, busy with all manner of carts and carriages about their business or their trade. A brewer's dray passed by him, great shire horses gleaming in the sun, decked in shining harness and with manes braided. Behind them were berlines and landaus and of course the ever-present hansoms.

He crossed the road opposite the Trinity Church and turned right into Albany Street, running parallel to the park, and set his mind to think as he strode the length of it to the Furnivals' house. He brushed past other pedestrians without noticing them: ladies flirting, gossiping; gentlemen taking the air, discussing sport or business; servants about errands, dressed in livery; the occasional peddler or newsboy. Carriages bowled past in both directions.

He looked a gentleman, and he had every intention of behaving as if he were one. When he arrived at Albany Street he presented himself at the front door of the Furnivals' house and asked the maid who answered it if he might speak with Mrs. Louisa Furnival. He also presented her with his card, which stated only his name and address, not his occupation.

"It concerns a legal matter in which Mrs. Furnival's assistance is required," he told her, seeing her very understandable indecision. She knew he had not called before, and in all probability her mistress did not know him. Still, he was very presentable . . .

"Yes sir. If you'll come in I'll find out if Mrs. Furnival's at home."

"Thank you," he accepted, not questioning the euphemism. "May I wait here?" he asked when they were in the hall.

"Yes sir, if you'd rather." She seemed to see nothing to object to, and as soon as she was gone he looked around. The stairway was very beautiful, sweeping down the right-hand wall as he stood facing it. The balcony stretched the full width of the landing above, a distance of about thirty-five feet as far as he could judge, and at least twenty feet above the hall. It would be an unpleasant fall, but not by any means necessarily a fatal one. In fact it would be quite possible to have overbalanced across the banister and dropped the distance without serious injury at all.

And the suit of armor was still there below the corner where the banister turned to come down. One would have had to fall over the very corner of it to land on the armor. It was a fine piece, although a trifle ostentatious, perhaps, in a London house. It belonged in a baronial hall with interior stonework and great open fireplaces, but it was extremely decorative here, and an excellent conversation piece, making the house one to remain in the memory, which was presumably the purpose of it. It was full late medieval knight's armor, covering the entire body, and the right-hand gauntlet was held as if to grasp a spear or pike of some sort, but was empty now. No doubt the police would have the halberd as evidence to be presented at Alexandra Carlyon's trial.

He looked around to see the disposition of the rest of the reception rooms. There was a door to his right, just beyond the foot of the stairs. If that were the withdrawing room, surely anyone in it must have heard that suit of armor fall to the ground, even though the hall was well scattered with carpets, either Bokhara or a good imitation. The metal pieces would crash against each other, even on cushions.

There was another door to the right, under the high point of the stairs, but that was more likely a library or billiard room. One did not often have a main reception room entrance so masked.

To the left was a very handsome double door. He went across and opened it softly. Since the maid had not gone to it, but towards the back of the house, he trusted it was empty at the moment.

He looked in. It was a very large, lavishly appointed dining room, with an oak table big enough to seat at least a dozen people. He pulled the door closed again quickly and stepped back. They could not have been dining when Thaddeus Carlyon fell onto the armor. Here too they could not have failed to hear it.

He had resumed his place in the center of the hall only just in time as the maid reappeared.

"Mrs. Furnival will see you, sir, if you like to come this way," she said demurely.

She led him to a wide corridor towards the back of the house, past another doorway, straight ahead to the withdrawing room, which opened onto the garden, as far as possible from the hall.

There was no time to look at the furnishings, except to get the briefest impression of crowding with overstuffed sofas and chairs in hot pinks and reds, rich curtains, some rather ordinary pictures, and at least two gilt-framed mirrors.

The woman who commanded his attention was actually physically quite small, but of such striking personality that she dominated the room. Her bones were slender, yet his overriding impression was of voluptuousness. She had a mass of dark hair, much fuller around her face than the current fashion; but it was also far more flattering to her broad, high cheekbones and long eyes, which were so narrow he could not at first be sure of their color, whether they were green or brown. She was not at all like a real cat, and yet there was an intensely feline quality in her, a grace and a detachment that made him think of small, fierce wild animals.

She would have been beautiful, in a sensuous and highly individual way, had not a meanness in her upper lip sent a tingling jar through him, like a warning.

"Good afternoon, Mr. Monk." Her voice was excellent, strong and level, much more immediate than he had expected, more candid. From such a woman he had expected something self-consciously childlike and artificially sweet. This was a most pleasant surprise. "How may I help you with a legal matter? I presume it is to do with poor General Carlyon?"

So she was both intelligent and forthright. He instantly altered what he had been going to say. He had imagined a sillier woman, a flirt. He was wrong. Louisa Furnival was much more powerful than he had supposed. And that made Alexandra Carlyon easier to understand. This woman in front of him was a rival to fear, not a casual pastime for an evening that might well have been heavy without a little frivolity.

"Yes," he agreed with equal frankness. "I am employed by Mr. Oliver Rathbone, counsel to Mrs. Carlyon, to make sure that we have understood correctly exactly what happened that evening."

She smiled only slightly, but there was humor in it, and her eyes were very bright.

"I appreciate your honesty, Mr. Monk. I do not mind interesting lies, but boring ones annoy me. What is it you wish to know?"

He smiled. He was not flirting with her—such a thing would not have entered his mind for himself—but he saw the spark of interest in her face, and instinctively used it.

"As much as you can remember of what happened that

evening, Mrs. Furnival," he replied. "And later, all you know, and are prepared to tell me, of General and Mrs. Carlyon and their relationship."

She lowered her gaze. "How very thorough of you, Mr. Monk. Although I fear thoroughness may be all you will be able to offer her, poor creature. But you must go through the motions, I understand. Where shall I begin? When they arrived?"

"If you please."

"Then sit down, Mr. Monk," she invited, indicating the overstuffed pink sofa. He obeyed, and she walked, with more swagger and sensuality than pure grace, over towards the window where the light fell on her, and turned to face him. In that moment he realized she knew her own power to an exactness, and enjoyed it.

He leaned back, waiting for her to begin.

She was wearing a rose-colored crinoline gown, cut low at the bosom, and against the lushly pink curtains she was strikingly dramatic to look at, and she smiled as she began her account.

"I cannot remember the order in which they arrived, but I recall their moods very clearly indeed." Her eyes never left his face, but even in the brilliance from the window he still could not see what color they were. "But I don't suppose times matter very much at that point, do they?" Her fine eyebrows rose.

"Not at all, Mrs. Furnival," he assured her.

"The Erskines were just as usual," she went on. "I suppose you know who they are? Yes, of course you do." She smoothed the fabric of her skirt almost unconsciously. "So was Fenton Pole, but Sabella was in quite a temper, and as soon as she was through the door she was rude to her father—oh! Which means he must already have been here, doesn't it?" She shrugged. "I think the last to arrive were Dr. and Mrs. Hargrave. Have you spoken to him?"

"No, you are the first."

She seemed about to comment on that, then changed her

mind. Her glance wandered away and she stared into the distance as if visualizing in her mind.

"Thaddeus—that is, the general—seemed as usual." A tiny smile flickered over her mouth, full of meaning and amusement. He noticed it, and thought it betrayed more of her than of the general or their relationship. "He was a very masculine man, very much the soldier. He had seen some very interesting action, you know?" This time she did look at Monk, her eyebrows high, her face full of vitality. "He spoke to me about it sometimes. We were friends, you know? Yes, I daresay you do. Alexandra was jealous, but she had no cause. I mean, it was not in the least improper." She hesitated for only an instant. She was far too sophisticated to wait for the obvious compliment, and he did not pay it, but it entered his mind. If General Carlyon had not entertained a few improper ideas about Louisa Furnival, then he was a very slow-blooded man indeed.

"But Alexandra seemed in something of an ill temper right from the beginning," she went on. "She did not smile at all, except briefly as was required by civility, and she avoided speaking to Thaddeus altogether. To tell you the truth, Mr. Monk, it strained my abilities as a hostess to keep the occasion from becoming embarrassing for my other guests. A family quarrel is a very ugly thing to have to witness and makes people most uncomfortable. I gather this one must have been very bitter, because all evening Alexandra was holding in an anger which no observant person could miss."

"But one-sided, you say?"

"I beg your pardon?"

"One-sided," he repeated. "According to you, the general was not angry with Mrs. Carlyon; he behaved as normal."

"Yes—that is true," she acknowledged with something like surprise. "Perhaps he had forbidden her something, or made a decision she did not like, and she was still smarting over it. But that is hardly reason to kill anyone, is it?"

"What would be reason to kill, Mrs. Furnival?"

She drew in her breath quickly, then shot him a bright, sharp smile.

"What unexpected things you say, Mr. Monk! I have no idea. I have never thought of killing anyone. That is not how I fight my battles."

He met her eyes without a flicker. "How do you fight them, Mrs. Furnival?"

This time the smile was wider. "Discreetly, Mr. Monk, and without forewarning people."

"And do you win?"

"Yes I do." Too late she wished to take it back. "Well, usually," she amended. "Of course if I did not, I should not . . ." She tailed off, realizing that to justify herself would be clumsy. He had not accused her; in fact he had not even allowed the thought to come through his words. She had raised it herself.

She continued with the story, looking up at the far wall again. "Then we all went in to dinner. Sabella was still making occasional bitter remarks, Damaris Erskine was behaving appallingly to poor Maxim, and Alex spoke to everyone except Thaddeus—oh, and very little to me. She seemed to feel I was on his side, which was foolish. Of course I was on no one's side, I was simply doing my duty as hostess."

"And after dinner?"

"Oh, as usual the gentlemen stayed at the table for port, and we went to the withdrawing room where we sat and gossiped for a while." She lifted her beautiful shoulders in an expression of both humor and boredom. "Sabella went upstairs, as I recall, something about a headache. She has not been entirely well since the birth of her child."

"Did you gossip about anything in particular?"

"I really cannot remember. It was rather difficult, as I said. Damaris Erskine had been behaving like a complete fool all evening. I have no idea why. Usually she is quite a sensible woman, but that evening she seemed on the point of hysteria ever since just before dinner. I don't know if she had quarreled with her husband, or something. They are very close, and she did seem to be avoiding him on this occasion, which is unusual. I really wondered once or twice if she had had rather too much wine before she came. I can't think what else would account for her manner, or why poor Maxim should be the principal victim. She is rather eccentric, but this was really too much!''

''I'll enquire into it,'' he remarked. ''Then what happened? At some point the general must have left the room.''

''Yes he did. I took him up to see my son, Valentine, who was at home because he has just recovered from the measles, poor boy. They were very fond of each other, you know. Thaddeus has always taken an interest in him, and of course Valentine, like any boy looking towards manhood, has a great admiration for the military and exploration and foreign travel.'' She looked at him very directly. ''He loved to hear Thaddeus's tales of India and the Far East. I am afraid my husband does not go in very much for that sort of thing.''

''You took General Carlyon upstairs to see your son. Did you remain with him?''

''No. My husband came up to find me, because the party needed some considerable management. As I said before, several people were behaving badly. Fenton Pole and Mrs. Hargrave were struggling to keep some sort of civilized conversation going. At least that is what Maxim said.''

''So you came down, leaving the general with Valentine?''

''Yes, that's right.'' Her face tightened. ''That is the last time I saw him.''

''And your husband?''

She shifted her position very slightly, but still stood against the rich swath of the curtain.

''He stayed upstairs. And almost as soon as I got back down here again, Alexandra went up. She looked furious, whitefaced and so tense I thought she was intending to have a terrible quarrel, but there was nothing any of us could do to stop her. I didn't know what it was about—and I still don't.''

He looked at her without any humor at all, directly and blankly.

''Mrs. Carlyon said she killed him because he was having an affair with you, and everyone knew it.''

Her eyes widened and she looked at him with complete incredulity, as if he had said something absurd, so ridiculous as to be funny rather than offensive.

"Oh really! That is too foolish! She couldn't possibly believe such a thing! It is not only untrue, it is not even remotely credible. We have been agreeable friends, no more. Nor would it ever have appeared to anyone that we were more—I assure you, no one else thought so. Ask them! I am an amusing and entertaining woman, I hope, and capable of friendship, but I am not irresponsible."

He smiled, still refusing to pay the implicit compliment, except with his eyes. "Can you think of any reason why Mrs. Carlyon would believe it?"

"No—none at all. None that are sane." She smiled at him, her eyes bright and steady. They were hazel after all. "Really, Mr. Monk, I think there must be some other reason for whatever she did—some quarrel we know nothing of. And honestly, I cannot see why it matters. If she killed him, and it seems inescapable that she did, then what difference does it make why?"

"It might make a difference to the judge, when he comes to sentence her, if and when she is convicted," he replied, watching her face for pity, anger, grief, any emotions he could read. He saw nothing but cool intelligence.

"I am not familiar with the law, except the obvious." She smiled. "I would have thought they would hang her regardless."

"Indeed they may," he conceded. "You left the story with your husband and the general upstairs, and Mrs. Carlyon just going up. What happened then?"

"Maxim came down, and then a little later, maybe ten minutes, Alexandra came down, looking dreadful. Shortly after that Maxim went out into the front hall—we had all used the back stairs as it is quicker to go up to Valentine's rooms that way—and almost immediately he came back to say Thaddeus had had an accident and was seriously hurt. Charles—that is, Dr. Hargrave, went to see if he could help.

He came back after the briefest time to say Thaddeus was dead and we should call the police."

"Which you did?"

"Of course. A Sergeant Evan came, and they asked us all sorts of questions. It was the worst night I can ever remember."

"So it is possible that Mrs. Carlyon, your husband, Sabella or yourself could have killed him—as far as opportunity is concerned?"

She looked surprised. "Yes—I suppose so. But why should we?"

"I don't know yet, Mrs. Furnival. When did Sabella Pole come downstairs?"

She thought for a moment. "After Charles said Thaddeus was dead. I cannot remember who went up for her. Her mother, I expect. I realize you are employed to help Alexandra, but I cannot see how you can. Neither my husband nor I had anything to do with Thaddeus's death. I know Sabella is very emotional, but I don't believe she killed her father—and no one else could have, apart from having no possible reason."

"Is your son still at home, Mrs. Furnival?"

"Yes."

"May I speak with him?"

There was a guarded look to her face which he found most natural in the circumstances.

"Why?" she asked.

"He may have seen or heard something which precipitated the quarrel resulting in the general's death."

"He didn't. I asked him that myself."

"I would still like to hear from him, if I may. After all, if Mrs. Carlyon murdered the general a few minutes afterwards, there must have been some indication of it then. If he is an intelligent boy, he must have been aware of something."

She hesitated for several moments. He thought she was weighing up the possible distress to her son, the justification for denying his request, and the light it would cast on her own motives and on Alexandra Carlyon's guilt.

"I am sure you would like this whole affair cleared up as soon as possible," he said carefully. "It cannot be pleasant for you to have it unresolved."

Her eyes did not waver from his face.

"It is resolved, Mr. Monk. Alexandra has confessed."

"But that is not the end," he argued. "It is merely the end of the first phase. May I see your son?"

"If you find it important. I shall take you up."

He followed her out of the withdrawing room, walking behind and watching her slight swagger, the elegant, feminine line of her shoulders, and the confident way she managed the big skirt with its stiff hoops. She led him along the passage, then instead of going up the main stairs, she turned right and went up the second staircase to the landing of the north wing. Valentine's rooms were separated from the main bedrooms by a guest suite, presently unused.

She knocked briefly but opened the door without waiting for a reply. Inside the large airy room was furnished as a schoolroom with tables, a large blackboard and several bookcases and a schoolteacher's desk. The windows opened onto other roofs, and the green boughs of a great tree. Inside, sitting on the bench by the window, was a slender dark boy of perhaps thirteen or fourteen years of age. His features were regular, with a long nose, heavy eyelids and clear blue eyes. He stood up as soon as he saw Monk. He was far taller than Monk expected, very close to six feet, and his shoulders were already broadening, foreshadowing the man he would become. He towered over his mother. Presumably Maxim Furnival was a tall man.

"Valentine, this is Mr. Monk. He works for Mrs. Carlyon's lawyer. He would like to ask you some questions about the evening the general died." Louisa was as direct as Monk would have expected. There was no attempt at evasion in her, no protection of him from reality.

The boy was tense, his face wary, and even as Louisa

spoke Monk saw a tension in his body, an anxiety narrowing his eyes, but he did not look away.

"Yes sir?" he said slowly. "I didn't see anything, or I would have told the police. They asked me."

"I'm sure." Monk made a conscious effort to be gentler than he would with an adult. The boy's face was pale and there were marks of tiredness around his eyes. If he had been fond of the general, admired him as both a friend and a hero, then this must have been a brutal shock as well as a bereavement. "Your mother brought the general up to see you?"

Valentine's body tightened and there was a bleakness in his face as if he had been dealt a blow deep inside him where the pain was hidden, only betraying itself as a change in his muscles, a dulling in his eyes.

"Yes."

"You were friends?"

Again the look was guarded. "Yes."

"So it was not unusual that he should call on you?"

"No, I've—I've known him a long time. In fact, all my life."

Monk wished to express some sympathy, but was uncertain what words to use. The relationship between a boy and his hero is a delicate thing, and at times very private, composed in part of dreams.

"His death must be a great blow to you. I'm sorry." He was uncharacteristically awkward. "Did you see your mother or your father at that time?"

"No. I—the general was—alone here. We were talking . . ." He glanced at his mother for an instant so brief Monk almost missed it.

"About what?" he asked.

"Er . . ." Valentine shrugged. "I don't remember now. Army—army life . . ."

"Did you see Mrs. Carlyon?"

Valentine looked very white. "Yes—yes, she came in."

"She came into your rooms here?"

"Yes." He swallowed hard. "Yes she did."

Monk was not surprised he was pale. He had seen a murderer and her victim a few minutes before the crime. He had almost certainly been the last one to see General Carlyon alive, except for Alexandra. It was a thought sufficient to chill anyone.

"How was she?" he asked very quietly. "Tell me what you can remember—and please be careful not to let your knowledge of what happened afterwards color what you say, if you can help it."

"No sir." Valentine looked squarely at him; his eyes were wide and vividly blue. "Mrs. Carlyon seemed very upset indeed, very angry. In fact she was shaking and she seemed to find it difficult to speak. I've seen someone drunk once, and it was rather like that, as if her tongue and her lips would not do what she wished."

"Can you remember what she said?"

Valentine frowned. "Not exactly. It was more or less that he should come downstairs, and that she had to speak to him—or that she had spoken, I don't remember which. I thought they had had a quarrel over something and it looked as if she wanted to start it up again. Sir?"

"Yes?"

This time he avoided his mother's eyes deliberately. "Can you do anything to help Mrs. Carlyon?"

Monk was startled. He had expected the opposite.

"I don't know yet. I have only just begun." He wanted to ask why Valentine should wish her helped, but he knew it would be clumsy in front of Louisa.

Valentine turned to the window. "Of course. I'm sorry."

"Not at all," Monk said quietly. "It is very decent of you to ask."

Valentine looked at him quickly, then away again, but in that instant Monk saw the flash of gratitude.

"Did the general seem upset?" he asked.

"No, not really."

"So you think he had no idea she was in such a fury?"

"No, I don't think so. Well if he had known, he wouldn't have turned his back on her, would he? He's a lot bigger than she is and he would have to have been caught by surprise . . ."

"You are quite right. It's a good point."

Valentine smiled unhappily.

Louisa interrupted for the first time.

"I don't think he can tell you anything more, Mr. Monk."

"No. Thank you." He spoke to Valentine. "I am grateful for your forbearance."

"You're welcome, sir."

They were back downstairs in the hall and Monk was ready to take his leave when Maxim Furnival came in, handing his hat and stick to the maid. He was a tall, slender man with hair almost black and deep-set dark brown eyes. He was very nearly handsome, except his lower lip was a trifle too full, and when he smiled there was a gap between his front teeth. It was a moody face, emotional, intelligent and without cruelty.

Louisa explained Monk's presence quickly. "Mr. Monk is working for Alexandra Carlyon's lawyer."

"Good afternoon, Mr. Furnival." Monk inclined his head. He needed this man's help. "I appreciate your courtesy."

Maxim's face darkened immediately, but it was with pity rather than irritation.

"I wish there was something we could do. But it's too late now." His voice was constricted, as though his distress were startlingly deep and full of anger. "We should have done it weeks ago." He moved towards the passage leading to the withdrawing room. "What is there now, Mr. Monk?"

"Only information," Monk answered. "Is there anything you remember of that evening that might explain things better?"

A flash of ironic humor crossed Maxim's face, and something that looked like self-blame. "Believe me, Mr. Monk, I've racked my brain trying to think of an explanation, and I know nothing now I didn't know then. It's a complete mystery to me. I know, of course, that Alex and Thaddeus had differences of opinion. In fact, to be honest, I know they did not get on particularly well; but that is true of a great many people, if not most, at some time or another. It does not excuse one breaking the marriage vows, and it certainly doesn't result in their killing each other."

"Mrs. Carlyon says she did it out of jealousy over her husband's attention towards Mrs. Furnival . . ."

Maxim's eyes widened in surprise. "That's absurd! They've been friends for years, in fact since before—before Valentine was born. Nothing has happened suddenly to make her jealous, nothing has changed at all." He looked genuinely confused. If he were an actor he was superb. It had crossed Monk's mind to wonder if it might have been he and not Alexandra who was the jealous spouse, or even for a wild moment if the general was Valentine's father. But he could think of no reason why Alexandra should confess to protect Maxim, unless they were lovers—in which case he had little cause to be jealous over the general and Louisa. In fact, it was in his interest it should continue.

"But Mrs. Carlyon was distressed that evening?" he asked aloud.

"Oh yes." Maxim poked his hands deep into his pockets and frowned. "Very. But I don't know what about, except that Thaddeus rather ignored her, but that is hardly cause for violence. Anyway, everyone seemed rather excitable that evening. Damaris Erskine was almost to the point of frenzy." He did not mention that she had singled him out for her abuse. "And I have no idea why about that either." He looked bewildered. "Nor had poor Peverell, to judge by his face. And Sabella was very overwrought as well—but then she has been rather often lately." His expression was rueful and more than a little embarrassed. "Altogether it was a pretty dreadful evening."

"But nothing happened to make you think it would end in murder?"

"Good God, no! No, nothing at all. It was just . . ." He stopped, his face bleak, lost for any words adequate to explain his feelings.

"Thank you, Mr. Furnival." Monk could think of nothing further to ask at this point. He thanked Louisa also and took his leave, going out into the patchy sunshine of Albany Street with his mind crowded with thoughts and impressions: Louisa's arrogant walk and her confident, inviting face with

90

an element of coldness in it in repose; Valentine's hidden pain; and Maxim's innocence.

Next Monk visited Alexandra Carlyon's younger daughter, Sabella. The elder daughter lived in Bath, and was no part of this tragedy, except as it deprived her of her father, and almost certainly in due course of the law, of her mother also. But Sabella might well be at the heart of it, either the true motive for Alexandra's crime or even the murderer herself.

The Poles' house was on George Street, only a short walk away, the other side of the Hampstead Road, and it took him ten minutes on foot to reach the step. When the door opened he explained to the parlormaid that he was engaged to do all he could to assist Mrs. Carlyon, and he would be obliged if he might speak to Mr. or Mrs. Pole to that end.

He was shown into the morning room, a small, chilly place even in the bright, gusty winds of May with a sudden rain squall battering against the heavily curtained windows. And to be fair, they were very newly in mourning for Sabella's father.

It was not Sabella who came, but Fenton Pole, a pleasant, unremarkable young man with strawberry fair hair and an earnest face, regular features and china-blue eyes. He was fashionably dressed in a shawl-collared waistcoat, very white shirt and somber suit. He closed the door behind him and regarded Monk with misgiving.

"I am sorry to disturb you in a time of such family grief," Monk began straightaway. "But the matter of helping Mrs. Carlyon cannot wait."

Fenton Pole's frown became deeper and he moved towards Monk with a candid expression, as if he would confide something, then stopped a few feet away.

"I cannot think what anyone can do to help her," he said anxiously. "Least of all my wife or I. We were present that evening, but anything I saw or heard only adds to her troubles. I think, Mr. Monk, that the least damage we can do would be to say as little as possible and let the end be as mercifully rapid as may be." He looked down at his shoes, then up at Monk with a frown. "My wife is not well, and I refuse to add anymore to her distress. She has lost both father and mother, in the most dreadful circumstances. I am sure you appreciate that?"

"I do, Mr. Pole," Monk conceded. "It would be hard to imagine anything worse than what appears to have happened. But so far it is only an appearance. We owe it to her, as well as ourselves, to see if there are other explanations, or mitigating circumstances. I am sure your wife, in love for her mother, would wish that too."

"My wife is not well . . ." Pole repeated rather sharply.

"I regret it profoundly," Monk interrupted. "But events will make no allowance for individual illness or grief." Then before Pole could protest again, "But perhaps if you would tell me what you recall of the evening, I will have to disturb your wife very little—only to see if she can add anything you do not know."

"I don't see that it can help." Pole's jaw hardened and there was a stubborn light in his blue eyes.

"Neither do I, until I hear what you have to say." Monk was beginning to grow irritated, and he concealed it with difficulty. He did not suffer foolishness, prejudice or complacency with any grace, and this man was exhibiting at least two of these faults. "But it is my profession to learn such things, and I have been employed by Mrs. Carlyon's barrister to discover what I can."

Pole regarded him without answering.

Deliberately Monk sat down on one of the higher chairs as if he intended to be there for some time.

"The dinner party, Mr. Pole," he insisted. "I understand your wife quarreled with her father almost as soon as she arrived at the Furnivals' house. Do you know what was the cause of that difference?"

Pole looked discomfited. "I cannot see what that has to do with the general's death, but since you ask, I don't know what the cause was. I imagine it was some old misunderstanding and nothing new or of any importance."

Monk looked at him with disbelief as civil as he could make it.

"Surely something was said? It is impossible to have a quarrel without mentioning what it is about, at least nominally, even if what is spoken of is not the real cause."

Pole's blond eyebrows rose. He pushed his hands even deeper into his pockets and turned away irritably. "If that is what you want. I thought from what you were saying that you wished to know the real cause—although it can hardly matter now."

Monk felt his anger rising. His muscles were tight and his voice was harsh when he replied.

"What did they say to each other, Mr. Pole?"

Pole sat down and crossed his legs. He looked at Monk coldly.

"The general made some observation about the army in India, and Sabella said she had heard there was a very tense situation there. The general told her it was nothing. In fact he was rather dismissive of her opinions, and it angered her. She felt he was being condescending and told him so. Sabella imagines that she knows something about India—and I am afraid that perhaps I have indulged her. At that point Maxim Furnival intervened and tried to turn the subject to something else, not entirely successfully. It was not anything remarkable, Mr. Monk. And it certainly had no bearing upon Mrs. Carlyon's quarrel with him."

"What was that about?"

"I have no idea!" he snapped. "I simply assume there was one, because she could not possibly have killed him unless there was a most violent difference between them. But none of us were aware of anything of the sort, or naturally we should have done something to prevent it." He looked annoyed, as if he could not believe Monk was so stupid intentionally.

Before Monk could reply the door opened and a lovely but disheveled young woman stood facing them, her fair hair over her shoulders, her gown wrapped around by a shawl.

93

She held it with one slender, pale hand grasped close to her throat. She stared at Monk, disregarding Pole.

"Who are you? Polly said you are trying to help Mama. How can you do that?"

Monk rose to his feet. "William Monk, Mrs. Pole. I am employed by your mother's barrister, Mr. Rathbone, to see if I can learn something to mitigate her case."

She stared at him in silence. Her eyes were very wide and fixed, and there was a hectic color in her cheeks.

Pole had risen when she came in, and now he turned to her gently. "Sabella, my dear, there is no cause to let this concern you. I think you should go back and lie down . . ."

She pushed him away angrily and came towards Monk. Pole put his hand on her arm and she snatched it away from him.

"Mr. Monk, is it possible you can do something to help my mother? You said 'mitigation.' Does that mean the law might take into account what manner of man he was? How he bullied us, forced us to his will regardless of our own desires?"

"Sabella . . ." Pole said urgently. He glared at Monk. "Really, Mr. Monk, this is all irrelevant and I—"

"It is not irrelevant!" Sabella said angrily, cutting across him. "Will you be good enough to answer me, Mr. Monk?"

He heard the rising hysteria in her voice and it was quite obvious she was on the edge of losing control altogether. It was hardly remarkable. Her family had been shattered by the most appalling double tragedy. She had effectively lost both her parents in a scandal which would ruin their reputations and tear her family life apart and expose it to public ignominy. What could he say to her that would not either make it worse or be totally meaningless? He forced his dislike of Pole out of his mind.

"I don't know, Mrs. Pole," he said very gently. "I hope so. I believe she must have had some reason to do such a thing—if indeed it was she who did it. I need to learn what the reason was: it may be grounds for some sort of defense."

"For God's sake, man!" Pole exploded furiously, his face

tight with rage. "Have you no sense of decency at all? My wife is ill—can you not see that? I am sorry, but Mrs. Carlyon's defense, if indeed there can be any, lies with her solicitors, not with us. You must do what you can and not involve my wife. Now I must ask you to leave, without causing any more distress than you already have." He stood, holding his position rather than moving towards Monk, but his threat was plain. He was a very angry man, and Monk thought he was also frightened, although his fear might well be for his wife's mental state and nothing more. Indeed she did look on the border of complete collapse.

Monk no longer had authority to insist, as he had when a policeman. He had no choice but to leave, and do it with as much dignity as possible. Being asked to leave was galling enough, being thrown out would be a total humiliation, which he would not endure. He turned from Pole to Sabella, but before he could collect his own excuses, she spoke.

"I have the deepest affection for my mother, Mr. Monk, and regardless of what my husband says, if there is anything at all I can do . . ." She stood rigidly, her body shaking, very deliberately ignoring Pole. "I shall do it! You may feel free to call upon me at any time. I shall instruct the servants that you are to be allowed in, and I am to be told."

"Sabella!" Pole was exasperated. "I forbid it! You really have no idea what you are saying—"

Before he could finish she swung around on him in fury, her face spotted with color, her eyes brilliant, lips twisted.

"How dare you forbid me to help my mother! You are just like Papa—arrogant, tyrannical, telling me what I may and may not do, regardless of my feelings or what I know to be right." Her voice was getting higher and more and more shrill. "I will not be dictated to—I—"

"Sabella! Keep your voice down!" he said furiously. "Remember who you are—and to whom you speak. I am your husband, and you owe me your obedience, not to mention your loyalty."

"Owe you?" She was shouting now. "I do not *owe* you

anything! I married you because my father commanded me and I had no choice.''

"You are hysterical!'' Pole's face was scarlet with fury and embarrassment. "Go to your room! That is an order, Sabella, and I will not be defied!'' He waved his arm towards the door. "Your father's death has unhinged you, which is understandable, but I will not have you behave like this in front of a—a—'' He was lost for words to describe Monk.

As if she had just remembered his presence, Sabella looked back at Monk, and at last realized the enormity of her behavior. Her color paled and with shuddering breath she turned and went out of the room without speaking again, leaving the door swinging.

Pole looked at Monk with blazing eyes, as if it were Monk's fault he had witnessed the scene.

"As you can see, Mr. Monk,'' he said stiffly, "my wife is in a very distressed state. It will be perfectly clear to you that nothing she says can be of any use to Mrs. Carlyon, or to anyone else.'' His face was hard, closed to all entreaty. "I must ask you not to call again. In spite of what she says, you will not be permitted in. I regret I cannot help, but it must be plain to anyone that we are in no state to do so. Good day to you. The maid will show you to the door.'' And so saying he turned around on his heel and went out, leaving Monk alone.

There was nothing to do but leave also, his mind filled with images and doubts. Surely Sabella Pole was passionate enough, and lightly balanced enough as Edith Sobell had apparently believed, to have pushed her father downstairs and then lifted that halberd and speared him to death. And she certainly seemed to have no idea at all of propriety, or what her station required of her, or perhaps even of sanity.

Monk met Hester Latterly, by arrangement, the following day. It was not that he entirely wanted to—his emotions were very mixed—but she was an excellent ally. She had acute observation, an understanding of women he would never achieve simply because he was a man. Also she was born of a different social class, and so would perceive and interpret nuances he might easily misunderstand. And of course in this instance she knew Edith Sobell, and had access to the Carlyon family, which might be invaluable if the case proved worth fighting and there was any weapon to use.

He had first met her in the Grey case nearly a year ago. She had been staying at Shelburne Court, the Grey country seat, and he had bumped into her when out walking on the estate. She had been conceited, opinionated, extremely bossy, far too outspoken, and as far as he was concerned, in no way attractive. She had proved to be resourceful, courageous, determined, and her candid tongue had at times been a blessing. She had bullied him out of defeat with her rudeness and her blind refusal to accept despair.

In fact there had been moments when he had felt a kind of friendship for her more totally honest than he had for anyone else, even John Evan. She saw him without any deluding mists of admiration, self-interest or fear for her own position, and there was something extraordinarily sweet and comfortable about a friend who knows you and accepts you at your worst, your most bitter, or defeated, who sees your emotional ugliness naked and is not afraid to call it by name, and yet does not turn from you or allow you to cease to struggle, who wills your survival as precious.

Therefore he went out in the early afternoon to meet Hester just outside Major Tiplady's apartment in Great Titchfield Street, and walk with her down to Oxford Street, where they could find an agreeable place to take tea or hot chocolate. Perhaps her company would even be pleasant.

He had barely arrived at Tiplady's house when she came down the steps, head high, back stiff as if she were on parade. It reminded him sharply of the first occasion on which they had met; she had a very individual way of carrying herself. It both jarred on him for its assurance and sense of purpose, not a feminine characteristic at all, rather more like a soldier; and also was oddly comforting because of its familiarity. It evoked most sharply the way she alone had been willing to fight the Grey case and had not recoiled from him in horror or disappointment when his part in it all had looked not only hopeless but inexcusable.

"Good afternoon, Mr. Monk," she said rather stiffly. She made no concession to ordinary civilities and the small trifles that most people indulged in as a preamble to more serious conversation. "Have you begun on the Carlyon case? I imagine it is not easy. I admit, from what Edith Sobell says, there can be little chance of a happy outcome. Still, to send the wrong person to the gallows would be even worse—as, I presume, we are agreed?" She shot him a sharp, very candid glance.

There was no need to make any comment; memory was a blade pointed between them, full of pain, but there was no blame in it, only shared emotion.

"I haven't seen Mrs. Carlyon herself yet." He set a smart pace and she kept up with him without difficulty. "I shall do that tomorrow. Rathbone has arranged it for me in the morning. Do you know her?"

"No—I know only the general's family, and that very slightly."

"What is your opinion?"

"That is a very large question." She hesitated, uncertain what her considered judgment was.

He looked at her with unconcealed scorn.

"You have become uncharacteristically genteel, Miss Latterly. You were never backwards in expressing your opinions of people in the past." He smiled wryly. "But of course that was when your opinion was unasked for. The fact that I am interested seems to have frozen your tongue."

"I thought you wanted a considered opinion," she retorted brusquely. "Not something merely given on the spur of the moment and without reflection."

"Assuming your opinions in the past have been on the spur of the moment, perhaps a considered opinion would be better," he agreed with a tight smile.

They came to the curb, hesitated while a carriage went past, harness gleaming, horses stepping high, then crossed Margaret Street into Market Place. Oxford Street was clearly visible ahead of them, crowded with traffic, all manner of vehicles of fashion, business, leisure and trade, pedestrians, idlers and street sellers of every sort.

"Mrs. Randolf Carlyon seems to be the most powerful member of the family," Hester answered when they reached the farther pavement. "A very forceful person, I should judge, ten years younger than her husband, and perhaps in better health—"

"It is unlike you to be so diplomatic," he interrupted. "Do you mean the old man is senile?"

"I—I'm not sure."

He glanced at her with surprise. "It is unlike you not to say what you mean. You used to err on the side of being far too frank. Have you suddenly become tactful, Hester? Why, for heaven's sake?"

"I am not tactful," she snapped back. "I am trying to be accurate—which is not at all the same thing." She lengthened her stride a fraction. "I am not sure whether he is senile or not. I have not seen him at sufficient length to judge. It is my opinion so far that he is definitely losing his vitality but that she was always the stronger personality of the two."

"Bravo," he said with slightly sarcastic approval. "And Mrs. Sobell, who seems to think her sister-in-law innocent? Is she a rose-gathering optimist? It seems, in the face of a confession, about the only sort of person who could still imagine there is anything to be done for Mrs. Carlyon, apart from pray for her soul."

"No she isn't," she replied with considerable acerbity. "She is a clear-sighted widow of considerable good sense. She thinks it far more likely Sabella Pole, the general's daughter, is the one who killed him."

"Not unreasonable," he conceded. "I have just met Sabella, and she is very highly emotional, if not outright hysterical."

"Is she?" Hester said quickly, turning to look at him, interest dismissing all her irritation. "What was your judgment of her? Might she have killed her father? I know from Damaris Erskine, who was at the party, that she had the opportunity."

They were at the corner of Market Street and Oxford Street, and turned into the thoroughfare, walking side by side along the footpath. He took her arm, largely to make sure they remained together and were not divided by passersby bustling in the opposite direction.

"I have no idea," he replied after a moment or two. "I form my opinions on evidence, not intuition."

"No you don't," she contradicted. "You cannot possibly be so stupid, or so pompous, as to disregard your intuitive judgment. Whatever you have forgotten, you remember enough of past experiences with people to know something of them merely by their faces and the way they behave to each other, and when you speak to them."

He smiled dryly. "Then I think Fenton Pole believes she could have done it," he replied. "And that is indicative."

"Then perhaps there is some hope?" Unconsciously she straightened up and lifted her chin a little.

"Hope of what? Is that any better an answer?"

She stopped so abruptly a gentleman behind bumped into her and growled under his breath, tripping over his cane and going around her with ill grace.

"I beg your pardon, sir?" Monk said loudly. "I did not catch your remark. I presume you apologized to the lady for jostling her?"

The man colored and shot him a furious glance.

"Of course I did!" he snapped, then glowered at Hester. "I beg your pardon, ma'am!" Then he turned on his heel and strode off.

"Clumsy fool," Monk said between his teeth.

"He was only a trifle awkward-footed," she said reasonably.

"Not him—you." He took her by the arm and moved her forward again. "Now attend to what we are doing, before you cause another accident. It can hardly be better that Sabella Pole should be guilty—but if it is the truth, then we must discover it. Do you wish for a cup of coffee?"

Monk entered the prison with a sharp stab of memory, not from the time before his accident, although surely he must have been in places like this on countless occasions, probably even this prison itself. The emotion that was so powerful now was from only a few months back, the case which had caused him to leave the police force, throw away all the long years of learning and labor, and the sacrifices to ambition.

He followed the turnkey along the grim passages, a chill on his skin. He still had little idea what he would say to Alexandra Carlyon, or indeed what kind of woman she would be—presumably something like Sabella.

They came to the cell and the turnkey opened the door.

"Call w'en yer want ter come aht," she said laconically. Making no further comment, she turned around without interest, and as soon as Monk was inside, slammed the door shut and locked it.

The cell was bare but for a single cot with straw pallet and gray blankets. On it was sitting a slender woman, pale-skinned, with fair hair tied loosely and pinned in a knot at the back of her head. As she turned to look at him he saw her face. It was not at all what he had expected; the features were nothing like Sabella's, far from being ordinarily pretty. She had a short, aquiline nose, very blue eyes and a mouth far too wide, too generous and full of sensuality and humor. Now she gazed at him almost expressionlessly and he knew in that single moment that she had no hope of reprieve of any sort. He did not bother with civilities, which could serve no purpose. He too had been mortally afraid and he knew its taste too well.

"I am William Monk. I expect Mr. Rathbone told you I would come."

"Yes," she said tonelessly. "But there is nothing you can do. Nothing you could discover would make any difference."

"Confessions alone are not sufficient evidence, Mrs. Carlyon." He remained standing in the center of the floor looking down at her. She did not bother to rise. "If you now wish to retract it for any reason," he went on, "the prosecution will still have to prove the case. Although admittedly it will be harder to defend you after your saying you had done it. Unless, of course, there is a good reason." He did not

101

make it a question. He did not think her hopelessness was due to a feeling that her confession condemned her so much as to some facts he as yet did not fully understand. But this was a place to begin.

She smiled briefly, without light or happiness. "The best of reasons, Mr. Monk. I am guilty. I killed my husband." Her voice was remarkably pleasing, low-pitched and a trifle husky, her diction very clear.

Without any warning he had an overwhelming sense of having done this before. Violent emotions overwhelmed him: fear, anger, love. And then as quickly it was gone again, leaving him breathless and confused. He was staring at Alexandra Carlyon as if he had only just seen her, the details of her face sharp and surprising, not what he expected.

"I beg your pardon?" He had missed whatever she had said.

"I killed my husband, Mr. Monk," she repeated.

"Yes—yes, I heard that. What did you say next?" He shook his head as if to clear it.

"Nothing." She frowned very slightly, puzzled now.

With a great effort he brought his mind back to the murder of General Carlyon.

"I have been to see Mr. and Mrs. Furnival."

This time her smile was quite different; there was sharp bitterness in it, and self-mockery.

"I wish I thought you could discover Louisa Furnival was guilty, but you cannot." There was a catch in her voice which at any other time he could have taken for laughter. "If Thaddeus had rejected her she might have been angry, even violently so, but I doubt she ever loved anyone enough to care greatly if he loved her or not. The only person I could imagine her killing would be another woman—a really beautiful woman, perhaps, who rivaled her or threatened her well-being." Her eyes widened as thoughts raced through her imagination. "Maybe if Maxim fell so deeply in love with someone he could not hide it—then people would know Louisa had been bested. Then she might kill."

"And Maxim was not fond of you?" he asked.

There was very faint color in her cheeks, so slight he noticed it only because she was facing the small high window and the light fell directly on her.

"Yes—yes, he was, in the past—but never to the degree where he could have left Louisa. Maxim is a very moral man. And anyway, I am alive. It is Thaddeus who is dead." She said the last words without feeling, certainly without any shred of regret. At least there was no playacting, no hypocrisy in her, and no attempt to gain sympathy. For that he liked her.

"I saw the balcony, and the banister where he went over." She winced.

"I assume he fell backwards?"

"Yes." Her voice was unsteady, little more than a whisper.

"Onto the suit of armor?"

"Yes."

"That must have made a considerable noise."

"Of course. I expected people to come and see what had happened—but no one did."

"The withdrawing room is at the back of the house. You knew that."

"Of course I did. I thought one of the servants might hear."

"Then what? You followed him down and saw he was struck senseless with the fall—and no one had come. So you picked up the halberd and drove it into his body?"

She was white-faced, her eyes like dark holes. This time her voice would hardly come at all.

"Yes."

"His chest? He was lying on his back. You did say he went over backwards?"

"Yes." She gulped. "Do we have to go over this? It cannot serve any purpose."

"You must have hated him very much."

"I didn't—" She stopped, drew in her breath and went on, her eyes down, away from his. "I already told Mr. Rathbone. He was having an affair with Louisa Furnival. I was . . . jealous."

He did not believe her.

"I also saw your daughter."

She froze, sitting totally immobile.

"She was very concerned for you." He knew he was being cruel, but he saw no alternative. He had to find the truth. With lies and defenses Rathbone might only make matters worse in court. "I am afraid my presence seemed to precipitate a quarrel between her and her husband."

She glared at him fiercely. For the first time there was real, violent emotion in her.

"You had no right to go to her! She is ill—and she has just lost her father. Whatever he was to me, he was her father. You . . ." She stopped, perhaps aware of the absurdity of her position, if indeed it was she who had killed the general.

"She did not seem greatly distressed by his death," he said deliberately, watching not only her face but also the tension in her body, the tight shoulders under the cotton blouse, and her hands clenched on her knees. "In fact, she made no secret that she had quarreled bitterly with him, and would do all she could to aid you—even at the cost of her husband's anger."

Alexandra said nothing, but he could feel her emotion as if it were an electric charge in the room.

"She said he was arbitrary and dictatorial—that he had forced her into a marriage against her will," he went on.

She stood up and turned away from him.

Then again he had a sudden jolt of memory so sharp it was like a physical blow. He had been here before, stood in a cell with a small fanlight like this, and watched another slender woman with fair hair that curled at her neck. She too had been charged with killing her husband, and he had cared about it desperately.

Who was she?

The image was gone and all he could recapture was a shaft of dim light on hair, the angle of a shoulder, and a gray dress, skirts too long, sweeping the floor. He could recall no more, no voice, certainly no faintest echo of a face, nothing—eyes, lips—nothing at all.

But the emotion was there. It had mattered to him so fiercely he had thrown all his mind and will into defending her.

But why? Who was she?

Had he succeeded? Or had she been hanged?

Was she innocent—or guilty?

Alexandra was talking, answering him at last.

"What?"

She swung around, her eyes bright and hard.

"You come in here with a cruel tongue and no—no gentleness, no—no sensibility at all. You ask the harshest questions." Her voice caught in her throat, gasping for breath. "You remind me of my daughter whom I shall probably never see again, except across the rail of a courtroom dock—and then you haven't even the honor to listen to my answers! What manner of man are you? What do you really want here?"

"I am sorry!" he said with genuine shame. "My thoughts were absent for only a moment—a memory . . . a—a painful one—of another time like this."

The anger drained out of her. She shrugged her shoulders, turning away again.

"It doesn't matter. None of it makes any difference."

He pulled his thoughts together with an effort.

"Your daughter quarreled with her father that evening . . ."

Instantly she was on guard again, her body rigid, her eyes wary.

"She has a very fierce temper, Mrs. Carlyon—she seemed to be on the edge of hysteria when I was there. In fact I gathered that her husband was anxious for her."

"I already told you." Her voice was low and hard. "She has not been well since the birth of her child. It happens sometimes. It is one of the perils of bearing children. Ask anyone who is familiar with childbirth—and . . ."

"I know that," he agreed. "Women quite often become temporarily deranged—"

"No! Sabella was ill—that's all." She came forward, so close he thought she was going to grasp his arm, then she stood still with her hands by her sides. "If you are trying to say that it was Sabella who killed Thaddeus, and not I, then you are wrong! I will confess it in court, and will certainly hang"—she said the word plainly and deliberately, like pushing her hand into a wound—"rather than allow my daughter to take the blame for my act. Do you understand me, Mr. Monk?"

There was no jar of memory, nothing even faintly familiar. The echo was as far away now as if he had never heard it.

"Yes, Mrs. Carlyon. It is what I would have expected you to say."

"It is the truth." Her voice rose and there was a note of desperation in it, almost of pleading. "You must not accuse Sabella! If you are employed by Mr. Rathbone—Mr. Rathbone is my lawyer. He cannot say what I forbid him to."

It was half a statement, half a reassurance to herself.

"He is also an officer of the court, Mrs. Carlyon," he said with sudden gentleness. "He cannot say something which he knows beyond question to be untrue."

She stared at him without speaking.

Could his memory have something to do with that older woman who wept without distorting her face? She had been the wife of the man who had taught him so much, upon whom he had modeled himself when he first came south from Northumberland. It was he who had been ruined, cheated in some way, and Monk had tried so hard to save him, and failed.

But the image that had come to him today was of a young woman, another woman like Alexandra, charged with murdering her husband. And he had come here, like this, to help her.

Had he failed? Was that why she no longer knew him? There was no record of her among his possessions, no letters, no pictures, not even a name written down. Why? Why had he ceased to know her?

The answers crowded in on him: because he had failed, she had gone to the gallows . . .

"I shall do what I can to help, Mrs. Carlyon," he said quietly. "To find the truth—and then you and Mr. Rathbone must do with it whatever you wish."

4

AT MID-MORNING ON MAY II, Hester received an urgent invitation from Edith to call upon her at Carlyon House. It was hand-written and delivered by a messenger, a small boy with a cap pulled over his ears and a broken front tooth. It requested Hester to come at her earliest convenience, and that she would be most welcome to stay for luncheon if she wished.

"By all means," Major Tiplady said graciously. He was feeling better with every day, and was now quite well enough to be ferociously bored with his immobility, to have read all he wished of both daily newspapers and books from his own collection and those he requested from the libraries of friends. He enjoyed Hester's conversation, but he longed for some new event or circumstance to intrude into his life.

"Go and see the Carlyons," he urged. "Learn something of what is progressing in that wretched case. Poor woman! Although I don't know why I should say that." His white eyebrows rose, making him look both belligerent and bemused. "I suppose some part of me refuses to believe she should kill her husband—especially in such a way. Not a woman's method. Women use something subtler, like poison—don't you think?" He looked at Hester's faintly surprised expression and did not wait for an answer. "Anyway, why should she kill him at all?'' He frowned. ''What could he have done to her to cause her to resort to such a—a—fatal and inexcusable violence?''

''I don't know,'' Hester admitted, putting aside the mending she had been doing. ''And rather more to the point, why does she not tell us? Why does she persist in this lie about jealousy? I fear it may be because she is afraid it is her daughter who is guilty, and she would rather hang than see her child perish.''

''You must do something,'' Tiplady said with intense feeling. ''You cannot allow her to sacrifice herself. At least . . .'' He hesitated, pity twisting his emotions so plainly his face reflected every thought that passed through his mind: the doubt, the sudden understanding and the confusion again. ''Oh, my dear Miss Latterly, what a terrible dilemma. Do we have the right to take from this poor creature her sacrifice for her child? If we prove her innocent, and her daughter guilty, surely that is the last thing she would wish? Do we then not rob her of the only precious thing she has left?''

''I don't know,'' Hester answered very quietly, folding the linen and putting the needle and thimble back in their case. ''But what if it was not either of them? What if she is confessing to protect Sabella, because she fears she is guilty, but in fact she is not? What hideous irony if we know, only when it is too late, that it was someone else altogether?''

He shut his eyes. ''How perfectly appalling. Surely this friend of yours, Mr. Monk, can prevent such a thing? You say he is very clever, most particularly in this field.''

A flood of memory and sadness washed over her. ''Cleverness is not always enough . . .''

''Then you had better go and see what you can learn for yourself,'' he said decisively. ''Find out what you can about this wretched General Carlyon. Someone must have hated him very dearly indeed. Go to luncheon with his family. Watch and listen, ask questions, do whatever it is detectives do. Go on!''

''I suppose you don't know anything about him?'' she asked without hope, looking around the room a last time before going to her own quarters to prepare herself. Everything he might need seemed to be available for him, the maid would serve his meal, and she should be back by midafternoon herself.

"Well, as I said before, I know him by repute," Tiplady replied somberly. "One cannot serve as long as I have and not know at least the names of all the generals of any note—and those of none."

She smiled wryly. "And which was he?" Her own opinion of generals was not high.

"Ah . . ." He breathed out, looking at her with a twisted smile. "I don't know for myself, but he had a name as a soldier's soldier, a good-enough leader, inspiring, personally heroic, but outside uniform not a colorful man, tactically neither a hero nor a disaster."

"He did not fight in the Crimea, then?" she said too quickly for thought or consideration to guard her tongue. "They were all one or the other—mostly the other."

A smile puckered his lips against his will. He knew the army's weaknesses, but they were a closed subject, like family faults, not to be exposed or even admitted to outsiders—least of all women.

"No," he said guardedly. "As I understand it he served most of his active time in India—and then spent a lot of years here at home, in high command, training younger officers and the like."

"What was his personal reputation? What did people think of him?" She straightened his blanket yet again, quite unnecessarily but from habit.

"I've no idea." He seemed surprised to be asked. "Never heard anything at all. I told you—he was not personally a colorful man. For heaven's sake, do go and see Mrs. Sobell. You have to discover the truth in the matter and save poor Mrs. Carlyon—or the daughter."

"Yes, Major. I am about to go." And without adding anything further except a farewell, she left him alone to think and imagine until she should return.

* * *

Edith met her with a quick, anxious interest, rising from the chair where she had been sitting awkwardly, one leg folded under her. She looked tired and too pale for her dark mourning dress to flatter her. Her long fair hair was already pulled untidy, as if she had been running her hand over her head and had caught the strands of it absentmindedly.

"Ah, Hester. I am so glad you could come. The major did not mind? How good of him. Have you learned anything? What has Mr. Rathbone discovered? Oh, please, do come and sit down—here." She indicated the place opposite where she had been, and resumed her own seat.

Hester obeyed, not bothering to arrange her skirts.

"I am afraid very little so far," she answered, responding to the last question, knowing it was the only one which mattered. "And of course there will be limits to what he could tell me anyway, since I have no standing in the case."

Edith looked momentarily confused, then quite suddenly she understood.

"Oh yes—of course." Her face was bleak, as if the different nature of things lent a grimmer reality to it. "But he is working on it?"

"Of course. Mr. Monk is investigating. I expect he will come here in due course."

"They won't tell him anything." Edith's brows rose in surprise.

Hester smiled. "Not intentionally, I know. But he is already engaged with the possibility that it was not Alexandra who killed the general, and certainly not for the reason she said. Edith . . ."

Edith stared at her, waiting, her eyes intent.

"Edith, it may be that it was Sabella after all—but is that going to be an answer that Alexandra will want? Should we be doing her any service to prove it? She has chosen to give her life to save Sabella—if indeed Sabella is guilty." She leaned forward earnestly. "But what if it was neither of them? If Alexandra simply thinks it is Sabella and she is confessing to protect her . . ."

"Yes," Edith said eagerly. "That would be marvelous! Hester, do you think it could be true?"

"Perhaps—but then who? Louisa? Maxim Furnival?"

"Ah." The light died out of Edith's eyes. "Honestly, I wish it could be Louisa, but I doubt it. Why should she?"

"Might she really have been having an affair with the general, and he threw her over—told her it was all finished? You said she was not a woman to take rejection lightly."

Edith's face reflected a curious mixture of emotions: amusement in her eyes, sadness in her mouth, even a shadow of guilt.

"You never knew Thaddeus, or you wouldn't seriously think of such a thing. He was . . ." She hesitated, her mind reaching for ideas and framing them into words. "He was . . . remote. Whatever passion there was in him was private, and chilly, not something to be shared. I never saw him deeply moved by anything."

A quick smile touched her mouth, imagination, pity and regret in it. "Except stories of heroism, loyalty and sacrifice. I remember him reading 'Sohrab and Rustum' when it was first published four years ago." She glanced at Hester and saw her incomprehension. "It's a tragic poem by Arnold." The smile returned, bleak and sad. "It's a complicated story; the point is they are father and son, both great military heroes, and they kill each other without knowing who they are, because they have wound up on opposite sides in a war. It's very moving."

"And Thaddeus liked it?"

"And the stories of the great heroes of the past—ours and other people's. The Spartans combing their hair before Thermopylae—they all died, you know, three hundred of them, but they saved Greece. And Horatius on the bridge . . ."

"I know," Hester said quickly. "Macaulay's 'Lays of Ancient Rome.' I begin to understand. There were the passions he could identify with: honor, duty, courage, loyalty—not bad things. I'm sorry . . ."

Edith gave her a look of sudden warmth. It was the first time they had spoken of Thaddeus as a person they could care about rather than merely as the center of a tragedy. "But I think he was a man of thought rather than feeling," she went on, returning to the business of it. "Usually he was very controlled, very civilized. I suppose in some ways he was not unlike Mama. He had an absolute commitment to what is right, and I never knew him to step outside it—in his speech or his acts."

She screwed up her face and shook her head a little. "If he had some secret passion for Louisa he hid it completely, and honestly I cannot imagine him so involved in it as to indulge himself in what he would consider a betrayal, not so much of Alexandra as of himself. You see, to him adultery would be wrong, against the sanctity of home and the values by which he lived. None of his heroes would do such a thing. It would be unimaginable."

She lifted her shoulders high in an exaggerated shrug. "But suppose if he had, and then grown tired of her, or had an attack of conscience. I really believe that Louisa—whom I don't much care for, but I must be honest, I think is quite clever enough to have seen it coming long before he said anything—would have preempted him by leaving him herself. She would choose to be the one to end it; she would never allow him to."

"But if she loved him?" Hester pressed. "And some women do love the unattainable with a passion they never achieve for what is in their reach. Might she not be reluctant to believe he would never respond—and care so much she would rather kill him than . . ."

Edith laughed jerkily. "Oh Hester. Don't be absurd! What a romantic you are. You live in a world of grand passions, undying love and devotion, and burning jealousy. Neither of them were remotely like that. Thaddeus was heroic, but he was also pompous, stuffy, very rigid in his views, and cold to talk to. One cannot always be reading epic poetry, you know. Most of the time he was a guarded, ungiving man. And Louisa is passionate only about herself. She likes to be loved, admired, envied—especially envied—and to be comfortable, to be the center of everyone's attention. She would never put involvement with anyone else before her own self-image. Added to that, she dresses gorgeously, parades around and flirts with her eyes, but Maxim is very proper about morality, you know? And he has the money. If Louisa went too far he wouldn't stand for it." She bit her soft lower lip. "He loved Alex very much, you know, but he denied himself anything with her. He wouldn't let Louisa play fast and loose now."

Hester watched Edith's face carefully; she did not wish to hurt, but the thoughts were high in her mind. "But Thaddeus had money surely? If Louisa married him, she wouldn't need Maxim's money?"

Edith laughed outright. "Don't be absurd! She'd be ruined if Maxim divorced her—and Thaddeus certainly wouldn't get involved in anything like that. The scandal would ruin him too."

"Yes, I suppose it would," Hester agreed sensibly. She sat silently for several minutes, thoughts churning around in her head.

"I hate even to think of this at all," Hester said with a shudder of memory. "But what if it were someone else altogether? Not any one of the guests, but one of the servants? Did he go to the Furnivals' house often?"

"Yes, I believe so, but why on earth should a servant want to kill him? That's too unlikely. I know you want to find something—but . . ."

"I don't know. Something in the past? He was a general—he must have made both friends and enemies. Perhaps the motive for his death lies in his career, and is nothing to do with his personal life."

Edith's face lit up. "Oh Hester. That's brilliant of you! You mean some incident on the battlefield, or in the barracks, that has at long last been revenged? We must find out all we can about the Furnivals' servants. You must tell him—Monk, did you say? Yes, Mr. Monk. You must tell him what we have thought of, and set him about it immediately!"

Hester smiled at the thought of so instructing Monk, but she acquiesced, and before Edith could continue with her ideas, the maid came to announce that luncheon was served and they were expected at table.

Apparently Edith had already informed the family that Hester was expected. No remarks were passed on her presence, except a cool acknowledgment of her arrival and an invitation to be seated at the specified place, and a rather perfunctory wish that she should enjoy her meal.

She thanked Felicia and took her seat otherwise in silence.

"I imagine you have seen the newspapers?" Randolf said, glancing around the table. He looked even wearier today than the last time Hester had seen him, but certainly had Monk asked her now if she thought him senile, she would have denied it without doubt. There was an angry intelligence in his eyes, and any querulousness around his mouth or droop to his features was set there by character as much as the mere passage of time.

"Naturally I have seen the headlines," Felicia said sharply. "I do not care for the rest. There is nothing we can do about it, but we do not have to discuss this with one another. It is like all evil speaking and distasteful speculation: one sets one's mind against it and refuses to be distressed. Would you be so good as to pass me the condiments, Peverell?"

Peverell did as he was bidden, and smiled from the corner of his vision at Hester. There was the same gentleness in his eyes, a mild awareness of humor, as she had observed before. He was an ordinary man—and yet far from ordinary. She could not imagine that Damaris had entertained romantic notions about Maxim Furnival; she was not foolish enough to destroy what she had for a cheap moment of entertainment. For all her flamboyance, she was not a stupid or shallow woman.

"I have not seen the newspapers," Edith said suddenly, looking at her mother.

"Of course you haven't." Felicia stared at her with wide eyes. "Nor shall you."

"What are they saying of Alexandra?" Edith persisted, apparently deaf to the warning note in Felicia's voice.

114

"Precisely what you would expect," Felicia answered. "Ignore it."

"You say that as if we could." Damaris's tone was sharp, almost an accusation. "Don't think about it, and it is of no importance. Just like that—it is dealt with."

"You have a great deal yet to learn, my dear," Felicia said with chill, looking at her daughter in something close to exasperation. "Where is Cassian? He is late. A certain amount of latitude may be allowed, but one must exercise discipline as well." She reached out her hand and rang the little silver bell.

Almost immediately a footman appeared.

"Go and fetch Master Cassian, James. Tell him he is required at luncheon."

"Yes ma'am." And obediently he left.

Randolf grunted, but spoke no words, and addressed himself again to his food.

"I imagine the newspapers write well of General Carlyon." Hester heard her own voice loud in the silence, sounding clumsy and terribly contrived. But how else was she to serve any purpose here? She could not hope any of them would say or do something in which she could find meaning, simply eating their luncheon. "He had a brilliant career," she went on. "They are bound to have written of it."

Randolf looked at her, his heavy face puckered.

"He did," he agreed. "He was an outstanding man, an ornament to his generation and his family. Although what you can possibly know about it, Miss Latterly, I fail to see. I daresay your remark is well meant, and intended as a kindness, and for your civility, I thank you." He looked anything but grateful.

Hester felt as if she had trespassed by praising him, as though they felt he was their particular property and only they might speak of him.

"I have spent a considerable time in the army myself, Colonel Carlyon," she said in defense.

"Army!" he snorted with quite open contempt. "Nonsense, young woman! You were a nurse, a skivvy to tend to the slops for the surgeons. Hardly the same thing!"

Her temper frayed raw, and she forgot Monk, Rathbone and Alexandra Carlyon.

"I don't know how you know anything about it," she said, mimicking his tone savagely and precisely. "You were not there. Or you would be aware that army nursing has changed a great deal. I have watched battles and walked the field afterwards. I have helped surgeons in field hospitals, and I daresay I have known as many soldiers in the space of a few years as you have."

His face was turning a rich plum color and his eyes were bulging.

"And I did not hear General Carlyon's name mentioned by anyone," she added coldly. "But I now work nursing a Major Tiplady, and he knew of General Carlyon, because he had also served in India, and he spoke of him in some detail. I did not speak without some knowledge. Was I misinformed?"

Randolf was torn between the desire to be thoroughly rude to her and the need to defend his son, his family pride, and to be at least reasonably civil to a guest, even one he had not invited. Family pride won.

"Of course not," he said grudgingly. "Thaddeus was exceptional. A man not only of military brilliance, but a man without a stain of dishonor on his name."

Felicia kept her eyes on her plate, her jaw tight. Hester wondered what inner grief tore at her at the loss of her only son, grief she would keep hidden with that same rigid discipline which had no doubt sustained her all her life, through the loneliness of long separations, perhaps service abroad in unfamiliar places, harsh climate, fear of injury and disease; and now scandal and devastating loss. On the courage and duty of such women had the soldiers of the Empire leaned.

The door opened and a small boy with fair hair and a thin, pale face came into the room; his first glance was to Randolf, then to Felicia.

"I'm sorry, Grandmama," he said very quietly.

"You are excused," Felicia replied formally. "Do not make a habit of it, Cassian. It is impolite to be late to meals. Please take your place, and James will bring your luncheon."

"Yes, Grandmama." He skirted wide around his grandfather's chair, around Peverell without looking at him, then sat in the empty seat next to Damaris.

Hester resumed eating her meal, but discreetly she looked at him as he kept his eyes down on his plate and without relish began his main course. Since he was too late for soup he was not to be spoiled by being permitted to catch up. He was a handsome child, with honey fair hair and fair skin with a dusting of freckles lending tone to his pallor. His brow was broad, his nose short and already beginning to show an aquiline curve. His mouth was wide and generous, still soft with childhood, but there was a sulkiness to it, an air of secrecy. Even when he looked up at Edith as she spoke to him, and to request the water or the condiments, there was something in his aspect that struck Hester as closed, more careful than she would have expected a child to be.

Then she remembered the appalling events of the last month, which must have scarred his senses with a pain too overwhelming to take in. In one evening his father was dead and his mother distraught and filled with her own terrors and griefs, and within a fortnight she was arrested and forcibly taken from him. Did he even know why yet? Had anyone told him the full extent of the tragedy? Or did he believe it was an accident, and his mother might yet be returned to him?

Looking at his careful, wary face it was impossible to know, but he did not look terrified and there were no glances of appeal at anyone, even though he was with his family, and presumably knew all of them moderately well.

Had anyone taken him in their arms and let him weep? Had anyone explained to him what was happening? Or was he wandering in a silent confusion, full of imaginings and fears? Did they expect him to shoulder his grief like a full-grown man, be stoic and continue his new and utterly changed life as if it needed no answers and no time for emotion? Was his adult air merely an attempt to be what they expected of him?

Or had they not even thought about it at all? Were food and clothes, warmth and a room of his own, considered to be all a boy his age required?

The conversation continued desultorily and Hester learned nothing from it. They spoke of trivialities of one sort or another, acquaintances Hester did not know, society in general, government, the current events and public opinion of the scandals and tragedies of the day.

The last course had been cleared away and Felicia was taking a mint from the silver tray when Damaris at last returned to the original subject.

"I passed a newsboy this morning, shouting about Alex," she said unhappily. "He was saying some awful things. Why are people so—so vicious? They don't even know yet if she did anything or not!"

"Shouldn't have been listening," Randolf muttered grimly. "Your mother's told you that before."

"I didn't know you were going out." Felicia looked across the table at her irritably. "Where did you go?"

"To the dressmakers'," Damaris replied with a flicker of annoyance. "I have to have another black dress. I'm sure you wouldn't wish me to mourn in purple."

"Purple is half mourning." Felicia's large, deep-set eyes rested on her daughter with disfavor. "Your brother is only just buried. You will maintain black as long as it is decent to do so. I know the funeral is over, but if I find you outside the house in lavender or purple before Michaelmas, I shall be most displeased."

The thought of black all summer was plain in Damaris's face, but she said nothing.

"Anyway, you did not need to go out," Felicia went on. "You should have sent for the dressmaker to come to you." A host of thoughts was plain in Damaris's face, most especially the desire to escape the house and its environs.

"What did they say?" Edith asked curiously, referring to the newspapers again.

"They seemed to have judged already that she was guilty," Damaris replied. "But it isn't that, it was the—the viciousness of it."

"What do you expect?" Felicia frowned. "She has confessed to the world that she has done something quite beyond understanding. It defies the order of everyone's lives, like madness. Of course people will be . . . angry. I think *vicious* is the wrong word to choose. You don't seem to understand the enormity of it." She pushed her salmon mousse to the side of her plate and abandoned it. "Can you imagine what would happen to the country if every woman whose husband flirted with someone else were to murder him? Really, Damaris, sometimes I wonder where your wits are. Society would disintegrate. There would be no safety, no decency or certainty in anything. Life would fall to pieces and we would be in the jungle."

She signaled peremptorily for the footman to remove the plate. "Heaven knows, Alexandra had nothing untoward to have to endure, but if she had then she should have done so, like thousands of other women before her, and no doubt after. No relationships are without their difficulties and sacrifices."

It was something of an exaggeration, and Hester looked around at their faces to see if anyone was going to reason with her. But Edith kept her eyes on her plate; Randolf nodded as if he agreed totally; and Damaris glanced up, her eyes on Hester, but she said nothing either. Cassian looked very grave, but no one seemed to bother that the allusions to his parents were made in front of him, and he showed no emotions at all.

It was Peverell who spoke.

"Fear, my dear," he said, looking at Edith with a sad smile. "People are frequently at their ugliest when they are afraid. Violence from garroters we expect, from the working classes among themselves, even now and then from gentlemen—a matter of insult and honor over a woman, or—in very bad taste, but it happens—over money.''

The footman removed all the fish plates and served the meat course.

"But when women start using violence," Peverell went on, "to dictate how men shall behave in the matter of morals or their appetites, then that threatens not only their freedom but the sanctity of their homes. And it strikes real terror into people, because it is the basic safety at the core of things, the refuge that all like to imagine we can retreat to from whatever forays into conflict we may make in the course of the day or the week.''

"I don't know why you use the word *imagine*." Felicia fixed him with a stony stare. "The home is the center of peace, morality, unquestioning loyalty, which is the refuge and the strength to all who must labor, or battle in an increasingly changing world." She waved away the meat course, and the footman withdrew to serve Hester. "Without it what would there be worth living for?" she demanded. "If the center and the heart give way, then everything else is lost. Can you wonder that people are frightened, and appalled, when a woman who has everything given her turns 'round and kills the very man who protected and provided for her? Of course they react displeased. One cannot expect anything else. You must ignore it. If you had sent for the dressmaker, as you should have, then you would not have witnessed it.''

Nothing further was said in the matter, and half an hour later when the meal was finished, Edith and Hester excused themselves. Shortly after that, Hester took her leave, having told Edith all she knew of progress so far, and promising to continue with every bit of the very small ability she possessed, and trying to assure her, in spite of her own misgivings, that there was indeed some hope.

Major Tiplady was staring towards the window waiting for her when she returned home, and immediately enquired to know the outcome of her visit.

"I don't know that it is anything really useful," she answered, taking off her cloak and bonnet and laying them on the chair for Molly to hang up. "But I learned quite a lot more about the general. I am not sure that I should have liked him, but at least I can feel some pity that he is dead."

"That is not very productive," Tiplady said critically. He regarded her narrowly, sitting very upright. "Could this Louisa woman have killed him?"

Hester came over and sat on the chair beside him.

"It looks very doubtful," she confessed. "He seems a man far more capable of friendship than romances; and Louisa apparently had too much to lose, both in reputation and finance, to have risked more than a flirtation." She felt suddenly depressed. "In fact it does seem as if Alexandra was the one—or else poor Sabella—if she really is deranged."

"Oh dear." Tiplady looked crushed. "Then where do we go from here?"

"Perhaps it was one of the servants," she said with sudden hope again.

"One of the servants?" he said incredulously. "Whatever for?"

"I don't know. Some old military matter?"

He looked doubtful.

"Well, I shall pursue it!" she said firmly. "Now, have you had tea yet? What about supper? What would you care for for supper?"

Two days later she took an afternoon off, at Major Tiplady's insistence, and went to visit Lady Callandra Daviot in order to enlist her help in learning more of General Carlyon's military career. Callandra had helped her with both counsel and friendship when she first returned from the Crimea, and it was with her good offices that she had obtained her hospital post. It was extremely gracious of Callandra not to have been a good deal harsher in her comments when Hester had then lost it through overstepping the bounds of her authority.

Callandra's late husband, Colonel Daviot, had been an army surgeon of some distinction; a quick-tempered, charming, stubborn, witty and somewhat arbitrary man. He had had a vast acquaintance and might well have known something of General Carlyon. Callandra, still with connections to the Army Medical Corps, might be able either to recall hearing of the general, or to institute discreet enquiries and learn something of his career and, more importantly, of his reputation. She might be able to find information about the unofficial events which just might lead to another motive for murder, either someone seeking revenge for a wrong, a betrayal on the field, or a promotion obtained unfairly—or imagined to be so, or even some scandal exposed or too harshly pursued. The possibilities were considerable.

They were sitting in Callandra's room, which could hardly be called a withdrawing room, since she would have received no formal visitors there. It was full of bright sunlight, desperately unfashionable, cluttered with books and papers, cushions thrown about for comfort, two discarded shawls and a sleeping cat which should have been white but was liberally dusted with soot.

Callandra herself, well into middle age, gray hair flying all over the place as if she were struggling against a high wind, her curious intelligent face long-nosed, full of humor, and quite out of fashion also, was sitting in the sunlight, which if it were habit might account for her indelicate complexion. She regarded Hester with amusement.

"My dear girl, do you not imagine Monk has already told me of the case? That was our bargain, if you recall. And quite naturally I have made considerable efforts to learn what I can of General Carlyon. And of his father. One may learn much of a man by knowing something of his parents—or of a woman, of course." She scowled ferociously. "Really, that cat is quite perverse. God intended him to be white, so what does he do but climb up chimneys! It quite sets my teeth on edge when I think that sooner or later he will lick all that out of his coat. I feel as if my own mouth were full of soot. But I can hardly bathe him, although I have thought of it—and told him so."

"I should think a great deal of it will come off on your

furniture," Hester said without disquiet. She was used to Callandra, and she had quite an affection for the animal anyway.

"Probably," Callandra agreed. "He is a refugee from the kitchen at the moment, and I must give the poor beast asylum."

"Why? I thought his job was in the kitchen, to keep the mice down."

"It is—but he is overfond of eggs."

"Can the cook not spare him an egg now and again?"

"Of course. But when she doesn't he is apt to help himself. He has just looped his paw 'round half a dozen this morning and sent them all to the floor, where quite naturally they broke, and he was able to eat his fill. We shall not now be having soufflé for dinner." She rearranged herself rather more comfortably and the cat moved itself gently in its sleep and began to purr. "I presume you wish to know what I have heard about General Carlyon?" Callandra asked.

"Of course."

"It is not very interesting. Indeed he was a remarkably uninteresting man, correct to a degree which amounts to complete boredom—for me. His father purchased his commission in the Guards. He was able and obeyed the letter of the law, very popular with his fellows, most of them, and in due course obtained promotion, no doubt a great deal to do with family influence and a certain natural ability with a weapon. He knew how to command his men's absolute loyalty—and that counts for a lot. He was an excellent horseman, which also helped."

"And his private reputation?" Hester said hopefully.

Callandra looked apologetic. "A complete blank," she confessed. "He married Alexandra FitzWilliam after a brief courtship. It was most suitable and both families were happy with the arrangement, which since they were the ones who were largely responsible for it, is not surprising. They had one daughter, Sabella, and many years later, their only son, Cassian. The general was posted to the Indian army, and remained abroad for many years, mostly in Bengal, and I have spoken to a friend of mine who served there also, but he had never heard anything the least bit disreputable about Carlyon, either his military duties or his personal life. His men respected him, indeed some intensely so.

"I did hear one small story which seems to indicate the character of the man. One young lieutenant, only been in India a few weeks, made an awful mess of a patrol, got himself lost and half of his men wounded. Carlyon, a major at the time, rode out with a couple of volunteers to look for this young fellow, at considerable risk to himself, found him, looked after the wounded and fought off an attack of some sort. He got nearly all of them safely back to the post. Tore the young fellow to shreds himself, but lied like a trooper to save him from coming up on a charge for total incompetence. Which all seems very unselfish, until you realize how it enhances his own reputation, and how his men admired him for it. He seems to have counted the hero worship of his men more than his own preferment, although that came too."

"Very human," Hester said thoughtfully. "Not entirely admirable, but not hard to understand."

"Not at all admirable," Callandra said grimly. "Not in a military leader. A general should be above all trusted; that is a far calmer emotion than hero worship, and far more to be relied on when the going is really hard."

"I suppose so—yes, of course." Hester reasserted her common sense. It was the same with any great leader. Florence Nightingale was not an especially lovable woman, being far too autocratic, insensitive to the vanities and foibles of others, intolerant of weakness and yet highly eccentric herself. But she was a leader even those who most loathed her would still follow, and the men she served regarded her as a saint—but then perhaps most saints were not easy people.

"I asked with some hope if he had gambled excessively," Callandra continued. "Been too rigid with discipline, espoused any barbaric sects of belief, earned any personal enemies, or had friendships that might lay him open to question—if you see what I mean?'' She looked at Hester dubiously.

''Yes, I see what you mean,'' Hester acknowledged with a wry smile. It was not a thought which had occurred to her, but it was a good one. What if the general's lover was not a woman, but a man? But it seemed that was not to be fruitful either. ''What a pity—that would be a powerful motive.''

''Indeed.'' Callandra's face tightened. ''But I could find no evidence whatsoever. And the person to whom I spoke was one who would not have minced words and pretended he would not have heard of such things. I am afraid, my dear, that General Carlyon was of totally traditional behavior in every way—and not a man who seems to have given anyone cause to hate him or to fear him.''

Hester sighed. ''Nor his father?''

''Much the same—very much the same, simply less successful. He served in the Peninsular War under the Duke of Wellington, and saw Waterloo—which one would think might make him interesting, but apparently it did not. The only difference between father and son seems to be that the colonel had his son first and his two daughters afterwards, whereas the general did it the other way 'round. And he reached a higher rank, no doubt because he had a father of influence to aid him. I'm sorry my enquiries have turned up so very little. It is most disappointing.''

And on that note, their conversation became more general, and they spent a most agreeable afternoon together until Hester rose to take her leave and return to Major Tiplady and her duties.

At the same time as Hester was dining with the Carlyon family, Monk was paying his first visit to Dr. Charles Hargrave, both as someone unrelated to the Carlyon family who had attended the party that evening and as the medical officer who had first seen the body of the general.

He had made an appointment in order not to find the doctor out on a call when he came, and therefore he approached with confidence, even at the unsuitable hour of half past eight in the evening. He was admitted by the maid and shown immediately to a pleasant and conventional study where he was received by Hargrave, an unusually tall man, lean and elegant of build, broad shouldered, and yet not athletic in manner. His coloring was nondescript fair, his eyes a little hooded and greenish blue in shade, his nose long and pointed, but not quite straight, as if at some time it had been broken and ill set. His mouth was small, his teeth when he smiled very regular. It was a highly individual face, and he seemed a man very much at his ease.

"Good evening, Mr. Monk. I doubt I can be of any assistance, but of course I shall do everything I can, although I have already spoken to the police—naturally."

"Thank you, sir," Monk accepted. "That is most generous of you."

"Not at all. A wretched business." Hargrave waved towards one of the large leather-covered chairs beside the fireplace, and as Monk sat in one, he sat in the other. "What can I tell you? I assume you already know the course of events that evening."

"I have several accounts, none seriously at variance with another," Monk replied. "But there remain some unanswered questions. For example, do you know what so distressed Mrs. Erskine?"

Hargrave smiled suddenly, a charming and candid gesture. "No idea at all. Quarrel with Louisa, I should think, but I haven't the faintest notion about what. Although it did seem to me she was quite uncharacteristically beastly to poor Maxim. Sorry not to be more helpful. And before you ask, neither do I know why Thaddeus and Alexandra quarreled."

"Could that also have been about Mrs. Furnival?" Monk asked.

Hargrave considered for a moment or two before replying, placing his fingers together in a steeple and looking at Monk over the point of them.

"I thought at first that it was unlikely, but on consideration perhaps it is not. Rivalry is a strange thing. People may fight passionately over something, not so much because they desire it for itself but because they wish to win the struggle, and be seen to win it—or at least not to lose.'' He regarded Monk closely, searching his face, his expression grave. ''What I was going to say is that although Alexandra was not deeply in love with the general, it may be that her pride was very precious to her, and to have her friends and family see him giving his attention to someone else may have been more than she was prepared to endure.'' He saw Monk's doubt, or imagined it. ''I realize murder is a very extreme reaction to that.'' He frowned, biting his lips. ''And solves nothing at all. But then it is absurd to imagine it would solve anything else either—but the general was undoubtedly murdered.''

''Was he?'' Monk did not ask the question with skepticism so much as enquiry for clarification. ''You examined the body; you did not perceive it as murder immediately, did you?''

Hargrave smiled wryly. ''No,'' he admitted. ''I would not have said anything that evening, whatever I had thought. I confess, I was considerably shaken when Maxim came back and said Thaddeus had had an accident, and then of course when I saw him I knew immediately that he was dead. It was a very nasty wound. My first thoughts, after it was obvious I could do nothing for him, were to break it as gently as possible to his family, many of whom were present, especially his wife. Of course I had no idea then that she was involved in it, and already knew better than any of us what had happened.''

''What had happened, Dr. Hargrave, in your medical opinion?''

Hargrave pursed his lips.

''Exactly,'' Monk added.

''Perhaps I had better describe the scene as I found it.'' Hargrave crossed his legs and stared at the low fire in the hearth, lit against the evening chill. ''The general was lying sprawled on the floor below the curve of the banister,'' he began. ''The suit of armor was on the floor beside him. As I remember, it had come to pieces, presumably from the impact of his body on it. It can have been held together only by rather perished leather straps, and a certain amount of sheer balance and weight of itself. One gauntlet was under his body, the other close to his head. The helmet had rolled away about eighteen inches.''

"Was the general on his back or his face?" Monk asked.

"His back," Hargrave said immediately. "The halberd was sticking out of his chest. I assumed he had gone over sideways, overbalanced and then twisted in the air in his effort to save himself, so that the point of the halberd had gone through his chest. Then when he hit the armor, it had deflected him and he had landed on his back. Awkward, I can see that now, but I wasn't thinking of murder at the time—only of what I could do to help.''

"And you saw immediately that he was dead?"

A bleak, rueful expression crossed Hargrave's face. "The first thing I did was to bend and reach for a pulse. Automatic, I assume. Pretty futile, in the circumstances. When I found none, I looked more closely at the wound. The halberd was still in it.'' He did not shiver, but the muscles of his body tightened and he seemed to draw into himself. "When I saw how far it had penetrated, I knew he could not possibly live more than a few moments with such an injury. It had sunk more than eight inches into his body. In fact when we moved him later we could see the mark where the point had scarred the floor underneath. She must have . . .'' His voice caught. He took a breath. "Death must have been more or less instantaneous.''

He swallowed and looked at Monk apologetically. "I've seen a lot of corpses, but mostly from age and disease. I haven't had to deal with violent death very often.''

"Of course not," Monk acknowledged with a softer tone. "Did you move him?"

"No. No, it was obvious it was going to require the police. Even an accident of that violence would have to be reported and investigated.''

"So you went back into the room and informed them he was dead? Can you recall their individual reactions?''

"Yes!" Hargrave looked surprised, his eyes widening.

"They were shocked, naturally. As far as I can remember, Maxim and Peverell were the most stunned—and my wife. Damaris Erskine had been preoccupied with her own emotions most of the evening, and I think it was some time before she really took in what I said. Sabella was not there. She had gone upstairs—I think honestly to avoid being in the room with her father, whom she loathed—"

"Do you know why?" Monk interrupted.

"Oh yes." Hargrave smiled tolerantly. "Since she was about twelve or thirteen she had had some idea of becoming a nun—sort of romantic idea some girls get." He shrugged, a shadow of humor across his face. "Most of them grow out of it—she didn't. Naturally her father wouldn't hear of such a thing. He insisted she marry and settle down, like any other young woman. And Fenton Pole is a nice enough man, well-bred, well-mannered, with more than sufficient means to keep her in comfort."

He leaned forward and poked the fire, steadying one of the logs with the poker. "To begin with it looked as if she had accepted things. Then she had a very difficult confinement and afterwards seemed not to regain her balance— mentally, that is. Physically she is perfectly well, and the child too. It can happen. Most unfortunate. Poor Alexandra had a very difficult time with her—not to mention Fenton."

"How did she take her father's death?"

"I'm afraid I really don't know. I was too preoccupied with Alexandra, and with sending for the police. You'll have to ask Maxim or Louisa."

"You were occupied with Mrs. Carlyon? Did she take the news very hard?"

Hargrave's eyes were wide and there was a grim humor there. "You mean was she surprised? It is impossible to tell. She sat frozen as if she could hardly comprehend what was happening. It might have been that she already knew—or equally easily it might have been shock. And even if she knew, or suspected murder, it may have been fear that it was Sabella who had done it. I have thought it was many times

129

since then, and I have no more certainty now than I did at the time."

"And Mrs. Furnival?"

Hargrave leaned back and crossed his legs.

"There I am on much surer ground. I am almost positive that she was taken totally by surprise. The evening had been very tense and not at all pleasant due to Alexandra's very evident quarrel with her husband, Sabella's continued rage with him, which she made almost no effort to conceal, in spite of the obvious embarrassment it caused everybody, and Damaris Erskine's quite unexplainable almost hysteria, and her rudeness to Maxim. She seemed to be so consumed with her own emotions she was hardly aware of what was going on with the rest of us."

He shook his head. "Peverell was naturally concerned with her, and embarrassed. Fenton Pole was annoyed with Sabella because she had made something of a habit of this recently. Indeed the poor man had every cause to find the situation almost intolerable.

"Louisa was, I confess, taking up the general's attention in a manner many wives would have found difficult to accommodate—but then women have their own resources with which to deal with these things. And Alexandra was neither a plain woman nor a stupid one. In the past Maxim Furnival paid more than a little attention to her—quite as much as the general was giving Louisa that evening—and I have a suspicion it was rooted in a far less superficial feeling. But that is only a notion; I know nothing."

Monk smiled, acknowledging the confidence.

"Dr. Hargrave, what is your opinion of the mental state of Sabella Pole? In your judgment, is it possible that she killed her father and that Alexandra has confessed to protect her?"

Hargrave leaned back very slowly, pursing his lips, his eyes on Monk's face.

"Yes, I think it is possible, but you will need a great deal more than a possibility before the police will take any notice of it. And I certainly cannot say she definitely did anything, or that her behavior betrays more than an emotional imbalance, which is quite well known in women who have recently given birth. Such melancholia sometimes takes the form of violence, but towards the child, not towards their own fathers.''

"And you also were the medical consultant to Mrs. Carlyon?"

"Yes, for what that is worth, which I fear is nothing in this instance." Again he shook his head. "I can offer no evidence of her sanity or the unlikelihood that she committed this crime. I really am sorry, Mr. Monk, but I believe you are fighting a lost cause."

"Can you think of any other reason whatever why she should have killed her husband?"

"No." Hargrave was totally serious. "And I have tried. So far as I am aware, he was never violent to her or overtly cruel in any way. I appreciate that you are seeking any mitigating circumstances—but I am truly sorry, I know of none. The general was a normal, healthy man, and as sane as any man alive. A trifle pompous, perhaps, and outside military matters, a bore—but that is not a capital sin."

Monk did not know what he had been hoping for; still he felt a deep sense of disappointment. The possibilities were narrowing, the chances to discover something of meaning were fading one by one, and each was so inconclusive.

"Thank you, Dr. Hargrave." Monk rose to his feet. "You have been very patient."

"Not at all." Hargrave stood up and moved towards the door. "I'm only sorry I could be of no assistance. What will you do now?"

"Retrace my steps," Monk said wearily. "Go back over police records of the investigation, recheck the evidence, times, places, answers to questions."

"I am afraid you are in for a disappointing time," Hargrave said ruefully. "I have very little idea why she should suddenly leave all sanity and self-interest, but I fear you will find in the end that Alexandra Carlyon killed her husband."

"Possibly," Monk conceded, opening the door. "But I have not given up yet!"

Monk had not so far been to the police about the case, and he would not go to Runcorn. The relationship between them had always been difficult, strained by Monk's ambition forever treading on Runcorn's heels, hungry for his rank, and making no secret that he believed he could do the job better. And Runcorn, afraid in his heart that that was true, had feared him, and out of fear had come resentment, bitterness, and then hatred.

Finally Monk had resigned in rage, refusing to obey an order he considered profoundly incompetent and morally mistaken. Runcorn had been delighted, free at last of his most dangerous subordinate. The fact that Monk had proved to be correct, as had happened so often before, had robbed him of victory, but not of the exquisite release from Monk's footsteps at his back and his shadow forever darkening his prospects.

John Evan was a totally different matter. He had not known Monk before the accident and had been assigned to work as his sergeant on his return from convalescence, when he began the Grey case. He had found a man discovering himself through evidence, the views and emotions of others, records of past cases, and not at all certain that he liked what he saw. Evan had learned Monk's vulnerability, and eventually guessed how little he knew of himself, and that he fought to keep his job because to lose it would be to lose not just his means of livelihood but the only certainty he possessed. Even at the very worst times, when Monk had doubted himself, not merely his competence but even his honor and his morality, Evan had never once betrayed him, to Runcorn or to anyone else. Evan and Hester Latterly had saved him when he himself had given it up as impossible.

John Evan was an unusual policeman, the son of a country parson, not quite a gentleman but certainly not a laborer or an artisan. Consequently Evan had an ease of manner that Monk admired and that irritated Runcorn, since both of them in their very different ways had aspirations to social advancement.

Monk did not wish to return to the police station to see Evan. It held too many memories of his own prowess and authority, and his final leaving, when juniors of all sorts had gathered, spellbound and awestruck, ears to the keyhole, to hear that last blazing quarrel, and then had scattered like rabbits when Monk threw open the door and strode out, leaving Runcorn scarlet-faced but victorious.

Instead he chose to seek him in the public house where Evan most frequently took his luncheon, if time and opportunity afforded. It was a small place, crowded with the good-natured chatter of street sellers, newsmen, petty clerks and the entrepreneurs on the edge of the underworld. The smells of ale and cider, sawdust, hot food and jostling bodies were pervasive and not unpleasant. Monk took a position where he could see the door, and nursed a pint of cider until Evan came in. Then he forced his way to the counter and pushed till he was beside him.

Evan swung around with surprise, and pleasure lit his face immediately. He was a lean young man with a long, aquiline nose, hazel eyes and an expression of gentle, lugubrious humor. Now he was quite openly delighted.

"Mr. Monk!" He had never lost the sense that Monk was his superior and must be treated with a certain dignity. "How are you? Are you looking for me?" There was a definite note of hope in his voice.

"I am," Monk confessed, more pleased at Evan's eagerness than he would willingly have expected, or conceded.

Evan ordered a pint of cider and a thick mutton-and-pickle sandwich, made with two crusty slices, and another pint for Monk, then made his way over to a corner where they could be relatively private.

"Yes?" he said as soon as they were seated. "Have you a case?"

Monk half hid his smile. "I'm not sure. But you have."

Evan's eyebrows shot up. "I have?"

"General Carlyon."

Evan's disappointment was apparent. "Oh—not much of a case there, I'm afraid. Poor woman did it. Jealousy is a cruel thing. Ruined a good many lives." His face puckered. "But how are you involved in it?" He took a large bite from his sandwich.

"Rathbone is defending her," Monk answered. "He hired me to try and find out if there are any mitigating circumstances—and even if it is possible that it was not she who killed him but someone else."

"She confessed," Evan said, holding his sandwich in both hands to keep the pickle from sliding out.

"Could be to protect the daughter," Monk suggested. "Wouldn't be the first time a person confessed in order to take the blame for someone they loved very deeply."

"No." Evan spoke with his mouth full, but even so his doubt was obvious. He swallowed and took a sip of his cider, his eyes still on Monk. "But it doesn't look like it in this case. We found no one who saw the daughter come downstairs."

"But could she have?"

"Can't prove that she didn't—just no cause to think she did. Anyway, why should she kill her father? It couldn't possibly gain her anything, as far as she was concerned; the harm was already done. She is married and had a child—she couldn't go back to being a nun now. If she'd killed him, then . . ."

"She'd have very little chance indeed of becoming a nun," Monk said dryly. "Not at all a good start to a life of holy contemplation."

"It was your idea, not mine." Evan defended himself, but there was an answering flick of humor in his eyes. "And as for anyone else—who? I can't see Mrs. Carlyon confessing to save Louisa Furnival from the gallows, can you?"

"Not intentionally, no, only unintentionally, if she thought it was Sabella." Monk took a long pull from his cider.

Evan frowned. "We thought it was Sabella to begin with," he conceded. "Mrs. Carlyon only confessed when it must have seemed to her we were going to arrest Sabella."

"Or Maxim Furnival," Monk went on. "Perhaps he was jealous. It looks as if he had more cause. It was Louisa who was doing the flirting, setting the pace. General Carlyon was merely responding."

Evan continued with his sandwich, and spoke with his mouth full again.

"Mrs. Furnival is the sort of woman who always flirts. It's her manner with most men. She even flirted with me, in a sort of way." He blushed very slightly, not at the memory—he was a most personable young man, and he had been flirted with before—but at reciting it to Monk. It sounded so unbecomingly immodest. "This can't have been the first time she made a public spectacle of exercising her powers. Why, if he put up with it all these years—the son is thirteen so they have been married fourteen years at least, and actually I gather quite a lot longer—why would Maxim Furnival suddenly lose his head so completely as to murder the general? From what I gather of him, General Carlyon was hardly a romantic threat to him. He was a highly respectable, rather pompous soldier well past his prime, stiff, not much sense of humor and not especially handsome. He had money, but so has Furnival."

Monk said nothing, and began to wish he had ordered a sandwich as well.

"Sorry," Evan said sincerely. "I really don't think there is anything you can do for Mrs. Carlyon. Society will not see any excuses for murdering a husband out of jealousy because he flirted. In fact, even if he had a full-blown affair and flaunted it publicly, she would still be expected to turn the other way, affect not to have seen anything amiss, and behave with dignity." He looked apologetic and his eyes were full of regret. "As long as she was provided for financially, and had the protection of his name, she would be considered to have a quite satisfactory portion in life, and must do her duty to keep the sanctity and stability of the home—whether he wished to return to it or not."

Monk knew he was right, and whatever his private thoughts of the morality of it, that was how she would be judged. And of course any jury would be entirely composed of men, and men of property at that. They would identify with the general. After all, what would happen to them if women were given the idea that if their husbands flirted they could get away with killing them? She would find very short shrift there.

"I can tell you the evidence as we found it if you like, but it won't do any good," Evan said ruefully. "There's nothing interesting in it; in fact nothing you couldn't have deduced for yourself."

"Tell me anyway," Monk said without hope.

Evan obliged, and as he had said, there was nothing of any use at all, nothing that offered even a thread to follow.

Monk went back to the bar and ordered a sandwich and two more pints of cider, then after a few more minutes of conversation about other things, bade Evan farewell and left the public house. He went out into the busy street with a sense of the warmth of friendship which was still a flavor to be relished with a lingering surprise, but even less hope for Alexandra Carlyon than before.

Monk would not go back to Rathbone and admit defeat. It was not proved. Really he had no more than Rathbone had told him in the beginning. A crime had three principal elements, and he cited them in his mind as he walked along the street between costermongers' barrows, young children of no more than six or seven years selling ribbons and matches. Sad-faced women held bags of old clothes; indigent and disabled men offered toys, small handmade articles, some carved of bone or wood, bottles of this and that, patent medicines. He passed by news vendors, singing patterers and every other inhabitant of the London streets. And he knew beneath them in the sewers there would be others hunting and scavenging a living, and along the river shore seeking the refuse and the lost treasures of the wealthier denizens of the great city.

Motive had failed him. Alexandra had a motive, even if it was a self-defeating and short-sighted one. She had not

136

looked like a woman torn by a murderously jealous rage. But that might be because it had been satisfied by his death, and now she could see the folly, and the price of it.

Sabella had motive, but it was equally self-defeating, and she had not confessed. Indeed she seemed genuinely concerned for her mother. Could it be she had committed the crime, in a fit of madness, and did not even remember it? From her husband's anxiety, it seemed not impossible he thought so.

Maxim Furnival? Not out of jealousy over Louisa, unless the affair were a great deal deeper than anyone had so far discovered. Or was Louisa so in love with the general she would have caused a public scandal and left her husband for him? On the evidence so far that was absurd.

Louisa herself? Because the general had flirted with her and then rejected her? There was no evidence whatsoever to suggest he had rejected her at all. On the contrary, there was every indication he was still quite definitely interested—although to what degree it was impossible to say.

Means. They all had the means. All it required was a simple push when the general was standing at the turn of the stairs with his back to the banister, as he might if he had stopped to speak to someone. He would naturally face them. And the halberd was there for anyone to use. It did not require strength or skill. Any person of adult height could have used his or her body's weight to force that blade through a man's chest, although it might take an overtowering passion to sink it to the floor.

Opportunity. That was his only course left. If the events of the dinner party had been retold accurately (and to imagine them all lying was too remote and forced an idea to entertain), then there were four people who could have done it, the four he had already considered: Alexandra, Sabella, Louisa and Maxim.

Who else was in the house and not at the party? All the servants—and young Valentine Furnival. But Valentine was little more than a child, and by all accounts very fond of the general. That left the servants. He must make one last effort to account for their whereabouts that evening. If nothing else, it might establish beyond question whether Sabella Pole could have come downstairs and killed her father.

He took a hansom—after all, Rathbone was paying for it—and presented himself at the Furnivals' front door. Although he wanted to speak to the servants, he must obtain permission first.

Maxim, home early, was startled to see him, and even more to hear his request, but with a smile that conveyed both surprise and pity he granted it without argument. Apparently Louisa was out taking tea with someone or other, and Monk was glad of it. She was far more acute in her suspicion, and might well have hindered him.

He began with the butler, a very composed individual well into his late sixties, with a broad nose and a tight, satisfied mouth.

"Dinner was served at nine o'clock." He was uncertain whether to add the "sir" or not. Precisely who was this person making enquiries? His master had been unclear.

"Which staff were on duty?" Monk asked.

The butler's eyes opened wide to convey his surprise at such an ignorant question.

"The kitchen and dining room staff, sir." His voice implied "of course."

"How many?" Monk kept his patience with difficulty.

"Myself and the two footmen," the butler replied levelly. "The parlormaid and the downstairs maid who serves sometimes if we have company. In the kitchen there were the cook, two kitchen maids and a scullery maid—and the boot-boy. He carries things if he's needed and does the occasional errand."

"In all parts of the house?" Monk asked quickly.

"That is not usually required," the butler replied somberly.

"And on this occasion?"

"He was in disgrace, sent to the scullery."

"What time in the evening was that?" Monk persisted.

"Long before the general's death—about nine o'clock, I gather."

"That would be after the guests arrived," Monk observed.

"It would," the butler agreed grimly.

It was only idle curiosity which made him ask, "What happened?"

"Stupid boy was carrying a pile of clean linen upstairs for one of the maids, who was busy, and he bumped into the general coming out of the cloakroom. Wasn't looking where he was going, I suppose—daydreaming—and he dropped the whole lot. Then instead of apologizing and picking them up, like any sensible person, he just turned on his heel and fled. The laundress had a few hard words to say to him, I can promise you! He spent the rest of the evening in the scullery. Didn't leave it."

"I see. What about the rest of the staff?"

"The housekeeper was in her sitting room in the servants' wing. The tweenies would be in their bedroom, the upstairs maids in theirs, the stillroom maid had an evening off to go and visit her mother, who's been took poorly. Mrs. Furnival's ladies' maid would be upstairs and Mr. Furnival's valet likewise."

"And the outside staff?"

"Outside, sir." The butler looked at him with open contempt.

"They have no access to the house?"

"No sir, they have no need."

Monk gritted his teeth. "And none of you heard the general fall onto the suit of armor, or the whole thing come crashing down?"

The butler's face paled, but his eyes were steady.

"No sir. I already told the police person who enquired. We were about our duties, and they did not necessitate any of us coming through the hall. As you may have observed, the withdrawing room is to the rear of the house, and by that time dinner was well finished. We had no cause to pass in that direction."

"After dinner were you all in the kitchen or the pantry clearing away?"

"Yes sir, naturally."

"No one left?"

"What would anyone leave for? We had more than sufficient to keep us busy if we were to get to bed before one."

"Doing what, precisely?" It galled Monk to have to persist in the face of such dignified but subtly apparent scorn. But he would not explain to the man.

Because his master had required it, the butler patiently answered these exceedingly tedious and foolish questions.

"I saw to the silver and the wine, with the assistance of the first footman. The second footman tidied up the dining room and set everything straight ready for morning, and fetched more coal up in case it was required—"

"The dining room," Monk interrupted. "The second footman was in the dining room. Surely he would have heard the armor go over?"

The butler flushed with annoyance. He had been caught out.

"Yes sir, I suppose he would," he said grudgingly. "If he'd been in the dining room when it happened."

"And you said he fetched up coal. Where from?"

"The coal cellar, sir."

"Where is the door to it?"

"Back of the scullery . . . sir." The "sir" was heavy with irony.

"Which rooms would he bring coal for?"

"I . . ." The butler stopped. "I don't know, sir." His face betrayed that he had realized the possibilities. For the dining room, the morning room, the library or billiard room the footman would have crossed the hall.

"May I speak with him?" Monk did not say please; the request was only a formality. He had every intention of speaking with the man regardless.

The butler was not going to put himself in the position of being wrong again.

"I'll send him to you." And before Monk could argue

that he would go to the man, which would give him an opportunity to see the servants' area, the butler was gone.

A few minutes later a very nervous young man came in, dressed in ordinary daytime livery of black trousers, shirt and striped waistcoat. He was in his early twenties, fair haired and fair skinned, and at the moment he was extremely ill at ease. Monk guessed the butler had reasserted his authority over the situation by frightening his immediate junior.

Out of perversity Monk decided to be thoroughly pleasant with the young man.

"Good morning," he said with a disarming smile—at least that was how it was intended. "I apologize for taking you from your duties, but I think you may be able to help me."

"Me sir?" His surprise was patent. " 'Ow can I do that, sir?"

"By telling me, as clearly as you can remember, everything you did the evening General Carlyon died, starting after dinner when the guests went to the withdrawing room."

The footman screwed up his face in painfully earnest concentration and recounted his usual routine.

"Then what?" Monk prompted.

"The withdrawing room bell rang," the footman answered. "And since I was passing right by there, I answered it. They wanted the fire stoked, so I did it."

"Who was there then?"

"The master wasn't there, and the mistress came in just as I was leaving."

"And then?"

"Then I—er . . ."

"Had another word with the kitchen maid?" Monk took a guess. He smiled as he said it.

The footman colored, his eyes downcast. "Yes sir."

"Did you fetch the coal buckets for the library?"

"Yes sir—but I don't remember how many minutes later it was." He looked unhappy. Monk guessed it was probably quite some time.

"And crossed the hall to do it?"

"Yes sir. The armor was still all right then."

141

So whoever it was, it was not Louisa. Not that he had held any real hope that it might be.

"Any other rooms you took coal for? What about upstairs?"

The footman blushed hotly and lowered his eyes.

"You were supposed to, and didn't?" Monk guessed.

The footman looked up quickly. "Yes I did, sir! Mrs. Furnival's room. The master doesn't care for a fire at this time o' the year."

"Did you see someone, or something, when you were upstairs?"

"No sir!"

What was the man lying about? There was something; it was there in his pink face, his downcast eyes, his awkward hands and feet. He was riddled with guilt.

"Where did you go upstairs? What rooms did you pass? Did you hear something, an argument?"

"No sir." He bit his lip and still avoided Monk's eyes.

"Well?" Monk demanded.

"I went up the front stairs—sir . . ."

Suddenly Monk understood. "Oh, I see—with the coal buckets?"

"Yes sir. Please sir . . ."

"I shan't tell the butler," Monk promised quickly.

"Thank you, sir! I—thank you sir." He swallowed. "The armor was still there, sir; and I didn't see the general—or anyone else, except the upstairs maid."

"I see. Thank you. You have helped me considerably."

"Have I sir?" He was doubtful, but relieved to be excused.

Next Monk went upstairs to find the off-duty housemaids. It was his last hope that one of them had seen Sabella.

The first maid offered no hope at all. The second was a bright girl of about sixteen with a mass of auburn hair. She seemed to grasp the significance of his questions, and answered readily enough, although with wary eyes, and he caught a sense of eagerness that suggested to him she had something to hide as well as something to reveal. Presumably she was the one the footman had seen.

"Yes, I saw Mrs. Pole," she said candidly. "She wasn't feeling well, so she lay down for a while in the green room."

"When was that?"

"I—I dunno, sir."

"Was it long after dinner?"

"Oh, yes sir. We 'as our dinner at six o'clock!"

Monk realized his mistake and tried to undo it.

"Did you see anyone else while you were on the landing?"

The color came to her face and suddenly the picture was clearer.

"I shan't report what you say, unless I have to. But if you lie, you may go to prison, because an innocent person could be hanged. You wouldn't want that, would you?"

Now she was ashen white, so frightened as to be robbed momentarily of words.

"So who did you see?"

"John." Her voice was a whisper.

"The footman who was filling the coal buckets?"

"Yes sir—but I didn't speak to him—honest! I jus' came to the top o' the stairs, like. Mrs. Pole were in the green room, 'cause I passed the door and it was open, an' I seen 'er like."

"You came all the way down from your own room at the top of the house?"

She nodded, guilt over her attempt to see the footman outweighing every other thought. She had no idea of the significance of what she was saying.

"How did you know when he was going to be there?"

"I . . ." She bit her lip. "I waited on the landing."

"Did you see Mrs. Carlyon go upstairs to Master Valentine's room?"

"Yes sir."

"Did you see Mrs. Carlyon come down again?"

"No sir, nor the general, sir—I swear to God!"

"Then what did you do?"

"I went as far as the top o' the stairs and looked for John, sir. I knew that was about the time 'e'd be fillin' the coal buckets."

"Did you see him?"

"No. I reckon I were too late. I 'ad to 'ang around cos of all the people comin' and goin'. I 'ad ter wait for the master ter go down again."

"You saw Mr. Furnival go down again?"

"Yes sir."

"When you were at the top of the stairs, looking for John—think very carefully, you may have to swear to this in court, before a judge, so tell the truth, as you know it . . ."

She gulped. "Yes sir?"

"Did you look down at the hallway below you?"

"Yes sir. I were looking for John."

"To come from the back of the house?"

"Yes sir—with the coal buckets."

"Was the suit of armor standing where it usually does?"

"I think so."

"It wasn't knocked over?"

"No—o' course it weren't, or I'd 'ave seen it. It'd be right between me and the corridor to the back."

"Then where did you go, after waiting for John and realizing you were too late?"

"Back upstairs again."

He saw the flicker in her eyes, barely discernible, just a tremor.

"Tell me the truth: did you pass anyone?"

Her eyes were downcast, the blush came again. "I heard someone comin', I don't know who. I didn't want to be caught there, so I went into Mrs. Pole's room to see if she needed anything. I was goin' ter say I thought I'd 'eard 'er call out, if anyone asked me."

"And the people passed, going along the passage to the front stairs?"

"Yes sir."

"When was that?"

"I dunno, sir. God help me, I don't! I swear it!"

"That's all right, I believe you." Alexandra and the general, minutes before she killed him.

"Did you hear anything?"

"No sir."

"You didn't hear voices?"

"No sir."

"Or the suit of armor crashing over?"

"No sir. The green room is a long way from the top o' the stairs, sir." She did not bother to swear—it was easily verifiable.

"Thank you," he said honestly.

So only Alexandra had the opportunity after all. It was murder.

"You've been a great help." He forced the words out. "A very great help. That's all—you can go." And Alexandra was guilty. Louisa and Maxim had already gone up and come down again, and the general was alive.

"Yes sir. Thank you, sir." And she turned on her heel and fled.

5

OLIVER RATHBONE AWAITED the arrival of Monk with some hope, in spite of his reason telling him that it was extremely unlikely he had been able to find any worthwhile evidence that it was not after all Alexandra Carlyon who had killed the general. He shared Monk's contempt for Runcorn personally, but he had a considerable respect for the police in general, and had found that when they brought a case to trial, they were seldom fundamentally in error. But he did hope that Monk might have turned up a stronger and more sympathetic motive than jealousy. And if he were honest, there was a lingering corner in his mind which cherished a vague idea that it might indeed have been someone else—although how it would be any better had it been Sabella, he had no idea, except that so far Sabella was not his client.

As well as Monk, he had invited Hester Latterly. He had hesitated before doing so. She had no official part in the case, nor indeed had she had in any other case. But she had opportunities for observation of the Carlyon family that neither he nor Monk possessed. And it had been she who had brought him the case in the first place and enlisted his help. She was owed some information as to the conclusion—if indeed there was a conclusion. Monk had sent him a message that he had incontrovertible evidence which he must share, so it was unquestionably a decisive point.

Apart from that, he felt a wish that she should be included, and he chose not to examine the cause of it. Therefore at ten minutes before eight on the evening of May 14, he was awaiting their arrival with uncharacteristic nervousness. He was sure he was concealing it perfectly, and yet it was there, once or twice a flutter in his stomach, a very slight tightening of his throat, and several changed decisions as to what he intended to say. He had chosen to receive them in his home rather than his office, because in the office time was precious and he would feel compelled simply to hear the bare outlines of what Monk had learned, and not to question him more deeply and to explore his understanding and his instinct. At home there was all evening, and no sense of haste, or of time being money.

And also, since it was in all probability a miserable tale, perhaps he owed Monk something more generous than simply a word of thanks and dismissal, and his money. And if she had heard from Monk directly what his discoveries were, it would be far easier for Hester to accept Rathbone's declining the case, if that were the only reasonable choice left to him. That was all most logical, nevertheless he found himself repeating it over and over, as if it required justification.

Although he was expecting them, their arrival caught him by surprise. He had not heard them come, presumably by hansom since neither of them had a carriage of their own. He was startled by the butler, Eames, announcing their presence, and a moment later they were in the room, Monk as beautifully tailored as usual. His suit must have cost as much as Rathbone's own, obviously bought in his police days when he had money for such luxuries. The waistcoat was modishly short with a shawl collar, and he wore a pointed, standing collar with a lavish bow tie.

Hester was dressed much more reservedly, in a cool teal-green gown with pointed waist and pagoda sleeves with separate gathered undersleeves of white broderie anglaise. There was no glamour to it, and yet he found it remarkably pleasing. It was both simple and subtle, and the shade accentuated the slight flush in her cheeks.

They greeted each other very formally, even stiffly, and he invited them to be seated. He noticed Hester's eyes glancing around the room, and suddenly it seemed to him less satisfactory than it had. It was bare of feminine touches. It was his, not inherited from his family, and there had been no woman resident in it since he came, some eleven years ago. His housekeeper and his cook he did not count. They maintained what he had, but introduced nothing new, nothing of their own taste.

He saw Hester look at the forest-green carpet and upholstery, and the plain white walls, the mahogany woodwork. It was very bare for current fashion, which favored oak, ornate carving and highly decorative china and ornaments. It was on the tip of his tongue to make some comment to her, but he could think of nothing that did not sound as if he were seeking a compliment, so he remained silent.

"Do you wish for my findings before dinner, or after?" Monk asked. "If you care what I say, I think you may prefer them after."

"I cannot but leap to the conclusion that they are unpleasant," Rathbone replied with a twisted smile. "In which case, do not let us spoil our meal."

"A wise decision," Monk conceded.

Eames returned with a decanter of sherry, long-stemmed glasses and a tray of savory tidbits. They accepted them and made trivial conversation about current political events, the possibility of war in India, until they were informed that dinner awaited them.

The dining room was in the same deep green, a far smaller room than that in the Furnivals' house; obviously Rathbone seldom entertained more than half a dozen people at the most. The china was imported from France, a delicately gold-rimmed pattern of extreme severity. The only concession to flamboyance was a magnificent Sevres urn covered in a profusion of roses and other flowers in blazing reds, pinks, golds and greens. Rathbone saw Hester look at it several times, but forbore from asking her opinion. If she praised it he would think it mere politeness; if not then he would be hurt, because he feared it was ostentatious, but he loved it.

Throughout the meal conversation centered on subjects of politics and social concern, which he would not personally have imagined discussing in front of a woman. He was well versed in the fashion and graces of Society, but Hester was different. She was not a woman in the customary sense of someone separate from the business of life outside the home, a person to be protected from the affairs or the emotions that involved the mind.

After the final course they returned to the withdrawing room and at last there was no reason any longer to put off the matter of the Carlyon case.

Rathbone looked across at Monk, his eyes wide.

"A crime contains three elements," Monk said, leaning back in his chair, a dour, ironic smile on his face. He was perfectly sure that Rathbone knew this, and quite possibly Hester did also, but he was going to tell them in his own fashion.

Rathbone could feel an irritation rising inside him already. He had a profound respect for Monk, and part of him liked the man, but there was also a quality in him which abraded the nerves like fine sandpaper, an awareness that at any time he might lash out with the unforeseeable, the suddenly disturbing, cutting away comforts and safely held ideas.

"The means were there to hand for anyone," Monk went on. "To wit, the halberd held by the suit of armor. They all had access to it, and they all knew it was there because any person entering the hall had to see it. That was its function—to impress."

"We knew they all could have done it," Rathbone said tersely. His irritation with Monk had provoked him into haste. "It does not take a powerful person to push a man over a banister, if he is standing next to it and is taken by surprise. And the halberd could have been used by anyone of average build—according to the medical report—although to penetrate the body and scar the floor beneath it must have been driven with extraordinary violence." He winced very slightly, and felt a chill pass through him at such a passion of hate. "At least four of them were upstairs," he hurried on. "Or otherwise out of the withdrawing room and unobserved during the time the general went upstairs until Maxim Furnival came in and said he had found him on the floor of the hall."

"Opportunity," Monk said somewhat officiously. "Not quite true, I'm afraid. That is the painful part. Apparently the police questioned the guests and Mr. and Mrs. Furnival at some length, but they only corroborated with the servants what they already knew."

"One of the servants was involved?" Hester said slowly. There was no real hope in her face, because of his warning that the news was not good. "I wondered that before, if one of them had a military experience, or was related to someone who had. The motive might be quite different, something in his professional life and nothing personal at all . . ." She looked at Monk.

There was a flicker in Monk's face, and Rathbone knew in that instant that he had not thought of that himself. Why not? Inefficiency—or had he reached some unarguable conclusion before he got that far?

"No." Monk glanced at him, then away again. "They did not question the movements of the servants closely enough. The butler said they had all been about their duties and noticed nothing at all, and since their duties were in the kitchen and servants' quarters, it was not surprising they had not heard the suit of armor fall. But on questioning him more closely, he admitted one footman tidied the dining room, which was not in the time period we are interested in. He was told to fill the coal scuttles for the rest of the house, including the morning room and the library, which are off the front hall."

Hester turned her head to watch him. Rathbone sat up a little straighter.

Monk continued impassively, only the faintest of smiles touching the corners of his mouth.

"The footman's observations as to the armor, and he could hardly have missed it had it been lying on the floor in pieces with the body of the general across it and the halberd sticking six feet out of his chest like a flagpole—"

"We take your point," Rathbone said sharply. "That reduces the opportunities of the suspects. I assume that is what you are eventually going to tell us?"

A flush of annoyance crossed Monk's face, then vanished and was replaced by satisfaction, not at the outcome, but at his own competence in proving it.

"That, and the romantic inclinations of the upstairs maid, and the fact that the footman had a lazy streak, and preferred to carry the scuttles up the front stairs instead of the back, for Mrs. Furnival's bedroom, make it impossible that anyone but Alexandra could have killed him. I'm sorry."

"Not Sabella?" Hester asked with a frown, leaning a little forward in her seat.

"No." He turned to her, his face softening for an instant. "The upstairs maid was waiting around the stair head to catch the footman, and when she realized she had missed him, and heard someone coming, she darted into the room where Sabella was resting, just off the first landing, on the pretext that she thought she had heard her call. And when she came out again the people had passed, and she went on back up to the servants' back stairs, and her own room. The people who passed her must have been Alexandra and the general, because after the footman had finished, he went down the back stairs, just in time to meet the news that General Carlyon had had an accident, and the butler had been told to keep the hall clear, and to send for the police."

Rathbone let out his breath in a sigh. He did not ask Monk if he were sure; he knew he would not have said it if there were the slightest doubt.

Monk bit his lip, glanced at Hester, who looked crushed, then back at Rathbone.

"The third element is motive," he said.

Rathbone's attention jerked back. Suddenly there was hope again. If not, why would Monk have bothered to mention it?

Damn the man for his theatricality! It was too late to pretend he was indifferent, Monk had seen his change of expression. To affect a casual air now would make himself ridiculous.

"I presume your discovery there is more useful to us?" he said aloud.

Monk's satisfaction evaporated.

"I don't know," he confessed. "One could speculate all sorts of motives for the others, but for her there seems only jealousy—and yet that was not the reason."

Rathbone and Hester stared at him. There was no sound in the quiet room but a leaf tapping against the window in the spring breeze.

Monk pulled a dubious face. "It was never easy to believe, in spite of one or two people accepting it, albeit reluctantly. I believed it myself for a while." He saw the sudden start of interest in their faces, and continued blindly. "Louisa Furnival is certainly a woman who would inspire uncertainty, self-doubt and then jealousy in another woman—and must have done so many times. And there is the possibility that Alexandra could have hated her not because she was so in love with the general but simply because she could not abide publicly being beaten by Louisa, being seen to be second best in the rivalry which cuts deepest to a person's self-esteem, most especially a woman's."

"But . . ." Hester could not contain herself. "But what? Why don't you believe it now?"

"Because Louisa was not having an affair with the general, and Alexandra must have known he was not."

"Are you sure?" Rathbone leaned forward keenly. "How do you know?"

"Maxim has money, which is important to Louisa," Monk replied, watching their faces carefully. "But even more important is her security and her reputation. Apparently some time ago Maxim was in love with Alexandra." He glanced up as Hester leaned forward, nodding quickly. "You knew that too?"

"Yes—yes, Edith told me. But he would not do anything

about it because he is very moral, and believes profoundly in his marriage vows, regardless of emotions afterwards.''

"Precisely," Monk agreed. "And Alexandra must have known that, because she was so immediately concerned. Louisa is not a woman to throw away anything—money, honor, home, Society's acceptance—for the love of a man, especially one she knew would not marry her. And the general would not; he would lose his own reputation and career, not to mention the son he adored. In fact I doubt Louisa ever threw away anything intentionally. Alexandra knew her, and knew the situation. If Louisa had been caught in an affair with the general, Maxim would have made life extremely hard for her. After all, he had already made a great sacrifice in order to sustain his marriage. He would demand the same of her. And all this Alexandra knew . . ." He left the rest unsaid, and sat staring at them, his face somber.

Rathbone sat back with a feeling of confusion and incompleteness in his mind. There must be so much more to this story they had not even guessed at. They had only pieces, and the most important one that held it all together was missing.

"It doesn't make sense," he said guardedly. He looked across at Hester, wondering what she thought, and was pleased to see the same doubt reflected in her face. Better than that, the attention in her eyes betrayed that she was still acutely involved in the matter. In no way had she resigned interest merely because the answer eluded them but left the guilt undeniable.

"And you have no idea what the real motive was?" he said to Monk, searching his face to see if he concealed yet another surprise, some final piece held back for a last self-satisfying dramatic effect. But there was nothing. Monk's face was perfectly candid.

"I've tried to think," he said frankly. "But there is nothing to suggest he used her badly in any way, nor has anyone else suggested anything." He also glanced at Hester.

Rathbone looked at her. "Hester? If you were in her place,

can you think of anything which would make you kill such a man?''

''Several things,'' she admitted with a twisted smile, then bit her lip as she realized what they might think of her for such feelings.

Rathbone grinned in sudden amusement. ''For example?'' he asked.

''The first thing that comes to mind is if I loved someone else.''

''And the second?''

''If he loved someone else.'' Her eyebrows rose. ''Frankly I should be delighted to let him go. He sounds so—so restricting. But if I could not bear the social shame of it, what my friends would say, or my enemies, the laughter behind my back, and above all the pity—and the other woman's victory . . .''

''But he was not having an affair with Louisa,'' Monk pointed out. ''Oh—you mean another woman entirely? Someone we have not even thought of? But why that night?''

Hester shrugged. ''Why not? Perhaps he taunted her. Perhaps that was the night he told her about it. We shall probably never know what they said to one another.''

''What else?''

The butler returned discreetly and enquired if there was anything more required. After asking his guests, Rathbone thanked him and bade him good-night.

Hester sighed. ''Money?'' she answered as the door closed. ''Perhaps she overspent, or gambled, and he refused to pay her debts. Maybe she was frightened her creditors would shame her publicly. The only thing . . .'' She frowned, looking first at one, then the other of them. Somewhere outside a dog barked. Beyond the windows it was almost dark. ''The thing is, why did she say she had done it out of jealousy of Louisa? Jealousy is an ugly thing, and in no way an excuse—is it?'' She turned to Rathbone again. ''Will the law take any account of that?''

''None at all,'' he answered grimly. ''They will hang her,

if they find her guilty, and on this evidence they will have no choice."

"Then what can we do?" Hester's face was full of anxiety. Her eyes held Rathbone's and there was a sharp pity in them. He wondered at it. She alone of them had never met Alexandra Carlyon. His own dragging void of pity he could understand; he had seen the woman. She was a real living being like himself. He had been touched by her hopelessness and her fear. Her death would be the extinguishing of someone he knew. For Monk it must be the same, and for all his sometime ruthlessness, Rathbone had no doubt Monk was just as capable of compassion as he was himself.

But for Hester she was still a creature of the imagination, a name and a set of circumstances, no more.

"What are we going to do?" Hester repeated urgently.

"I don't know," he replied. "If she doesn't tell us the truth, I don't know what there is that I can do."

"Then ask her," Hester retorted. "Go to her and tell her what you know, and ask her what the truth is. It may be better. It may offer some . . ." Her voice tailed off. "Some mitigation," she finished lamely.

"None of your suggestions were any mitigation at all," Monk pointed out. "She would hang just as surely as if it had been what she claims."

"What do you want to do, give up?" Hester snapped.

"What I want is immaterial," Monk replied. "I cannot afford the luxury of meddling in other people's affairs for entertainment."

"I'll go and see her again," Rathbone declared. "At least I will ask her."

Alexandra looked up as he came into the cell. For an instant her face lit with hope, then knowledge prevailed and fear took its place.

"Mr. Rathbone?" She swallowed with difficulty, as though there were some constriction in her throat. "What is it?"

The door clanged shut behind him and they both heard the

lock fall and then the silence. He longed to be able to comfort her, at least to be gentle, but there was no time, no place for evasion.

"I should not have doubted you, Mrs. Carlyon," he answered, looking straight at her remarkable blue eyes. "I thought perhaps you had confessed in order to shield your daughter. But Monk has proved beyond any question at all that it was, as you say, you who killed your husband. However, it was not because he was having an affair with Louisa Furnival. He was not—and you knew he was not."

She stared at him, white-faced. He felt as if he had struck her, but she did not flinch. She was an extraordinary woman, and the feeling renewed in him that he must know the truth behind the surface facts. Why in heaven's name had she resorted to such hopeless and foredoomed violence? Could she ever have imagined she would get away with it?

"Why did you kill him, Mrs. Carlyon?" he said urgently, leaning towards her. It was raining outside and the cell was dim, the air clammy.

She did not look away, but closed her eyes to avoid seeing him.

"I have told you! I was jealous of Louisa!"

"That is not true!"

"Yes it is." Still her eyes were closed.

"They will hang you," he said deliberately. He saw her wince, but she still kept her face towards his, eyes tight shut. "Unless we can find some circumstance that will at least in part explain what you did, they will hang you, Mrs. Carlyon! For heaven's sake, tell me why you did it." His voice was low, grating and insistent. How could he get through the shield of denial? What could he say to reach her mind with reality? He wanted to touch her, take her by those slender arms and shake sense into her. But it would be such a breach of all possible etiquette, it would shatter the mood and become more important, for the moment, than the issue that would save or lose her life.

"Why did you kill him?" he repeated desperately.

"Whatever you say, you cannot make it worse than it is already."

"I killed him because he was having an affair with Louisa," she repeated flatly. "At least I thought he was."

And he could get nothing further from her. She refused to add anything, or take anything from what she had said.

Reluctantly, temporarily defeated, he took his leave. She remained sitting on the cot, immobile, ashen-faced.

Outside in the street the rain was a steady downpour, the gutter filling, people hurrying by with collars up. He passed a newsboy shouting the latest headlines. It was something to do with a financial scandal and the boy caressed the words with relish, seeing the faces of passersby as they turned. "Scandal, scandal in the City! Financier absconds with fortune. Secret love nest! Scandal in the City!"

Rathbone quickened his pace to get away from it. They had temporarily forgotten Alexandra and the murder of General Carlyon, but as soon as the trial began it would be all over every front page and every newsboy would be crying out each day's revelations and turning them over with delight, poring over the details, imagining, condemning.

And they would condemn. He had no delusion that there would be any pity for her. Society would protect itself from threat and disruption. They would close ranks, and even the few who might feel some twinge of pity for her would not dare to admit it. Any woman who was in the same situation, or imagined herself so, would have even less compassion. If she herself had to endure it, why should Alexandra be able to escape? And no man whose eyes or thoughts had ever wandered, or who considered they might in the future, would countenance the notion that a wife could take such terrible revenge for a brief and relatively harmless indulgence of his very natural appetites. Carlyon's offense of flirtation, not even proved to be adultery, would be utterly lost in her immeasurably deeper offense of murder.

Was there anything at all Rathbone could do to help her? She had robbed him of every possible weapon he might have

157

used. The only thing still left to him was time. But time to do what?

He passed an acquaintance, but was too absorbed in thought to recognize him until he was twenty yards farther along the pavement. By then it was too late to retrieve his steps and apologize for having ignored his greeting.

The rain was easing into merely a spring squall. Bright shafts of sunlight shone fitfully on the wet pavement.

If he went into court with all he had at present he would lose. There would be no doubt of it. He could imagine it vividly, the feeling of helplessness as the prosecution demolished his case effortlessly, the derision of the spectators, the quiet and detached concern of the judge that there should be some semblance of a defense, the crowds in the gallery, eager for details and ultimately for the drama of conviction, the black cap and the sentence of death. Worse than those, he could picture the jury, earnest men, overawed by the situation, disturbed by the story and the inevitability of its end, and Alexandra herself, with the same white hopelessness he had seen in her face in the cell.

And afterwards his colleagues would ask him why on earth he had given such a poor account of himself. What ailed him to have taken so foregone a case? Had he lost his skills? His reputation would suffer. Even his junior would laugh and ask questions behind his back.

He hailed a cab and rode the rest of the way to Vere Street in a dark mood, almost resolved to decline the case and tell Alexandra Carlyon that if she would not tell him the truth then he was sorry but he could not help her.

At his offices he alighted, paid the driver and went in to be greeted by his clerk, who informed him that Miss Latterly was awaiting him.

Good. That would give him the opportunity to tell her now that he had seen Alexandra, and failed to elicit from her a single thing more than the idiotic insistence of the story they all knew to be untrue. Perhaps Peverell Erskine could persuade her to speak, but if even he could not, then the case was at an end as far as he was concerned.

Hester stood up as soon as he was inside, her face curious, full of questions.

He felt a flicker of doubt. His certainty wavered. Before he saw her he had been resolved to decline the case. Now her eagerness confounded him.

"Did you see her?" She made no apology for having come. The matter was too important to her, and she judged to him also, for her to pretend indifference or make excuses.

"Yes, I have just come from the prison . . ." he began.

"Oh." She read from his expression, the weariness in him, that he had failed. "She would not tell you." For a moment she was taken aback; disappointment filled her. Then she took a deep breath and lifted her head a little. A momentary compassion for him was replaced by anxiety again. "Then the reason must be very deep—something she would rather die than reveal." She shuddered and her face pulled into an expression of pain. "It had to be something very terrible—and I cannot help believing it must concern some other person."

"Then please sit down," he asked, moving to the large chair behind the desk himself.

She obeyed, taking the upright chair opposite him. When she was unconscious of herself she was curiously graceful. He brought his mind back to the case.

"Or be so ugly that it would only make her situation worse," he went on reasonably, then wished he had not. "I'm sorry," he said quickly. "But Hester—we must be honest."

She did not even seem to notice his use of her Christian name. Indeed it seemed very natural to her.

"As it is there is nothing I can do for her. I have to tell Erskine that. I would be defrauding him if I allowed him to think I could say anything more than the merest novice barrister could."

If she suspected fear for his reputation, the dread of losing, it did not show in her face, and he felt a twinge of shame that the thoughts had been there in his own mind.

"We have to find it!" she said uncertainly, convincing herself as well as him. "There is still time, isn't there?"

"Till the trial? Yes, some weeks. But what good will it do, and where do we begin?"

"I don't know, but Monk will." Her eyes never wavered from his face. She saw the shadow in his expression at mention of Monk's name, and wished she had been less clumsy. "We cannot give up now," she went on. There was no time for self-indulgence. "Whatever it is, surely we must find out if she is protecting someone else. Oh I know she did it—the proof is beyond argument. But why? Why was she prepared to kill him, and then to confess to it, and if necessary face the gallows? It has to be something—something beyond bearing. Something so terrible that prison, trial and the rope are better!"

"Not necessarily, my dear," he said gently. "Sometimes people commit even the most terrible crimes for the most trivial of reasons. Men have killed for a few shillings, or in a rage over a petty insult . . ."

"Not Alexandra Carlyon," she insisted, leaning across the desk towards him. "You have met her! Did she? Do you believe she sacrificed all she had—her husband, her family, her home, her position, even her life—over something trivial?" She shook her head impatiently. "And what woman cares about an insult? Men fight duels of honor—women don't! We are perfectly used to being insulted; the best defense is to pretend you haven't noticed—then you need not reply. Anyway, with a mother-in-law like Felicia Carlyon, I imagine Alexandra had sufficient practice at being insulted to be mistress of anything. She is not a fool, is she?"

"No."

"Or a drunkard?"

"No."

"Then we must find out why she did it! If you are thinking of the worst, what has she to lose? What better way to spend her money than to try to save her life?"

"I doubt I can . . ." he began. Then not only Hester's face but memory of Alexandra herself, the remarkable eyes,

160

the strong, intelligent features and sensuous mouth, the possibility of humor came back to him. He wanted to know; it would hurt him as long as he did not.

"I'll try," he conceded, and felt a surprising stab of pleasure as her eyes softened and she smiled, relaxing at last.

"Thank you."

"But it may do no good," he warned her, hating to curb her hope, and afraid of the darker despair and anger with him if he misled her.

"Of course," she assured him. "I understand. But at least we shall try."

"For what it may be worth . . ."

"Shall you tell Monk?"

"Yes—yes, I shall instruct him to continue his search."

She smiled, a sudden brilliant gesture lighting her face.

"Thank you—thank you very much."

Monk was surprised that Rathbone should request him to continue in the case. As a matter of personal curiosity he would like to have known the real reason why Alexandra Carlyon had killed her husband. But he could afford neither the time nor the finance to seek an answer when it could scarcely affect the outcome of any trial, and would almost certainly be a long and exhausting task.

But Rathbone had pointed out that if Erskine wished it, as her solicitor and acting in her best interest, then that was possibly the best use for her money. Certainly there was no other use that could serve her more. And presumably her heirs and the general's were all cared for.

Perhaps that was a place to begin—money? He doubted it would show anything of use, but if nothing else, it must be eliminated, and since he had not even a guess as to what the answer might be, this was as good a place as any. He might be fortunately surprised.

It was not difficult to trace the Carlyon estate, since wills were a matter of public record. Thaddeus George Randolf Carlyon had died possessed of a very considerable wealth. His family had invested fortunately in the past. Although his father was still alive, Thaddeus had always had a generous allowance, which he in turn had spent sparingly and invested on excellent advice, largely in various parts of the Empire: India, southern Africa and the Anglo-Egyptian Sudan, in export business which had brought him a more than handsome return. And he had lived comfortably, but at very moderate expense in view of his means.

It occurred to Monk while reading the financial outlines that he had not yet seen Carlyon's house, and that was an omission which must be rectified. One occasionally learned a great deal about people from their choice of books, furnishings, pictures, and the small items on which they did or did not spend their money.

He turned his attention to the disposition the general had chosen for his estate. The house was Alexandra's to live in for the duration of her life, then it passed to their only son, Cassian. He also bequeathed her sufficient income to ensure the upkeep of the house and a reasonable style of living for the duration of her life, adequately, but certainly not extravagantly, and there was no provision made should she wish to undertake any greater expense. She would not be able to purchase any new horses or carriages without considerable savings on other things, nor would she be able to take any extended journeys, such as a tour of Italy or Greece or any other sunny climate.

There were small bequests to his daughters, and personal mementos to his two sisters and to Maxim and Louisa Furnival, to Valentine Furnival, and to Dr. Charles Hargrave. But the vast bulk of his estate, both real and financial, went to Cassian, during his minority to be held in trust for him by a firm of solicitors, and administered by them. Alexandra had no say in the matter and there was no stipulation that she should even be consulted.

It was an inescapable conclusion that she had been far better off while Thaddeus was alive. The only question was, had she been aware of that prior to his death, or had she expected to become a wealthy woman?

Was there any purpose in asking the solicitors who had

drawn the will, and who were to administer the estate? They might tell him, in the interests of justice. There was no point to be served by hiding such a thing now.

An hour later he presented himself at Messrs. Goodbody, Pemberton and Lightfoot. He found Mr. Lightfoot, the only surviving original partner, to be quite agreeable to informing him that on hearing of the general's death—such a sad affair, heaven only knew what the world was coming to when respectable women like Mrs. Carlyon sank to such depths—of course he could not believe it at the time. When he had called upon her to acquaint her with her position and assure her of his best services, she showed no surprise or distress at the news. Indeed she had seemed scarcely to be interested. He had taken it then to be shock and grief at the death of her husband. Now, of course! He shook his head, and wondered again what had happened to civilized society that such things came to pass.

It was on the edge of Monk's tongue to tell him that she had not yet been tried, let alone convicted of anything, but he knew it would be a waste of time. She had confessed, and as far as Mr. Lightfoot was concerned, that was the end of the matter. And indeed, he might well be right. Monk had no reasonable argument to offer.

He was hurrying along Threadneedle Street, past the Bank of England, and turned left down Bartholomew Lane, then suddenly did not know where he was going. He stopped, momentarily confused. He had turned the corner with absolute confidence, and now he did not know where he was. He looked around. It was familiar. There was an office opposite him; the name meant nothing, but the stone doorway with a brass plate in it woke in him a sense of anxiety and profound failure.

Why? When had he been here before, and for whom? Was it something to do with that other woman he had remembered briefly and so painfully in the prison with Alexandra Carlyon? He racked his mind for any link of memory that might have to do with her: prison, courtroom, police station, a house, a street . . . Nothing came—nothing at all.

163

An elderly gentleman passed him, walking briskly with a silver-topped cane in his hand. For an instant Monk thought he knew him, then the impression faded and he realized the set of the shoulder was wrong, the breadth of the man. Only the gait and the silver-topped cane were somehow familiar.

Of course. It was nothing to do with the woman that tugged at his mind. It was the man who had helped him in his youth, his mentor, the man whose wife wept silently, stricken with a grief he had shared, and had had helpless inability to prevent.

What had happened? Why was—was . . . Walbrook!

With singing triumph he knew the name quite clearly and without doubt. Walbrook—that had been his name. Frederick Walbrook . . . banker—commercial banker. Why did he have this terrible feeling of failure? What had his part been in the disaster that had struck?

He had no idea.

He gave up for the moment and retraced his steps back to Threadneedle Street, and then Cheapside and up towards Newgate.

He must bring back his mind to Alexandra Carlyon. What he could learn might be her only chance. She had begged him to help her, save her from the gallows and clear her name. He quickened his pace, visualizing her anguished face and the terror in her, her dark eyes . . .

He cared about it more intensely than anything he had ever known before. The emotion surging up inside him was so urgent he was hardly even aware of his feet on the pavement or the people passing by him. He was jostled by bankers and clerks, errand runners, peddlers and newsboys without even being aware of them. Everything hung on this.

He suddenly recalled a pair of eyes so clearly, wide and golden brown—but the rest of her face was a blank—no lips, no cheeks, no chin, just the golden eyes.

He stopped and the man behind him bumped into him, apologized bitterly, and moved on. Blue eyes. He could picture Alexandra Carlyon's face in his mind quite clearly, and it was not what his inner eye had seen: wide mouth full of humor and passion, short aquiline nose, high cheekbones and blue eyes, very blue. And she had not begged him to help, in fact she seemed almost indifferent about it, as if she knew his efforts were doomed.

He had met her only once, and he was pursuing the case because Oliver Rathbone asked him, not because he cared about her, more than a general compassion because she was in desperate trouble.

Who was it that came so vividly to his mind, and with such a powerful emotion, filling him with urgency, and terror of failure?

It must be someone from that past which haunted him and which he so ached to retrieve. It was certainly nothing since his accident. And it was not Imogen Latterly. Her face he could recall without any effort at all, and knew his relationship with her had been simply her trust in him to help clear her father's name—which he had failed to do.

Had he failed to help this other woman also? Had she hanged for a murder she did not commit? Or did she?

He started to walk rapidly again. At least he would do everything humanly possible to help Alexandra Carlyon—with her help or without it. There must be some passionate reason why she had pushed the general over the stairs, and then followed him down and as he lay senseless at her feet, picked up the halberd and driven it through his body.

It seemed money could not have been the cause, because she had known she would be less well off with him dead than she had been when he was alive. And socially she would be a widow, which would mean at least a year of mourning, then in all probability several more years of dark gowns, modest behavior and few if any social engagements. Apart from the requirements of mourning, she would be invited very infrequently to parties. Widows were something of a disadvantage, having no husband to escort them; except wealthy and eligible widows, which Alexandra was not, nor had she expected to be.

He must enquire into her life and habits as her friends knew her. To be of any value, those enquiries should be with those who were as unbiased as possible and would give a fair view. Perhaps Edith Sobell would be the person most likely to help. After all, it was she who had sought Hester's aid, convinced that Alexandra was innocent.

Edith proved more than willing to help, and after an enforced idleness on Sunday, for the next two days Monk pursued various friends and acquaintances who all gave much the same observations. Alexandra was a good friend, agreeable in nature but not intrusive, humorous but never vulgar. She appeared to have no vices except a slight tendency to mockery at times, a tongue a little sharp, and an interest in subjects not entirely suitable for ladies of good breeding, or indeed for women at all. She had been seen reading political periodicals, which she had very rapidly hidden when disturbed. She was impatient with those of slower wit and could be very abrupt when questions were inquisitive or she felt pressed to an opinion she preferred not to give. She was overfond of strawberries and loud band music, and she liked to walk alone—and speak to unsuitable strangers. And yes— she had on occasion been seen going into a Roman Catholic church! Most odd. Was she of that faith? Certainly not!

Was she extravagant?

Occasionally, with clothes. She loved color and form.

With anything else? Did she gamble, like new carriages, fine horses, furniture, silver, ornate jewelry?

Not that anyone had remarked. Certainly she did not gamble.

Did she flirt?

No more than anyone.

Did she owe money?

Definitely not.

Did she spend inordinate periods of time alone, or where no one knew where she was?

Yes—that was true. She liked solitude, the more especially in the last year or so.

Where did she go?

To the park.

Alone?

166

Apparently. No one had observed her with someone else.

All the answers seemed frank and without guile; the women who gave them bemused, sad, troubled—but honest. And all were unprofitable.

As he went from one smart house to another, echoes of memory drifted across his mind, like wraiths of mist, and as insubstantial. As soon as he grasped them they became nothing. Only the echo of emotion remained, fierce and painful, love, fear, terrible anxiety and a dread of failure.

Had Alexandra gone to seek counsel or comfort from a Roman Catholic priest? Possibly. But there was no point in looking for such a man; his secrets were inviolable. But it must surely have been something profound to have driven her to find a priest of a different faith, a stranger in whom to confide.

There were two other outstanding possibilities to investigate. First, that Alexandra had been jealous not of Louisa Furnival but of some other woman, and in this case justifiably so. From what he had learned of him, Monk could not see the general as an amorous adventurer, or even as a man likely to fall passionately in love to a degree where he would throw away his career and his reputation by abandoning his wife and his only son, still a child. And a mere affair was not cause for most wives to resort to murder. If Alexandra had loved her husband so possessively as to prefer him dead rather than in the arms of another woman, then she was a superb actress. She appeared intelligent and somewhat indifferent to the fact that her husband was dead. She was stunned, but not racked with grief; frightened for herself, but even more frightened for her secret being discovered. Surely a woman who had just killed a man she loved in such a fashion would show some traces of such a consuming love— and the devastation of grief.

And why hide it? Why pretend it was Louisa if it was not? It made no sense.

Nevertheless he would investigate it. Every possibility must be explored, no matter how remote, or seemingly nonsensical.

The other possibility—and it seemed more likely—was that Alexandra herself had a lover; and now that she was a widow, she intended in due course to marry whoever it was. That made far more sense. It would be understandable, in those circumstances, if she hid the facts. If Thaddeus had betrayed her with another woman, she was at least the injured party. She might have, in some wild hope, imagined society would excuse her.

But if she wished to betray him with a lover of her own, and had murdered him to free herself, no one on earth would excuse that.

In fact the more Monk thought about it, the more did it seem the only solution that fitted all they knew. It was an exceedingly ugly thought—but imperative he learn if it were the truth.

He decided to begin at Alexandra Carlyon's home, which she had shared with the general for the last ten years of his life, since his return from active service abroad. Since Monk was indirectly in Mrs. Carlyon's employ, and she had so far not been convicted of any crime, he felt certain he would find a civil, even friendly reception.

The house on Portland Place was closed and forbidding in appearance, the blinds drawn in mourning and a black wreath on the door. For the first time he could recall, he presented himself at the servants' entrance, as if he had been hawking household goods or was calling to visit some relative in service.

The back door was opened by a bootboy of perhaps twelve years, round-faced, snub-nosed and wary.

"Yes sir?" he said guardedly. Monk imagined he had probably been told by the butler to be very careful of inquisitive strangers, most especially if they might be from the newspapers. Had he been butler he would have said something of the sort.

"Wotcher want?" the boy added as Monk said nothing.

"To speak with your butler, and if he is not available, with your housekeeper," Monk replied. He hoped fervently that Alexandra had been a considerate mistress, and her staff were loyal enough to her to wish her well now and give what assistance they might to someone seeking to aid her cause, and that they would have sufficient understanding to accept that that was indeed his aim.

"Woffor?" The boy was not so easily beguiled. He looked Monk up and down, the quality of his suit, his stiff-collared white shirt and immaculate boots. " 'Oo are yer, mister?"

"William Monk, employed by Mrs. Carlyon's barrister."

The boy scowled. "Wot's a barrister?"

"Lawyer—who speaks for her in court."

"Oh—well, yer'd better come in. I'll get Mr. 'Agger." And he opened the door wider and permitted Monk into the back kitchen. He was left to stand there while the boy went for the butler, who was in charge of the house now that both master and mistress were gone, until either Mrs. Carlyon should be acquitted or the executors should dispose of the estate.

Monk stared about him. He could see through the open doorway into the laundry room, where the dolly tub was standing with its wooden dolly for moving, lifting and turning the clothes, the mangle for squeezing out the water, and the long shelf with jars of various substances for washing the different kinds of cloth: boiled bran for sponging chintz; clean horses' hoof parings for woollens; turpentine and ground sheep's trotters, or chalk, to remove oil and grease; lemon or onion juice for ink; warm cows' milk for wine or vinegar stains; stale bread for gold, silver or silken fabrics; and of course some soap.

There were also jars of bleach, a large tub of borax for heavy starching, and a board and knife for cutting up old potatoes to soak for articles to be more lightly starched.

Monk recognized them all from dim memories, habit, and recollections of more recent investigations which had taken him into kitchens and laundry rooms. This was apparently a well-run household, with all the attentions to detail one would expect from an efficient staff.

Sharply he recalled his mother with the luxury of home made soap from fat and wood ash. For the laundry, like other poorer women, she used lye, the liquid made from wood ash collected from furnaces and open fires and then mixed with water. Sometimes urine, fowl dung or bran were added to make it more effective. In 1853 the tax had been taken off soap, but that was long after he left home. She would have been overwhelmed by all this abundance.

He turned his attention to the room he was in, but had little time to see more than the racks piled with brussels sprouts, asparagus, cabbage and strings of stored onions and potatoes kept from last autumn, when the butler appeared, clad in total black and looking grim. He was a man in his middle years, short, sandy-haired, with mustache, thick side whiskers, and balding on top. His voice when he spoke was very precise.

"Yes, Mr.—er, Monk? What can we do for you? Any way in which we can help the mistress, of course we will. But you understand I shall need some proof of your identity and your purpose in coming here?" He clicked his teeth. "I don't mean to be uncivil, sir, but you must understand we have had some charlatans here, pretending to be who they were not, and out to deceive us for their own purposes."

"Of course." Monk produced his card, and a letter from Rathbone, and one from Peverell Erskine. "Very prudent of you, Mr. Hagger. You are to be commended."

Hagger closed his eyes again, but the pink in his cheeks indicated that he had heard the compliment, and appreciated it.

"Well, sir, what can we do for you?" he said after he had read the letters and handed them back. "Perhaps you would care to come into the pantry where we can be private?"

"Thank you, that would be excellent," Monk accepted, and followed him into the small room, taking the offered seat. Hagger sat opposite him and looked enquiringly.

As a matter of principle, Monk told him as little as possible. One could always add more later; one could not retract.

He must begin slowly, and hope to elicit the kind of information he wanted, disguised among more trivial details.

170

"Perhaps you would begin by telling me something of the running of the house, Mr. Hagger? How many staff have you? How long have they been here, and if you please, something of what you know of them—where they were before here, and so on."

"If you wish, sir." Hagger looked dubious. "Although I cannot see how that can possibly help."

"Nor I—yet," Monk conceded. "But it is a place to begin."

Dutifully Hagger named the staff, their positions in the household and what their references said of them. Then at Monk's prompting he began to outline a normal week's events.

Monk stopped him once or twice to ask for more detail about a dinner party, the guests, the menu, the general's attitude, how Mrs. Carlyon had behaved, and on occasions when she and the general had gone out, whom they had visited.

"Did Mr. and Mrs. Pole dine here often?" he asked as artlessly as he could.

"No sir, very seldom," Hagger replied. "Mrs. Pole only came when the general was away from home." His face clouded. "I am afraid, sir, that there was some ill feeling there, owing to an event in the past, before Miss Sabella's marriage."

"Yes, I am aware of it. Mrs. Carlyon told me." It was an extension of the truth. Alexandra had told Edith Sobell, who had told Hester, who in turn had told him. "But Mrs. Carlyon and her daughter remained close?"

"Oh yes sir." Hagger's face lightened a little. "Mrs. Carlyon was always most fond of all her children, and relations were excellent—" He broke off with a frown so slight Monk was not sure if he had imagined it.

"But . . . ." he said aloud.

Hagger shook his head. "Nothing, sir. They were always excellent."

"You were going to add something."

"Well, only that she seemed a trifle closer to her daughters, but I imagine that is natural in a woman. Master Cassian was very fond of his father, poor child. Thought the world o' the general, he did. Very natural 'e should. General took a lot o' care with 'im; spent time, which is more than many a man will with 'is son, 'specially a man as busy as the general, and as important. Admired him for that, I did.''

"A fine trait," Monk agreed. "One many a son might envy. I assume from what you say that these times did not include Mrs. Carlyon's presence?''

"No, sir, I can't recall as they ever did. I suppose they spoke of man's affairs, not suitable for ladies—the army, acts o' heroism and fighting, adventures, exploration and the like." Hagger shifted in his seat a trifle. "The boy used to come downstairs with stars in his eyes, poor child—and a smile on his lips." He shook his head. "I can't think what he must be feeling, fair stunned and lost, I shouldn't wonder.''

For the first time since seeing Alexandra Carlyon in prison Monk felt an overwhelming anger against her, crowding out pity and divorcing him utterly from the other woman who haunted the periphery of his mind, and whose innocence he had struggled so intensely to prove. She had had no child— of that he was quite certain. And younger—yes, she had been younger. He did not know why he was so sure of that, but it was a certainty inside him like the knowledge one has in dreams, without knowing where it came from.

He forced himself back to the present. Hagger was staring at him, a flicker of anxiety returning to his face.

"Where is he?" Monk asked aloud.

"With his grandparents, sir, Colonel and Mrs. Carlyon. They sent for him as soon as 'is mother was took.''

"Did you know Mrs. Furnival?''

"I have seen her, sir. She and Mr. Furnival dined here on occasion, but that's all I could say—not exactly 'know.' She didn't come 'ere very often.''

"I thought the general was a good friend of the Furnivals'?''

"Yes sir, so 'e was. But far more often 'e went there.''

"How often?"

Hagger looked harassed and tired, but there was no guilt in his expression and no evasion. "Well, as I understand it from Holmes, that's 'is valet, about once or twice a week. But if you're thinking it was anything improper, sir, all I can say is I most sincerely think as you're mistaken. The general 'ad business with Mr. Furnival, and 'e went there to 'elp the gentleman. And most obliged Mr. Furnival was too, from what I hear."

Monk asked the question he had been leading towards, the one that mattered most, and whose answer now he curiously dreaded.

"Who were Mrs. Carlyon's friends, if not Mrs. Furnival? I imagine she had friends, people she called upon and who came here, people with whom she attended parties, dances, the theater and so on?"

"Oh yes, sir, naturally."

"Who are they?"

Hagger listed a dozen or so names, most of them married couples.

"Mr. Oundel?" Monk asked. "Was there no Mrs. Oundel?" He felt surprisingly miserable as he asked it. He did not want the answer.

"No sir, she died some time ago. Very lonely, he was, poor gentleman. Used to come 'ere often."

"I see. Mrs. Carlyon was fond of him?"

"Yes sir, I think she was. Sorry for 'im, I should say. 'E used to call in the afternoons sometimes, and they'd sit in the garden and talk for ages. Went 'ome fairly lifted in spirits." He smiled as he said it, and looked at Monk with a sudden sadness in his eyes. "Very good to 'im, she was."

Monk felt a little sick.

"What is Mr. Oundel's occupation? Or is he a gentleman of leisure?"

"Bless you, sir, 'e's retired. Must be eighty if 'e's a day, poor old gentleman."

"Oh." Monk felt such an overwhelming relief it was absurd. He wanted to smile, to say something wild and happy.

Hagger would think he had taken leave of his wits—or at the very least his manners. "Yes—yes, I see. Thank you very much. You have been most helpful. Perhaps I should speak to her ladies' maid? She is still in the house?"

"Oh yes sir, we wouldn't presume to let any of the staff go until—I mean . . ." Hagger stopped awkardly.

"Of course," Monk agreed. "I understand. Let us hope it doesn't come to that." He rose to his feet.

Hagger also rose to his feet, his face tightened, and he fumbled awkwardly. "Is there any hope, sir, that . . ."

"I don't know," Monk said candidly. "What I need to know, Mr. Hagger, is what reason Mrs. Carlyon could possibly have for wishing her husband dead."

"Oh—I'm sure I can't think of any! Can't you—I mean, I wish . . ."

"No," Monk cut off hope instantly. "I am afraid she is definitely responsible; there can be no doubt."

Hagger's face fell. "I see. I had hoped—I mean . . . someone else . . . and she was protecting them."

"Is that the sort of person she was?"

"Yes sir, I believe so—a great deal of courage, stood up to anyone to protect 'er own . . ."

"Miss Sabella?"

"Yes sir—but . . ." Hagger was caught in a dilemma, his face pink, his body stiff.

"It's all right," Monk assured him. "Miss Sabella was not responsible. That is beyond question."

Hagger relaxed a little. "I don't know 'ow to 'elp," he said miserably. "There isn't any reason why a decent woman kills her husband—unless he threatened her life."

"Was the general ever violent towards her?"

Hagger looked shocked. "Oh no sir! Most certainly not."

"Would you know, if he had been?"

"I believe so, sir. But you can ask Ginny, what's Mrs. Carlyon's maid. She'd know beyond question."

"I'll do that, Mr. Hagger, if you will be so good as to allow me to go upstairs and find her?"

"I'll 'ave 'er sent for."

174

"No—I should prefer to speak to her in her normal place of work, if you please. Make her less nervous, you understand?" Actually that was not the reason. Monk wished to see Alexandra's bedroom and if possible her dressing room and something of her wardrobe. It would furnish him a better picture of the woman. All he had seen her wearing was a dark skirt and plain blouse; far from her usual dress, he imagined.

"By all means," Hagger concurred. "If you'll follow me, sir." And he led the way through a surprisingly busy kitchen, where the cook was presiding over the first preparation for a large dinner. The scullery maid had apparently already prepared the vegetables, the kitchen maid was carrying dirty pots and pans to the sink for the scullery maid to wash, and the cook herself was chopping large quantities of meat ready to put into a pie dish, lined with pastry, and the crust ready rolled to go on when she had finished.

A packet of Purcel's portable jelly mixture, newly available since the Great Exhibition of 1851, was lying ready to make for a later course, along with cold apple pie, cream and fresh cheese. It looked as if the meal would feed a dozen.

Then of course Monk remembered that even when all the family were at home, they only added three more to the household, which was predominantly staff, and with upstairs and downstairs, indoor and outdoor, must have numbered at least twelve, and they continued regardless of the death of the general or the imprisonment of Mrs. Carlyon, at least for the moment.

Along the corridor they passed the pantry, where a footman was cleaning the knives with India rubber, a buff leather knife board and a green-and-red tin of Wellington knife polish. Then past the housekeeper's sitting room with door closed, the butler's sitting room similarly, and through the green baize door to the main house. Of course most of the cleaning work would normally be done before the family rose for breakfast, but at present there was hardly any need, so the maids had an extra hour in bed, and were now occupied in sweeping, beating carpets, polishing floors with melted candle ends and turpentine, cleaning brass with boiling vinegar.

Up the stairs and along the landing Monk followed Hagger until they came to the master bedroom, apparently the general's, past his dressing room next door, and on to a very fine sunny and spacious room which he announced as being Mrs. Carlyon's. Opening off it to the left was a dressing room where cupboard doors stood open and a ladies' maid was busy brushing down a blue-gray outdoor cape which must have suited Alexandra's fair coloring excellently.

The girl looked up in surprise as she saw Hagger, and Monk behind him. Monk judged her to be in her mid-twenties, thin and dark, but with a remarkably pleasant countenance.

Hagger wasted no time. "Ginny, this is Mr. Monk. He is working for the mistress's lawyers, trying to find out something that will help her. He wants to ask you some questions, and you will answer him as much as you can—anything 'e wants to know. Understand?"

"Yes, Mr. Hagger." She looked very puzzled, but not unwilling.

"Right." Hagger turned to Monk. "You come down when you're ready, an' if there's ought else as can 'elp, let me know."

"I will, thank you, Mr. Hagger. You have been most obliging," Monk accepted. Then as soon as Hagger had departed and closed the door, he turned to the maid.

"Go on with what you are doing," he requested. "I shall be some time."

"I'm sure I don't know what I can tell you," Ginny said, obediently continuing to brush the cape. "She was always a very good mistress to me."

"In what way good?"

She looked surprised. "Well . . . considerate, like. She apologized if she got anything extra dirty, or if she kept me up extra late. She gave me things as she didn't want no more, and always asked after me family, and the like."

"You were fond of her?"

"Very fond of 'er, Mr.—"

"Monk."

"Mr. Monk, can you 'elp 'er now? I mean, after she said as she done it?" Her face was puckered with anxiety.

"I don't know," Monk admitted. "If there were some reason why, that people could understand, it might help."

"What would anybody understand, as why a lady should kill 'er 'usband?" Ginny put away the cape and brought out a gown of a most unusual deep mulberry shade. She shook it and a perfume came from its folds that caught Monk with a jolt of memory so violent he saw a whole scene of a woman in pink, standing with her back to him, weeping softly. He had no idea what her face was like, except he found it beautiful, and he recalled none of her words. But the feeling was intense, an emotion that shook him and filled his being, an urgency amounting to passion that he must find the truth, and free her from a terrible danger, one that would destroy her life and her reputation.

But who was she? Surely she had nothing to do with Walbrook? No—one thing seemed to resolve in his mind. When Walbrook was ruined, and Monk's own career in commerce came to an end, he had not at that point even thought of becoming a policeman. That was what had decided him— his total inability to either help Walbrook and his wife, or even to avenge them and put his enemy out of business.

The woman in pink had turned to him because he was a policeman. It was his job to find the truth.

But he could not bring her face to mind, nor anything to do with the case, except that she was suspected of murder— murdering her husband—like Alexandra Carlyon.

Had he succeeded? He did not even know that. Or for that matter, if she was innocent or guilty. And why had he cared with such personal anguish? What had been their relationship? Had she cared for him as deeply, or was she simply turning to him because she was desperate and terrified?

"Sir?" Ginny was staring at him. "Are you all right, sir?"

"Oh—oh yes, thank you. What did you say?"

"What would folks reckon was a reason why it might be all right for a lady to kill 'er 'usband? I don't know of none."

"Why do you think she did it?" Monk asked baldly, his wits still too scattered to be subtle. "Was she jealous of Mrs. Furnival?"

"Oh no sir." Ginny dismissed it out of hand. "I don't like to speak ill of me betters, but Mrs. Furnival weren't the kind o' person to—well, sir, I don't rightly know 'ow to put it—"

"Simply." Monk's attention was entirely on her now, the memory dismissed for the time being. "Just in your own words. Don't worry if it sounds ill—you can always take it back, if you want."

"Thank you, sir, I'm sure."

"Mrs. Furnival."

"Well, sir, she's what my granny used to call a flighty piece, sir, beggin' yer pardon, all smiles and nods and eyes all over the place. Likes the taste o' power, but not one to fall what you'd call in love, not to care for anyone."

"But the general might have cared for her? Was he a good judge of women?"

"Lord, sir, he didn't hardly know one kind o' woman from another, if you take my meaning. He wasn't no ladies' man."

"Isn't that just the sort that gets taken in by the likes of anyone such as Mrs. Furnival?"

"No sir, because 'e weren't susceptible like. I seen 'er when she was 'ere to dinner, and he weren't interested 'ceptin' business and casual talking like to a friend. And Mrs. Carlyon, she knew that, sir. There weren't no cause for 'er to be jealous, and she never imagined there were. Besides . . ." She stopped, the pink color up her cheeks.

"Besides what, Ginny?"

Still she hesitated.

"Ginny, Mrs. Carlyon's life is at stake. As it is, if we don't find some good reason, she'll hang! Surely you don't think she did it without a good reason, do you?"

"Oh no sir! Never!"

"Well then . . ."

"Well, sir, Mrs. Carlyon weren't that fond o' the general anyway, as to mind all that terrible if occasionally 'e took 'is pleasures elsewhere, if you know what I mean?"

"Yes, I know what you mean. Quite a common enough arrangement, when a couple have been married a long time, no doubt. And did Mrs. Carlyon—have other interests?"

She colored very faintly, but did not evade the subject.

"Some time ago, sir, I did rather think as she favored a Mr. Ives, but it was only a little flattery, and enjoying his company, like. And there was Mr. McLaren, who was obviously very taken with 'er, but I don't think she more than passing liked him. And of course she was always fond of Mr. Furnival, and at one time . . ." She lowered her eyes. "But that was four years ago now. And if you ask if she ever did anything improper, I can tell you as she didn't. And bein' 'er maid, like, an' seein' all 'er most private things, I would know, I'll be bound."

"Yes, I imagine you would," Monk said. He was inclined to believe her, in spite of the fact that she could only be biased. "Well, if the general was not overly fond of Mrs. Furnival, is it possible he was fond of someone else, another lady, perhaps?"

"Well, if he was, sir, 'e hid it powerful well," she said vehemently. "Holmes, that's his valet, didn't know about it—an' I reckon he'd have at least an idea. No sir, I'm sorry, I can't 'elp you at all. I truly believe as the general was an exemplary man in that respect. Everything in loyalty an' honor a woman would want."

"And in other respects?" Monk persisted. He glanced along the row of cupboards. "It doesn't look as if he kept her short of money?"

"Oh no, sir. I don't think 'e was very interested in what the mistress wore, but 'e weren't never mean about it one bit. Always 'ad all she wanted, an' more."

"Sounds like a model husband," Monk said dispiritedly.

"Well, yes, I suppose so—for a lady, that is," she conceded, watching his face.

"But not what you would like?" he asked.

"Me? Well—well sir, I think as I'd want someone who—maybe this sounds silly, you bein' a gentleman an' all—but I'd want someone as I could 'ave fun with—talk to, like. A man who'd . . ." She colored fiercely now. "Who'd give me a bit of affection—if you see what I mean, sir."

"Yes, I see what you mean." Monk smiled at her without knowing quite why. Some old memory of warmth came back to him, the kitchen in his mother's house in Northumberland, her standing there at the table with her sleeves rolled up, and cuffing him gently around the ear for being cheeky, but it was more a caress than a discipline. She had been proud of him. He knew that beyond doubt in that moment. He had written regularly from London, letting her know how he was doing, of his career and what he hoped to achieve. And she had written back, short, oddly spelled letters in a round hand, but full of pride. He had sent money when he could, which was quite often. It pleased him to help her, after all the lean, sacrificing years, and it was a mark of his success.

Then after Walbrook's ruin, there had been no more money. And in embarrassment he had ceased to write. What utter stupidity! As if that would have mattered to her. What a pride he had. What an ugly, selfish pride.

"Of course I know what you mean," he said again to the maid. "Perhaps Mrs. Carlyon felt the same way, do you suppose?"

"Oh I wouldn't know, sir. Ladies is different. They don't—well . . ."

"They didn't share a room?"

"Oh no, sir—not since I been here. And I 'eard from Lucy, as I took over from, not before that neither. But then gentry don't, do they? They got bigger 'ouses than the likes of my ma and pa."

"Or mine," Monk agreed. "Was she happy?"

Ginny frowned, looking at him guardedly. "No sir, I don't think as she were."

"Did she change lately in any way?"

"She's been awful worried over something lately. An' she

and the general 'ad a terrible row six months ago—but there's no use askin' me what about, because I don't know. She shut the doors and sent me away. I just know because o' the way she was all white-faced and spoke to no one, and the way she looked like she seen death face-to-face. But that was six months ago, an' I thought it was all settled again.''

"Did he ever hurt her physically, Ginny?"

"Great 'eaven's, no!'' She shook her head, looking at him with deep distress. "I can't 'elp you, sir, nor 'er. I really don't know of anything at all as why she should 'ave killed 'im. He were cold, and terrible tedious, but 'e were generous with 'is money, faithful to 'er, well-spoken, didn't drink too much nor gamble nor keep fast company. And although 'e were terrible 'ard to Miss Sabella over that going into a nunnery business, he were the best father to young master Cassian as a boy could ask. And terrible fond of 'im Master Cassian were, poor little thing. If it weren't that I know as she wasn't a wicked woman, I'd think—well, I'd think as she were.''

"Yes,'' Monk said miserably. "Yes—I am afraid I would too. Thank you for your time, Ginny. I'll take myself downstairs.''

It was not until Monk had fruitlessly interviewed the rest of the staff, who bore out what Hagger and Ginny had said, partaken of luncheon in the servants' hall, and was outside in the street that he realized just how much of his own life had come back to him unbidden: his training in commerce, his letters home, Walbrook's ruin and his own consequent change of fortune—but not the face of the woman who so haunted him, who she was, or why he cared so intensely . . . or what had happened to her.

6

With Major Tiplady's enthusiastic permission, Hester accepted an invitation to dine with Oliver Rathbone in the very proper circumstances of taking a hansom to the home in Primrose Hill of Rathbone's father, who proved to be an elderly gentleman of charm and distinction.

Hester, determined not to be late, actually arrived before Rathbone himself, who had been held up by a jury taking far longer to return than foreseen. She alighted at the address given her, and when she was admitted by the manservant, found herself in a small sitting room. It opened onto a garden in which late daffodils were blowing in the shade under the trees and a massive honeysuckle vine all but drowned the gate in the wall leading into a very small, overgrown orchard whose apples, in full blossom, she could just see over the top.

The room itself was crowded with books of various shapes and sizes, obviously positioned according to subject matter and not to please the eye. On the walls were several paintings in watercolors, one which she noticed immediately because it held a place of honor above the mantel. It was of a youth in costume of leather doublet and apron, sitting on the base of a pillar. The whole work was in soft earth colors, ochers and sepia, except for the dark red of his cap, and it was unfinished; the lower half of his body, and a small dog he reached out to stroke, were still in sketch form.

"You like it?" Henry Rathbone asked her. He was taller than his son, and very lean, shoulders stooped as from many years of intensive study. His face was aquiline, all nose and jaw, and yet there was a serenity in it, a mildness that set her at ease the moment she saw him. His gray hair was very sparse, and he looked at her with shortsighted blue eyes.

"Yes I do, very much," she answered honestly. "The more I look at it, the more it pleases me."

"It is my favorite," he agreed. "Perhaps because it is unfinished. Completed it might have been harder, more final. This leaves room for the imagination, almost a sense of collaboration with the artist."

She knew precisely what he meant, and found herself smiling at him.

They moved on to discuss other things, and she questioned him shamelessly because she was so interested, and because she was so comfortable with him. He had traveled in many foreign places, and indeed spoke the German language fluently. He seemed not to have been enraptured with scenery, totally unlike herself, but he had met and fallen into conversations with all manner of unlikely people in little old shops which he loved rummaging through. No one was too outwardly ordinary to excite his interest, or for him to have discovered some aspect of their lives which was unique.

She barely noticed that Rathbone was an hour late, and when he came in in a flurry of apologies, she was amused to see the consternation in his face that no one had missed him, except the cook, whose preparations were discommoded.

"Never mind," Henry Rathbone said easily, rising to his feet. "It is not worth being upset about. It cannot be helped. Miss Latterly, please come into the dining room; we shall do the best we can with what there is."

"You should have started without me," Oliver said with a flash of irritation across his face. "Then you would have had it at its best."

"There is no need to feel guilty," his father replied. He

indicated where Hester was to sit, and the manservant held her chair for her. "We know you were detained unavoidably. And I believe we were enjoying ourselves."

"Indeed I was," Hester said sincerely, and took her place.

The meal was served. The soup was excellent, and Rathbone made no comment; to do so now would be so obviously ungracious. When the fish was brought, a little dry from having had to wait, he bit into it and met Hester's eye, but refrained from comment.

"I spoke with Monk yesterday," he said at length. "I am afraid we have made almost no progress."

Hester was disappointed, yet the mere fact that he had kept from mentioning the subject for so long had forewarned her that the news would be poor.

"That only means that we have not yet discovered the reason," she said doggedly. "We shall have to look harder."

"Or persuade her to tell us," Oliver added, placing his knife and fork together and indicating to the manservant that he might remove the plates.

The vegetables were a trifle overdone by any standard, but the cold saddle of mutton was perfect, and the array of pickles and chutneys with it rich and full of variety and interest.

"Are you acquainted with the case, Mr. Rathbone?" Hester turned to Henry enquiringly, not wishing him to be excluded from the conversation.

"Oliver has mentioned it," he replied, helping himself liberally to a dark chutney. "What is it you hope to find?"

"The true reason why she killed him. Unfortunately it is beyond question that she did."

"What reason has she given you?"

"Jealousy of her hostess of that evening, but we know that is not true. She said she believed her husband was having an affair with this woman, Louisa Furnival, but we know that he was not, and that she knew that."

"But she will not tell you the truth?"

"No."

He frowned, cutting off a piece of meat and spreading it liberally with the chutney and mashed potato.

"Let us be logical about it," he said thoughtfully. "Did she plan this murder before she committed it?"

"We don't know. There is nothing to indicate whether she did or not."

"So it might have been a spur-of-the-moment act—lacking forethought, and possibly not considering the consequences either."

"But she is not a foolish woman," Hester protested. "She cannot have failed to know she would be hanged."

"If she was caught!" he argued. "It is possible an overwhelming fury possessed her and she acted unreasonably."

Hester frowned.

"My dear, it is a mistake to imagine we are all reasonable all of the time," he said gently. "People act from all sorts of impulses, sometimes quite contrary to their own interests, had they stopped to think. But so often we don't, we do what our emotions drive us to. If we are frightened we either run or freeze motionless, or we lash out, according to our nature and past experience."

He ignored his food, looking at her with concentration. "I think most tragedies happen when people have had too little time to think or weigh one course against another, or perhaps even to assess the real situation. They leap in before they have seen or understood. And then it is too late." Absentmindedly he pushed the pickle toward Oliver. "We are full of preconceptions; we judge from our own viewpoint. We believe what we have to, to keep the whole edifice of our views of things to be as they are. A new idea is still the most dangerous thing in the world. A new idea about something close to ourselves, coming quite suddenly and without warning, can make us so disconcerted, so frightened at the idea of all our beliefs about ourselves and those around us crumbling about our ears that we reach to strike at the one who has introduced this explosion into our lives—to deny it, violently if need be."

"Perhaps we don't know nearly enough about Alexandra Carlyon," she said thoughtfully, staring at her plate.

"We know a great deal more now than we did a week

ago," Oliver said quietly. "Monk has been to her house and spoken with her servants, but the picture that emerges of both her and the general does nothing to set her in a better light, or explain why she should kill him. He was chilly, and possibly a bore, but he was faithful to her, generous with his money, had an excellent reputation, indeed almost perfect— and he was a devoted father to his son, and not unreasonable to his daughters."

"He refused to allow Sabella to devote herself to the Church," Hester said hotly. "And forced her to marry Fenton Pole."

Oliver smiled. "Not unreasonable, really. I think most fathers might well do the same. And Pole seems a decent enough man."

"He still ordered her against her will," she protested.

"That is a father's prerogative, especially where daughters are concerned."

She drew in her breath sharply, longing to remonstrate, even to accuse him of injustice, but she did not want to appear abrasive and ungracious to Henry Rathbone. It was an inappropriate time to pursue her own causes, however justifiable. She liked him more than she had expected, and his ill opinion of her would hurt. He was utterly unlike her own father, who had been very conventional, not greatly given to discussion; and yet in his company she was reminded, with comfort and a stab of pain, of all the wealth of belonging, the ease of family. Her own loneliness was sharpened by the sudden awareness. She had forgotten, perhaps deliberately, how good it had been when her parents were alive, in spite of the restrictions, the discipline and the staid and old-fashioned views. She had chosen to forget, to accommodate her grief.

Now, unaccountably, with Henry Rathbone the best of it returned.

Henry interrupted her thoughts, jerking her back to the present and the Carlyon case. "But that all happened some time ago. The daughter is married already, from what you say?"

186

"Yes. They have a child," she said hastily.

"So this may rankle still, but it will not be the motive for murder so long after?"

"No."

"Let us suggest a hypothesis," Henry said thoughtfully, his meal almost forgotten. "The crime seems to have been committed on the spur of the moment. Alexandra saw the opportunity and took it—rather clumsily, as it turns out. Which means, if we are correct, either that she learned something that evening which so distressed her that she lost all sense of reason or self-preservation, or that she already wished to kill him but had not previously found an opportunity to do it." He looked at Hester. "Miss Latterly, in your judgment, what might shake a woman so? In other words, what would a woman hold so dear that she would kill to protect it?"

Oliver stopped eating, his fork in the air.

"We haven't looked at it that way," he said, turning to her. "Hester?"

She thought, wishing to give the most careful and intelligent answer she could.

"Well, I suppose the thing that would make me most likely to act without thinking, even of the risk to myself, would be some threat to the people I loved most—which in Alexandra's case would surely be her children." She allowed herself a half smile. "Regrettably it was obviously not her husband. To me it would have been my parents and brothers, but all of them except Charles are dead anyway." She said it because it was high in her mind, not to seek sympathy, then immediately wished she had not. She went on before they could offer any. "But let us say family—and in the case where there are children, I imagine one's home as well. There are some homes that go back for generations, even centuries. I would imagine one might care about them so extremely as to kill to preserve them, or to keep them from falling into the possession of others. But that does not apply here."

"Not according to Monk," Oliver agreed, watching with

187

dark, intent eyes. "And anyway, the house is his, not hers—and not an ancestral home in any way. What else?"

Hester smiled wryly, very aware of him. "Well, if I were beautiful, I suppose my looks would also be precious to me. Is Alexandra beautiful?"

He thought for a moment, his face reflecting a curious mixture of humor and pain. "Not beautiful, strictly speaking. But she is most memorable, and perhaps that is better. She has a face of distinct character."

"So far you have only mentioned one thing which she might care about sufficiently," Henry Rathbone pointed out. "What about her reputation?"

"Oh yes," Hester agreed quickly. "If one's honor is sufficiently threatened, if one were to be accused of something wrongfully, that could make one lose one's temper and control and every bit of good sense. It is one of the things I hate above all else. That is a distinct possibility. Or the honor of someone I loved—that would cut equally deeply."

"Who threatened her honor?" Oliver asked with a frown. "We have heard nothing at all to suggest anyone did. And if it were so, why should she not tell us? Or could it have been someone else's honor? Who? Not his, surely?"

"Blackmail," Hester said immediately. "A person blackmailed would naturally not tell—or it would reveal the very subject she had killed to hide."

"By her husband?" Oliver said skeptically. "That would be robbing one pocket to pay the other."

"Not for money," she said quickly, leaning forward over the table. "Of course that would make no sense. For something else—perhaps simply power over her."

"But who would he tell, my dear Hester? Any scandal about her would reflect just as badly upon him. Usually if a woman has disgraced herself, it is the husband whom the blackmailer would tell."

"Oh." She saw the point of what he was saying and it made excellent sense. "Yes." She looked at his eyes, expecting criticism, and saw a gentleness and a humor that for an instant robbed her of her concentration. She was far too comfortable here with the two of them she liked so much. It would be so easy to wish to stay, to wish to belong. She recalled herself rapidly to the subject.

"It doesn't make sense as it is," she said quietly, lowering her eyes and looking away from him. "You said he was an excellent father, with the exception a couple of years ago of forcing Sabella to marry instead of taking the veil."

"Then if it doesn't make sense as it is," Henry said thoughtfully, "it means that either there is some element which you have not thought of, or else you are seeing something wrongly."

Hester looked at his mild, ascetic face and realized what intelligence there was in his eyes. It was the cleverest face she had seen that held absolutely nothing spiteful or ungenerous whatever. She found herself smiling, without any specific reason.

"Then we had better go back and look at it again," she resolved aloud. "I think perhaps it is the second of those two cases, and we are seeing something wrongly."

"Are you sure it is worth it?" Henry asked her gently. "Even if you do discover why she killed him, will it alter anything? Oliver?"

"I don't know. Quite possibly not," Oliver confessed. "But I cannot go into court with no more than I know now."

"That is your pride," Henry said frankly. "What about her interests? Surely if she wished you to defend her with the truth, she would have told it you?"

"I suppose so," he conceded. "But I should be the judge of what is her best defense in law, not she."

"I think you simply don't wish to be beaten," his father said, returning to his plate. "But I fear you may find the victory very small, even if you can obtain it. Who will it serve? It may merely demonstrate that Oliver Rathbone can discover the truth and lay it bare for all to see, even if the wretched accused would rather be hanged than reveal it herself."

"I shan't reveal it if she does not give me permission," Oliver said quickly, his face pink, his dark eyes wide. "For heaven's sake, what do you take me for?"

"Occasionally hotheaded, my dear boy," Henry replied. "And possessed of an intellectual arrogance and curiosity, which I fear you have inherited from me."

They continued the evening very pleasantly speaking of any number of things other than the Carlyon case. They discussed music, of which all were fond. Henry Rathbone was quite knowledgeable, having a great love of Beethoven's late quartets, composed when Beethoven himself was already severely deaf. They had a darkness and a complexity he found endlessly satisfying, and a beauty wrought out of pain which excited his pity but also reached a deeper level of his nature and fed a hunger there.

They also spoke of political events, the news from India and the growing unrest there. They touched only once on the Crimean War, but Henry Rathbone was so infuriated by the incompetence and the unnecessary deaths that after a quick glance at each other, Hester and Oliver changed the subject and did not hark back to it again.

Before leaving Hester and Oliver took a slow stroll around the garden and down to the honeysuckle hedge at the border of the orchard. The smell of the first flowers was close and sweet in the hazy darkness and she could see only the outline of the longest upflung branches against the starlit sky. For once they did not talk of the case.

"The news from India is very dark," she said, staring across at the pale blur of the apple blossoms. "It is so peaceful here it seems doubly painful to think of mutiny and battle. I feel guilty to have such beauty . . ."

He was standing very close to her and she was aware of the warmth of him. It was an acutely pleasant feeling.

"There is no need for guilt," he replied. She knew he was smiling although she had her back to him, and could scarcely have seen him in the dark anyway. "You could not help them," he went on, "by not appreciating what you have. That would merely be ungrateful."

"Of course you are right," she agreed. "It is self-indulgent for the sake of conscience, but actually achieves nothing at all, except ingratitude, as you say. I used to walk near the battlefields sometimes, in the Crimea, and knew what had happened so close by, and yet I needed the silence and the flowers, or I could not have gone on. If you don't keep your strength, both physical and spiritual, you are of no help to those who need you. All my intelligence knows that.''

He took her elbow gently and they walked towards the herbaceous border, lupin spears just visible against the pale stones of the wall and the dusky outline of a climbing rose.

''Do you find hard cases affect you like that?'' she asked presently. ''Or are you more practical? I don't know—do you often lose?''

''Certainly not.'' There was laughter in his voice.

''You must lose sometimes!''

The laughter vanished. ''Yes, of course I do. And yes—I find myself lying awake imagining how the prisoner must feel, tormenting myself in case I did not do everything I could have, and I was lying in my warm bed, and will do the next night, and the next . . . and that poor devil who depended on me will soon lie in the cold earth of an unhallowed grave.''

''Oliver!'' She swung around and stared at him, without thinking, reaching for both his hands.

He clasped her gently, fingers closing over hers.

''Don't your patients die sometimes, my dear?''

''Yes, of course.''

''And don't you wonder if you were to blame? Even if you could not have saved them, could not have eased their pain, their fear?''

''Yes. But you have to let it go, or you would cripple yourself, and then be of no more use to the next patient.''

''Of course.'' He raised her hands and touched his lips to them, first the left, and then the right. ''And we shall both continue to do so, all we can. And we shall both also look at the moonlight on the apple trees, and be glad of it without guilt that no one else can see it precisely as we do. Promise me?''

"I promise," she said softly. "And the stars and the honeysuckle as well."

"Oh, don't worry about the stars," he said with laughter back in his voice. "They are universal. But the honeysuckle on the orchard fence and the lupins against the wall belong peculiarly to an English garden. This is ours."

Together they walked back to where Henry was standing by the French doors of the sitting room just as the clear song of a nightingale trilled through the night once and vanished.

Half an hour later Hester left. It was remarkably late, and she had enjoyed the evening more than any other she could recall for a very long time indeed.

It was now May 28, and more than a month since the murder of Thaddeus Carlyon and since Edith had come to Hester asking her assistance in finding some occupation that would use her talents and fill her time more rewardingly than the endless round of domestic pleasantries which now occupied her. And so far Hester had achieved nothing in that direction.

And quite apart from Edith Sobell, Major Tiplady was progressing extremely well and in a very short time would have no need of her services, and she would have to look for another position herself. And while for Edith it was a matter of finding something to use her time to more purpose, for Hester it was necessary to earn her living.

"You are looking much concerned, Miss Latterly," Major Tiplady said anxiously. "Is something wrong?"

"No—oh no. Not at all," she said quickly. "Your leg is healing beautifully. There is no infection now, and in a week or two at the outside, I think you may begin putting your weight on it again."

"And when is the unfortunate Carlyon woman coming to trial?"

"I'm not sure, precisely. Some time in the middle of June."

"Then I doubt I shall be able to dispense with you in two

weeks." There was a faint flush in his cheeks as he said it, but his china-blue eyes did not waver.

She smiled at him. "I would be less than honest if I remained here once you are perfectly well. Then how could you recommend me, should anyone ask?"

"I shall give you the very highest recommendation," he promised. "When the time comes—but it is not yet. And what about your friend who wishes for a position? What have you found for her?"

"Nothing so far. That is why I was looking concerned just now." It was at least partially true, if not the whole truth.

"Well, you had better look a little harder," he said seriously. "What manner of person is she?"

"A soldier's widow, well-bred, intelligent." She looked at his innocent face. "And I should think most unlikely to take kindly to being given orders."

"Awkward," he agreed with a tiny smile. "You will not find it an easy task."

"I am sure there must be something." She busied herself tidying away three books he had been reading, without asking him if he were finished or not.

"And you haven't done very well with Mrs. Carlyon either, have you," he went on.

"No—not at all. We must have missed something." She had related much of her discussions to him to while away the long evenings, and to help put it all in order in her own mind.

"Then you had better go back and see the people again," he advised her solemnly, looking very pink and white in his dressing robe with his face scrubbed clean and his hair a trifle on end. "I can spare you in the afternoons. You have left it all to the men. Surely you have some observations to offer? Take a look at the Furnival woman. She sounds appalling!"

He was getting very brave in offering his opinions, and she knew that if Monk and Rathbone were right, Louisa Furnival was the sort of woman who would terrify Major Tiplady into a paralyzed silence. Still, he was quite correct.

She had left it very much to other people's judgment. She could at least have seen Louisa Furnival herself.

"That is an excellent idea, Major," she concluded. "But what excuse can I give for calling upon a woman I have never met? She will show me the door instantly—and quite understandably."

He thought very gravely for several minutes, and she disappeared to consult the cook about dinner. In fact the subject was not raised again until she was preparing to leave him for the night.

"She is wealthy?" the major said suddenly as she was assisting him into bed.

"I beg your pardon?" She had no idea what he was talking about.

"Mrs. Furnival," he said impatiently. "She is wealthy?"

"I believe so—yes. Apparently her husband does very well out of military contracts. Why?"

"Well go and ask her for some money," he said reasonably, sitting rigidly and refusing to be assisted under the blankets. "For crippled soldiers from the Crimea, or for a military hospital or something. And if by any chance she gives you anything, you can pass it on to an appropriate organization. But I doubt she will. Or ask her to give her time and be a patron of such a place."

"Oh no," Hester said instinctively, still half pushing at him. "She would throw me out as a medicant."

He resisted her stubbornly. "Does it matter? She will speak to you first. Go in Miss Nightingale's name. No self-respecting person would insult her—she is revered next to the Queen. You do want to see her, don't you, this Furnival woman?"

"Yes," Hester agreed cautiously. "But . . ."

"Where's your courage, woman? You saw the charge of the Light Brigade." He faced her defiantly. "You've told me about it! You survived the siege of Sebastopol. Are you afraid of one miserable woman who flirts?"

"Like many a good soldier before me." Hester grinned. "Aren't you?"

He winced. "That's a foul blow."

"But it hit the mark," she said triumphantly. "Get into bed."

"Irrelevant! I cannot go—so you must!" He still sat perched on the edge. "You must fight whatever the battle is. This time the enemy has picked the ground, so you must gird yourself, choose your weapons well, and attack when he least expects it." Finally he swung his feet up and she pulled the blankets over him. He finished with fervor. "Courage."

She grimaced at him, but he gave no quarter. He lay back in the bed while she tucked the sheets around him, and smiled at her seraphically.

"Tomorrow late afternoon, when her husband may be home also," he said relentlessly. "You should see him too."

She glared at him. "Good night."

However the following afternoon at a little before five, dressed in a blue-gray gown of great sobriety, no pagoda sleeves, no white broderie, and looking as if she had indeed just come off duty in Miss Nightingale's presence, Hester swallowed her pride and her nerves, telling herself it was a good cause, and knocked on Louisa Furnival's front door. She hoped profoundly the maid would tell her Mrs. Furnival was out.

However she was not so fortunate. She was conducted into the hall after only the briefest of pauses while the maid announced her name and business. She barely had time to register the doors in the hallway and the handsome banister sweeping across the balcony at the far end and down the stairs. The suit of armor had been replaced; however, without the halberd. Alexandra must have stood with the general at the top on the landing, perhaps silently, perhaps in the last, bitter quarrel, and then she had lunged forward and he had gone over. He must have landed with an almighty crash. However had they not heard him?

The floor was carpeted, a pale Chinese rug with heavy pile. That would have softened the noise to some extent. Even so . . .

She got no further. The maid returned to say that Mrs.

Furnival would be pleased to receive her, and led her through the long corridor to the back of the house and the withdrawing room opening onto the garden.

She did not even bother to look at the sunlight on the grass, or the mass of flowering bushes. All her attention was on the woman who awaited her with unconcealed curiosity. She assumed in that instant that she had gained admittance so easily because Louisa was bored.

"Good afternoon, Miss Latterly. The Florence Nightingale Hospital? How interesting. In what way can I possibly be of help to you?"

Hester regarded her with equal curiosity. She might have only a few moments in which to form an opinion before she was asked to leave. The woman in front of her standing by the mantel wore a full crinoline skirt, emphasizing the extreme femininity of her form. It was up to the minute in fashion: pointed waist, pleated bodice, floral trimmings. She looked both voluptuous and fragile, with her tawny skin and mass of fine dark hair, dressed immaculately but far fuller than the fashion dictated. She was one of those few women who can defy the current mode and make her own style seem the right one, and all others ordinary and unimaginative. Self-confidence surrounded her, making Hester already feel dowdy, unfeminine, and remarkably foolish. She knew immediately why Alexandra Carlyon had expected people to believe in a passionate jealousy. It must have happened dozens of times, whatever the reality of any relationship.

She changed her mind as to what she had been going to say. She was horrified as she heard her own voice. It was bravado, and it was totally untrue. Something in Louisa Furnival's insolence provoked her.

"We learned a great deal in the Crimea about just how much good nursing can save the lives of soldiers," she said briskly. "Of course you are probably aware of this already." She widened her eyes innocently. "But perhaps you have not had occasion to think on the details of the matter. Miss Nightingale herself, as you well know, is a woman of excellent family, her father is well known and respected, and Miss Nightingale is

196

highly educated. She chose nursing as a way of dedicating her life and her talents to the service of others—''

"We all agree that she is a most excellent woman, Miss Latterly," Louisa interrupted impatiently. Praise of other women did not appeal to her. "What has this to do with you, or me?"

"I will come immediately to the point." Hester looked at Louisa's long, slanting eyes, saw the fire of intelligence in them. To take her for a fool because she was a flirt would be a profound mistake. "If nursing is to become the force for saving life that it could be, we must attract into its service more well-bred and well-educated young women."

Louisa laughed, a rippling, self-conscious sound, made from amusement but tailored over years to have exactly the right effect. Had any man been listening he might well have found her wild, exotic, fascinating, elusive—all the things Hester was not. With a flash of doubt she wondered what Oliver Rathbone would have made of her.

"Really, Miss Latterly. You surely cannot imagine I would be interested in taking up a career in nursing?" Louisa said with something close to laughter. "That is ridiculous. I am a married woman!"

Hester bit back her temper with considerable difficulty. She could very easily dislike this woman.

"Of course I did not imagine you would be." She wished she could add her opinion of the likelihood of Louisa's having the courage, the skill, the unselfishness or the stamina to do anything of the sort. But this was not the time. It would defeat her own ends. "But you are the sort of woman that other women wish to model themselves upon." She squirmed inwardly as she said it. It was blatant flattery, and yet Louisa did not seem to find it excessive.

"How kind of you," she said with a smile, but her eyes did not leave Hester's.

"Such a woman, who is both well known and widely . . ." She hesitated. "And widely envied, would find that her words were listened to with more attention, and given more weight, than most other people's." She did not flinch from Louisa's brown-hazel eyes. She was speaking the truth now, and would dare anyone with it. "If you were to let it be known that you thought nursing a fine career for a young woman, not unfeminine or in any way degraded, then I believe more young women, hesitating about choosing it, might make their decisions in favor. It is only a matter of words, Mrs. Furnival, but they might make a great deal of difference."

"You are very persuasive, Miss Latterly." Louisa moved gracefully and arrogantly to the window, swinging her skirts as if she were walking outside along an open path. She might play at the coquette, but Hester judged there was nothing yielding or submissive in her. If she ever pretended it, it would be short-lived and to serve some purpose of her own.

Hester watched her, and remained seated where she was, silently.

Louisa was looking out of the window at the sun on the grass. The light on her face betrayed no age lines yet, but there was a hardness to the expression she could not have noticed, or she would not have stood so. And there was a meanness in her thin upper lip.

"You wish me to allow it to be known in those social circles I frequent that I admire nursing as an occupation for a woman, and might have followed it myself, were I not married?" she asked. The humor of it still appealed to her, the amusement was there in her face.

"Indeed," Hester agreed. "Since quite obviously you could not do it now, no one can expect you to prove what you say by offering your services, only your support."

Laughter flickered over Louisa's mouth. "And you think they would believe me, Miss Latterly? It seems to me you imagine them a little gullible."

"Do you often find yourself disbelieved, Mrs. Furnival?" Hester asked as politely as she could, given such a choice of words.

Louisa's smile hardened.

"No—no, I cannot say I can recall ever having done so. But I have never claimed to admire nursing before."

Hester raised her eyebrows. "Nor anything else that was an . . . an extending—of the truth?"

Louisa turned to face her.

"Don't be mealymouthed, Miss Latterly. I have lied outright, and been utterly believed. But the circumstances were different."

"I am sure."

"However, if you wish, I shall do as you suggest," Louisa cut her off. "It would be quite entertaining—and certainly different. Yes, the more I think of it, the more it appeals to me." She swung around from the window and walked back across towards the mantel. "I shall begin a quiet crusade to have young women of breeding and intelligence join the nurses. I can imagine how my acquaintances will view my new cause." She turned swiftly and came back over to Hester, standing in front of her and staring down. "And now, if I am to speak so well of this wonderful career, you had better tell me something about it. I don't wish to appear ignorant. Would you care for some refreshment while we talk?"

"Indeed, that would be most agreeable," Hester accepted.

"By the way, who else are you approaching?"

"You are the only one, so far," Hester said with absolute veracity. "I haven't spoken to anyone else as yet. I don't wish to be blatant."

"Yes—I think this could be most entertaining." Louisa reached for the bell and rang it vigorously.

Hester was still busy recounting everything she could to make nursing seem dramatic and glamorous when Maxim Furnival came home. He was a tall, slender man with a dark face, emotional, and made in lines that could as easily sulk or be dazzlingly bright. He smiled at Hester and enquired after her health in the normal manner of politeness, and when Louisa explained who Hester was, and her purpose in coming, he seemed genuinely interested.

They made polite conversation for some little time, Maxim charming, Louisa cool, Hester talking more about her experiences in the Crimea. Only half her attention was upon

199

her answers. She was busy wondering how deeply Maxim had loved Alexandra, or if he had been jealous over Louisa and the ease with which she flirted, her total self-confidence. She did not imagine Louisa being gentle, yielding with pleasure to other than the purely physical. She seemed a woman who must always retain the emotional power. Had Maxim found that cold, a lonely thing when the initial passion had worn off, and then sought a gentler woman, one who could give as well as take? Alexandra Carlyon?

She had no idea. She realized again with a jolt of surprise that she had never seen Alexandra. All she knew of her was Monk's description, and Rathbone's.

Her attention was beginning to flag and she was repeating herself. She saw it in Louisa's face. She must be careful.

But before she could add much more the door opened and a youth of about thirteen came in, very tall and gangling as if he had outgrown his strength. His hair was dark but his eyes were heavy-lidded and clear blue, his nose long. In manner he was unusually diffident, hanging back half behind his father, and looking at Hester with shy curiosity.

"Ah, Valentine." Maxim ushered him forward. "My son, Valentine, Miss Latterly. Miss Latterly was in the Crimea with Miss Nightingale, Val. She has come to persuade Mama to encourage other young women of good family and education to take up nursing."

"How interesting. How do you do, Miss Latterly," Valentine said quietly.

"How do you do," Hester replied, looking at his face and trying to decide whether the gravity in his eyes was fear or a natural reticence. There was no quickening of interest in his face, and he looked at her with a sort of weary care. The spontaneity she would have expected from someone of his years was absent. She had looked to see an emotion, even if it was boredom or irritation at being introduced to someone in whom he had no interest. Instead he seemed guarded.

Was that a result of there having been a murder in his house so recently, and by all accounts of a man of whom he was very fond? It did not seem unreasonable. He was suffering from shock. Fate had dealt him an extraordinary blow, unseen in its coming, and having no reasonable explanation. Perhaps he no longer trusted fate to be either kind or sensible. Hester's pity was quickened, and again she wished intensely that she understood Alexandra's crime, even if there were no mitigation for it.

They said little more. Louisa was growing impatient and Hester had exhausted all that she could say on the subject, and after a few more polite trivialities she thanked them for their forbearance and took her leave.

"Well?" Major Tiplady demanded as soon as she reached Great Titchfield Street again. "Did you form any opinion? What is she like, this Mrs. Furnival? Would you have been jealous of her?"

Hester was barely through the door and had not yet taken off her cloak or bonnet.

"You were quite right," she conceded, placing her bonnet on the side table and undoing the button of her cloak and placing it on the hook. "It was definitely a good idea to meet her, and it went surprisingly well." She smiled at him. "In fact I was astoundingly bold. You would have been proud of me. I charged the enemy to the face, and carried the day, I think."

"Well don't stand there smirking, girl." He was thoroughly excited and the pink color rose in his cheeks. "What did you say, and what was she like?"

"I told her"—Hester blushed at the recollection—"that since all women admire her, her influence would be very powerful in encouraging young ladies of breeding and education to take up nursing—and would she use her good offices to that end."

"Great heavens. You said that?" The major closed his eyes as if to digest this startling piece of news. Then he opened them again, bright blue and wide. "And she believed you?"

"Certainly." She came over and sat on the chair opposite him. "She is a dashing and very dominant personality, very sure of herself, and quite aware that men admire her and women envy her. I could flatter her absurdly, and she would believe me, as long as I stayed within the bounds of her own field of influence. I might have been disbelieved had I told her she was virtuous or learned—but not that she was capable of influencing people."

"Oh dear." He sighed, not in unhappiness, but mystification. The ways of women were something he would never understand. Just when he thought he had begun to grasp them, Hester went and did something completely incomprehensible, and he was back to the beginning again. "And did you come to any conclusions about her?"

"Are you hungry?" she asked him.

"Yes I am. But first tell me what you concluded!"

"I am not certain, except I am quite sure she was not in love with the general. She is not a woman who has had to change her plans, or has been deeply bereaved. Actually the only person who seemed really shaken was her son, Valentine. The poor boy looked quite stunned."

Major Tiplady's face registered a sudden bleak pity, as if mention of Valentine had brought the reality of loss back to him, and it ceased to be a puzzle for the intellect and became a tragedy of people again, and their pain and confusion.

Hester said no more. Her mind was still busy trying to make a deeper sense out of her impressions of the Furnivals, hoping against experience to see something which she had missed before, something Monk had missed—and Rathbone.

The following morning she was surprised when at about eleven o'clock the maid announced that she had a visitor.

"I have?" she asked dubiously. "You mean the major has?"

"No, Miss Latterly, ma'am. It's a lady to see you, a Mrs. Sobell."

"Oh! Oh yes." She glanced at Major Tiplady. He nodded, his eyes alive with interest. She turned back to the maid. "Yes, please ask her to come in."

A moment later Edith came in, dressed in a deep lilac silk gown with a wide skirt and looking surprisingly attractive.

There was only sufficient black to pay lip service to mourning, and the rich color enhanced her somewhat sallow skin. For once her hair was beautifully done and apparently she had come by carriage, because the wind had not pulled any of it loose.

Hester introduced her to the major, who flushed with pleasure—and annoyance at still being confined to his chaise longue and unable to stand to greet her.

"How do you do, Major Tiplady," Edith said with courtesy. "It is very gracious of you to receive me."

"How do you do, Mrs. Sobell. I am delighted you have called. May I extend my condolences on the death of your brother. I knew him by repute. A fine man."

"Oh thank you. Yes—it was a tragedy altogether, in every respect."

"Indeed. I hope the solution may yet prove less awful than we fear."

She looked at him curiously, and he colored under her gaze.

"Oh dear," he said hastily. "I fear I have been intrusive. I am so sorry. I know of it only because Miss Latterly has been so concerned on your behalf. Believe me, Mrs. Sobell, I did not mean to sound—er . . ." He faltered, not sure what word to use.

Edith smiled at him suddenly, a radiant, utterly natural expression. Under its warmth he became even pinker, stammered without saying anything at all, then slowly relaxed and smiled hesitantly back.

"I know Hester is doing all she can to help," Edith went on, looking at the major, not at Hester, who was busy taking her bonnet and shawl and giving them to the maid. "And indeed she has obtained for Alexandra the most excellent barrister, who in his turn has employed a detective. But I fear they have not yet discovered anything which will alter what appears to be a total tragedy."

"Do not give up hope yet, my dear Mrs. Sobell," Major Tiplady said eagerly. "Never give up until you are beaten and have no other course open to you. Miss Latterly went only yesterday afternoon to see Mrs. Furnival and form some opinion of her own as to her character.''

''Did you?'' Edith turned to Hester with a lift in her voice. ''What did you think of her?''

Hester smiled ruefully. ''Nothing helpful, I'm afraid. Would you like tea? It would be no trouble at all.''

Edith glanced at the major. It was not a usual hour for tea, and yet she very much wished to have an excuse to stay awhile.

''Of course,'' the major said hastily. ''Unless you are able to remain for luncheon? That would be delightful.'' He stopped, realizing he was being too forward. ''But you probably have other things to do—people to call on. I did not mean to be . . .''

Edith turned back to him. ''I should be delighted, if it is not an imposition?''

Major Tiplady beamed with relief. ''Not at all—not at all. Please sit down, Mrs. Sobell. I believe that chair is quite comfortable. Hester, please tell Molly we shall be three for luncheon.''

''Thank you,'' Edith accepted, sitting on the big chair with uncharacteristic grace, her back straight, her hands folded, both feet on the floor.

Hester departed obediently.

Edith glanced at the major's elevated leg on the chaise longue.

''I hope you are recovering well?''

''Oh excellently, thank you.'' He winced, but not with pain at any injury, rather at his incapacity, and the disadvantage at which it placed him. ''I am very tired of sitting here, you know. I feel so . . .'' He hesitated again, not wishing to burden her with his complaints. After all, she had merely asked in general politeness, not requiring a detailed answer. The color swept up his cheeks again.

''Of course,'' she agreed with a quick smile. ''You must be terribly . . . caged. I am used to spending all my time in one house, and I feel as if I were imprisoned. How much worse must you feel, when you are a soldier and used to traveling all over the world and doing something useful all the time." She leaned forward a little, and unconsciously made herself more comfortable. "You must have been to some marvelous places."

"Well . . ." The pink spots in his cheeks grew deeper. "Well, I had not thought of it quite like that, but yes, I suppose I have. India, you know?"

"No, I don't know," she said frankly. "I wish I did."

"Do you really?" He looked surprised and hopeful.

"Of course!" She regarded him as if he had asked a truly odd question. "Where in India have you been? What is it like?"

"Oh it was all the usual thing, you know," he said modestly. "Scores of other people have been there too—officers' wives, and so on, and written letters home, full of descriptions. It isn't very new, I'm afraid." He hesitated, looking down at the blanket over his knees, and his rather bony hands spread across them. "But I did go to Africa a couple of times."

"Africa! How marvelous!" She was not being polite; eagerness rang in her voice like music. "Where in Africa? To the south?"

He watched her face keenly to make sure he was not saying too much.

"At first. Then I went north to Matabeleland, and Mashonaland . . ."

"Did you?" Her eyes were wide. "What is it like? Is that where Dr. Livingstone is?"

"No—the missionary there is a Dr. Robert Moffatt, a most remarkable person, as is his wife, Mary." His face lit with memory, as if the vividness of it were but a day or two since. "Indeed I think perhaps she is one of the most admirable of women. Such courage to travel with the word of God and to carry it to a savage people in an unknown land."

Edith leaned towards him eagerly. "What is the land like, Major Tiplady? Is it very hot? Is it quite different from England? What are the animals like, and the flowers?"

"You have never seen so many different kinds of beasts in all your life," he said expressively, still watching her. "Elephants, lions, giraffes, rhinos, and so many species of deer and antelope you cannot imagine it, and zebras and buffalo. Why, I have seen herds so vast they darkened the ground." He leaned towards her unconsciously, and she moved a fraction closer.

"And when something frightens them," he went on, "like a grass fire, and they stampede, then the earth shakes and roars under tens of thousands of hooves, and the little creatures dart in every direction before them, as before a tidal wave. Which reminds me, most of the ground there is red—a rich, brilliant soil. Oh, and the trees." He shrugged his shoulders. "Of course most of the veldt is just grassland and acacia trees, with flat tops—but there are flowering trees to dazzle the eyes so you scarcely can believe what they see. And—" He stopped suddenly as Hester came back into the room. "Oh dear—I am afraid I am monopolizing the conversation. You are too generous, Mrs. Sobell."

Hester stopped abruptly, then a slow smile spread over her face and she continued in.

"Not at all," Edith denied immediately. "Hester, has Major Tiplady ever told you about his adventures in Mashonaland and Matabeleland?"

"No," Hester said with some surprise, looking at the major. "I thought you served in India."

"Oh yes. But he has been to Africa too," Edith said quickly. "Major"—she faced him again eagerly—"you should write down everything about all these places you have been to, so we all may hear about them. Most of us don't even leave our miserable little parts of London, let alone see wild and exotic places such as you describe. Think how many people could while away a winter afternoon with imagination on fire with what you could tell them."

He looked profoundly abashed, and yet there was an eagerness in him he could not hide.

"Do you really think so, Mrs. Sobell?"

"Oh yes! Indeed I do," Edith said urgently. "It is quite apparent that you can recall it most clearly, and you recount it so extraordinarily well."

Major Tiplady colored with pleasure, and opened his

mouth to deny it, as modesty required. Then apparently he could think of nothing that did not sound ungracious, and so remained silent.

"An excellent idea," Hester agreed, delighted for the major and for Edith, and able to endorse it with some honesty as well. "There is so much rubbish written, it would be marvelous that true adventures should be recorded not only for the present day, but for the future as well. People will always want to know the explorations of such a country, whatever may happen there."

"Oh—oh." Major Tiplady looked very pleased. "Perhaps you are right. However, there are more pressing matters which I can see you need to discuss, my dear Mrs. Sobell. Please do not let your good manners prevent you from doing so. And if you wish to do so in private . . ."

"Not at all," Edith assured him. "But you are right, of course. We must consider the case." She turned to Hester again, her brightness of expression vanished, the pain replacing it. "Hester, Mr. Rathbone has spoken to Peverell about the trial. The date is set for Monday, June twenty-second, and we still have nothing to say but the same miserable lie with which we began. Alexandra did not do it"—she avoided using the word *kill*—"because of anything to do with Louisa Furnival. Thaddeus did not beat her, or leave her short of money. She had no other lover that we can find trace of. I cannot easily believe she is simply mad—and yet what else is there?" She sighed and the distress in her face deepened. "Perhaps Mama is right." She dragged her mouth down, as if even putting form to the thought was difficult, and made it worse.

"No, my dear, you must not give up," Major Tiplady said gently. "We shall think of something." He stopped, aware that it was not his concern. He knew of it only by virtue of his injured leg, and Hester's presence to nurse him. "I'm sorry," he apologized, embarrassed that he had intruded again, a cardinal sin in his own view. No gentleman intruded into another person's private affairs, especially a woman's.

"Don't apologize," Edith said with a hasty smile. "You

are quite right. I was disheartened, but that is when courage counts, isn't it? Anyone can keep going when all is easy.''

"We must use logic." Hester sat down on the remaining chair. "We have been busy running 'round gathering facts and impressions, and not applying our brains sufficiently."

Edith looked puzzled, but did not argue. Major Tiplady sat up a little straighter on the chaise longue, his attention total.

"Let us suppose," Hester continued, "that Alexandra is perfectly sane, and has done this thing from some powerful motive which she is not prepared to share with anyone. Then she must have a reason for keeping silent. I was speaking with someone the other day who suggested she might be protecting someone or something she valued more than life."

"She is protecting someone else," Edith said slowly. "But who? We have ruled out Sabella. Mr. Monk proved she could not have killed her father."

"She could not have killed her father," Hester agreed quickly. "But we have not ruled out that there may be some other reason why she was in danger, of some sort, and Alexandra killed Thaddeus to save her from it."

"For example?"

"I don't know. Perhaps she has done something very odd, if childbirth has turned her mind, and Thaddeus was going to have her committed to an asylum."

"No, Thaddeus wouldn't do that," Edith argued. "She is Fenton's wife—he would have to do it."

"Well maybe he would have—if Thaddeus had told him to." Hester was not very happy with the idea, but it was a start. "Or it might be something quite different, but still to do with Sabella. Alexandra would kill to protect Sabella, wouldn't she?"

"Yes, I believe so. All right—that is one reason. What else?"

"Because she is so ashamed of the reason she does not wish anyone to know," Hester said. "I'm sorry—I realize that is a distasteful thought. But it is a possibility."

Edith nodded.

"Or," suggested Major Tiplady, looking from one to the other of them, "it is some reason which she believes will not make her case any better than it is now, and she would prefer that her real motive remain private if it cannot save her."

They both looked at him.

"You are right," Edith said slowly. "That also would be a reason." She turned to Hester. "Would any of that help?"

"I don't know," Hester said grimly. "Perhaps all we can look for now is sense. At least sense would stop it hurting quite so much." She shrugged. "I cannot get young Valentine Furnival's face out of my mind's eye; the poor boy looked so wounded. As if everything the adult world had led him to believe only confused him and left him with nowhere to turn!"

Edith sighed. "Cassian is the same. And he is only eight, poor child, and he's lost both his parents in one blow, as it were. I have tried to comfort him, or at least not to say anything which would belittle his loss, that would be absurd, but to spend time with him, talk to him and make him feel less alone." She shook her head and a troubled expression crossed her face. "But it hasn't done any good. I think he doesn't really like me very much. The only person he really seems to like is Peverell."

"I suppose he misses his father very much," Hester said unhappily. "And he may have heard whispers, no matter how much people try to keep it from him, that it was his mother who killed him. He may view all women with a certain mistrust."

Edith sighed and bent her head, putting her hands over her face as if she could shut out not only the light but some of what her mind could see as well.

"I suppose so," she said very quietly. "Poor little soul— I feel so totally helpless. I think that is the worst part of all this—there is nothing whatever we can do."

"We will just have to hope." Major Tiplady reached out a hand as if to touch Edith's arm, then suddenly realized what he was doing and withdrew it. "Until something occurs to us," he finished quietly.

But nearly a week later, on June 4, nothing had occurred.

Monk was nowhere to be seen. Oliver Rathbone was working silently in his office in Vere Street, and Major Tiplady was almost recovered, although loth to admit it.

Hester received a message from Clarence Gardens in Edith's rather sprawling script asking her to come to luncheon the following day. She was to come, not as a formal guest so much as Edith's friend, with a view to persuading her parents that it would not be unseemly for Edith to become a librarian to some discreet gentleman of unspotted reputation, should such a position be found.

"I cannot endure this idleness any longer," she had written. "Merely to sit here day after day, waiting for the trial and unable to lift a finger to assist anyone, is more than I can bear, and keep a reasonable temper or frame of mind."

Hester was also concerned about where she herself would find her next position. She had hoped Major Tiplady might know of some other soldier recently wounded or in frail health who would need her services, but he had been extremely unforthcoming. In fact all his attention lately seemed to be on the Carlyons and the case of the general's death.

However, he made no demur at all when she asked him if he would be agreeable to her taking luncheon with Edith the following day; in fact he seemed quite eager that she should.

Accordingly noon on the fifth saw her in Edith's sitting room discussing with her the possibilities of employment, not only as librarian but as companion if a lady of suitable occupation and temperament could be found. Even teaching foreign languages was not beyond consideration if the worse came to the worst.

They were still arguing the possibilities and seeking for more when luncheon was announced and they went downstairs to find Dr. Charles Hargrave in the withdrawing room. He was lean, very tall, and even more elegant than Hester had imagined from Edith's brief description of him. Introductions were performed by Felicia, and a moment later Randolf came in with a fair, handsome boy with a face still soft with the bloom of childhood, his hair curling back from his brow, his blue eyes wary and a careful, closed expression.

210

He was introduced, although Hester knew he was Cassian Carlyon, Alexandra's son.

"Good morning, Cassian," Hargrave said courteously, smiling at the boy.

Cassian dropped his shoulder and wriggled his left foot up his right ankle. He smiled back. "Good morning, sir."

Hargrave looked directly at him, ignoring the adults in the room and speaking as if they were alone, man to man.

"How are you getting on? Are you quite well? I hear your grandfather has given you a fine set of lead soldiers."

"Yes sir, Wellington's army at Waterloo," the boy answered with a flicker of enthusiasm at last touching his pale face. "Grandpapa was at Waterloo, you know? He actually saw it, isn't that tremendous?"

"Absolutely," Hargrave agreed quickly. "I should think he has some splendid stories he can tell you."

"Oh yes sir! He saw the emperor of the French, you know. And he was a funny little man with a cocked hat, and quite short when he wasn't on his white horse. He said the Iron Duke was magnificent. I would love to have been there." He dropped his shoulder again and smiled tentatively, his eyes never leaving Hargrave's face. "Wouldn't you, sir?"

"Indeed I would," Hargrave agreed. "But I daresay there will be other battles in the future, marvelous ones where you can fight, and see great events that turn history, and great men who win or lose nations in a day."

"Do you think so, sir?" For a moment his eyes were wide and full of unclouded excitement as the vision spread before his mind.

"Why not?" Hargrave said casually. "The whole world lies in front of us, and the Empire gets bigger and more exciting every year. There's all of Australia, New Zealand, Canada. And in Africa there's Gambia, Sierra Leone, the Gold Coast, South Africa; and in India there's the Northwest Province, Bengal, Oudh, Assam, Arakan, Mysore, and all the south, including Ceylon and islands in every ocean on earth."

"I'm not sure I even know where all those places are, sir," Cassian said with wonderment.

"Well then I had better show you, hadn't I?" Hargrave said, smiling broadly. He looked at Felicia. "Do you still have a schoolroom here?"

"It has been closed a long time, but we intend to open it again for Cassian's use, as soon as this unsettled time is over. We will engage a suitable tutor for him of course. I think a complete change is advisable, don't you?"

"A good idea," Hargrave agreed. "Nothing to remind him of things best put away." He turned back to Cassian. "Then this afternoon I shall take you up to the old schoolroom and we shall find a globe, and you shall show me all those places in the Empire that you know, and I shall show you all the ones you don't. Does that appeal to you?"

"Yes sir—thank you sir," Cassian accepted quickly. Then he glanced at his grandmother, saw the approval in her eyes, and moved around so that his back was to his grandfather, studiously avoiding looking at him.

Hester found herself smiling and a little prickle of warmth coming into her for the first time on behalf of the child. It seemed he had at least one friend who was going to treat him as a person and give him the uncritical, undemanding companionship he so desperately needed. And from what he said, his grandfather too was offering him some thoughts and tales that bore no relationship to his own tragedy. It was a generosity she would not have expected from Randolf, and she was obliged to view him with a greater liking than before. From Peverell she had expected it anyway, but he was out on business most of the day, when Cassian had his long hours alone.

They were about to go into the dining room when Peverell himself came in, apologized for being late and said he hoped he had not delayed them. He greeted Hester and Hargrave, then looked around for Damaris.

"Late again," Felicia said with tight lips. "Well we certainly cannot wait for her. She will have to join us wherever we are at the time she gets here. If she misses her meal it is her own doing." She turned around and without looking at any of them led the way into the dining room.

They were seated and the maid had come with soup when Damaris opened the door and stood on the threshold. She was dressed in a very slender gown, almost without hoops they were so small, the whole outfit in black and dove-gray, her hair pulled back from her long, thoughtful face with its lovely bones and emotional mouth.

For a moment there was silence, and the maid stopped with the soup ladle in the air.

"Sorry I'm late," she said with a tiny smile curling her lips, her eyes going first to Peverell, then to Edith and Hester, finally to her mother. She was leaning against the lintel.

"Your apologies are wearing a little thin!" Felicia said tartly. "This is the fifth time this fortnight that you have been late for a meal. Please continue to serve, Marigold."

The maid resumed her duty.

Damaris straightened up and was about to move forward and take her seat when she noticed Charles Hargrave for the first time. He had been partly shielded by Randolf. Her whole body froze and the blood drained from her skin. She swayed as if dizzy, and put both hands onto the door lintel to save herself.

Peverell rose to his feet immediately, scraping his chair back.

"What is it, Ris? Are you ill? Here, sit down, my dear." He half dragged her to his own abandoned chair and eased her into it. "What has happened? Are you faint?"

Edith pushed across her glass of water and he seized it and held it up to Damaris's lips.

Hargrave rose and came forward to kneel beside her, looking at her with a professional calm.

"Oh really," Randolf said irritably, and continued with his soup.

"Did you have any breakfast?" Hargrave asked, frowning at Damaris. "Or were you late for that also? Fasting can be dangerous, you know, make you light-headed."

She lifted her face and met his eyes slowly. For seconds they stared at each other in a strange, frozen immobility, he with concern, she with a look of bewilderment as if she barely knew where she was.

"Yes," she said at last, her voice husky. "That must be what it is. I apologize for making such a nuisance of myself." She swallowed awkwardly. "Thank you for the water Pev— Edith. I am sure I shall be perfectly all right now."

"Ridiculous!" Felicia said furiously, glaring at her daughter. "Not only are you late, but you come in here making an entrance like an operatic diva and then half swoon all over the place. Really, Damaris, your sense of the melodramatic is both absurd and offensive, and it is time you stopped drawing attention to yourself by any and every means you can think of!"

Hester was acutely uncomfortable; it was the sort of scene an outsider should not be privy to.

Peverell looked up, his face suddenly filled with anger.

"You are being unjust, Mama-in-law. Damaris had no intention of making herself ill. And I think if you have some criticism to make, it would be more fitting if you were to do it in private, when neither Miss Latterly nor Dr. Hargrave would be embarrassed by our family differences."

It was a speech delivered in a gentle tone of voice, but it contained the most cutting criticism that could be imagined. He accused her of behaving without dignity, without loyalty to her family's honor, and perhaps worst of all, of embarrassing her guests, sins which were socially and morally unforgivable.

She blushed scarlet, and then the blood fled, leaving her ashen. She opened her mouth to retaliate with something equally vicious, and was lost to find it.

Peverell turned from his mother-in-law to his wife. "I think it would be better if you were to lie down, my dear. I will have Gertrude bring you up a tray."

"I . . ." Damaris sat upright again, turning away from Hargrave. "I really . . ."

"You will feel better if you do," Peverell assured her, but there was a steel in his voice that brooked no argument. "I will see you to the stairs. Come!"

Obediently, leaning a little on his arm, she left, muttering "Excuse me" over her shoulder.

Edith began eating again and gradually the table returned

to normal. A few moments later Peverell came back and made no comment as to Damaris, and the episode was not referred to again.

They were beginning dessert of baked apple and caramel sauce when Edith caused the second violent disruption.

"I am going to find a position as a librarian, or possibly a companion to someone," she announced, looking ahead at the centerpiece of the table. It was an elaborate arrangement of irises, full-blown lupins from some sheltered area of the garden, and half-open white lilac.

Felicia choked on her apple.

"You are what?" Randolf demanded.

Hargrave stared at her, his face puckered, his eyes curious.

"I am going to seek a position as a librarian," Edith said again. "Or as a companion, or even a teacher of French, if all else fails."

"You always had an unreliable sense of humor," Felicia said coldly. "As if it were not enough that Damaris has to make a fool of herself, you have to follow her with idiotic remarks. What is the matter with you? Your brother's death seems to have deprived all of you of your wits. Not to mention your sense of what is fitting. I forbid you to mention it again. We are in a house of mourning, and you will remember that, and behave accordingly." Her face was bleak and a wave of misery passed over it, leaving her suddenly older and more vulnerable, the brave aspect that she showed to the world patently a veneer. "Your brother was a fine man, a brilliant man, robbed of the prime of his life by a wife who lost her reason. Our nation is the poorer for his loss. You will not make our suffering worse by behaving in an irresponsible manner and making wild and extremely trying remarks. Do I make myself clear?"

Edith opened her mouth to protest, but the argument died out of her. She saw the grief in her mother's face, and pity and guilt overrode her own wishes, and all the reasons she had been so certain of an hour ago talking to Hester in her own sitting room.

"Yes, Mama, I . . ." She let out her breath in a sigh.

"Good!" Felicia resumed eating, forcing herself to swallow with difficulty.

"I apologize, Hargrave," Randolf said with a frown. "Family's hit hard, you know. Grief does funny things to women—at least most women. Felicia's different—remarkable strength—a most outstanding woman, if I do say so."

"Most remarkable." Hargrave nodded towards Felicia and smiled. "You have my greatest respect, ma'am; you always have had."

Felicia colored very slightly and accepted the compliment with an inclination of her head.

The meal continued in silence, except for the most trivial and contrived of small talk.

When it was over and they had left the table and Hester had thanked Felicia and bidden them farewell, she and Edith went upstairs to the sitting room. Edith was thoroughly dejected; her shoulders were hunched and her feet heavy on the stairs.

Hester was extremely sorry for her. She understood why she had offered no argument. The sight of her mother's face so stripped, for an instant, of all its armor, had left her feeling brutal, and she was unable to strike another blow, least of all in front of others who had already seen her wounded once.

But it was no comfort to Edith, and offered only a long, bleak prospect ahead of endless meals the same, filled with little more than duty. The world of endeavor and reward was closed off as if it were a view through a window, and someone had drawn the curtains.

They were on the first landing when they were passed, almost at a run, by an elderly woman with crackling black skirts. She was very lean, almost gaunt, at least as tall as Hester. Her hair had once been auburn but now was almost white; only the tone of her skin gave away her original coloring. Her dark gray eyes were intent and her brows drawn down. Her thin face, highly individual, was creased with temper.

"Hallo, Buckie," Edith said cheerfully. "Where are you off to in such a rush? Been fighting with Cook again?"

"I don't fight with Cook, Miss Edith," she said briskly. "I simply tell her what she ought to know already. She takes it ill, even though I am right, and loses her temper. I cannot abide a woman who cannot control her temper—especially when she's in service."

Edith hid a smile. "Buckie, you don't know my friend, Hester Latterly. Miss Latterly was in the Crimea, with Florence Nightingale. Hester, this is Miss Buchan, my governess, long ago."

"How do you do, Miss Buchan," Hester said with interest.

"How do you do, Miss Latterly," Miss Buchan replied, screwing up her face and staring at Hester. "The Crimea, eh? Well, well. I'll have to have Edith tell me all about it. Right now I'm off up to see Master Cassian in the schoolroom."

"You're not going to teach him, are you, Buckie?" Edith said in surprise. "I thought you gave up that sort of thing years ago!"

"Of course I did," Miss Buchan said tartly. "Think I'm going to take up lessons again at my age? I'm sixty-six, as you well know. I taught you to count, myself, and your brother and sister before you!"

"Didn't Dr. Hargrave go up with him, to show him the globe?"

Miss Buchan's face hardened, a curious look of anger in her eyes and around her mouth.

"Indeed he did. I'll go and find out if he's there, and make sure nothing gets broken. Now if you will excuse me, Miss Edith, I'll be on my way. Miss Latterly." And without waiting to hear anything further she almost pushed past them, and walked very briskly, her heels clicking on the floor, and took the second flight of stairs to the schoolroom at something inelegantly close to a dash.

Monk was finding the Carlyon case, as Rathbone had said, a thankless one. But he had given his word that he would do all he could for as long as it was asked of him. There were over two weeks yet until the trial, and so far he had found nothing that could be of use in helping even to mitigate the case against Alexandra, let alone answer it. It was a matter of pride not to give up now, and his own curiosity was piqued. He did not like to be beaten. He had not been beaten on a serious case since the accident, and he thought seldom before it.

And there was also the perfectly practical fact that Rathbone was still paying him, and he had no other case pending.

In the afternoon Monk went again to see Charles Hargrave. He had been the Carlyon family doctor for many years. If anyone knew the truth, or the elements from which the truth could be deduced, it would be he.

He was received courteously, and as soon as he explained why he believed Hargrave could help, he was led through into the same pleasing room as before. Hargrave instructed the servants he was not to be interrupted except for an emergency, and then offered Monk a seat and made himself available to answer any questions he was free to.

"I cannot tell you any personal facts about Mrs. Carlyon,

you understand," he said with an apologetic smile. "She is still my patient, and I have to assume that she is innocent until the law says otherwise, in spite of that being patently ridiculous. But I admit, if I thought there was anything at all that would be of help in your case, I should break that confidence and give you all the information I had." He lifted his shoulders a trifle. "But there is nothing. She has had only the very ordinary ailments that most women have. Her confinements were without incident. Her children were born normally, and thrived. She herself recovered her health as soon and as happily as most women do. There is really nothing to tell."

"Not like Sabella?"

His face shadowed. "No—no, I am afraid Sabella was one of those few who suffer profoundly. No one knows why it happens, but occasionally a woman will have a difficult time carrying a child, during confinement, or afterwards. Sabella was quite well right up until the last week. Her confinement was long and extremely painful. At one time I was fearful lest we lose her."

"Her mother would be most distressed."

"Of course. But then death in childbirth is quite common, Mr. Monk. It is a risk all women take, and they are aware of it."

"Was that why Sabella did not wish to marry?"

Hargrave looked surprised. "Not that I know of. I believe she genuinely wished to devote her life to the Church." Again he raised his shoulders very slightly. "It is not unknown among girls of a certain age. Usually they grow out of it. It is a sort of romance, an escape for a young and overheated imagination. Some simply fall in love with an ideal of man, a figure from literature or whatever, some with the most ideal of all—the Son of God. And after all"—he smiled with a gentle amusement touched only fractionally with bitterness—"it is the one love which can never fall short of our dreams, never disillusion us, because it lies in illusion anyway." He sighed. "No, forgive me, that is not quite right. I mean it is mystical, its fulfillment does not rest with any real person but in the mind of the lover.''

"And after the confinement and the birth of her child?" Monk prompted.

"Oh—yes, I'm afraid she suffered a melancholia that occasionally occurs at such times. She became quite deranged, did not want her child, repelled any comfort or offer of help, any friendship; indeed any company except that of her mother." He spread his hands expressively. "But it passed. These things do. Sometimes they take several years, but usually it is only a matter of a month or two, or at most four or five."

"There was no question of her being incarcerated as insane?"

"No!" Hargrave was startled. "None at all. Her husband was very patient, and they had a wet nurse for the child. Why?"

Monk sighed. "It was a possibility."

"Alexandra? Don't see how. What are you looking for, Mr. Monk? What is it you hope to find? If I knew, perhaps I could save your time, and tell you if it exists at all."

"I don't know myself," Monk confessed. Also he did not wish to confide in Hargrave, or anyone else, because the whole idea involved some other person who was a threat to Alexandra. And who better than her doctor, who must know so many intimate things?

"What about the general?" he said aloud. "He is dead and cannot care who knows about him, and his medical history may contain some answer as to why he was killed."

Hargrave frowned. "I cannot think what. It is very ordinary indeed. Of course I did not attend him for the various injuries he received in action." He smiled. "In fact I think the only time I attended him at all was for a cut he received on his upper leg—a rather foolish accident."

"Oh? It must have been severe for him to send for you."

"Yes, it was a very nasty gash, ragged and quite deep. It was necessary to clean it, stop the bleeding with packs, then to stitch it closed. I went back several times to make quite sure it healed properly, without infection."

"How did it happen?" A wild thought occurred to Monk

that it might have been a previous attack by Alexandra, which the general had warded off, sustaining only a thigh injury.

A look of puzzlement crossed Hargrave's face.

"He said he had been cleaning an ornamental weapon, an Indian knife he had brought home as a souvenir, and taken it to give to young Valentine Furnival. It had stuck in its scabbard, and in forcing it out it slipped from his grasp and gashed him on the leg. He was attempting to clean it, or something of the sort."

"Valentine Furnival? Was Valentine visiting him?"

"No—no, it happened at the Furnivals' house. I was sent there."

"Did you see the weapon?" Monk asked.

"No—I didn't bother. He assured me the blade itself was clean, and that since it was such a dangerous thing he had disposed of it. I saw no reason to pursue it, because even in the unlikely event it was not self-inflicted, but a domestic quarrel, it was none of my affair, so long as he did not ask me to interfere. And he never did. In fact he did not mention it again as long as I knew him." He smiled slightly. "If you are thinking it was Alexandra, I must say I think you are mistaken, but even if so, he forgave her for it. And nothing like it ever occurred again."

"Alexandra was at the Furnivals' house?"

"I've no idea. I didn't see her."

"I see. Thank you, Dr. Hargrave."

And although he stayed another forty-five minutes, Monk learned nothing else that was of use to him. In fact he could find no thread to follow that might lead him to the reason why Alexandra had killed her husband, and still less why she should remain silent rather than admit it, even to him.

He left in the late afternoon, disappointed and puzzled.

He must ask Rathbone to arrange for him to see the woman again, but while that was in hand, he would go back to her daughter, Sabella Pole. The answer as to why Alexandra had killed her husband must lie somewhere in her nature, or in

221

her circumstances. The only course that he could see left to him was to learn still more about her.

Accordingly, eleven o'clock in the morning saw him at Fenton Pole's house in Albany Street, again knocking on the door and requesting to see Mrs. Pole, if she would receive him, and handing the maid his card.

He had chosen his time carefully. Fenton Pole was out on business, and as he had hoped, Sabella received him eagerly. As soon as he came into the morning room where she was she rose from the green sofa and came towards him, her eyes wide and hopeful, her hair framing her face with its soft, fair curls. Her skirts were very wide, the crinoline hoops settling themselves straight as she rose and the taffeta rustling against itself with a soft, whispering sound.

Without any warning he felt a stab of memory that erased his present surroundings of conventional green and placed him in a gaslit room with mirrors reflecting a chandelier, and a woman talking. But before he could focus on anything it was gone, leaving nothing behind but confusion, a sense of being in two places at once, and a desperate need to recapture it and grasp the whole of it.

"Mr. Monk," Sabella said hastily. "I am so glad you came again. I was afraid after my husband was so abrupt to you that you would not return. How is Mama? Have you seen her? Can you help? No one will tell me anything, and I am going nearly frantic with fear for her."

The sunlight in the bright room seemed unreal, as if he were detached from it and seeing it in a reflection rather than reality. His mind was struggling after gaslight, dim corners and brilliant splinters of light on crystal.

Sabella stood in front of him, her lovely oval face strained and her eyes full of anxiety. He must pull his wits together and give her his attention. Every decency demanded it. What had she said? Concentrate!

"I have requested permission to see her again as soon as possible, Mrs. Pole," he replied, his words sounding far away. "As to whether I can help, I am afraid I don't know yet. So far I have learned little that seems of any use."

She closed her eyes as if the pain were physical, and stepped back from him.

"I need to know more about her," he went on, memory abandoned for the moment. "Please, Mrs. Pole, if you can help me, do so. She will not tell us anything, except that she killed him. She will not tell us any reason but the one we know is not true. I have searched for any evidence of another cause, and I can find none. It must be in her nature, or in your father's. Or in some event which as yet we know nothing of. Please—tell me about them!"

She opened her eyes and stared at him; slowly a little of the color came back into her face.

"What sort of thing do you wish to know, Mr. Monk? I will tell you anything I can. Just ask me—instruct me!" She sat down and waved to a seat for him.

He obeyed, sinking into the deep upholstery and finding it more comfortable than he had expected.

"It may be painful," he warned. "If it distresses you please say so. I do not wish to make you ill." He was gentler with her than he had expected to be, or was his habit. Perhaps it was because she was too concerned with her mother to think of being afraid of him for herself. Fear brought out a pursuing instinct in him, a kind of anger because he thought it was unwarranted. He admired courage.

"Mr. Monk, my mother's life is in jeopardy," she replied with a very direct gaze. "I do not think a little distress is beyond my bearing."

He smiled at her for the first time, a quick, generous gesture that came quite spontaneously.

"Thank you. Did you ever hear your parents quarreling, say, in the last two or three years?"

She smiled back at him, only a ghost, and then was gone.

"I have tried to think of that myself," she said seriously. "And I am afraid I have not. Papa was not the sort of man to quarrel. He was a general, you know. Generals don't quarrel." She pulled a little face. "I suppose that is because the only person who would dare to quarrel with a general would be another general, and you so seldom get two in any one place. There is presumably a whole army between one general and the next.''

She was watching his face. "Except in the Crimea, so I hear. And then of course they did quarrel—and the results were catastrophic. At least that is what Maxim Furnival says, although everybody else denies it and says our men were fearfully brave and the generals were all very clever. But I believe Maxim . . .''

"So do I,'' he agreed. "I believe some were clever, most were brave enough, but far too many were disastrously ignorant and inexcusably stupid!''

"Oh do you think so?'' The fleeting smile crossed her face again. "Not many people will dare to say that generals are stupid, especially so close to a war. But my father was a general, and so I know how they can be. They know some things, but others they have no idea of at all, the most ordinary things about people. Half the people in the world are women, you know?'' She said it as if the fact surprised even herself.

He found himself liking her. "Was your father like that?'' he asked, not only because it mattered, but because he was interested.

"Very much.'' She lifted her head and pushed back a stray strand of hair. The gesture was startlingly familiar to him, bringing back not a sight or a sound, but an emotion of tenderness rare and startling to him, and a longing to protect her as if she were a vulnerable child; and yet he knew beyond question that the urgency he felt was not that which he might have towards any child, but only towards a woman.

But which woman? What had happened between them, and why did he not know her now? Was she dead? Had he failed to protect her, as he had failed with the Walbrooks? Or had they quarreled over something; had he been too precipitate with his feelings? Did she love someone else?

If only he knew more of himself, he might know the answer to that. All he had learned up until now showed him that he was not a gentle man, not used to bridling his tongue to protect other people's feelings, or to stifling his own wants, needs, or opinions. He could be cruel with words. Too many cautious and bruised inferiors had borne witness to that. He recalled with increasing discomfort the wariness with which they had greeted him when he returned from the hospital after the accident. They admired him, certainly, respected his professional ability and judgment, his honesty, skill, dedication and courage. But they were also afraid of him—and not only if they were lax in duty or less than honest, but even if they were in the right. Which meant that a number of times he must have been unjust, his sarcastic wit directed against the weak as well as the strong. It was not a pleasant knowledge to live with.

"Tell me about him." He looked at Sabella. "Tell me about his nature, his interests, what you liked best about him, and what you disliked."

"Liked best about him?" She concentrated hard. "I think I liked . . ."

He was not listening to her. The woman he had loved— yes, *loved* was the word—why had he not married her? Had she refused him? But if he had cared so much, why could he not now even recall her face, her name, anything about her beyond these sharp and confusing flashes?

Or had she been guilty of the crime after all? Was that why he had tried to expunge her from his mind? And she returned now only because he had forgotten the circumstances, the guilt, the dreadful end of the affair? Could he have been so mistaken in his judgment? Surely not. It was his profession to detect truth from lies—he could not have been such a fool!

". . . and I liked the way he always spoke gently," Sabella was saying. "I can't recall that I ever heard him shout, or use language unbecoming for us to hear. He had a lovely voice." She was looking up at the ceiling, her face softer, the anger gone from it, which he had only dimly registered when she must have been speaking of some of the things she disliked in her father. "He used to read to us from the Bible— the Book of Isaiah especially," she went on. "I don't remember what he said, but I loved listening to him because

225

his voice wrapped all 'round us and made it all seem important and good.''

''And your greatest dislike?'' he prompted, hoping she had not already specified it when he was not listening.

''I think the way he would withdraw into himself and not even seem to notice that I was there—sometimes for days,'' she replied without hesitation. Then a look of sorrow came into her eyes, and a self-conscious pain. ''And he never laughed with me, as if—as if he were not altogether comfortable in my company.'' Her fair brows puckered as she concentrated on Monk. ''Do you know what I mean?''

Then as quickly she looked away. ''I'm sorry, that is a foolish question, and embarrassing. I fear I am being no help at all—and I wish I could.'' This last was said with such intense feeling that Monk ached to be able to reach across the bright space between them and touch her slender wrist, to assure her with some more immediate warmth than words, that he did understand. But to do so would be intrusive, and open to all manner of misconstruction. All he could think of was to continue with questions that might lead to some fragment of useful knowledge. He did not often feel so awkward.

''I believe he had been friends with Mr. and Mrs. Furnival for a long time?''

She looked up, recalling herself to the matter in hand and putting away memory and thought of her own wounds.

''Yes—about sixteen or seventeen years, I think, something like that. They had been much closer over the last seven or eight years. I believe he used to visit them once or twice a week when he was at home.'' She looked at him with a slight frown. ''But he was friends with both of them, you know. It would be easy to believe he was having an affair with Louisa—I mean easy as far as his death is concerned, but I really do not think he was. Maxim was very fond of Mama, you know? Sometimes I used to think—but that is another thing, and of no use to us now.

''Maxim is in the business of dealing in foodstuffs, you know, and Papa put a very great deal of army contracts his way. A cavalry regiment can use a marvelous amount of corn, hay, oats and so on. I think he also was an agent for saddlery and other things of that sort. I don't know the details, but I know Maxim profited greatly because of it, and has become a very respected power in the trade, among his fellows. I think he must be very good at it."

"Indeed." Monk turned it over in his mind; it was an interesting piece of information, but he could not see how it was of any use to Alexandra Carlyon. It did not sound in any way corrupt; presumably a general might suggest to his quartermaster that he obtain his stores from one merchant rather than another, if the price were fair. But even had it not been, why should that cause Alexandra any anger or distress—still less drive her to murder?

But it was another thread leading back to the Furnivals.

"Do you remember the incident where your father was stabbed with the ornamental knife? It happened at the Furnivals' house. It was quite a deep injury."

"He wasn't stabbed," she said with a tiny smile. "He slipped and did it himself. He was cleaning the knife, or something. I can't imagine why. It wasn't even used."

"But you remember it?"

"Yes of course. Poor Valentine was terribly upset. I think he saw it happen. He was only about eleven or twelve, poor child."

"Was your mother there?"

"At the Furnivals'? Yes, I think so. I really don't remember. Louisa was there. She sent for Dr. Hargrave to come immediately because it was bleeding pretty badly. They had to put a lot of bandages on it, and he could barely get his trousers back on, even with Maxim's valet to help him. When he came down the stairs, assisted by the valet and the footman, I could see the great bulges under the cloth of his trousers. He looked awfully pale and he went straight home in the carriage."

Monk tried to visualize it. A clumsy accident. But was it relevant? Could it conceivably have been an earlier attempt to kill him? Surely not—not in the Furnivals' house and so long ago. But why not in the Furnivals' house? She had finally killed him there. But why no attempt between then and now?

Sabella had said she saw the swell of the bandages under his trousers. Not the bloodstained tear where the knife had gone through! Was it possible Alexandra had found him in bed with Louisa and taken the knife to him in a fit of jealous rage? And they had conspired to conceal it—and the scandal? There was no point in asking Sabella. She would naturally deny it, to protect her mother.

He stayed a further half hour, drawing from her memories of her parents, some quite varied, but not showing him anything he had not already learned from his talk with the servants in Alexandra's own home. She and the general had been reasonably content in their relationship. It was cool but not intolerable. He had not abused her in any way, he had been generous, even-tempered, and had no apparent vices; he was simply an unemotional man who preferred his own interests and his own company. Surely that was the position of many married women, and nothing to warrant serious complaint, let alone violence.

He thanked her, promised her again that he would not cease to do all he could for her mother, right to the last possible moment, then took his leave with a deep regret that he could offer her no real comfort.

He was outside on the warm pavement in the sun when the sudden fragrance of lilac in bloom made him stop so abruptly a messenger boy moving along the curb nearly fell over him. The smell, the brightness of the light and the warmth of the paving stones woke in him a feeling of such intense loneliness, as if he had just this moment lost something, or realized it was beyond his reach when he had thought it his, that he found his heart pounding and his breath caught in his throat.

But why? Who? Whose closeness, whose friendship or love had he lost? How? Had they betrayed him—or he them? He had a terrible fear that it was he who had betrayed them!

One answer he knew already, as soon as the question formed in his mind—it was the woman whom he had tried to defend from a charge of killing her husband. The woman with the fair hair and dark amber eyes. That was certain: but only that—no more.

He must find out! If he had investigated the case then there would be police records of it: names, dates, places—conclusions. He would find out who the woman was and what had happened to her, if possible what they had felt for each other, and why it had ended.

He moved forward with a fresh, determined stride. Now he had purpose. At the end of Albany Street he turned into the Euston Road and within a few minutes had hailed a cab. There was only one course open. He would find Evan and get him to search through the records for the case.

But it was not so easy. He was not able to contact Evan until early in the evening, when he came back tired and dispirited from a fruitless chase after a man who had embezzled a fortune and fled with it across the Channel. Now began the burdensome business of contacting the French police to apprehend him.

When Monk caught up with Evan leaving the police station on his way home, Evan was sufficiently generous of spirit to be pleased to see him, but he was obviously tired and discouraged. For once Monk put his own concern out of his immediate mind, and simply walked in step with Evan for some distance, listening to his affairs, until Evan, knowing him well, eventually asked why he had come.

Monk pulled a face.

"For help," he acknowledged, skirting his way around an old woman haggling with a coster.

"The Carlyon case?" Evan asked, stepping back onto the pavement.

"No—quite different. Have you eaten?"

"No. Given up on the Carlyon case? It must be coming to trial soon."

"Care to have dinner with me? There's a good chophouse 'round the corner."

Evan smiled, suddenly illuminating his face. "I'd love to. What is it you want, if it's not the Carlyons?"

229

"I haven't given up on it, I'm still looking. But this is a case in the past, something I worked on before the accident."

Evan was startled, his eyes widened. "You remember!"

"No—oh, I remember more, certainly. Bits and pieces keep coming back. But I can remember a woman charged with murdering her husband, and I was trying to solve the case, or to be more precise, I was trying to clear her."

They turned the corner into Goodge Street and halfway along came to the chophouse. Inside was warm and busy, crowded with clerks and businessmen, traders and men of the minor professions, all talking together and eating, a clatter of knives, forks, chink of plates and the pleasant steam of hot food.

Monk and Evans were conducted to a table and took their seats, giving their orders without reference to a menu. For a moment an old comfort settled over Monk. It was like the best of the past, and for all the pleasure of being rid of Runcorn, he realized how lonely he was without the comradeship of Evan, and how anxious he was lurching from one private case to another, with never the certainty of anything further, and only a week or two's money in hand.

"What is it?" Evan asked, his young face full of interest and concern. "Do you need to find the case because of Mrs. Carlyon?"

"No." Monk did not even think of being dishonest with him, and yet he was self-conscious about exposing his vulnerability. "I keep getting moments of memory so sharp, I know I cared about it profoundly. It is simply for myself; I need to know who she was, and what happened to her." He watched Evan's face for pity, dreading it.

"Her?" Evan said casually.

"The woman." Monk looked down at the white tablecloth. "She keeps coming back into my mind, obscuring what I am thinking of at the time. It is my past, part of my life I need to reclaim. I must find the case."

"Of course." If Evan felt any curiosity or compassion he hid it, and Monk was profoundly grateful.

Their meals arrived and they began to eat, Monk with indifference, Evan hungrily.

"All right," Evan said after a few moments, when the edge of his appetite had been blunted. "What do you want me to do?"

Monk had already thought of this carefully. He did not want to ask more of Evan than he had to, or to place him in an intolerable position.

"Look through the files of my past cases and see which ones fit the possibilities. Then give me what information you can, and I'll retrace my steps. Find whatever witnesses there still are available, and I'll find her."

Evan put some meat in his mouth and chewed thoughtfully. He did not point out that he was not permitted to do this, or what Runcorn would say if he found out, or even that it would be necessary to practice a certain amount of deception to his colleagues in order to obtain such files. They both knew it. Monk was asking a very considerable favor. It would be indelicate to make it obvious, and Evan was not an unkind man, but a small smile did curl the corners of his sensitive mouth, and Monk saw it and understood. His resentment died even as it was born. It was grossly unfair.

Evan swallowed.

"What do you know about her?" he asked, reaching for his glass of cider.

"She was young," Monk began, saw the flash of humor in Evan's face, and went on as if he had not. "Fair hair, brown eyes. She was accused of murdering her husband, and I was investigating the case. That's all. Except I must have spent some time on it, because I knew her quite well—and I cared about her."

Evan's laughter died completely, replaced by a complexity of expression which Monk knew was an attempt to hide his sympathy. It was ridiculous, and sensitive, and admirable. And from anyone else Monk would have loathed it.

"I'll find all the cases that answer these criteria," Evan promised. "I can't bring the files, but I'll write down the details that matter and tell you the outline."

"When?"

"Monday evening. That will be my first chance. Can't tell you what time. This chop is very good." He grinned. "You can give me dinner here again, and I'll tell you what I know."

"I'm obliged," Monk said with a very faint trace of sarcasm, but he meant it more than it was easy for him to say.

"There's the first," Evan said the following Monday evening, passing a folded piece of paper across the table to Monk. They were sitting in the cheerful hubbub of the chophouse with waiters, diners and steaming food all around them. "Margery Worth, accused of murdering her husband by poison in order to run off with a younger man." Evan pulled a face. "I'm afraid I don't know what the result of the trial was. Our records only show that the evidence you collected was pretty good, but not conclusive. I'm sorry."

"You said the first." Monk took the paper. "There are others?"

"Two more. I only had the time to copy one of them, and that is only the bare outline, you know. Phyllis Dexter. She was accused of killing her husband with a carving knife." He shrugged expressively. "She claimed it was self-defense. From what you have in your notes there is no way of telling whether it was or not, nor what you thought of it. Your feelings are plain enough; you sympathized with her and thought he deserved all he got. But that doesn't mean that she told the truth."

"Any notes on the verdict?" Monk tried to keep the excitement out of his voice. This sounded as if it could be the case about which he cared so much, if only by reading his notes from the file Evan could sense the emotion through it. "What happened to her? How long ago was it?"

"No idea what happened to her," Evan replied with a rueful smile. "Your notes didn't say, and I didn't dare ask anyone in case they realized what I was doing. I had no reason to know."

"Of course. But when did it happen? It must have been dated."

"1853."

"And the other one, Margery Worth?"

"1854." Evan passed over the second piece of paper. "There is everything in there I could copy in the time. All the places and principal people you interviewed."

"Thank you." Monk meant it and did not know how to say it without being clumsy, and embarrassing Evan. "I . . ."

"Good," Evan said quickly with a grin. "So you should. What about getting me another mug of cider?"

The next morning, with an unusual mixture of excitement and fear, Monk set off on the train for Suffolk and the village of Yoxford. It was a brilliant day, sky with white towers of cloud in the sunlight, fields rolling in green waves from the carriage windows, hedges burgeoning with drifts of hawthorn blossoms. He wished he could be out to walk among it and smell the wild, sweet odor of it, instead of in this steaming, belching, clanking monster roaring through the countryside on a late spring morning.

But he was driven by a compulsion, and the only thatched village nestling against the folded downs or half hidden by its trees which held any interest for him was the one which might yield up his past, and the woman who haunted him.

He had read Evan's notes as soon as he got to his rooms the previous evening. He tried this one first simply because it was the closer of the two. The second lay in Shrewsbury, and would be a full day's journey away, and since Shrewsbury was a far larger town, might be harder to trace now it was three years old.

The notes on Margery Worth told a simple story. She was a handsome young woman, married some eight years to a man nearly twice her age. One October morning she had reported to the local doctor that her husband had died in the night, she knew not how. He had made no disturbance and she was a heavy sleeper and had been in the next room since she had taken a chill and did not wish to waken him with her sneezing.

The doctor duly called around with expressions of sympathy, and pronounced that Jack Worth was indeed dead, but he was unsatisfied as to the cause. The body was removed and a second opinion called for. The second opinion, from a doctor in Saxmundham, some four and a half miles away, was of the view that Jack Worth had not died naturally but of some poison. However he could not be certain, he could not name the poison, nor could he state positively when it had been administered, and still less by whom.

The local police had been called in, and confessed themselves confused. Margery was Jack Worth's second wife, and he had two grown sons by the first who stood to inherit the farm, which was of considerable size, and extremely fertile. Margery was to have the house for the duration of her life, or until she remarried, and a small income, barely sufficient to survive.

Scotland Yard was sent for. Monk had arrived on November 1, 1854. He had immediately seen the local police, then had interviewed Margery herself, the first doctor, the second doctor, both the surviving sons, and several other neighbors and shopkeepers. Evan had not been able to make copies of any of his questions, or their answers, only the names, but it would be sufficient to retrace his steps, and the villagers would doubtless remember a great deal about a celebrated murder only three years old.

The journey took him rather more than two hours, and he alighted at the small station and walked the road some three quarters of a mile back to the village. There was one main street stretching westward, with shops and a public house, and as far as he could see only one side street off it. It was a little early for luncheon, but not at all inappropriate to go to the public house and have a glass of cider.

He was greeted with silent curiosity and it was ten minutes before the landlord finally spoke to him.

"Mornin', Mr. Monk. What be you doin' back 'ere, then? We in't 'ad no more murders you know."

"I'm glad to hear it," Monk said conversationally. "I'm sure one is enough."

"More'n so," the landlord agreed.

Another few minutes passed in silence. Two more men came in, hot and thirsty, bare arms brown from the wind and sun, eyes blinking in the interior darkness after the brilliance outside. No one left.

"So what you 'ere for then?" the landlord said at last.

"Tidying up a few things," Monk replied casually.

The landlord eyed him suspiciously. "Like wot, then? Poor Margery 'anged. Wot else is there to do?"

That was the last question answered first, and brutally. Monk felt a sick chill, as if something had slipped out of his grasp already. And yet the name meant nothing to him. He could vaguely recall this street, but what use was that? There was no question that he had been here; the question was, was Margery Worth the woman he had cared about so intensely? How could he find out? Only her form, her face would tell him, and they were destroyed with her life on the gallows rope.

"A few questions must be asked," he said as noncommittally as he could, but his throat was tight and his heart raced, and yet he felt cold. Was that why he could not remember—bitter dreadful failure? Was it pride that had blocked it out, and the woman who had died with it?

"I want to retrace some of my steps and be sure I recall it rightly." His voice was husky and the excuse sounded lame even as he said it.

" 'Oo's asking?" The landlord was wary.

Monk compromised the truth. "Their lordships in London. That's all I can say. Now if you'll excuse me, I'll go and see if the doctor's still about."

" 'E's still about." The landlord shook his head. "But ol' Doc Sillitoe from Saxmundham's dead now. Fell off 'is 'orse and cracked 'is 'ead wide open."

"I'm sorry to hear it." Monk went out and turned left along the road, trusting memory and good luck would find the right house for him. Everyone knew where the doctor lived.

He spent that day and the following one in Yoxford. He spoke to the doctor and to both Jack Worth's sons, now in possession of his farm; the police constable, who greeted him with fear and embarrassment, eager to please him even now;

and to his landlord for the night. He learned much about his first investigation which was not recorded in his notes, but none of it struck any chord in memory except a vague familiarity with a house or a view along a street, a great tree against the sky or the wave of the land. There was nothing sharp, no emotion except a sort of peace at the beauty of the place, the calm skies filled with great clouds sailing across the width of heaven in towers like splashed and ruffled snow, the green of the land, deep huddled oaks and elms, the hedges wide, tangled with wild roses and dappled with cow parsley that some of the locals called ladies' lace. The may blossom was heavy and its rich scent reached out and clung around him. The flowering chestnuts raised myriad candles to the sun, and already the corn was springing green and strong.

But it was utterly impersonal. He felt no lurch of emotion, no tearing inside that loss or drowning loneliness was ahead.

His retraced footsteps taught him that he had been hard on the local constable, critical of the inability to collect evidence and deduce facts from it. He rued his harsh words but it was too late to undo them now. He did not know exactly what he had said; only the man's nervousness and his repeated apologies, his eagerness to please made the past obvious. Why had he been so harsh? He might have been accurate, but it was unnecessary, and had not made the man a better detective, only hurt him. What did he need to be a detective for, here in a tiny village where the worst he would deal with would be a few drunken quarrels, a little poaching, the occasional petty theft? But to apologize now would be absurd, and do no good. The harm was done. He could not ease his conscience with belated patronage.

It was from the local doctor, unprepared to see him back, and full of respect, that he learned how unremitting had been his pursuit of the case and how his attention to detail, his observation of mannerisms and subtle, intuitive guesses had finally learned the poison used, the unsuspected lover who had driven Margery to rid herself of her husband, and sent her to her own early death.

"Brilliant," the doctor had said again, shaking his head.

"Brilliant, you were, and no mistake. Never used to 'ave time for Lunnon folk myself, before that. But you surely showed us a thing or two." He eyed Monk with interest untouched by liking. "And bought that picture from Squire Leadbetter for a pretty penny. Spent your money like you 'ad no end of it, you did. Folks still talk about it."

"Bought the picture . . . ?" Monk frowned, trying to recall. There was no picture of any great beauty among his things. Had he given it to the woman?

"Lord bless me, don't you remember?" The doctor looked amazed, his sandy eyebrows raised in incredulity. "Cost more'n I make in a month, it did, an' no mistake. I suppose you were that pleased with yourself in your case. An' it was a clever piece o' work, I'll give you that. We all knew no one else could 'ave done it, an' p'raps the poor creature got all she deserved, God forgive 'er."

And that was the final seal on his disappointment. If he had gone out and committed some extravagance, of which he now had no trace, to celebrate his success in the case, he could hardly have anguished over Margery Worth's death. This was another ruthlessly brilliant case for Inspector Monk, but it was no clue to the woman who trespassed again and again into his mind these days, who intruded when he thought of Alexandra Carlyon, and who stirred in him such memories of loneliness, of hope, and of having struggled so hard to help her, and not knowing now whether he had failed or succeeded, or how—or even why.

It was late. He thanked the doctor, stayed one more night, and on the morning of Thursday the eleventh, caught the earliest train back to London. He was tired not by physical effort, but by disappointment and a crowding sense of guilt, because he had less than two weeks left before the trial, and he had wasted over two days pursuing a wild goose of his own. Now he still had no idea why Alexandra had killed the general, or what he could tell Oliver Rathbone to help him.

In the afternoon he used the permission Rathbone had obtained for him and went again to the prison to see Alexandra. Even as he was going in the vast gates and the gray walls towered over him, he had little idea what he could say to her beyond what he or Rathbone had already said, but he had to try at least one more time. It was June 11, and on June 22 the trial was to begin.

Was this history repeating itself—another fruitless attempt with time running out, scrambling for evidence to save a woman from her own acts?

He found her in the same attitude, sitting on the cot, shoulders hunched, staring at the wall but seeing something in her own mind. He wished he knew what it was.

"Mrs. Carlyon . . ."

The door slammed behind him and they were alone.

She looked up, a slight flicker of surprise over her face as she recognized him. If she had expected anyone, it must have been Rathbone. She was thinner than last time, wearing the same blouse, but the fabric of it pulled tighter, showing the bones of her shoulders. Her face was very pale. She did not speak.

"Mrs. Carlyon, we have only a short time left. It is too late to deal in pleasantries and evasions. Only the truth will serve now."

"There is only one truth that matters, Mr. Monk," she said wearily. "And that is that I killed my husband. There are no other truths they will care about. Please don't pretend otherwise. It is absurd—and doesn't help."

He stood still in the middle of the small stone floor, staring down at her.

"They might care why you did it!" he said with a hard edge to his voice, "if you stopped lying about it. You are not mad. There was some reason behind it. Either you had a quarrel there at the top of the stairs, and you lunged at him and pushed him over backwards, and then when he fell you were still so possessed with rage you ran down the stairs after him and as he lay on the floor, tangled in the suit of armor in its pieces, you picked up the halberd and finished him off." He watched her face and saw her eyes widen and her mouth wince, but she did not look away from him. "Or else you planned it beforehand and led him to the stairs deliberately, intending to push him over. Perhaps you hoped he would break his neck in the fall, and you went down after him to make sure he had. Then when you found he was relatively unhurt, you used the halberd to do what the fall had failed to.''

''You are wrong,'' she said flatly. ''I didn't think of it until we were standing at the top of the stairs—oh, I wanted to find a way. I meant to kill him some time, I just hadn't thought of the stairs until then. And when he stood there at the top, with his back to the banister and that drop behind him, and I knew he would never . . .'' She stopped and the flicker of light which had been in her blue eyes died. She looked away from him.

''I pushed him,'' she went on. ''And when he went over and hit the armor I thought he was dead. I went down quite slowly. I thought it was the end, all finished. I expected people to come, because of the noise of the armor going over. I was going to say he fell—overbalanced.'' Her face showed a momentary surprise. ''But no one came. Not even any of the servants, so I suppose no one heard after all. When I looked at him, he was senseless, but he was still alive. His breathing was quite normal.'' She sighed and the muscles of her jaw tightened. ''So I picked up the halberd and ended it. I knew I would never have a better chance. But you are wrong if you think I planned it. I didn't—not then or in that way.''

He believed her. He had no doubt that what she said was the truth.

''But why?'' he said again. ''It wasn't over Louisa Furnival, or any other woman, was it?''

She stood up and turned her back to him, staring at the tiny single window, high in the wall and barred against the sky.

''It doesn't matter.''

''Have you ever seen anyone hanged, Mrs. Carlyon?'' It was brutal, but if he could not reason her into telling him, then there was little left but fear. He hated doing it. He saw her body tighten and the hands by her sides clench. Had he done this before? It brought no memory. Everything in his mind was Alexandra, the present, the death of Thaddeus Carlyon and no one else, no other time or place. "It's an ugly thing. They don't always die immediately. They take you from the cell to the yard where the noose is . . ." He swallowed hard. Execution repelled him more than any other act he knew of, because it was sanctioned by law. People would contemplate it, commit it, watch it and feel justified. They would gather together in groups and congratulate each other on its completion and say that they upheld civilization.

She stood without moving, thin and slight, her body painfully rigid.

"They lay the rope 'round your neck, after they have put a hood over your head, so you can't see it—that's what they say it is for. Actually I think it is so they cannot see you. Perhaps if they could look at your face, your eyes, they couldn't do it themselves."

"Stop it!" she said between her teeth. "I know I will hang. Do you have to tell me every step to the gallows rope so I do it more than once in my mind?"

He wanted to shake her, to reach out and take her by the arms, force her to turn around and face him, look at him. But it would only be an assault, pointless and stupid, perhaps closing the last door through which he might yet find something to help her.

"Did you try to stab him once before?" he asked suddenly.

She looked startled. "No! Whatever makes you think that?"

"The knife wound in his thigh."

"Oh that. No—he did that himself, showing off for Valentine Furnival."

"I see."

She said nothing.

"Is it blackmail?" he said quietly. "Is there someone who holds some threat over you?"

"No."

"Tell me! Perhaps we can stop them. At least let me try."

240

"There is no one. What more could anyone do to me than the law will already do?"

"Nothing to you—but to someone you love? Sabella?"

"No." There was a lift in her voice, almost like a bitter laugh, had she the strength left for it.

He did not believe her. Was this it at last? She was prepared to die to protect Sabella, in some way they had not yet imagined.

He looked at her stiff back and knew she would not tell him. He would still have to find out, if he could. There were twelve days left before the trial.

"I won't stop trying," he said gently. "You'll not hang if I can prevent it—whether you wish me to or not. Good day, Mrs. Carlyon."

"Good-bye, Mr. Monk."

That evening Monk dined with Evan again and told him of his abortive trip to Suffolk, and Evan gave him notes of one more case which might have been the woman he had tried so hard to save. But tonight his mind was still on Alexandra, and the incomprehensible puzzle she presented.

The following day he went to Vere Street and told Oliver Rathbone of his interview in the prison, and his new thoughts. Rathbone was surprised, and then after a moment's hesitation, more hopeful than he had been for some time. It was at least an idea which made some sense.

That evening he opened the second set of notes Evan had given him and looked at them. This was the case about Phyllis Dexter, of Shrewsbury, who had knifed her husband to death. The Shrewsbury police had had no trouble establishing the facts. Adam Dexter was a large man, a heavy drinker and known to get into the occasional brawl, but no one had heard that he had beaten his wife, or in any other way treated her more roughly than most men. Indeed, he seemed in his own way quite fond of her.

On his death the local police had been puzzled as to how they might prove, one way or the other, whether Phyllis was speaking the truth. All their efforts, expended over the first week, had left them no wiser than at the beginning. They had sent for Scotland Yard, and Runcorn had dispatched Monk.

The notes were plain that Monk had interviewed Phyllis herself, immediate neighbors who might have heard a quarrel or threat, the doctor who had examined the body, and of course the local police.

Apparently he had remained in Shrewsbury for three weeks, going relentlessly over and over the same ground until he found a weakness here, a change of emphasis there, the possibility of a different interpretation or a shred of new evidence. Runcorn had sent for him to come back; everything they had indicated guilt, and justice should be allowed to take its course, but Monk had defied him and remained.

Eventually he had pieced together a story, with the most delicate of proof, that Phyllis Dexter had had three miscarriages and two stillbirths, and had eventually refused her husband's attentions because she could no longer bear the pain it caused her. In a drunken fury at her rejection, as if it were of him, not of her pain, he had attempted to force her. On this occasion his sense of outrage had driven him to assault her with the broken end of a bottle, and she had defended herself with the carving knife. In his clumsiness he had got the worst of the brief battle, and within moments of his first charge, he lay dead on the floor, the knife in his chest and the broken bottle shattered—a scatter of shards over the floor.

There was no note as to the outcome of the case. Whether the Shrewsbury police had accepted Monk's deduction or not was not noted. Nor was there any record as to a trial.

There was nothing for Monk to do but purchase a ticket and take the train to Shrewsbury. The people there at least would remember such a case, even if few others did.

On the late afternoon of the thirteenth, in golden sunlight, Monk alighted at Shrewsbury station and made his way through the ancient town with its narrow streets and magnificent Elizabethan half-timbered houses to the police station.

The desk sergeant's look of polite enquiry turned to one of wary self-defense, and Monk knew he had been recognized, and not with pleasure. He felt himself harden inside, but he could not justify himself because he had no memory of what he had done. It was a stranger with his face who had been here four years before.

"Well, Mr. Monk, I'm sure I don't know," the desk sergeant said to his enquiry. "That case is all over and done with. We thought as she was guilty, but you proved as she weren't! It's not for us to say, but it don't do for a woman to go murderin' 'er 'usband because she takes it into 'er 'ead as to refuse 'im what's 'is by right. Puts ideas of all sorts in women's 'eads. We'll have them murderin' their 'usbands all over the place!"

"You're quite right," Monk said tartly.

The desk sergeant looked surprised, and pleased.

"It's not for you to say," Monk finished.

The sergeant's face tightened and his skin flushed red.

"Well I don't know what you'll be wanting from us. If you'd be so good as to tell me, I'll mebbe see what I can do for you."

"Do you know where Phyllis Dexter is now?" Monk asked.

The sergeant's eyes lit with satisfaction.

"Yes I do. She left these parts right after the trial. Acquitted, she was; walked out o' the courtroom and packed 'er things that night."

"Do you know where she went?" Monk kept his temper with difficulty. He would like to wipe the smug smile off the man's face.

The man's satisfaction wavered. He met Monk's eyes and his courage drained away.

"Yes sir. I heard as it were somewhere in France. I don't rightly know where, but there's them in the town as can tell you, I expect. At least where she went to from 'ere. As to where she is now, I expect being the detective you are, you'll be able to learn that when you get there."

There was nothing more to be learned here, so Monk duly thanked him and took his leave.

He spent the evening at the Bull Inn and in the morning went to find the doctor who had been concerned in the case. He went with some trepidation. Apparently he had made himself unpopular here; the desk sergeant's aggression had been born of those weeks of fear and probably some humiliation as well. Monk knew his own behavior at his station in London under Runcorn, his sarcastic tongue, his impatience with men of less ability than himself. He was not proud of it.

He walked down the street where the doctor's house was and found with a sharp sense of satisfaction that he knew it. The particular pattern of beams and plastering was familiar. There was no need to look for the name or a number; he could remember being here before.

With excitement catching in his throat he knocked on the door. It seemed an age before it was answered by an aged man with a game leg. Monk could hear it dragging on the floor. His white hair was thinly plastered across his skull and his teeth were broken, but his face lit with pleasure as soon as his eyes focused on Monk.

"My, if it in't Mr. Monk back again!" he said in a cracked falsetto voice. "Well bless my soul! What brings you back to these parts? We in't 'ad no more murders! Least, not that I knows of. 'Ave we?"

"No Mr. Wraggs, I don't think so." Monk was elated to an absurd degree that the old man was so pleased to see him, and that he in turn could recall his name. "I'm here on a private matter, to see the doctor, if I may?"

"Ah no, sir." Wraggs's face fell. "You're never poorly, are you, sir? Come in and set yourself down, then. I'll get you a drop o' summink!"

"No, no, Mr. Wraggs, I'm very well, thank you," Monk said hastily. "I just want to see him as a friend, not professionally."

"Ah, well." The old man breathed a sigh of relief. "That's all right then! Still, come on in just the same. Doctor's out on a call right now, but 'e'll be back by an' by. Now what can I get you, Mr. Monk? You just name it, and if we got it, it's yours."

It would have been churlish to refuse so generous an offer.

"Well, I'll have a glass of cider, and a slice of bread and cheese, if you've got it," he accepted.

" 'Course we got it!" Wraggs said delightedly, and led the way in, hobbling lopsidedly ahead of Monk into the parlor.

Monk wondered with a silent blessing what kindness he had shown this old man that he was so welcome here, but he could not ask. He hoped profoundly it was not simply the old man's nature that was so blithely giving, and he was glad he could not put it to the test. Instead he accepted the hospitality and sat talking with him for well over an hour until the doctor returned. Actually in that space he learned from him almost all he wished to know. Phyllis Dexter had been a very pretty woman with soft honey-brown hair and golden brown eyes, a gentle manner and a nice wit. Opinion in the town had been violently divided about her innocence or guilt. The police had felt her guilty, as had the mayor and many of the gentry. The doctor and the parson had taken her side, so had the innkeeper, who had had more than enough of Adam Dexter's temper and sullen complaints. Wraggs was emphatic that Monk himself had pursued his enquiries night and day, bullying, exhorting, pleading with witnesses, driving himself to exhaustion, sitting up into the small hours of the morning poring over the statements and the evidence till his eyes were red.

"She owes 'er life to you, Mr. Monk, and no mistake," Wraggs said with wide eyes. "A rare fighter you were. No woman, nor man neither, ever had a better champion in their cause, I'll swear to that on my Bible oath, I will."

"Where did she go to, Mr. Wraggs, when she left here?"

"Ah, that she didn't tell no one, poor soul!" Wraggs shook his head. "An' who can blame 'er, I ask you, after what some folk said."

Monk's heart sank. After the hope, the warmth of Wraggs's welcome and the sudden sight of some better part of himself, it had all slipped away again.

"You've no idea?" He was horrified to hear a catch in his voice.

"No sir, none at all." Wraggs peered at him with anxiety

and sorrow in his old eyes. "Thanked you with tears, she did, an' then just packed 'er things and went. Funny, you know, but I thought as you knew where she'd gone, 'cause I 'ad a feeling as you 'elped her go! But there, I suppose I must a' bin wrong."

"France—the desk sergeant in the police station said he thought it was France."

"Well I shouldn't wonder." Wraggs nodded his head. "Poor lady would want to be out o' England, now wouldn't she, after all what folks said about 'er!"

"If she went south, who would know where she was?" Monk said reasonably. "She would take a new name and be lost in the crowd."

"Ah no sir, not hardly. Not with the pictures of her in the newspapers! An' 'andsome as she was, people'd soon see the likeness. No, better she go abroad. And I for one hopes she's found a place for 'erself."

"Pictures?"

"Yes sir—all in the illustrated news they was. Here, don't you remember? I'll get it for you. We kept them all." And without waiting for Monk he scrambled to his feet and went over to the desk in the corner. He rummaged around for several minutes, then came back proudly holding a piece of paper which he put in front of Monk.

It was a clear picture of a remarkably pretty woman of perhaps twenty-five or twenty-six, with wide eyes and a long, delicate face. Seeing it he remembered her quite clearly. Emotion came back: pity, some admiration, anger at the pain she had endured and at people's ignorance and refusal to understand it, determination that he would see her acquitted, intense relief when he had succeeded, and a quiet happiness. But nothing more; no love, no despair—no haunting, persistent memory.

8

By JUNE 15 there was a bare week to go before the trial commenced and the newspapers had again taken up the subject. There was much speculation as to what would be revealed, surprise witnesses for the defense, for the prosecution, revelations about character. Thaddeus Carlyon had been a hero, and his murder in such circumstances shocked people profoundly. There must be some explanation which would provide an answer and restore the balance of their beliefs.

Hester dined again at the Carlyon house, not because she was considered a close enough friend of the family to be welcome even at such a time, but because it was she who had recommended Oliver Rathbone, and they all now wished to know something more about him and what he was likely to do to try and defend Alexandra.

It was an uncomfortable meal. Hester had accepted although she could not tell them anything of Rathbone, except his integrity and his past success, which presumably at least Peverell already knew. But she still hoped she might learn some tiny shred of fact which would, together with other things, lead to Alexandra's true motive. Anything about the general surely ought to be useful in some fashion?

"I wish I knew more about this man Rathbone," Randolf

said morosely, staring down the length of the table at no one in particular. "Who is he? Where does he come from?"

"What on earth does that matter, Papa?" Edith said, blinking at him. "He's the best there is. If anyone can help Alexandra, he will."

"Help Alexandra!" He faced her angrily, his eyes wide, his brows furrowed. "My dear girl, Alexandra murdered your brother because she had some insane idea he was amorously involved with another woman. If he had been, she should have borne it like a lady and kept her silence, but as we all know, he was not." His voice was thick with distress. "There is nothing in the world more unbecoming in a woman than jealousy. It has been the curse of many an otherwise more than acceptable character. That she should carry it to the extreme of murder, and against one of the finest men of his generation, is a complete tragedy."

"What we need to know," Felicia said very quietly, "is what kind of implications and suggestions he is likely to make to try and defend her." She turned to Hester. "You are familiar with the man, Miss Latterly." She caught Damaris's eye. "I beg your pardon," she said stiffly. "*Familiar* was an unfortunate choice of word. That was not what I intended." She blinked; her wide eyes were cold and direct. "You are sufficiently acquainted with him to have recommended him to us. To what degree can you answer for his . . . his moral decency? Can you assure us that he will not attempt to slander our son's character in order to make there seem to be some justification for his wife having murdered him?"

Hester was taken aback. This was not what she had expected, but after only an instant's thought she appreciated their view. It was not a foolish question.

"I am not answerable for his conduct in any way, Mrs. Carlyon," she replied gravely. "He is not employed by any of us here, but by Alexandra herself." She was acutely conscious of Felicia's grief. The fact that she could not like her did not lessen her awareness of its reality, or her pity for it. "But it would not be in her interest to make any charge against the general that could not be substantiated with proof," she went on. "I believe it would predispose the jury against her. But quite apart from that, had the general been the most totally wretched, inconsiderate, coarse and vile man, unless he threatened her life, or that of her child, it would be pointless to raise it, because it would be no excuse for killing him."

Felicia sat back in her chair, her face calmer.

"That is good, and I presume in the circumstances, certainly all we can hope for. If he has any sense, he will claim she is insane and throw her on the mercy of the court." She swallowed hard and her chin lifted; her eyes were wide and very blue. She looked ahead of her, at no one. "Thaddeus was a considerate man, a gentleman in every way." Her voice was harsh with emotion. "He never raised a hand against her, even when at times she sorely provoked him. And I know she did. She has been flighty, inconsiderate, and refused to understand the necessity of his leaving her when his career took him abroad in the life to which he dedicated himself for the service of his Queen and country."

"You should see some of the letters of condolence we have received," Randolf added with a sigh. "Only this morning one came from a sergeant who used to be in the Indian army with him. Just heard, poor fellow. Devastated. Said Thaddeus was the finest officer he ever served with. Spoke of his courage, his inspiration to the men." He blinked hard and his head sank a little lower. His voice became thicker, and Hester was not sure whether it was purely from grief or grief mixed with self-pity. "Said how he had kept all the men cheerful when they were pinned down by a bunch of savages, howling like demons." He was staring into the distance as if he saw not the sideboard with the elaborate Coalport china on it, but some baking plain under an Indian sun. "Almost out of ammunition, they were, and waiting to die. Said Thaddeus gave them heart, made them proud to be British and give their lives for the Queen." He sighed again.

Peverell smiled sadly. Edith pulled a face, partly sorrow, partly embarrassment.

"That must be a great comfort to you," Hester said, then

found it sounded hollow the moment her words were out. "I mean to know that he was so admired."

"We knew it anyway," Felicia said without looking at her. "Everyone admired Thaddeus. He was a leader among men. His officers thought he was a hero, his troops would follow him anywhere. Had the gift of command, you see?" She looked at Hester, eyes wide. "He knew how to inspire loyalty because he was always fair. He punished cowardice and dishonesty; he praised courage and honor, and duty. He never denied a man his right, and never charged a man unless he was sure that man was guilty. He kept total discipline, but the men loved him for it."

"Have to in the army," Randolf added, glaring at Hester. "Do you know what happens when there is no discipline, girl? Army falls to pieces under fire. Every man for himself. Un-British! Frightful! A soldier must obey his superior at all times—instantly."

"Yes I do know," Hester said without thinking, but from the depth of her own feeling. "Sometimes it's glorious, and sometimes it's unmitigated disaster."

Randolf's face darkened. "What the devil do you mean, girl? What on earth do you know about it? Damned impertinence! I'll have you know I fought in the Peninsular War, and at Waterloo against the emperor of the French, and beat him too."

"Yes, Colonel Carlyon." She met his eyes without flinching. She felt a pity for him as a man; he was old, bereaved, muddle-headed and becoming more than a little maudlin. But soldierlike she stood her ground. "And magnificent campaigns they were, none more brilliant in all our history. But times have changed. And some of our commanders have not changed with them. They fought the Crimea with the same tactics, and they were not good enough. A soldier's blind obedience is only as good as his commander's knowledge of the situation and skill in combat."

"Thaddeus was brilliant," Felicia said icily. "He never lost a major campaign and no soldier forfeited his life because of any incompetence of his."

250

"Certainly not," Randolf added, and slid a fraction farther down in his seat, hiccuping.

"We all know he was a very good soldier, Papa," Edith said quietly. "And I am glad that men who served with him have written to say how grieved they are he is gone. It is a wonderful thing to have been so admired."

"He was more than admired," Felicia said quickly. "He was also loved."

"The obituaries have been excellent," Peverell put in. "Few men have had their passing marked by such respect."

"It is appalling that this whole disaster was ever allowed to progress this far," Felicia said with a tight expression in her face, blinking as if to avoid tears.

"I don't know what you mean." Damaris looked at her perplexedly. "Progress to what?"

"To trial, of course." Felicia's face puckered with anger and distress. "It should have been dealt with long before it ever got so far." She turned to Peverell. "I blame you for that. I expected you to cope with it and see that Thaddeus's memory was not subjected to vulgar speculation; and that Alexandra's madness, and it must be said, wickedness, was not made a public sensation for the worst elements of humanity to revel in. As a lawyer, you should have been able to do it, and as a member of this family, I would have thought your loyalty to us would have seen that you did."

"That's unfair," Damaris said immediately, her face hot and her eyes bright. "Just because one is a lawyer does not mean one can do anything one likes with the law. In fact just the opposite. Peverell has a trust towards the law, an obligation, which none of the rest of us have. I don't know what you think he could have done!"

"I think he could have certified Alexandra as insane and unfit to stand trial," Felicia snapped. "Instead of encouraging her to get a lawyer who will drag all our lives before the public and expose all our most private emotions to the gaze of the common people so they can decide something we all know anyway—that Alexandra murdered Thaddeus. For God's sake, she doesn't deny it!"

Cassian sat white-faced, his eyes on his grandmother.

"Why?" he said, a very small voice in the silence.

Hester and Felicia spoke at once.

"We don't know," Hester said.

"Because she is sick," Felicia cut across her. She turned to Cassian. "There are sicknesses of the body and sicknesses of the mind. Your mother is ill in her brain, and it caused her to do a very dreadful thing. It is best you try not to think of it, ever again." She reached out towards him tentatively, then changed her mind. "Of course it will be difficult, but you are a Carlyon, and you are brave. Think of your father, what a great man he was and how proud he was of you. Grow up to be like him." For a moment her voice caught, too thick with tears to continue. Then she mastered herself with an effort so profound it was painfully visible. "You can do that. We shall help you, your grandfather and I, and your aunts."

Cassian said nothing, but turned and looked very carefully at his grandfather, his eyes somber. Then slowly he smiled, a shy, uncertain smile, and his eyes filled with tears. He sniffed hard, swallowed, and everyone turned away from him so as not to intrude.

"Will they call him at the trial?" Damaris asked anxiously.

"Of course not." Felicia dismissed the idea as absurd. "What on earth could he know?"

Damaris turned to Peverell, her eyes questioning.

"I don't know," he answered. "But I doubt it."

Felicia stared at him. "Well for heaven's sake do something useful! Prevent it! He is only eight years old!"

"I cannot prevent it, Mama-in-law," he said patiently. "If either the prosecution or the defense wishes to call him, then the judge will decide whether Cassian is competent to give evidence or not. If the judge decides he is, then Cassian will do so."

"You shouldn't have allowed it to come to trial," she repeated furiously. "She has confessed. What good can it do anyone to parade the whole wretched affair before a court? They will hang her anyway." Her eyes hardened and she glanced across the table. "And don't look at me like that, Damaris! The poor child will have to know one day. Perhaps it is better we don't lie to him, and he knows now. But if Peverell had seen to it that she was put away in Bedlam, it wouldn't be necessary to face the problem at all."

"How could he do that?" Damaris demanded. "He isn't a doctor."

"I don't think she is mad anyway," Edith interrupted.

"Be quiet," Felicia snapped. "Nobody wants to know what you think. Why would a sane woman murder your brother?"

"I don't know," Edith admitted. "But she has a right to defend herself. And Peverell, or anyone else, ought to wish that she gets it . . ."

"Your brother should be your first concern," Felicia said grimly. "And the honor of your family your next. I realize you were very young when he first left home and went into the army, but you knew him. You were aware what a brave and honorable man he was." Her voice quivered for the first time in Hester's hearing. "Have you no love in you? Does his memory mean no more to you than some smart intellectual exercise in what is legally this or that? Where is your natural feeling, girl?"

Edith flushed hotly, her eyes miserable.

"I cannot help Thaddeus now, Mama."

"Well you certainly cannot help Alexandra," Felicia added.

"We know Thaddeus was a good man," Damaris said gently. "Of course Edith knows it. But she is a lot younger, and she never knew him as I did. He was always just a strange young man in a soldier's uniform whom everyone praised. But I know how kind he could be, and how understanding. And although he disciplined his men in the army, and made no allowances or bent any rules, with other people he could be quite different, I know. He was . . ." Suddenly she stopped, gave a funny little half smile, half sigh, and bit her lip. There was intense pain in her face. She avoided Peverell's eyes.

"We are aware of your appreciation of your brother, Damaris," Felicia said very quietly. "But I think you have said enough. That particular episode is far better not discussed—I'm sure you agree?"

Randolf looked confused. He started to speak, then stopped again. No one was listening to him anyway.

Edith looked from Damaris to her mother and back again.

Peverell made as if to say something to his wife, but she looked everywhere but at him, and he changed his mind.

Damaris stared at her mother as if some realization almost beyond belief had touched her. She blinked, frowned, and remained staring.

Felicia met her gaze with a small, wry smile, quite unwavering.

Gradually the amazement waned and another even more powerful emotion filled Damaris's long, sensitive, turbulent face, and Hester was almost sure it was fear.

"Ris?" Edith said tentatively. She was confused as to the reason, but aware that her sister was suffering in some fierce, lonely way, and she wanted to help.

"Of course," Damaris said slowly, still staring at her mother. "I wasn't going to discuss it." She swallowed hard. "I was just remembering that Thaddeus could be . . . very kind. It seemed . . . it seemed an appropriate time to—think of it."

"You have thought of it," Felicia pointed out. "It would have been better had you done so silently, but since you have not, I should consider the matter closed, if I were you. We all appreciate your words on your brother's virtues."

"I don't know what you are talking about," Randolf said sulkily.

"Kindness." Felicia looked at him with weary patience. "Damaris is saying that Thaddeus was on occasion extremely kind. It is not always remembered of him, when we are busy saying what a brave soldier he was." Then again without warning emotion flooded her face. "All a man's good qualities should be remembered, not just the public ones," she finished huskily.

"Of course." He frowned at her, aware that he had been sidetracked, but not sure how, still less why. "No one denies it."

Felicia considered the matter sufficiently explained. If he did not understand, it was quite obvious she did not intend to enlighten him. She turned to Hester, her emotion gone, her expression perfectly controlled.

"Miss Latterly. Since, as my husband has said, jealousy is one of the ugliest and least sympathetic of all human emotions, and becomes a woman even less than a man, can you tell us what manner of defense this Mr. Rathbone intends to put forward?" She looked at Hester with the same cool, brave face she might have presented to the judge himself. "I imagine he is not going to be rash enough to attempt to lay the blame elsewhere, and say she did not do it at all?"

"That would be pointless," Hester answered, aware that Cassian was watching her with a guarded, almost hostile expression. "She has confessed, and there is unarguable proof that she did it. The defense must rest in the circumstances, the reason why."

"Indeed." Felicia's eyebrows rose very high. "And just what sort of a reason does this Mr. Rathbone believe would excuse such an act? And how does he propose to prove it?"

"I don't know." Hester faced her pretending a confidence far from anything she felt. "It is not my prerogative to know, Mrs. Carlyon. I have no part in this tragedy, other than as a friend of Edith's, and I hope of yours. I mentioned Mr. Rathbone's name to you before I knew that there was no question that Alexandra was guilty of the act. But even had I known it, I would still have told you, because she needs a lawyer to speak for her, whatever her situation."

"She does not need someone to persuade her to fight a hopeless cause," Felicia said acidly. "Or lead her to imagine that she can avoid her fate. That is an unnecessary cruelty, Miss Latterly, tormenting some poor creature and stringing out its death in order to entertain the crowd!"

Hester blushed hotly, but there was far too much guilt in her for her to find any denial.

It was Peverell who came to her rescue.

"Would you have every accused person put to death quickly, Mama-in-law, to save them the pain of struggle? I doubt that that is what they would choose."

"And how would you know that?" she demanded. "It might well have been exactly what Alexandra would choose. Only you have all taken that opportunity away from her with your interference."

"We offered her a lawyer," Peverell replied, refusing to back away. "We have not told her how to plead."

"Then you should have. Perhaps if she had pleaded guilty then this whole sorry business would be over with. Now we shall have to go into court and conduct ourselves with all the dignity we can muster. I presume you will be testifying, since you were there at that wretched party?"

"Yes. I have no choice."

"For the prosecution?" she enquired.

"Yes."

"Well at least if you go, one imagines Damaris will be spared. That is something. I don't know what you can possibly tell them that will be of use." There was half a question in her voice, and Hester knew, watching her tense face and brilliant eyes, that she was both asking Peverell what he intended saying, and warning him of family loyalties, trusts, unspoken ties that were deeper than any single occasion could test or break.

"Neither do I, Mama-in-law," he agreed. "Presumably only my observations as to who was where at any particular time. And maybe the fact that Alex and Thaddeus did seem to be at odds with each other. And Louisa Furnival took Thaddeus upstairs alone, and Alex seemed extraordinarily upset about it."

"You'll tell them that?" Edith said, horrified.

"I shall have to, if they ask me," he said apologetically. "That is what I saw."

"But Pev—"

He leaned forward. "My dear, they already know it.

256

Maxim and Louisa were there, and they will say that. And Fenton Pole, and Charles and Sarah Hargrave . . .''

Damaris was very pale. Edith buried her face in her hands.

''This is going to be awful.''

''Of course it is going to be awful,'' Felicia said thickly. ''That is the reason why we must think carefully what we are going to say beforehand, speak only the truth, say nothing malicious or undignified, whatever we may feel, answer only what we are asked, exactly and precisely, and at all times remember who we are!''

Damaris swallowed convulsively.

Cassian stared at her with huge eyes, his lips parted.

Randolf sat up a trifle straighter.

''Offer no opinions,'' Felicia continued. ''Remember that the vulgar press will write down everything you say, and quite probably distort it. That you cannot help. But you can most certainly help your deportment, your diction, and the fact that you do not lie, prevaricate, giggle, faint, weep or otherwise disgrace yourself by being less than the ladies you are—or the gentlemen, as the case is. Alexandra is the one who is accused, but the whole family will be on trial.''

''Thank you, my dear.'' Randolf looked at her with a mixture of obligation, gratitude and an awe which for one ridiculous moment Hester imagined was akin to fear. ''As always you have done what is necessary.''

Felicia said nothing. A flicker of pain passed across her rigid features, but it was gone again almost as soon as it was there. She did not indulge in such things; she could not afford to.

''Yes, Mama,'' Damaris said obediently. ''We will all do our best to acquit ourselves with dignity and honesty.''

''You will not be required,'' Felicia said, but there was a slight melting in her tone, and their eyes met for a moment. ''But of course if you choose to attend, you will be noticed, and no doubt some busybody will recognize you as a Carlyon.''

''Will I go, Grandmama?'' Cassian asked, his face troubled.

"No, my dear, you will certainly not go. You will remain here with Miss Buchan."

"Won't Mama expect me to be there?"

"No, she will wish you to be here where you can be comfortable. You will be told all you need to know." She turned away from him to Peverell again and continued to discuss the general's last will and testament. It was a somewhat simple document that needed little explanation, but presumably she chose to argue it as a final closing of any other subject.

Everyone bent to continue with the meal, hitherto eaten entirely mechanically. Indeed Hester had no idea what any of the courses had been or even how many there were.

Now her mind turned to Damaris, and the intense, almost passionate emotion she had seen in her face, the swift play from sorrow to amazement to fear, and then the deep pain.

And according to Monk, several people had said she had behaved in a highly emotional manner on the evening of the general's death, bordering on the edge of hysteria, and been extremely offensive to Maxim Furnival.

Why? Peverell seemed to know nothing of its cause, nor had he been able to comfort her or offer any help at all.

Was it conceivable that she knew there was going to be violence, even murder? Or had she seen it? No—no one else had seen it, and Damaris had been distracted with some deep torment of her own long before Alexandra had followed Thaddeus upstairs. And why the rage at Maxim?

But then if the motive for the murder was something other than the stupid jealousy Alexandra had seized on, perhaps Damaris knew what it was? And knowing it, she might have foreseen it would end as it did.

Why had she said nothing? Why had she not trusted that Peverell and she together might have prevented it? It was perfectly obvious Peverell had no idea what troubled her; the expression in his eyes as he looked at her, the way he half spoke, and then fell silent, were all eloquent witness of that.

Was it the same horror, force, or fear that kept Alexandra silent even in the shadow of the hangman's rope?

In something of a daze Hester left the table and together

with Edith went slowly upstairs to her sitting room. Damaris and Peverell had their own wing of the house, and frequently chose to be there rather than in the main rooms with the rest of the family. Hester thought it was extremely long-suffering of Peverell to live in Carlyon House at all, but possibly he could not afford to keep Damaris in this style, or anything like it, otherwise. It was a curious side to Damaris's character that she did not prefer independence and privacy, at the relatively small price of a modest household, instead of this very lavish one. But then Hester had never been used to luxury, so she did not know how easy it was to become dependent upon it.

As soon as the door was closed in the sitting room Edith threw herself onto the largest sofa and pulled her legs up under her, regardless of the inelegance of the position and the ruination of her skirt. She stared at Hester, her curious face with its aquiline nose and gentle mouth filled with consternation.

"Hester—it's going to be terrible!"

"Of course it is," Hester agreed quietly. "Whatever the result, the trial is going to be ghastly. Someone was murdered. That can only ever be a tragedy, whoever did it, or why."

"Why . . ." Edith hugged her knees and stared at the floor. "We don't even know that, do we." It was not a question.

"We don't," Hester said thoughtfully, watching Edith's face. "But do you think Damaris might?"

Edith jerked up, her eyes wide. "Damaris? Why? How would she? Why do you say that?"

"She knew something that evening. She was almost distracted with emotion—on the verge of hysteria, they said."

"Who said? Pev didn't tell us."

"It doesn't seem as if he knew why," Hester replied. "But according to what Monk was able to find out, from quite early in the evening, long before the general was killed, Damaris was so frantic about something she could barely keep control of herself. I don't know why I didn't think of it before, but maybe she knew why Alexandra did it. Perhaps she even feared it would happen, before it did.''

''But if she knew . . .'' Edith said slowly, her face filled with distress and dawning horror. ''No—she would have stopped it. Are you—are you saying Damaris was part of it?''

''No. No, certainly not,'' Hester denied quickly. ''I mean she may have feared it would happen, because perhaps what caused her to be so terribly upset was the knowledge of why Alexandra would do such a thing. And if it is something so secret that Alexandra would rather hang than tell anyone, then I believe Damaris will honor her feelings and keep the secret for her.''

''Yes,'' Edith agreed slowly, her face very white. ''Yes, she would. It would be her sense of honor. But what could it be? I can't think of anything so—so terrible, so dark that . . .'' She tailed off, unable to find words for the thought.

''Neither can I,'' Hester agreed. ''But it exists—it must—or why will Alexandra not tell us why she killed the general?''

''I don't know.'' Edith bent her head to her knees.

There was a knock on the door, nervous and urgent.

Edith looked up, surprised. Servants did not knock.

''Yes?'' She unwound herself and put her feet down. ''Come in.''

The door opened and Cassian stood there, his face pale, his eyes frightened.

''Aunt Edith, Miss Buchan and Cook are fighting again!'' His voice was ragged and a little high. ''Cook has a carving knife!''

''Oh—'' Edith stifled an unladylike word and rose. Cassian took a step towards her and she put an arm around him. ''Don't worry, I'll take care of it. You stay here. Hester . . .''

Hester was on her feet.

''Come with me, if you don't mind,'' Edith said urgently. ''It may take two of us, if it's as bad as Cass says. Stay here, Cass! It will be all right, I promise!'' And without waiting any further she led the way out of the sitting room, along

260

towards the back landing. Before they had reached the servants' stairs it was only too apparent that Cassian was right.

"You've no place 'ere, yer miserable old biddy! You should a' bin put out ter grass like the dried-up old mare yer are!"

"And you should have been left in the sty in the first place, you fat sow," came back the stinging reply.

"Fat indeed, is it? And what man'd look at you, yer withered old bag o' bones? No wonder yer spend yer life looking after other folks' children! Nobody'd ever get any on you!"

"And where are yours, then? Litters of them. One every season—running around on all fours in the byre, I shouldn't wonder. With snouts for noses and trotters for feet."

"I'll cut yer gizzard out, yer sour old fool! Ah!"

There was a shriek, then laughter.

"Oh damnation!" Edith said exasperatedly. "This sounds worse than usual."

"Missed!" came the crow of delight. "You drunken sot! Couldn't hit a barn door if it was in front of you—you cross-eyed pig!"

"Ah!"

Then a shriek from the kitchen maid and a shout from the footman.

Edith scrambled down the last of the stairs, Hester behind her. Almost immediately they saw them, the upright figure of Miss Buchan coming towards them, half sideways, half backwards, and a couple of yards away the rotund, red-faced cook, brandishing a carving knife in her hand.

"Vinegar bitch!" the cook shouted furiously, brandishing the knife at considerable risk to the footman, who was trying to get close enough to restrain her.

"Wine belly," Miss Buchan retorted, leaning forward.

"Stop it!" Edith shouted sternly. "Stop it at once!"

"Yer want to get rid of 'er." The cook stared at Edith but waved the knife at Miss Buchan. "She's no good for that poor boy. Poor little child."

Behind them the kitchen maid wailed again and stuffed the corners of her apron into her mouth.

"You don't know what you're talking about, you fat fool,"

Miss Buchan shouted back at her, her thin, sharp face full of fury. "All you do is stuff him full of cakes—as if that solved anything."

"Be quiet," Edith said loudly. "Both of you, be quiet at once!"

"And all you do is follow him around, you dried-up old witch!" The cook ignored Edith completely and went on shouting at Miss Buchan. "Never leave the poor little mite alone. I don't know what's the matter with you."

"Don't know," Miss Buchan yelled back at her. "Don't know. Of course you don't know, you stupid old glutton. You don't know anything. You never did."

"Neither do you, you miserable old baggage!" She waved the knife again, and the footman darted backwards, missing his step and overbalancing. "Sit up there all by yourself dreaming evil thoughts," the cook went on, oblivious of the other servants gathering in the passage. "And then come down here to decent folk, thinking you know something." She was well into her stride and Edith might as well not have been there. "You should 'ave bin born an 'undred years ago— then they'd 'ave burned you, they would. And served you right too. Poor little child. They shouldn't allow you anywhere near 'im."

"Ignorant you are," Miss Buchan cried back at her. "Ignorant as the pigs you look like—nothing but snuffle around all day eating and drinking. All you think about is your belly. You know nothing. Think if a child's got food on his plate he's got everything, and if he eats it he's well. Ha!" She looked around for something to throw, and since she was standing on the stairs, nothing came to hand. "Think you know everything, and you know nothing at all."

"Buckie, be quiet!" Edith shrieked.

"That's right, Miss Edith," the cook said, cheering her on. "You tell 'er to keep 'er wicked mouth closed! You should get rid of 'er! Put 'er out! Daft, she is. All them years with other folks' children have turned 'er wits. She's no good for that poor child. Lost 'is father and 'is mother, poor little mite, and now 'e 'as to put up with that old witch. It's enough to drive 'im mad. D'yer know what she's bin tellin' 'im? Do yer?''

"No—nor do I want to," Edith said sharply. "You just be quiet!"

"Well you should know!" The cook's eyes were blazing and her hair was flying out of nearly all its pins. "An' if nobody else'll tell yer, I will! Got the poor little child so confused 'e don't know anything anymore. One minute 'is grandmama tells 'im 'is papa's dead and 'e's gotter ferget 'is mama because she's a madwoman what killed 'is papa an' will be 'anged for it. Which God 'elp us is the truth.''

The footman had rearmed himself and approached her again. She backhanded him almost unconsciously.

"Then along comes that wizened-up ol' bag o' bones," she continued regardless, "an' tells 'im 'is mama loves 'im very much and in't a wicked woman at all. Wot's 'e to think?'' Her voice was rising all the time. "Don't know whether 'e's comin' or goin', nor 'oo's good nor bad, nor what's the truth about anything.'' She finally took the damp dish towel out of her apron pocket and hurled it at Miss Buchan.

It hit Miss Buchan in the chest and slid to the floor. She ignored it completely. Her face was pale, her eyes glittering. Her thin, bony hands were knotted into fists.

"You ugly, interfering old fool," she shouted back. "You know nothing about it. You should stay with your pots and pans in the kitchen where you belong. Cleaning out the slop pots is your place. Scrubbing the pans, slicing the vegetables, food, food, food! Keep their stomachs full—you leave their minds to me.''

"Buckie, what have you been saying to Master Cassian?" Edith asked her.

Miss Buchan went very white. "Only that his mother's not a wicked woman, Miss Edith. No child should be told his mother's wicked and doesn't love him.''

"She murdered his father, you daft old bat!" the cook yelled at her. "They'll hang her for it! How's 'e goin' to understand that, if he doesn't know she's wicked, poor little creature?''

"We'll see," Miss Buchan said. "She's got the best lawyer in London. It's not over yet."

" 'Course it's over," the cook said, scenting victory. "They'll 'ang 'er, and so they should. What's the city coming to if women can murder their 'usbands any time they take a fancy to—and walk away with it?"

"There's worse things than killing people," Miss Buchan said darkly. "And you know nothing."

"That's enough!" Edith slipped between the two of them. "Cook, you are to go back to the kitchen and do your own job. Do you hear me?"

"She should be got rid of," the cook repeated, looking over Edith's shoulder at Miss Buchan. "You mark my words, Miss Edith, she's a—"

"That's enough." Edith took the cook by the arm and physically turned her around, pushing her down the stairs.

"Miss Buchan," Hester said quickly, "I think we should leave them. If there is to be any dinner in the house, the cook should get back to her duties."

Miss Buchan stared at her.

"And anyway," Hester went on, "I don't think there's really any point in telling her, do you? She isn't listening, and honestly I don't think she'd understand even if she were."

Miss Buchan hesitated, looking at her with slow consideration, then back at the retreating cook, now clasped firmly by Edith, then at Hester again.

"Come on," Hester urged. "How long have you known the cook? Has she ever listened to you, or understood what you were talking about?"

Miss Buchan sighed and the rigidity went out of her. She turned and walked back up the stairs with Hester. "Never," she said wearily. "Idiot," she said again under her breath.

They reached the landing and went on up again to the schoolroom floor and Miss Buchan's sitting room. Hester followed her in and closed the door. Miss Buchan went to the dormer window and stared out of it across the roof and into the branches of the trees, leaves moving in the wind against the sky.

Hester was not sure how to begin. It must be done very carefully, and perhaps so subtly that the actual words were never said. But perhaps, just perhaps, the truth was at last within her grasp.

"I'm glad you told Cassian not to think his mother was wicked," she said quietly, almost casually. She saw Miss Buchan's back stiffen. She must go very carefully. There was no retreat left now, nothing must be said in haste or unguardedly. Even in fury she had betrayed nothing, still less would she here, and to a stranger. "It is an unbearable thing for a child to think."

"It is," Miss Buchan agreed, still staring out of the window.

"Even though, as I understand it, he was closer to his father."

Miss Buchan said nothing.

"It is very generous of you to speak well of Mrs. Carlyon to him," Hester went on, hoping desperately that she was saying the right thing. "You must have had a special affection for the general—after all, you must have known him since his childhood." Please heaven her guess was right. Miss Buchan had been their governess, hadn't she?

"I had," Miss Buchan agreed quietly. "Just like Master Cassian, he was."

"Was he?" Hester sat down as if she intended to stay some time. Miss Buchan remained at the window. "You remember him very clearly? Was he fair, like Cassian?" A new thought came into her mind, unformed, indefinite. "Sometimes people seem to resemble each other even though their coloring or their features are not alike. It is a matter of gesture, mannerism, tone of voice . . ."

"Yes," Miss Buchan agreed, turning towards Hester, a half smile on her lips. "Thaddeus had just the same way of looking at you, careful, as if he were measuring you in his mind."

"Was he fond of his father too?" Hester tried to picture Randolf as a young man, proud of his only son, spending time with him, telling him about his great campaigns, and the boy's face lighting up with the glamour and the danger and the heroism of it.

"Just the same," Miss Buchan said with a strange, sad expression in her face, and a flicker of anger coming and going so rapidly Hester only just caught it.

"And to his mother?" Hester asked, not knowing what to say next.

Miss Buchan looked at her, then away again and out of the window, her face puckered with pain.

"Miss Felicia was different from Miss Alexandra," she said with something like a sob in her voice. "Poor creature. May God forgive her."

"And yet you find it in your heart to be sorry for her?" Hester said gently, and with respect.

"Of course," Miss Buchan replied with a sad little smile. "You know what you are taught, what everyone tells you is so. You are all alone. Who is there to ask? You do what you think—you weigh what you value most. Unity: one face to the outside world. Too much to lose, you see. She lacked the courage . . ."

Hester did not understand. She groped after threads of it, and the moment she had them the next piece made no sense. But how much dare she ask without risking Miss Buchan's rebuffing her and ceasing to talk at all? One word or gesture of seeming intrusion, a hint of curiosity, and she might withdraw altogether.

"It seems she had everything to lose, poor woman," she said tentatively.

"Not now," Miss Buchan replied with sudden bitterness. "It's all too late now. It's over—the harm is all done."

"You don't think the trial might make a difference?" Hester said with fading hope. "You sounded before as if you did."

Miss Buchan was silent for several minutes. Outside a gardener dropped a rake and the sound of the wood on the path came up through the open window.

"It might help Miss Alexandra," Miss Buchan said at last. "Please God it will, although I don't see how. But what will it do to the child? And God knows, it can't alter the past for anyone else. What's done is done."

Hester had a curious sensation, almost like a tingling in the brain. Suddenly shards of a pattern fell together, incomplete, vague, but with a tiny, hideous thread of sense.

"That is why she won't tell us," she said very slowly. "To protect the child?"

"Tell you?" Miss Buchan faced Hester, a pucker of confusion between her brows.

"Tell us the real reason why she killed the general."

"No—of course not," she said slowly. "How could she? But how did you know? No one told you."

"I guessed."

"She'll not admit it. God help her, she thinks that is all there is to it—just the one." Her eyes filled with tears of pity and helplessness, and she turned away again. "But I know there are others, of course there are. I knew it from his face, from the way he smiles, and tells lies, and cries at night." She spoke very quietly, her voice full of old pain. "He's frightened, and excited, and grown up, and a tiny child, and desperately, sickeningly alone, all at the same time like his father before him, God damn him!" Miss Buchan took a long, shuddering breath, so deep it seemed to rack her whole, thin body. "Can you save her, Miss Latterly?"

"I don't know," Hester said honestly. All the pity in the world now would not permit a lie. It was not the time. "But I will do everything I can—that I swear to you."

Without saying anything else she stood up and left the room, closing the door behind her and walking away towards the rest of the small rooms in the wing. She was looking for Cassian.

She found him standing in the corridor outside the door to his bedroom, staring up at her, his face pale, his eyes careful.

"You did the right thing to get Edith to stop the fight," she said matter-of-factly. "Do you like Miss Buchan?"

He continued to stare at her without speaking, his eyelids heavy, his face watchful and uncertain.

"Shall we go into your room?" she suggested. She was

not sure how she was going to approach the subject, but nothing now would make her turn back. The truth was almost reached, at least this part of it.

Wordlessly he turned around and opened the door. She followed him in. Suddenly she was furious that the burden of so much tragedy, guilt and death should rest on the narrow, fragile shoulders of such a child.

He walked over to the window; the light on his face showed the marks of tears on his soft, blemishless skin. His bones were still not fully formed, his nose just beginning to strengthen and lose its childish outline, his brows to darken.

"Cassian," she began quietly.

"Yes ma'am?" He looked at her, turning his head slowly.

"Miss Buchan was right, you know. Your mother is not a wicked person, and she does love you very much."

"Then why did she kill my papa?" His lip trembled and with great difficulty he stopped himself from crying.

"You loved your papa very much?"

He nodded, his hand going up to his mouth.

The rage inside her made her tremble.

"You had some special secrets with your papa, didn't you?"

His right shoulder came up and for an instant a half smile brushed over his mouth. Then there was fear in his eyes, a guarded look.

"I'm not going to ask you about it," she said gently. "Not if he told you not to tell anyone. Did he make you promise?"

He nodded again.

"That must have been very difficult for you?"

"Yes."

"Because you couldn't tell Mama?"

He looked frightened and backed away half a step.

"Was that important, not to tell Mama?"

He nodded slowly, his eyes on her face.

"Did you want to tell her, at first?"

He stood quite still.

Hester waited. Far outside she heard faint murmurs from the street, carriage wheels, a horse's hooves. Beyond the window the leaves flickered in the wind and threw patterns of light across the glass.

Slowly he nodded.

"Did it hurt?"

Again the long hesitation, then he nodded.

"But it was a very grown-up thing to do, and being a man of honor, you didn't tell anyone?"

He shook his head.

"I understand."

"Are you going to tell Mama? Papa said if she ever knew she'd hate me—she wouldn't love me anymore, she wouldn't understand, and she'd send me away. Is that what happened?" His eyes were very large, full of fear and defeat, as if in his heart he had already accepted it was true.

"No." She swallowed hard. "She went because they took her, not because of you at all. And I'm not going to tell her, but I think perhaps she knows already—and she doesn't hate you. She'll never hate you."

"Yes she will! Papa said so!" His voice rose in panic and he backed away from her.

"No she won't! She loves you very much indeed. So much she is prepared to do anything she can for you."

"Then why has she gone away? She killed Papa, Grandmama told me—and Grandpapa said so too. And they'll take her away and she'll never come back. Grandmama said so. She said I've got to forget her, not think about her anymore! She's never coming back!"

"Is that what you want to do—forget her?"

There was a long silence.

His hand came up to his mouth again. "I don't know."

"Of course you don't, I'm sorry. I should not have asked. Are you glad now no one is doing that to you anymore—what Papa did?"

His eyelids lowered again and he hunched his right shoulder and looked at the ground.

Hester felt sick.

"Someone is. Who?"

He swallowed hard and said nothing.

"Someone is. You don't have to tell me who—not if it's secret."

He looked up at her.

"Someone is?" she repeated.

Very slowly he nodded.

"Just one person?"

He looked down again, frightened.

"All right—it's your secret. But if you want any help any time, or someone to talk to, you go to Miss Buchan. She's very good at secrets, and she understands. Do you hear me?"

He nodded.

"And remember, your mama loves you very much, and I am going to try to do everything I can to see that she comes back to you. I promise you."

He looked at her with steady blue eyes, slowly filling with tears.

"I promise," she repeated. "I'm going to start right now. Remember, if you want to be with somebody, talk to them, you go to Miss Buchan. She's here all the time, and she understands secrets—promise me?"

Again he nodded, and turned away as his eyes brimmed over.

She longed to go over and put her arms around him, let him weep, but if he did he might not be able to regain the composure, the dignity and self-reliance he must have in order to survive the next few days or weeks.

Reluctantly she turned and went out of the door, closing it softly behind her.

Hester excused herself to Edith as hastily as possible and without any explanation, then as soon as she was on the pavement she began to walk briskly towards William Street. She hailed the very first hansom she saw and requested the driver to take her to Vere Street, off Lincoln's Inn Fields, then she sat back to compose herself until she should arrive at Rathbone's office.

Once there she alighted, paid the driver and went in. The clerk greeted her civilly, but with some surprise.

"I have no appointment," she said quickly. "But I must see Mr. Rathbone as soon as possible. I have discovered the motive in the Carlyon case, and as you must know, there is no time to be lost."

He rose from his seat, setting down his quill and closing the ledger.

"Indeed, ma'am. Then I will inform Mr. Rathbone. He is with a client at the moment, but I am sure he will be most obliged if you are able to wait until he is free."

"Certainly." She sat down and with the greatest difficulty watched the hands on the clock go around infinitely slowly until twenty-five minutes later the inner office door opened. A large gentleman came out, his gold watch chain across an extensive stomach. He glanced at her without speaking, wished the clerk good-day, and went out.

The clerk went in to Rathbone immediately, and within a moment was out again.

"If you please, Miss Latterly?" He stood back, inviting her in.

"Thank you." She barely glanced at him as she passed.

Oliver Rathbone was sitting at his desk and he rose to his feet before she was across the threshold.

"Hester?"

She closed the door behind her and leaned against it, suddenly breathless.

"I know why Alexandra killed the general!" She swallowed hard, an ache in her throat. "And my God, I think I would have done it too. And gone to the gallows before I would have told anyone why."

"Why?" His voice was husky, little more than a whisper. "For God's sake why?"

"Because he was having carnal knowledge of his own son!"

"Dear heaven! Are you sure?" He sat down suddenly as though all the strength had gone out of him. "General Carlyon—was . . . ? Hester . . . ?"

"Yes—and not only he, but probably the old colonel as well—and God knows who else."

Rathbone shut his eyes and his face was ashen.

"No wonder she killed him," he said very quietly.

Hester came over and sat down on the chair opposite the desk. There was no need to spell it out. They both knew the helplessness of a woman who wanted to leave her husband without his agreement, and that even if she did, all children were legally his, not hers. By law she would forfeit all right to them, even nursing babies, let alone an eight-year-old son.

"What else could she do?" Hester said blankly. "There was no one to turn to—I don't suppose anyone would have believed her. They'd lock her up for slander, or insanity, if she tried to say such a thing about a pillar of the military establishment like the general."

"His parents?" he said, then laughed bitterly. "I don't suppose they'd ever believe it, even if they saw the act."

"I don't know," she admitted. "The old colonel does it too—so he would be no help. Presumably Felicia never knew? I don't know how Alexandra did; the child certainly didn't tell her. He was sworn to secrecy, and terrified. He'd been told his mother wouldn't love him anymore, that she'd hate him and send him away if she ever found out."

His face was pale, the skin drawn tight.

"How do you know?"

Detail by detail she related to him the events of the afternoon. The clerk knocked on the door and said that the next client was here. Rathbone told him to go away again.

"Oh God," he said quietly when she had finished. He turned from the window where he had moved when she was halfway through. His face was twisted with pity, and anger for the pain and loneliness and the fear of it. "Hester . . ."

"You can help her, can't you?" she pleaded. "She'll hang for it, if you don't, and he'll have no one. He'll be left in that house—for it to go on."

"I know!" He turned away and looked out of the window. "I'll do what I can. Let me think. Come back tomorrow, with Monk." His hands clenched by his sides. "We have no proof."

She wanted to cry out that there must be, but she knew he

272

did not speak lightly, or from defeat, only from the need to be exact. She rose to her feet and stood a little behind him.

"You've done what seemed impossible before," she said tentatively.

He looked back at her, smiling, his eyes very soft.

"My dear Hester . . ."

She did not flinch or ease the demand in her face.

"I'll try," he said quietly. "I promise you I will try."

She smiled quickly, reached up her hand and brushed his cheek, without knowing why, then turned and left, going out into the clerk's office with her head high.

The following day, late in the morning, Rathbone, Monk and Hester sat in the office in Vere Street with all doors closed and all other business suspended until they should have reached a decision. It was June 16.

Monk had just heard from Hester what she had learned at the Carlyon house. He sat pale-faced, his lips tight, his knuckles clenched. It marred his opinion of himself that he was shocked, but he was, too deeply to conceal it. It had not occurred to him that someone of the breeding and reputation of General Carlyon should indulge in such a devastating abuse. He was too angry even to resent the fact that it had not occurred to him to look for such an answer. All his thoughts were outward, to Alexandra, to Cassian, and to what was to come.

"Is it a defense?" he demanded of Rathbone. "Will the judge dismiss it?"

"No," Rathbone said quietly. He was very grave this morning and his long face was marked by lines of tiredness; even his eyes looked weary. "I have been reading cases all night, checking every point of law I can find on the subject, and I come back each time to what is, I think, our only chance, and that is a defense of provocation. The law states that if a person receives extraordinary provocation, and that may take many forms, then the charge of murder may be reduced to manslaughter."

"That's not good enough," Monk interrupted, his voice

rising with his emotion. "This was justifiable. For God's sake, what else could she do? Her husband was committing incest and sodomy against her child. She had not only a right but a duty to protect him. The law gave her nothing—she has no rights in her son. In law it is his child, but the law never intended he should be free to do that to him."

"Of course not," Rathbone agreed quietly, the effort of restraint trembling behind it. "Nevertheless, the law gives a woman no rights in her child. She has no means to support it, and no freedom to leave her husband if he does not wish her to, and certainly no way to take her child with her."

"Then what else can she do but kill him?" Monk's face was white. "How can we tolerate a law which affords no possible justice? And the injustice is unspeakable."

"We change it, we don't break it," Rathbone replied.

Monk swore briefly and violently.

"I agree," Rathbone said with a tight smile. "Now may we proceed with what is practical?"

Monk and Hester stared at him wordlessly.

"Manslaughter is the best we can hope for, and that will be extremely difficult to prove. But if we succeed, the sentence is largely at the discretion of the judge. It can be as little as a matter of months, or as great as ten years."

Both Hester and Monk relaxed a little. Hester smiled bleakly.

"But we must prove it," Rathbone went on. "And that will be very hard to do. General Carlyon is a hero. People do not like their heroes tarnished, let alone utterly destroyed." He leaned back a little, sliding his hands into his pockets. "And we have had more than enough of that with the war. We have a tendency to see people as good or evil; it is so much easier both on the brain and on the emotions, but especially the emotions, to place people into one or the other category. Black or white. It is a painful adjustment to have to recognize and accommodate into our thinking the fact that people with great qualities which we have admired may also have ugly and profoundly repellent flaws."

He did not look at either of them, but at a space on the

farther wall. "One then has to learn to understand, which is difficult and painful, unless one is to swing completely 'round, tear up one's admiration, and turn it into hate—which is also painful, and wrong, but so much easier. The wound of disillusion turns to rage because one has been let down. One's own sense of betrayal outweighs all else."

His delicate mouth registered wry pity.

"Disillusion is one of the most difficult of all emotions to wear gracefully, and with any honor. I am afraid we will not find many who will do it. People will be very reluctant to believe anything so disturbing. And we have had far too much disturbance to our settled and comfortable world lately as it is—first the war, and all the ugly whispers there are of inefficiency and needless death, and now wind of mutiny in India. God knows how bad that will turn out to be."

He slid a little farther down in his chair. "We need our heroes. We don't want them proved to be weak and ugly, to practice vices we can barely even bring ourselves to name—let alone against their own children."

"I don't care a damn whether people like it or not," Monk said violently. "It is true. We must force them to see it. Would they rather we hang an innocent woman, before we oblige them to see a truth which is disgusting?"

"Some of them well might." Rathbone looked at him with a faint smile. "But I don't intend to allow them that luxury."

"If they would, then there is not much hope for our society," Hester said in a small voice. "When we are happy to turn from evil because it is ugly, and causes us distress, then we condone it and become party to its continuance. Little by little, we become as guilty of it as those who commit the act—because we have told them by our silence that it is acceptable."

Rathbone glanced at her, his eyes bright and soft.

"Then we must prove it," Monk said between his teeth. "We must make it impossible for anyone to deny or evade."

"I will try." Rathbone looked at Hester, then at Monk. "But we haven't enough here yet. I'll need more. Ideally I need to name the other members of the ring, if there is one, and from what you say"—he turned to Hester—"there may be several members. And of course I dare not name anyone without proof. Cassian is only eight. I may be able to call him; that will depend upon the judge. But his testimony alone will certainly not be sufficient."

"I think Damaris might know," Hester said thoughtfully. "I'm not certain, but she undoubtedly discovered something at the party that evening, and it shook her so desperately she was hardly able to keep control of herself."

"We have several people's testimony to that," Monk added.

"If she will admit it, that will go a long way towards belief," Rathbone said guardedly. "But it will not be easy to make her. She is called as a witness for the prosecution."

"Damaris is?" Hester was incredulous. "But why? I thought she was on our side."

Rathbone smiled without pleasure. "She has no choice. The prosecution has called her, and she must come, or risk being charged with contempt of court. So must Peverell Erskine, Fenton and Sabella Pole, Maxim and Louisa Furnival, Dr. Hargrave, Sergeant Evan, and Randolf Carlyon."

"But that's everyone." Hester was horrified. Suddenly hope was being snatched away again. "What about us? That's unjust. Can't they testify for us too?"

"No, a witness can be called by only one side. But I shall have an opportunity to cross-examine them," Rathbone replied. "It will not be as easy as if they were my witnesses. But it is not everyone. We can call Felicia Carlyon—although I am not sure if I will. I have not subpoenaed her, but if she is there I may call her at the last moment—when she has had an opportunity to hear the other testimony."

"She won't tell us anything," Hester said furiously. "Even if she could. And I don't suppose she knows. But if she did, can you imagine her standing up in court and admitting that any member of her family committed incest and sodomy, let alone her heroic son, the general!"

"Not willingly." Rathbone's face was grim, but there was a faint, cold light in his eyes. "But it is my art, my dear, to make people admit what they do not wish to, and had not intended to.''

"You had better be damnably good at it," Monk said angrily.

"I am." Rathbone met his eyes and for a moment they stared at each other in silence.

"And Edith," Hester said urgently. "You can call Edith. She will help all she can."

"What does she know?" Monk swung around to her. "Willingness won't help if she doesn't know anything."

Hester ignored him. "And Miss Buchan. She knows."

"A servant." Rathbone bit his lip. "A very elderly woman with a hot temper and a family loyalty . . . If she turns against them they won't forgive her. She will be thrown out without a roof over her head or food to eat, and too old to work anymore. Not an enviable position."

Hester felt hopelessness wash over her anger. A black defeat threatened to crush her.

"Then what can we do?"

"Find some more evidence," Rathbone replied. "Find out who else is involved."

Monk thought for a few moments, his hands knotted hard in his lap.

"That should be possible: either they came to the house or the child was taken to them. The servants will know who called. The footmen ought to know where the boy went." His face pinched with anger. "Poor little devil!" He looked at Rathbone critically. "But even if you prove other men used him, will that prove that his father did, and that Alexandra knew it?"

"You give me the evidence," Rathbone replied. "Everything you get, whether you think it is relevant or not. I'll decide how to use it."

Monk rose to his feet, scraping back his chair, his whole body hard with anger.

"Then we have no time to lose. God knows there is little enough."

"And I shall go to try and persuade Alexandra Carlyon to

allow us to use the truth," Rathbone said with a tight little smile. "Without her consent we have nothing."

"Oliver." Hester was aghast.

He turned to her, touching her very gently.

"Don't worry, my dear. You have done superbly. You have discovered the truth. Now leave me to do my part."

She met his eyes, dark and brilliant, took a deep breath and let it out slowly, forcing herself to relax.

"Of course. I'm sorry. Go and see Alexandra. I shall go and tell Callandra. She will be as appalled as we are."

Alexandra Carlyon turned from the place where she had been standing, staring up at the small square of light of the cell window. She was surprised to see Rathbone.

The door swung shut with a hollow sound of metal on metal, and they were alone.

"You are wasting your time, Mr. Rathbone," she said huskily. "I cannot tell you anything more."

"You don't need to, Mrs. Carlyon," he said very gently. "I know why you killed your husband—and God help me, had I been in your place I might have done the same."

She stared at him uncomprehendingly.

"To save your son from further unnatural abuse . . ."

What little color there was left fled from her face. Her eyes were wide, so hollow as to seem black in the dim light.

"You—know . . ." She sank onto the cot. "You can't. Please . . ."

He sat on the bottom of the cot, facing her.

"My dear, I understand that you were prepared to go to the gallows rather than expose your son to the world's knowledge of his suffering. But I have something very dreadful to tell you, which must change your mind."

Very slowly she raised her head and looked at him.

"Your husband was not the only one to use him in that way."

Her breath caught in her throat, and she seemed unable to find it again. He thought she was going to faint.

"You must fight," he said softly but with intense urgency.

"It seems most probable that his grandfather is another—and there is at least a third, if not more. You must use all the courage you have and tell the truth about what happened, and why. We must destroy them, so they can never harm Cassian again, or any other child."

She shook her head, still struggling to breathe.

"You must!" He took both her hands. At first they were limp, then slowly tightened until they clung onto him as if she were drowning. "You must! Otherwise Cassian will go to his grandparents, and the whole tragedy will continue. You will have killed your husband for nothing. And you yourself will hang—for nothing."

"I can't." The words barely passed her lips.

"Yes you can! You are not alone. There are people who will be with you, people as horrified and appalled as you are, who know the truth and will help us fight to prove it. For your son's sake, you must not give up now. Tell the truth, and I will fight to see that it is believed—and understood."

"Can you?"

He took a deep breath and met her eyes.

"Yes—I can."

She stared at him, exhausted beyond emotion.

"I can," he repeated.

9

THE TRIAL OF ALEXANDRA CARLYON began on the morning of Monday, June 22. Major Tiplady had intended to be present, not out of cheap curiosity; normally he shunned such proceedings as he would have an accident had a horse bolted in the street and thrown and trampled its rider. It was a vulgar intrusion into another person's embarrassment and distress. But in this case he felt a deep and personal concern for the outcome, and he wished to demonstrate his support for Alexandra, and for the Carlyon family, or if he were honest, for Edith; not that he would have admitted it, even to himself.

When he put his foot to the ground he was well able to bear his weight on it. It seemed the leg had healed perfectly. However, when he attempted to bend it to climb the step up into a hansom, he found, to his humiliation, that it would not support him as he mounted. And he knew dismounting at the other end might well be even worse. He was both abashed and infuriated, but he was powerless to do anything about it. It obviously needed at least another week, and trying to force the issue would only make it worse.

Therefore he deputed Hester to report to him, since she was still in his employ and must do what she could for his comfort. He insisted this was crucial to it. She was to report to him everything that happened, not only the evidence that was given by each witness but their manner and bearing, and whether in her best judgment they were telling the truth or not. Also she was to observe the attitudes of everyone else who appeared for the prosecution and for the defense, and most particularly the jury. Naturally she should also mark well all other members of the family she might see. To this end she should equip herself with a large notebook and several sharp pencils.

"Yes Major," she said obediently, hoping she would be able to fulfil so demanding an assignment adequately. He asked a great deal, but his earnestness and his concern were so genuine she did not even try to point out the difficulties involved.

"I wish to know your opinions as well as the facts," he said for the umpteenth time. "It is a matter of feelings, you know? People are not always rational, especially in matters like this."

"Yes, I know," she said with magnificent understatement. "I will watch expressions and listen to tones of voice—I promise you."

"Good." His cheeks pinkened a trifle. "I am most obliged." He looked down. "I am aware it is not customarily part of a nurse's duties . . ."

She hid a smile with great difficulty.

"And it will not be pleasant," he added.

"It is merely a reversal of roles," she said, allowing her smile to be seen.

"What?" He looked at her quickly, not understanding. He saw her amusement, but did not know what caused it.

"Had you been able to go, then I should have had to ask you to repeat it all to me. I have no authority to require it of you. This is far more convenient."

"Oh—I see." His eyes filled with perception and amusement as well. "Yes—well, you had better go, or you might be late and not obtain a satisfactory seat."

"Yes Major. I shall be back when I am quite sure I have

281

observed everything. Molly has your luncheon prepared, and . . .''

"Never mind." He waved his hands impatiently. "Go on, woman."

"Yes Major."

She was early, as she had said; even so the crowds were eager and she only just got a seat from which she could see all the proceedings, and that was because Monk had saved it for her.

The courtroom was smaller than she had expected, and higher-ceilinged, more like a theater with the public gallery far above the dock, which itself was twelve or fifteen feet above the floor where the barristers and court officials had their leather-padded seats at right angles to the dock.

The jury was on two benches, one behind the other, on the left of the gallery, several steps up from the floor, and with a row of windows behind them. On the farther end of the same wall was the witness box, a curious affair up several steps, placing it high above the arena, very exposed.

At the farther wall, opposite the gallery and the dock, was the red-upholstered seat on which the judge sat. To the right was a further gallery for onlookers, newsmen and other interested parties.

There was a great amount of wooden paneling around the dock and witness box, and on the walls behind the jury and above the dock to the gallery rail. It was all very imposing and as little like an ordinary room as possible, and at the present was so crowded with people one was able to move only with the greatest difficulty.

"Where have you been?" Monk demanded furiously. "You're late."

She was torn between snapping back and gratitude to him for thinking of her. The first would be pointless and only precipitate a quarrel when she least wanted one, so she chose the latter, which surprised and amused him.

The Bill of Indictment before the Grand Jury had already

been brought at an earlier date, and a true case found and Alexandra charged.

"What about the jury?" she asked him. "Have they been chosen?"

"Friday," he answered. "Poor devils."

"Why poor?"

"Because I wouldn't like to have to decide this case," Monk answered. "I don't think the verdict I want to bring in is open to me."

"No," she agreed, more to herself than to him. "What are they like?"

"The jury? Ordinary, worried, taking themselves very seriously," he replied, not looking at her but straight ahead at the judge's bench and the lawyers' tables below.

"All middle-aged, I suppose? And all men of course."

"Not all middle-aged," he contradicted. "One or two are youngish, and one very old. You have to be between twenty-one and sixty, and have a guaranteed income from rents or lands, or live in a house with not less than fifteen windows—"

"What?"

"Not less than fifteen windows," he repeated with a sardonic smile, looking sideways at her. "And of course they are all men. That question is not worthy of you. Women are not considered capable of such decisions, for heaven's sake. You don't make any legal decisions at all. You don't own property, you don't expect to be able to decide a man's fate before the law, do you?"

"If one is entitled to be tried before a jury of one's peers, I expect to be able to decide a woman's fate," she said sharply. "And rather more to the point, I expect if I come to trial to have women on the jury. How else could I be judged fairly?"

"I don't think you'd do any better with women," he said, pulling his face into a bitter expression and looking at the fat woman in front of them. "Not that it would make the slightest difference if you did."

She knew it was irrelevant. They must fight the case with

the jury as it was. She turned around to look at others in the crowd. They seemed to be all manner of people, every age and social condition, and nearly as many women as men. The only thing they had in common was a restless excitement, a murmuring to one another, a shifting from foot to foot where they were standing, or a craning forward if they were seated, a peering around in case they were to miss something.

"Of course I really shouldn't be 'ere," a woman said just behind Hester. "It won't do me nerves any good at all. Wickedest thing I ever 'eard of, an' 'er a lady too. You expec' better from them as ought ter know 'ow ter be'ave theirselves."

"I know," her companion agreed. "If gentry murders each other, wot can yer expec' of the lower orders? I ask yer."

"Wonder wot she's like? Vulgar, I shouldn't wonder. Of course they'll 'ang 'er."

"O' course. Don't be daft. Wot else could they do?"

"Right and proper thing too."

" 'Course it is. My 'usband don't always control 'isself, but I don't go murderin' 'im."

" 'Course you don't. No one does. What would 'appen to the world if we did?"

"Shockin'. And they're sayin' as there's mutiny in India too. People killin' an' murderin' all over the place. I tell yer, we live in terrible times. God 'isself only knows what'll be next!"

"An' that's true for sure," her companion agreed, sagely nodding her head.

Hester longed to tell them not to be so stupid, that there had always been virtue and tragedy—and laughter, discovery and hope—but the clerk called the court to order. There was a rustle of excitement as the counsel for the prosecution came in dressed in traditional wig and black gown, followed by his junior. Wilberforce Lovat-Smith was not a large man, but he had a walk which was confident, even a trifle arrogant, and full of vitality, so that everyone was immediately aware of

284

him. He was unusually dark of complexion and under the white horsehair wig very black hair was easily visible. Even at this distance, Hester could see with surprise as he turned that his eyes were cold gray-blue. He was certainly not a handsome man, but there was something compelling in his features: sharp nose, humorous mouth and heavy-lidded eyes which suggested sensuality. It was the face of a man who had succeeded in the past, and expected to again.

He had barely taken his place when there was another murmur of excitement as Rathbone came in, also gowned and wigged and followed by a junior. He looked unfamiliar to Hester, lately used to seeing him in ordinary clothes and informal in his manner. Now he was quite obviously thinking only of the contest ahead on which depended not only Alexandra's life but perhaps the quality of Cassian's also. Hester and Monk had done all they could; now it lay with Rathbone. He was a lone gladiator in the arena, and the crowd was hungering for blood. As he turned she saw the familiar profile with its long nose and delicate mouth so ready to change from pity to anger, and back to wry, quick humor again.

"It's going to begin," someone whispered behind her. "That's the defense. It's Rathbone—I wonder what he's going to say?"

"Nothing 'e can say," came the reply from a man somewhere to her left. "Don't know why 'e bothers. They should 'ang 'er, save the government the money."

"Save us, more like."

"Ssh!"

"Ssh yerself!"

Monk swung around, his voice vicious. "If you don't want a trial you should vacate the seat and allow someone who does to sit in it. There are plenty of slaughterhouses in London if all you want is blood."

There was a gasp of fury.

" 'Ow dare you speak to my wife like that?" the man demanded.

"I was speaking to you, sir," Monk retorted. "I expect you to be responsible for your own opinions."

"Hold your tongue," someone else said furiously. "Or we'll all be thrown out! The judge is coming."

And indeed he was, splendid in robes touched with scarlet, white wig only slightly fuller than those of the lawyers. He was a tallish man with a broad brow and fine strong nose, short jaw and good mouth, but he was far younger than Hester had expected, and for no reason that she understood, her heart sank. In some way she had imagined a fatherly man might have more compassion, a grandfatherly man even more again. She found herself sitting forward on the edge of the hard bench, her hands clenched, her shoulders tight.

There was a rising wave of excitement, then a sudden silence as the prisoner was brought in, a craning forward and turning of heads on the benches behind the lawyers, of all except one woman dressed entirely in black, and veiled. Beneath the gallery in the dock the prisoner had been brought in.

Even the jury, seemingly against their will, found their eyes moving towards her.

Hester cursed the arrangement which made it impossible to see the dock from the gallery.

"We should have got seats down there," she said to Monk, nodding her head towards the few benches behind the lawyers' seats.

"We?" he said acidly. "If it weren't for me you'd be standing outside."

"I know—and I'm grateful. All the same, we should still try to get a seat down there."

"Then come an hour earlier next time."

"I will. But it doesn't help now."

"What do you want to do?" he whispered sarcastically. "Lose these seats and go out and try to get in downstairs?"

"Yes," she hissed back. "Of course I do. Come on!"

"Don't be ridiculous. You'll end up with nothing."

"You can do as you please. I'm going."

The woman in front swung around. "Be quiet," she said furiously.

286

"Mind your own business, madam," Monk said, freezing calm, then grasped Hester by the elbow and propelled her out past the row of protesting onlookers. Up the aisle and outside in the hallway he maintained silence. They went down the stairs, and at the door of the lower court he let go of her.

"All right," he said with a scathing stare. "Now what do you propose to do?"

She gulped, glared back at him, then swung around and marched to the doors.

A bailiff appeared and barred the way. "I'm sorry. You can't go in there, miss. It's all full up. You should 'a come earlier. You'll 'ave ter read about it in the papers."

"That will not be satisfactory," she said with all the dignity she could muster. "We are involved in the case, retained by Mr. Rathbone, counsel for the defense. This is Mr. Monk," she inclined her head slightly. "He is working with Mr. Rathbone, and Mr. Rathbone may need to consult with him during the course of the evidence. I am with him."

The bailiff looked over her head at Monk. "Is that true, sir?"

"Certainly it is," Monk said without a flicker, producing a card from his vest pocket.

"Then you'd better go in," the bailiff agreed cautiously. "But next time, get in 'ere a bit sooner, will you."

"Of course. We apologize," Monk said tactfully. "A little late business, you understand."

And without arguing the point any further, he pushed Hester inside and allowed the bailiff to close the doors.

The court looked different from this level, the judge's seat higher and more imposing, the witness box oddly more vulnerable, and the dock very enclosed, like a wide cage with wooden walls, very high up.

"Sit down," Monk said sharply.

Hester obeyed, perching on the end of the nearest bench and forcing the present occupants to move up uncomfortably close to each other. Monk was obliged to stand, until someone graciously changed places to the next row and gave him space.

For the first time, with something of a start, Hester saw the haggard face of Alexandra Carlyon, who was permitted to sit because the proceedings were expected to take several days. It was not the face she had envisioned at all; it was far too immediate and individual, even pale and exhausted as it was. There was too much capacity for intelligence and pain in it; she was acutely aware that they were dealing with the agonies and desires of a unique person, not merely a tragic set of circumstances.

She looked away again, feeling intrusive to be caught staring. She already knew more of her much too intimate suffering than anyone had a right to.

The proceedings began almost straightaway. The charge had already been made and answered. The opening speeches were brief. Lovat-Smith said the facts of the case were only too apparent, and he would prove step by step how the accused had deliberately, out of unfounded jealousy, murdered her husband, General Thaddeus Carlyon, and attempted to pass off her crime as an accident.

Rathbone said simply that he would answer with such a story that would shed a new and terrible light on all they knew, a light in which no answer would be as they now thought, and to look carefully into both their hearts and their consciences before they returned a verdict.

Lovat-Smith called his first witness, Louisa Mary Furnival. There was a rustle of excitement, and then as she appeared a swift indrawing of breath and whisper of fabric against fabric as people craned forward to see her. And indeed she presented a spectacle worth their effort. She was dressed in the darkest purple touched with amethyst, dignified, subdued in actual tones, and yet so fashionably and flamboyantly cut with a tiny waist and gorgeous sleeves. Her bonnet was perched so rakishly on her wide brushed dark hair as to be absolutely dashing. Her expression should have been demure, that of an elegant woman mourning the shocking death of a friend, and yet there was so much vitality in her, such awareness of her own beauty and magnetism, that no one thought of such an emotion for more than the first superficial instant.

She crossed the space of floor in front of the lawyers and climbed the flight of steps up into the witness box, negotiating her skirts through the narrow rails with considerable skill, then turned to face Lovat-Smith.

She swore as to her name and residence in a low, husky voice, looking down at him with shining eyes.

"Mrs. Furnival"—he moved forward towards her, hands in his pockets under his gown—"will you tell the court what you can recall of the events of that dreadful evening when General Carlyon met his death? Begin with the arrival of your guests, if you please."

Louisa looked perfectly composed. If the occasion intimidated her in any way, there was not the slightest sign of it in her face or her bearing. Even her hands on the witness box railing were quite relaxed.

"The first to arrive were Mr. and Mrs. Erskine," she started. "The next were General Carlyon and Alexandra." She did not glance at the dock as she said it.

Lovat-Smith was talking to Louisa.

Alexandra might not have been present for any emotional impact Louisa showed.

"At that time, Mrs. Furnival," Lovat-Smith was saying, "what was the attitude between General and Mrs. Carlyon? Did you notice?"

"The general seemed as usual," Louisa replied levelly. "I thought Alexandra very tense, and I was aware that the evening might become difficult." She allowed the ghost of a smile to cross her face. "As hostess, I was concerned that the party should be a success."

There was a ripple of laughter around the court, dying away again immediately.

Hester glanced up at Alexandra, but her face was expressionless.

"Who arrived next?" Lovat-Smith asked.

"Sabella Pole and her husband, Fenton Pole. She was immediately rude to her father, the general." Louisa's face shadowed very slightly but she forbore from more than the vaguest of implied criticism. She knew it was ugly and above all she would avoid that. "Of course she has not been well," she added. "So one forgave her readily. It was an embarrassment, no more."

"You did not fear it indicated any dangerous ill will?" Lovat-Smith asked with apparent concern.

"Not at all." Louisa dismissed it with a gesture.

"Who else arrived at this dinner of yours?"

"Dr. Charles Hargrave and Mrs. Hargrave; they were the last."

"And no one else called that evening?"

"No one."

"Can you tell us something of the course of events, Mrs. Furnival?"

She shrugged very delicately and half smiled.

Hester watched the jury. They were fascinated with her and Hester had no doubt she knew it.

"We spent some time in the withdrawing room," Louisa said casually. "We talked of this and that, as we will on such occasions. I cannot recall what we said, only that Mrs. Carlyon picked a quarrel with the general, which he did all he could to avoid, but she seemed determined to bring the matter to an open dispute."

"Do you know what it was about?"

"No, it seemed to be very nebulous, just a longstanding ill feeling, so far as I could judge. Of course I did not overhear it all . . ." She left it hanging delicately, not to rule out the possibility of a raging jealousy.

"And at dinner, Mrs. Furnival," Lovat-Smith prompted. "Was the ill feeling between General and Mrs. Carlyon still apparent?"

"Yes, I am afraid it was. Of course at that time I had no idea it was anything serious . . ." For an instant she looked contrite, abashed at her own blindness. There was a murmur of sympathy around the courtroom. People turned to look at the dock. One of the jurors nodded sagely.

"And after dinner?" Lovat-Smith asked.

"The ladies withdrew and left the men to take port and cigars," Louisa continued. "In the withdrawing room we simply spoke of trivial things again, a little gossip, and a few opinions of fashion and so on. Then when the men rejoined us I took General Carlyon upstairs to visit my son, who admired him greatly, and to whom he had been a good friend." A spasm of pain passed over her immaculate features and again there was a buzz of sympathy and anger around the room.

Hester looked at Alexandra in the dock, and saw hurt and puzzlement in her face.

The judge lifted his eyes and stared over the heads of the counsel to the body of the court. The sound subsided.

"Continue, Mr. Lovat-Smith," he ordered.

Lovat-Smith turned to Louisa. "Did this occasion any response that you observed, Mrs. Furnival?"

Louisa looked downwards modestly, as if embarrassed to admit it now.

"Yes. I am afraid Mrs. Carlyon was extremely angry. I thought at the time it was just a fit of pique. Of course I realize now that it was immeasurably deeper than that."

Oliver Rathbone rose to his feet.

"I object, my lord. The witness—"

"Sustained," the judge interrupted him. "Mrs. Furnival, we wish to know only what you observed at the time, not what later events may have led you to conclude, correctly or incorrectly. It is for the jury to interpret, not for you. At this time you felt it to be a fit of pique—that is all."

Louisa's face tightened with annoyance, but she would not argue with him.

"My lord," Lovat-Smith acknowledged the rebuke. He turned back to Louisa. "Mrs. Furnival, you took General Carlyon upstairs to visit with your son, whose age is thirteen, is that correct? Good. When did you come downstairs again?"

"When my husband came up to tell me that Alexandra—Mrs. Carlyon—was extremely upset and the party was becoming very tense and rather unpleasant. He wished me to return to try to improve the atmosphere. Naturally I did so.''

"Leaving General Carlyon still upstairs with your son?"

"Yes."

"And what happened next?"

"Mrs. Carlyon went upstairs."

"What was her manner, Mrs. Furnival, from your own observation?" He glanced at the judge, who made no comment.

"She was white-faced," Louisa replied. Still she ignored Alexandra as if the dock had been empty and she were speaking of someone absent. "She appeared to be in a rage greater than any I have ever seen before, or since. There was nothing I could do to stop her, but I still imagined that it was some private quarrel and would be settled when they got home."

Lovat-Smith smiled. "We assume you did not believe it would lead to violence, Mrs. Furnival, or you would naturally have taken steps to prevent it. But did you still have no idea as to its cause? You did not, for example, think it was jealousy over some imagined relationship between the general and yourself?"

She smiled, a fleeting, enigmatic expression. For the first time she glanced at Alexandra, but so quickly their eyes barely met. "A trifle, perhaps," she said gravely. "But not serious. Our relationship was purely one of friendship—quite platonic—as it had been for years. I thought she knew that, as did everyone else." Her smile widened. "Had it been more, my husband would hardly have been the friend to the general he was. I did not think she was . . . obsessive about it. A little envious, maybe—friendship can be very precious. Especially if you feel you do not have it."

"Exactly so." He smiled at her. "And then?" he asked, moving a little to one side and putting his hands deeper into his pockets.

Louisa took up the thread. "Then Mrs. Carlyon came downstairs, alone."

"Had her manner changed?"

"I was not aware of it . . ." She looked as if she were

waiting for him to lead her, but as he remained silent, she continued unasked. "Then my husband went out into the hall." She stopped for dramatic effect. "That is the front hall, not the back one, which we had been using to go up to my son's room—and he came back within a moment, looking very shaken, and told us that General Carlyon had had an accident and was seriously hurt."

"Seriously hurt," Lovat-Smith interrupted. "Not dead?"

"I think he was too shocked to have looked at him closely," she answered, a faint, sad smile touching her mouth. "I imagine he wanted Charles to come as soon as possible. That is what I would have done."

"Of course. And Dr. Hargrave went?"

"Yes—after a few moments he was back to say that Thaddeus was dead and we should call the police—because it was an accident that needed explaining, not because any of us suspected murder then."

"Naturally," Lovat-Smith agreed. "Thank you, Mrs. Furnival. Would you please remain there, in case my learned friend has any questions to ask you." He bowed very slightly and turned to Rathbone.

Rathbone rose, acknowledged him with a nod, and moved forward towards the witness box. His manner was cautious, but there was no deference in it and he looked up at Louisa very directly.

"Thank you for a most clear description of the events of that tragic evening, Mrs. Furnival," he began, his voice smooth and beautifully modulated. As soon as she smiled he continued gravely. "But I think perhaps you have omitted one or two events which may turn out to be relevant. We can hardly overlook anything, can we?" He smiled back at her, but there was no lightness in the gesture, and it died instantly, leaving no trace in his eyes. "Did anyone else go up to see your son, Valentine?"

"I . . ." She stopped, as if uncertain.

"Mrs. Erskine, for example?"

Lovat-Smith stirred, half rose as if to interrupt, then changed his mind.

"I believe so," Louisa conceded, her expression making it plain she thought it irrelevant.

"And how was her manner when she came down?" Rathbone said softly.

Louisa hesitated. "She seemed . . . upset."

"Just upset?" Rathbone sounded surprised. "Not distressed, unable to keep her mind on a conversation, distracted by some inner pain?"

"Well . . ." Louisa lifted her shoulder delicately. "She was in a very strange mood, yes. I thought perhaps she was not entirely well."

"Did she give any explanation for the sudden change from her usual manner to such a distracted, offensive, near-frenzied mood?"

Lovat-Smith rose to his feet.

"Objection, my lord! The witness did not say Mrs. Erskine was offensive or near frenzied, only that she was distressed and unable to command her attention to the conversation."

The judge looked at Rathbone. "Mr. Lovat-Smith is correct. What is your point, Mr. Rathbone? I confess, I fail to see it."

"It will emerge later, my lord," Rathbone said, and Hester had a strong feeling he was bluffing, hoping that by the time Damaris was called, they would have learned precisely what it was that she had discovered. Surely it must have to do with the general.

"Very well. Proceed," the judge directed.

"Did you find the cause of Mrs. Erskine's distress, Mrs. Furnival?" Rathbone resumed.

"No."

"Nor of Mrs. Carlyon's distress either? Is it an assumption that it had to do with you, and your relationship with the general?"

Louisa frowned.

"Is that not so, Mrs. Furnival? Did Mrs. Carlyon ever say anything either to you, or in your hearing, to suggest that she was distressed because of a jealousy of you and your friendship with her husband? Please be exact.''

Louisa drew in her breath deeply, her face shadowed, but still she did not glance towards the dock or the motionless woman in it.

"No."

Rathbone smiled, showing his teeth.

"Indeed, you have testified that she had nothing of which to be jealous. Your friendship with the general was perfectly proper, and a sensible woman might conceivably have regarded it as enviable that you could have such a comfortable regard, perhaps, but not cause for distress, let alone a passionate jealousy or hatred. Indeed there seems no reason for it at all. Is that not so?''

"Yes." It was not a flattering description, and certainly not glamorous, or the image Hester had seen Louisa project. Hester smiled to herself and glanced at Monk, but Monk had not caught the inflection. He was watching the jury.

"And this friendship between yourself and the general had existed for many years, some thirteen or fourteen years, in fact?''

"Yes."

"With the full knowledge and consent of your husband?''

"Of course."

"And of Mrs. Carlyon?''

"Yes."

"Did she at any time at all approach you on the matter, or let you know that she was displeased about it?''

"No." Louisa raised her eyebrows. "This came without any warning at all."

"What came, Mrs. Furnival?''

"Why the . . . the murder, of course." She looked a little disconcerted, not entirely sure whether he was very simple or very clever.

He smiled blandly, a slight curling of the lips. "Then on what evidence do you suppose that jealousy of you was the cause?''

She breathed in slowly, giving herself time, and her expression hardened.

"I—I did not think it, until she herself claimed it to be so. But I have experienced unreasonable jealousies before, and it was not hard to believe. Why should she lie about it? It is not a quality one would wish to claim—it is hardly attractive."

"A profound question, Mrs. Furnival, which in time I will answer. Thank you." He half turned away. "That is all I have to ask you. Please remain there, in case my learned friend has any questions to redirect to you."

Lovat-Smith rose, smiling, a small, satisfied gesture.

"No thank you, I think Mrs. Furnival by her very appearance makes the motive of jealousy more than understandable."

Louisa flushed, but it was quite obviously with pleasure, even a vindication. She shot a hard glance at Rathbone as she very carefully came down the steps, negotiating the hoops of her wide skirts with a swaggering grace, and walked across the small space of the floor.

There was a rustle of movement in the crowd and a few clearly audible shouts of admiration and approval. Louisa sailed out with her head high and an increasing satisfaction in her face.

Hester found her muscles clenching and a totally unreasonable anger boiling up inside her. It was completely unfair. Louisa could not know the truth, and in all likelihood she believed that Alexandra had murdered the general out of exactly the sudden and violent jealousy she envisioned. But Hester's anger remained exactly the same.

She looked up at the dock and saw Alexandra's pale face. She could see no hatred in it, no easy contempt. There was nothing there but tiredness and fear.

The next witness to be called was Maxim Furnival. He took the stand very gravely, his face pale. He was stronger than Hester had remembered, with more gravity and power to his features, more honest emotion. He had not testified yet, but she found herself disposed towards him. She glanced up at Alexandra again, and saw a momentary breaking of her self-control, a sudden softening, as if memories, and perhaps a sweetness, came through with bitter contrast. Then it was gone again, and the present reasserted itself.

Maxim was sworn in, and Lovat-Smith rose to address him.

"Of course you were also at this unfortunate dinner party, Mr. Furnival?"

Maxim looked wretched; he had none of Louisa's panache or flair for appearing before an audience. His bearing, the look in his face, suggested his mind was filled with memory of the tragedy, an awareness of the murder that still lay upon them. He had looked at Alexandra once, painfully, without evasion and without anger or blame. Whatever he thought of her, or believed, it was not harsh.

"Yes," he replied.

"Naturally," Lovat-Smith agreed. "Will you please tell us what you remember of that evening, from the time your first guests arrived."

In a quiet voice, but without hesitation, Maxim recounted exactly the same events as Louisa had, only his choice of words was different, laden with his knowledge of what had later occurred. Lovat-Smith did not interrupt him until he came to the point where Alexandra returned from upstairs, alone.

"What was her manner, Mr. Furnival? You did not mention it, and yet your wife said that it was worthy of remark." He glanced at Rathbone; he had forestalled objection, and Rathbone smiled back.

"I did not notice," Maxim replied, and it was so obviously a lie there was a little gasp from the crowd and the judge glanced at him a second time in surprise.

"Try your memory a little harder, Mr. Furnival," Lovat-Smith said gravely. "I think you will find it comes to you." Deliberately he kept his back to Rathbone.

Maxim frowned. "She had not been herself all evening." He met Lovat-Smith's eyes directly. "I was concerned for her, but not more so when she came down than earlier."

Lovat-Smith seemed on the edge of asking yet again, but heard Rathbone rise from his seat to object and changed his mind.

"What happened next?" he said instead.

"I went to the front hall, I forget what for now, and I saw Thaddeus lying on the floor with the suit of armor in pieces all around him—and the halberd in his chest." He hesitated only to compose himself, and Lovat-Smith did not prompt him. "It was quite obvious he had been very seriously hurt, far too seriously for me to do anything useful to help him, so I went back to the withdrawing room to get Charles Hargrave—the doctor . . ."

"Yes, naturally. Was Mrs. Carlyon there?"

"Yes."

"How did she take the news that her husband had had a serious, possibly even fatal accident, Mr. Furnival?"

"She was very shocked, very pale indeed and I think a trifle faint, what do you imagine? It is a fearful thing to have to tell any woman."

Lovat-Smith smiled and looked down at the floor, pushing his hands into his pockets again.

Hester looked at the jury. She could see from the puckered brows, the careful mouths, that their minds were crowded with all manner of questions, sharper and more serious for being unspoken. She had the first intimation of Lovat-Smith's skill.

"Of course," Lovat-Smith said at last. "Fearful indeed. And I expect you were deeply distressed on her behalf." He turned and looked up at Maxim suddenly. "Tell me, Mr. Furnival, did you at any time suspect that your wife was having an affair with General Carlyon?"

Maxim's face was pale, and he stiffened as if the question were distasteful, but not unexpected.

"No, I did not. If I said I trusted my wife, you would no doubt find that of no value, but I had known General Carlyon for many years, and I knew that he was not a man to enter into such a relationship. He had been a friend to both of us for some fifteen years. Had I at any time suspected there to

298

be anything improper I should not have allowed it to continue. That surely you can believe?"

"Of course, Mr. Furnival. Would it be true then to say that you would find Mrs. Carlyon's jealousy in that area to be unfounded, not an understandable passion rooted in a cause that anyone might sympathize with?"

Maxim looked unhappy, his eyes downcast, avoiding Lovat-Smith.

"I find it hard to believe she truly thought there was an affair," he said very quietly. "I cannot explain it."

"Your wife is a very beautiful woman, sir; jealousy is not always a rational emotion. Unreasonable suspicion can—"

Rathbone was on his feet.

"My lord, my honorable friend's speculations on the nature of jealousy are irrelevant to this case, and may prejudice the jury's opinions, since they are being presented as belonging to Mrs. Carlyon in this instance."

"Your objection is sustained," the judge said without hesitation, then turned to Lovat-Smith. "Mr. Lovat-Smith, you know better than that. Prove your point, do not philosophize."

"I apologize, my lord. Thank you, Mr. Furnival, that is all."

"Mr. Rathbone?" the judge invited.

Rathbone rose to his feet and faced the witness box.

"Mr. Furnival, may I take you back to earlier in the evening; to be precise, when Mrs. Erskine went upstairs to see your son. Do you recall that?"

"Yes." Maxim looked puzzled.

"Did she tell you, either then or later, what transpired when she was upstairs?"

Maxim frowned. "No."

"Did anyone else—for example, your son, Valentine?"

"No."

"Both you and Mrs. Furnival have testified that when Mrs. Erskine came down again she was extremely distressed, so much so that she was unable to behave normally for the rest of the evening. Is that correct?"

"Yes." Maxim looked embarrassed. Hester guessed not for himself but for Damaris. It was indelicate to refer to someone's emotional behavior in public, particularly a woman, and a friend. Gentlemen did not speak of such things.

Rathbone flashed him a brief smile.

"Thank you. Now back to the vexing question of whether Mrs. Furnival and General Carlyon were having any nature of relationship which was improper. You have sworn that at no time during the fifteen years or so of their friendship did you have any cause to believe it was not perfectly open and seemly, and all that either you as Mrs. Furnival's husband, or the accused as the general's wife, would have agreed to— as indeed you did agree. Do I understand you correctly, sir?"

Several of the jurors were looking sideways up at Alexandra, their faces curious.

"Yes, you do. At no time did I have any cause whatsoever to believe it was anything but a perfectly proper friendship," Maxim said stiffly, his eyes on Rathbone, his brows drawn down in concentration.

Hester glanced at the jury and saw one or two of them nodding. They believed him; his honesty was transparent, as was his discomfort.

"Did you suppose Mrs. Carlyon to feel the same?"

"Yes! Yes I did!" Maxim's face became animated for the first time since the subject had been raised. "I—I still find it hard—"

"Indeed," Rathbone cut him off. "Did she ever say anything in your hearing, or do anything at all, to indicate that she thought otherwise? Please—please be quite specific. I do not wish for speculation or interpretation in the light of later events. Did she ever express anger or jealousy of Mrs. Furnival with regard to her husband and their relationship?"

"No—never," Maxim said without hesitation. "Nothing at all." He had avoided looking across at Alexandra, as if afraid the jury might misinterpret his motives or doubt his honesty, but now he could not stop his eyes from flickering for a moment towards her.

"You are quite certain?" Rathbone insisted.

300

"Quite."

The judge frowned, looking closely at Rathbone. He leaned forward as if to say something, then changed his mind.

Lovat-Smith frowned also.

"Thank you, Mr. Furnival." Rathbone smiled at him. "You have been very frank, and it is much appreciated. It is distasteful to all of us to have to ask such questions and open up to public speculation what should remain private, but the force of circumstances leaves us no alternative. Now unless Mr. Lovat-Smith has some further questions for you, you may leave the stand."

"No—thank you," Lovat-Smith replied, half rising to his feet. "None at all."

Maxim left, going down the steps slowly, and the next witness was called, Sabella Carlyon Pole. There was a ripple of expectation around the court, murmurs of excitement, rustles of fabric against fabric as people shifted position, craned forward in the gallery, jostling each other.

"That's the daughter," someone said to Hester's left. "Mad, so they say. 'Ated her father."

"I 'ate my father," came the reply. "That don't make me mad!"

"Sssh," someone else hissed angrily.

Sabella came into the court and walked across the floor, head high, back stiff, and took the stand. She was very pale, but her face was set in an expression of defiance, and she looked straight at her mother in the dock and forced herself to smile.

For the first time since the trial had begun, Alexandra looked as if her composure would break. Her mouth quivered, the steady gaze softened, she blinked several times. Hester could not bear to watch her; she looked away, and felt a coward, and yet had she not turned, she would have felt intrusive. She did not know which was worse.

Sabella swore to her name and place of residence, and to her relationship with the accused.

"I realize this must be painful for you, Mrs. Pole," Lovat-Smith began courteously. "I wish it were possible for me to

301

spare you it, but I regret it is not. However I will try to be brief. Do you recall the evening of the dinner party at which your father met his death?"

"Of course! It is not the sort of thing one forgets."

"Naturally." Lovat-Smith was a trifle taken aback. He had been expecting a woman a little tearful, even afraid of him, or at the very least awed by the situation. "I understand that as soon as you arrived you had a disagreement with your father, is that correct?"

"Yes, perfectly."

"What was that about, Mrs. Pole?"

"He was patronizing about my views that there was going to be trouble in the army in India. As it turns out, I was correct."

There was a murmur of sympathy around the room, and another sharper one of irritation that she should presume to disagree with a military hero, a man, and her father—and someone who was dead and could not answer for himself; still worse, that the appalling news coming in on the India and China mail ships should prove her right.

"Is that all?" Lovat-Smith raised his eyebrows.

"Yes. It was a few sharp words, no more."

"Did your mother quarrel with him that evening?"

Hester looked sideways at the dock. Alexandra's face was tense, filled with anxiety, but Hester believed it was fear for Sabella, not for herself.

"I don't know. Not in my hearing," Sabella answered levelly.

"Have you ever heard your parents quarrel?"

"Of course."

"On what subject, in the last six months, let us say?"

"Particularly, over whether my brother Cassian should be sent away to boarding school or remain at home and have a tutor. He is eight years old."

"Your parents disagreed?"

"Yes."

"Passionately?" Lovat-Smith looked curious and surprised.

"Yes," she said tartly. "Apparently they felt passionately about it."

"Your mother wished him to remain at home with her, and your father wished him to begin his training for adulthood?"

"Not at all. It was Father who wanted him at home. Mama wanted him to go away to school."

Several jurors looked startled, and more than one turned to look at Alexandra.

"Indeed!" Lovat-Smith also sounded surprised, but uninterested in such details, although he had asked for them. "What else?"

"I don't know. I have my own home, Mr. Lovat-Smith. I visited my parents very infrequently. I did not have a close relationship with my father, as I am sure you know. My mother visited me in my home often. My father did not."

"I see. But you were aware that the relationship between your parents was strained, and on the evening of the unfortunate dinner party, particularly so?"

Sabella hesitated, and in so doing betrayed her partiality. Hester saw the jury's faces harden, as if something inside had closed; from now on they would interpret a difference in her answers. One man turned curiously and looked at Alexandra, then away again, as if caught peeping. It too was a betraying gesture.

"Mrs. Pole?" Lovat-Smith prompted her.

"Yes, of course I was aware of it. Everyone was."

"And the cause? Think carefully: knowing your mother, as close to you as she was, did she say anything which allowed you to understand the cause of her anger?"

Rathbone half rose to his feet, then as the judge glanced at him, changed his mind and sank back again. The jury saw it and their faces lit with expectancy.

Sabella spoke very quietly. "When people are unhappy with each other, there is not necessarily a specific cause for each disagreement. My father was very arbitrary at times, very dictatorial. The only subject of quarrel I know of was over Cassian and his schooling."

"Surely you are not suggesting your mother murdered your father because of his choice of education for his son, Mrs. Pole?" Lovat-Smith's voice, charming and distinctive, was filled with incredulity only just short of the offensive.

In the dock Alexandra moved forward impulsively, and the wardress beside her moved also, as if it were even conceivable she should leap over the edge. The gallery could not see it, but the jurors started in their seats.

Sabella said nothing. Her soft oval face hardened and she stared at him, not knowing what to say and reluctant to commit an error.

"Thank you, Mrs. Pole. We quite understand." Lovat-Smith smiled and sat down again, leaving the floor to Rathbone.

Sabella looked at Rathbone guardedly, her cheeks flushed, her eyes wary and miserable.

Rathbone smiled at her. "Mrs. Pole, have you known Mrs. Furnival for some time, several years in fact?"

"Yes."

"Did you believe that she was having an affair with your father?"

There was a gasp of indrawn breath around the courtroom. At last someone was getting to the crux of the situation. Excitement rippled through them.

"No," Sabella said hotly. Then she looked at Rathbone's expression and repeated it with more composure. "No, I did not. I never saw or heard anything to make me think so."

"Did your mother ever say anything to you to indicate that she thought so, or that the relationship gave her any anxiety or distress of any sort?"

"No—no, I cannot recall that she ever mentioned it at all."

"Never?" Rathbone said with surprise. "And yet you were very close, were you not?"

For the first time Sabella quite openly looked up towards the dock.

"Yes, we were—we are close."

"And she never mentioned the subject?"

"No."

"Thank you." He turned back to Lovat-Smith with a smile.

Lovat-Smith rose.

"Mrs. Pole, did you kill your father?"

The judge held up his hand to prevent Sabella from replying, and looked at Rathbone, inviting him to object. It was an improper question, since it had not been part of the examination in chief, and also she should be warned of the possibility of incriminating herself.

Rathbone shrugged.

The judge sighed and lowered his hand, frowning at Lovat-Smith.

"You do not need to answer that question unless you wish to," he said to Sabella.

"No, I did not," Sabella said huskily, her voice little more than a whisper.

"Thank you." Lovat-Smith inclined his head; it was all he had required.

The judge leaned forward. "You may go, Mrs. Pole," he said gently. "There is nothing further."

"Oh," she said, as if a little lost and wishing to find something more to say, something to help. Reluctantly she came down, assisted for the last two steps by the clerk of the court, and disappeared into the crowd, the light catching for a moment on her pale hair before she was gone.

There was an adjournment for luncheon. Monk and Hester found a man with a sandwich cart, purchased a sandwich each and ate them in great haste before returning to find their seats again.

As soon as the court reassembled and came to order the next witness was summoned.

"Fenton Pole!" the bailiff said loudly. "Calling Fenton Pole!"

Fenton Pole climbed up the stairs to the stand, his face set, his jaw hard in lines of utter disapproval. He answered Lovat-Smith tersely but very much as though he believed his mother-in-law to be guilty, but insane. Never even for an instant did he turn his head and look up at her. Twice Lovat-

305

Smith had to stop him from expressing his view in so many words, as if it excused the family from any connection. After all madness was like a disease, a tragedy which might strike anyone, therefore they were not accountable. His resentment of the whole matter was apparent.

There were murmurs of sympathy from the crowd, even one quite audible word of agreement; but looking at the jury again Hester could see at least one man's face cloud over and a certain disapproval touch him. He seemed to take his duty very seriously, and had probably been told much about not judging the case before all the evidence was in. And for all he sought impartiality, he did not admire disloyalty. He shot Fenton Pole a look of deep dislike. For an instant Hester felt unreasonably comforted. It was silly, and her wiser self knew it, and yet it was a straw in the wind, a sign that at least one man had not yet condemned Alexandra outright.

Rathbone asked Fenton Pole very little, only if he had any precise and incontrovertible evidence that his father-in-law was having an affair with Louisa Furnival.

Pole's face darkened with contempt for such vulgarity, and with offense that the matter should have been raised at all.

"Certainly not," he said vigorously. "General Carlyon was not an immoral man. To suppose that he indulged in such adulterous behavior is quite unbalanced, not rational at all, and without any foundation in fact."

"Quite so," Rathbone agreed. "And have you any cause, Mr. Pole, to suppose that your mother-in-law, Mrs. Carlyon, believed him to be so deceiving her, and betraying his vows?"

Pole's lips tightened.

"I would have thought our presence here today was tragically sufficient proof of that."

"Oh no, Mr. Pole, not at all," Rathbone replied with a harsh sibilance to his voice. "It is proof only that General Carlyon is dead, by violence, and that the police have some cause, rightly or wrongly, to bring a case against Mrs. Carlyon."

There was a rustle of movement in the jury. Someone sat up a trifle straighter.

Fenton Pole looked confused. He did not argue, although the rebuttal was plain in his face.

"You have not answered my question, Mr. Pole," Rathbone pressed him. "Did you see or hear anything to prove to you that Mrs. Carlyon believed there to be anything improper in the relationship between Mrs. Furnival and the general?"

"Ah—well . . . said like that, I suppose not. I don't know what you have in mind."

"Nothing, Mr. Pole. And it would be quite improper for me to suggest anything to you, as I am sure his lordship would inform you."

Fenton Pole did not even glance at the judge.

He was excused.

Lovat-Smith called the footman, John Barton. He was overawed by the occasion, and his fair face was flushed hot with embarrassment. He stuttered as he took the oath and gave his name, occupation and residence. Lovat-Smith was extremely gentle with him and never once condescended or treated him with less courtesy than he had Fenton Pole or Maxim Furnival. To the most absolute silence from the court and the rapt attention of the jury, he elicited from him the whole story of the clearing away after the dinner party, the carrying of the coal buckets up the front stairs, the observation of the suit of armor still standing on its plinth, who was in the withdrawing room, his meeting with the maid, and the final inevitable conclusion that only either Sabella or Alexandra could possibly have killed Thaddeus Carlyon.

There was a slow letting out of a sigh around the courtroom, like the first chill air of a coming storm.

Rathbone rose amid a crackling silence. Not a juryman moved.

"I have no questions to ask this witness, my lord."

There was a gasp of amazement. Jurors swiveled around to look at one another in disbelief.

The judge leaned forward. "Are you sure, Mr. Rathbone? This witness's evidence is very serious for your client."

"I am quite sure, thank you, my lord."

The judge frowned. "Very well." He turned to John. "You are excused."

Lovat-Smith called the upstairs maid with the red hair, and sealed beyond doubt the incontestable fact that it could only have been Alexandra who pushed the general over the stairs, and then followed him down and plunged the halberd into his body.

"I don't know why this has to go on," a man said behind Monk. "Waste o' time."

"Waste o' money," his companion agreed. "Should just call it done, 'ang 'er now. Nothing anyone can say to that."

Monk swung around, his face tight, hard, eyes blazing.

"Because Englishmen don't hang people without giving them a chance to explain," he said between his teeth. "It's a quaint custom, but we give everyone a hearing, whatever we think of them. If that doesn't suit you, then you'd better go somewhere else, because there's no place for you here!"

" 'Ere! 'Oo are you callin' foreign? I'm as English as you are! An' I pay me taxes, but not for the likes of 'er to play fast an' loose wi' the law. I believe in the law, I do. Can't 'ave women going 'round murderin' their 'usbands every time they get a fit o' jealousy. No one in England'd be safe!"

"You don't believe in the law," Monk accused bitterly. "You believe in the rope, and mob rule, you just said so."

"I never did. You lyin' bastard!"

"You said forget the trial, overthrow the courts, hang her now, without waiting for a verdict." Monk glared at him. "You want to do away with judge and jury and be both yourself."

"I never said that!"

Monk gave him a look of total disgust, and turned to Hester, as they rose on adjournment, taking her a trifle roughly by the elbow, and steering her out through the noisy, shoving crowd.

There was nothing to say. It was what they could have expected: a crowd who knew no more than the newspapers had led them to believe; a judge who was fair, impartial and unable to help; a prosecuting counsel who was skilled and would be duped or misled by no one. The evidence proved that Alexandra had murdered her husband. That should not depress them or make them the least discouraged. It was not in question.

Monk was pushing his way through the people who jostled and talked, swirling around like dead leaves in an eddy of wind, infuriating him because he had purpose and was trying to force his way out as if somehow haste could help them to escape what was in their minds.

They were out in Old Bailey and turning onto Ludgate Hill when at last he spoke.

"I hope to God he knows what he is doing."

"That is a stupid thing to say," she replied angrily, because she was frightened herself, and stung for Rathbone. "He's doing his best—what we all agreed on. And anyway, what alternative is there? There isn't any other plan. She did do it. It would be pointless to try to deny it. There's nothing else to say, except the reason why."

"No," he agreed grimly. "No, there isn't. Damn, but it's cold. June shouldn't be this cold."

She managed to smile. "Shouldn't it? It frequently is."

He glared at her wordlessly.

"It'll get better." She shrugged and pulled her cloak higher. "Thank you for saving me a seat. I'll be here tomorrow."

She parted from him and set off into the chill air. She took a hansom, in spite of the expense, to Callandra Daviot's house.

"What has happened?" Callandra asked immediately, rising from her chair, her face anxious as she regarded Hester, seeing her tiredness, the droop of her shoulders and the fear in her eyes. "Come sit down—tell me."

Hester sat obediently. "Only what we expected, I suppose. But they all seem so very rational and set in their ideas. They know she did it—Lovat-Smith has proved that already. I just feel as if no matter what we say, they'll never believe he was anything but a fine man, a soldier and a hero. How can we prove he sodomized his own son?" Deliberately she used the hardest word she could find, and was perversely

309

annoyed when Callandra did not flinch. "They'll only hate her the more fiercely that we could say such a thing about such a fine man." She spoke with heavy sarcasm. "They'll hang her higher for the insult."

"Find the others," Callandra said levelly, her gray eyes sad and hard. "The alternative is giving up. Are you prepared to do that?"

"No, of course not. But I'm trying to think, if we are realistic, we should be prepared to be beaten."

Callandra stared at her, waiting, refusing to speak.

Hester met her look silently, then gradually began to think.

"The general's father abused him." She was fumbling towards something, a thread to begin pulling. "I don't suppose he started doing it himself suddenly, do you?"

"I have no idea—but sense would suggest not."

"There must be something to find in the past, if only we knew where to look," she went on, trying to make herself believe. "We've got to find the others; the other people who do this abysmal thing. But where? It's no use saying the old colonel did—we'll never prove that. He'll deny it, so will everyone else, and the general is dead."

She leaned back slowly. "Anyway, what would be the use? Even if we proved someone else did, that would not prove it of the general, or that Alexandra knew. I don't know where to begin. And time is so short." She stared at Callandra miserably. "Oliver has to start the defense in a couple of days, at the outside. Lovat-Smith is proving his case to the hilt. We haven't said a single thing worth anything yet—only that there was no evidence Alexandra was jealous."

"Not the others who abuse," Callandra said quietly. "The other victims. We must search the military records again."

"There's no time," Hester said desperately. "It would take months. And there might be nothing anyway."

"If he did that in the army, there will be something to find." Callandra's voice had no uncertainty in it, no quaver of doubt. "You stay at the trial. I'll search for some slip he's made, some drummer boy or cadet who's been hurt enough for it to show."

310

"Do you think . . . ?" Hester felt a quick leap of hope, foolish, quite unreasonable.

"Calm down, order your mind," Callandra commanded. "Tell me again everything that we know about the whole affair!"

Hester obeyed.

When the court was adjourned Oliver Rathbone was on his way out when Lovat-Smith caught up with him, his dark face sharp with curiosity. There was no avoiding him, and Rathbone was only half certain he wanted to. He had a need to speak with him, as one is sometimes compelled to probe a wound to see just how deep or how painful it is.

"What in the devil's name made you take this one?" Lovat-Smith demanded, his eyes meeting Rathbone's, brilliant with intelligence. There was a light in the back of them which might have been a wry kind of pity, or any of a dozen other things, all equally uncomfortable. "What are you playing at? You don't even seem to be trying. There are no miracles in this, you know. She did it!"

Somehow the goad lifted Rathbone's spirits; it gave him something to fight against. He looked back at Lovat-Smith, a man he respected, and if he were to know him better, might even like. They had much in common.

"I know she did," he said with a dry, close little smile. "Have I worried you, Wilberforce?"

Lovat-Smith smiled with answering tightness, his eyes bright. "Concerned me, Oliver, concerned me. I should not like to see you lose your touch. Your skill hitherto has been one of the ornaments of our profession. It would be . . . disconcerting"—he chose the word deliberately—"to have you crumble to pieces. What certitude then would there be for any of us?"

"How kind of you," Rathbone murmured sarcastically. "But easy victories pall after a while. If one always wins, perhaps one is attempting only what is well within one's capabilities—and there lies a kind of death, don't you think?

That which does not grow may well be showing the first signs of atrophy.''

They were passed by two lawyers, heads close together. They both turned to look at Rathbone, curiosity in their faces, before they resumed their conversation.

"All probably true," Lovat-Smith conceded, his eyes never leaving Rathbone's, a smile curling his mouth. "But though it is fine philosophy, it has nothing to do with the Carlyon case. Are you going to try for diminished responsibility? You've left it rather late—the judge will not take kindly to your not having said so at the beginning. You should have pleaded guilty but insane. I would have been prepared to consider meeting you somewhere on that."

"Do you think she's insane?" Rathbone enquired with raised eyebrows, disbelief in his voice.

Lovat-Smith pulled a face. "She didn't seem so. But in view of your masterly proof that no one thought there was an affair between Mrs. Furnival and the general, not even Mrs. Carlyon herself, by all accounts, what else is there? Isn't that what you are leading to: her assumption was groundless, and mad?''

Rathbone's smile broadened into a grin. "Come along, Wilberforce. You know better than that! You'll hear my defense when the rest of the court does.''

Lovat-Smith shook his head, a furrow between his black eyebrows.

Rathbone gave him a tiny mock salute with more bravado than he felt, and took his leave. Lovat-Smith stood on the spot on the great courtroom steps, deep in thought, seemingly unaware of the coming and going around him, the crush of people, the chatter of voices.

Instead of going home, which perhaps he ought to have done, Rathbone took a hansom and went out to Primrose Hill to take supper with his father. He found Henry Rathbone standing in the garden looking at the young moon pale in the sky above the orchard trees, and half listening to the birdsong as the late starlings swirled across the sky and here and there a thrush or a chaffinch gave a warning cry.

For several moments they both stood in silence, letting the peace of the evening smooth out the smallest of the frets and wrinkles of the day. The bigger things, the pains and disappointments, took a firmer shape, less angry. Temper drained away.

"Well?" Henry Rathbone said eventually, half turning to look at Oliver.

"I suppose as well as could be expected," Oliver replied. "Lovat-Smith thinks I have lost my grip in taking the case at all. He may be right. In the cold light of the courtroom it seems a pretty wild attempt. Sometimes I even wonder if I believe in it myself. The public image of General Thaddeus Carlyon is impeccable, and the private one almost as good." He remembered vividly his father's anger and dismay, his imagination of pain, when he had told him of the abuse. He did not look at him now.

"Who testified today?" Henry asked quietly.

"The Furnivals. Lord, I loathe Louisa Furnival!" he said with sudden vehemence. "She is the total antithesis of everything I find attractive in a woman. Devious, manipulative, cocksure of herself, humorless, materialistic and completely unemotional. But I cannot fault her in the witness box." His face tightened. "And how I wanted to. I would take the greatest possible pleasure in tearing her to shreds!"

"How is Hester Latterly?"

"What?"

"How is Hester?" Henry repeated.

"What made you ask that?" Oliver screwed up his face.

"The opposite of everything you find attractive in a woman," Henry replied with a quiet smile.

Oliver blushed, a thing he did not do often. "I didn't see her," he said, feeling ridiculously evasive although it was the absolute truth.

Henry said nothing further, and perversely Oliver felt worse than if he had pursued the matter and allowed him to argue.

313

Beyond the orchard wall another cloud of starlings rose chattering into the pale sky and circled around, dark specks against the last flush of the sun. The honeysuckle was coming into bloom and the perfume of it was so strong the breeze carried it across the lawn to where they were standing. Oliver felt a rush of emotion, a sweetness, a longing to hold the beauty and keep it, which was impossible and always would be, a loneliness because he ached to share it, and pity, confusion and piercing hope all at once. He remained silent because silence was the only space large enough to hold it without crushing or bruising the heart of it.

The following morning he went to see Alexandra before court began. He did not know what he could say to her, but to leave her alone would be inexcusable. She was in the police cell, and as soon as she heard his step she swung around, her eyes wide, her face drained of all color. He could feel the fear in her touching him like a palpable thing.

"They hate me," she said simply, her voice betraying the tears so close to the surface. "They have already made up their minds. They aren't even listening. I heard one woman call out 'Hang her!' " She struggled to keep her control and almost failed. She blinked hard. "If women feel like that, what hope is there for me with the jury, who are all men?"

"More hope," he said very gently, and was amazed at the certainty in his own voice. Without thinking he took her hands in his, at first quite unresisting, like those of someone too ill to respond. "More hope," he said again with even greater assurance. "The woman you heard was frightened because you threaten her own status if you are allowed to go free and Society accepts you. Her only value in her own eyes is the certainty of her unquestionable purity. She has nothing else marketable, no talent, no beauty, no wealth or social position, but she has her impeccable virtue. Therefore virtue must keep its unassailable value. She does not understand virtue as a positive thing—generosity, patience, courage, kindness—only as the freedom from taint. That is so much easier to cope with."

She smiled bleakly. "You make it sound so very reasonable, and I don't feel it is at all. I feel it as hate." Her voice quivered.

"Of course it is hate, because it is fear, which is one of the ugliest of emotions. But later, when they have the truth, it will swing 'round like the wind, and blow just as hard from the other direction."

"Do you think so?" There was no belief in her and no lightness in her eyes.

"Yes," he said with more certainty than he was sure of. "Then it will be compassion and outrage—and fear lest such a thing happen to those they love, their own children. We are capable of great ugliness and stupidity," he said gently. "But you will find many of the same people just as capable of courage and pity as well. We must tell them the truth so they can have the chance."

She shivered and half turned away.

"We are singing in the dark, Mr. Rathbone. They aren't going to believe you, for the very reasons you talk about. Thaddeus was a hero, the sort of hero they need to believe in, because there are hundreds like him in the army, and they are what keep us safe and build our Empire." She hunched a little farther into herself. "They protect us from the real armies outside, and from the armies of doubt inside. If you destroy the British soldier in his red coat, the men who stood against all Europe and defeated Napoleon, saved England from the French, acquired Africa, India, Canada, quarter of the world, what have you left? No one is going to do that for one woman who is a criminal anyway."

"All you are saying is that the odds are heavy against us." He deliberately made his voice harder, suppressing the emotion he felt. "That same redcoat would not have turned away from battle because he was not sure of winning. You haven't read his history if you can entertain that thought for a second. His finest victories have been when outnumbered and against the odds."

"Like the charge of the Light Brigade?" she said with sudden sarcasm. "Do you know how many of them died? And for nothing at all!"

"Yes, one man in six of the entire Brigade—God knows how many were injured," he replied flatly, aware of a dull heat in his cheeks. "I was thinking more of the 'thin red line'—which if you recall stood a single man deep, and repulsed the enemy and held its ground till the charge broke and failed."

There was a smile on her wide mouth, and tears in her eyes, and no belief.

"Is that what you intend?"

"Certainly."

He could see she was still frightened, he could almost taste it in the air, but she had lost the will to fight him anymore. She turned away; it was surrender, and dismissal. She needed her time alone to prepare for the fear and the embarrassment, and the helplessness of the day.

The first witness was Charles Hargrave, called by Lovat-Smith to confirm the events of the dinner party already given, but primarily to retell his finding of the body of the general, with its terrible wound.

"Mr. Furnival came back into the room and said that the general had had an accident, is that correct?" Lovat-Smith asked.

Hargrave looked very serious, his face reflecting both his professional gravity and personal distress. The jury listened to him with a respect they reserved for the more distinguished members of certain professions: medicine, the Church, and lawyers who dealt with the bequests of the dead.

"Quite correct," Hargrave replied with a flicker of a smile across his rakish, rather elegant sandy face. "I presume he phrased it that way because he did not want to alarm people or cause more distress than necessary."

"Why do you say that, Doctor?"

"Because as soon as I went into the hallway myself and saw the body it was perfectly apparent that he was dead. Even a person with no medical training at all must have been aware of it."

"Could you describe his injuries—in full, please, Dr. Hargrave?"

The jury all shifted fractionally in their seats, attention and unhappiness vying in their expressions.

A shadow crossed Hargrave's face, but he was too practiced to need any explanation as to the necessity for such a thing.

"Of course," he agreed. "At the time I found him he was lying on his back with his left arm flung out, more or less level with one shoulder, but bent at the elbow. The right arm was only a short distance from his side, the hand twelve or fourteen inches from his hip. His legs were bent, the right folded awkwardly under him, and I judged it to be broken below the knee, his left leg severely twisted. These guesses later turned out to be correct." An expression crossed his face it was impossible to name, but it did not seem to be complacency. His eyes remained always on Lovat-Smith, never once straying upwards towards Alexandra in the dock opposite him.

"The injuries?" Lovat-Smith prompted.

"At the time all that was visible was bruising to the head, bleeding from the scalp at the left temple where he had struck the ground. There was a certain amount of blood, but not a great deal."

People in the gallery were craning their necks to stare up at Alexandra. There was a hiss of indrawn breath and a muttering.

"Let me understand you, Doctor." Lovat-Smith held up his hand, strong, short-fingered and slender. "There was only one injury to the head that you could see?"

"That is correct."

"As a medical man, what do you deduce from that?"

Hargrave lifted his wide shoulders very slightly. "That he fell straight over the banister and struck his head only once."

Lovat-Smith touched his left temple.

"Here?"

"Yes, within an inch or so."

"And yet he was lying on his back, did you not say?"

"I did," Hargrave said very quietly.

"Dr. Hargrave, Mr. Furnival has told us that the halberd was protruding from his chest." Lovat-Smith paced across

317

the floor and swung around, staring up at Hargrave on the witness box, his face creased in concentration. "How could a man fall from a balcony onto a weapon held upright in the hands of a suit of armour, piercing his chest, and land in such a way as to bruise himself on the front of his temple?"

The judge glanced at Rathbone.

Rathbone pursed his lips. He had no objections. He did not contest that Alexandra had murdered the general. This was all necessary, but beside the point of the real issue.

Lovat-Smith seemed surprised there was no interruption. Far from making it easier for him, it seemed to throw him a trifle off his stride.

"Dr. Hargrave," he said, shifting his balance from one foot to the other.

A juror fidgeted. Another scratched his nose and frowned.

"I have no idea," Hargrave replied. "It would seem to me as if the only explanation must be that he fell backwards, as one would naturally, and in some way twisted in the air after—" He stopped.

Lovat-Smith's black eyebrows rose curiously.

"You were saying, Doctor?" He spread his arms out. "He fell over backwards, turned in the air to allow the halberd to pierce his chest, and then somehow turned again so he could strike the floor with his temple? All without breaking the halberd or tearing it out of the wound. And then he rolled over to lie on his back with one leg folded under the other? You amaze me."

"Of course not," Hargrave said seriously, his temper unruffled, only a deep concern reflected in his face.

Rathbone glanced at the jury and knew they liked Hargrave, and Lovat-Smith had annoyed them. He also knew it was intentional. Hargrave was his witness, he wished him to be not only liked but profoundly believed.

"Then what are you saying, Dr. Hargrave?"

Hargrave was very serious. He looked at no one but Lovat-Smith, as if the two of them were discussing some tragedy in their gentlemen's club. There were faint mutters of approval from the crowd.

"That he must have fallen and struck his head, and then spun, the halberd been driven into his body when he was lying on the ground. Perhaps he was moved, but not necessarily. He could quite naturally have struck his head and then rolled a little to lie on his back. His head was at an odd angle—but his neck was not broken. I looked for that, and I am sure it was not so."

"You are saying it could not have been an accident, Dr. Hargrave?"

Hargrave's face tightened. "I am."

"How long did it take you to come to this tragic conclusion?"

"From the time I first saw the body, about—about one or two minutes, I imagine." A ghost of a smile moved his lips. "Time is a peculiar commodity on such an occasion. It seems both to stretch out endlessly, like a road before and behind with no turning, and at the same time to crush in on you and have no size at all. To say one or two minutes is only a guess, made afterwards using intelligence. It was one of the most dreadful moments I can recall."

"Why? Because you knew someone in that house, one of your personal friends, had murdered General Thaddeus Carlyon?"

Again the judge glanced at Rathbone, and Rathbone made no move. A frown crossed the judge's face, and still Rathbone did not object.

"Yes," Hargrave said almost inaudibly. "I regret it, but it was inescapable. I am sorry." For the first and only time he looked up at Alexandra.

"Just so," Lovat-Smith agreed solemnly. "And accordingly you informed the police?"

"I did."

"Thank you."

Rathbone looked at the jury again. Not one of them looked at the dock. She sat there motionless, her blue eyes on Rathbone, without anger, without surprise, and without hope.

He smiled at her, and felt ridiculous.

10

MONK LISTENED TO LOVAT-SMITH questioning Charles Hargrave with a mounting anxiety. Hargrave was creating an excellent impression with the jury; he could see their grave, attentive faces. He not only had their respect but their belief. Whatever he said about the Carlyons they would accept.

There was nothing Rathbone could do yet, and Monk's intelligence knew it; nevertheless he fretted at the helplessness and the anger rose in him, clenching his hands and hardening the muscles of his body.

Lovat-Smith stood in front of the witness box, not elegantly (it was not in him), but with a vitality that held attention more effectively, and his voice was fine, resonant and individual, an actor's instrument.

"Dr. Hargrave, you have known the Carlyon family for many years, and indeed been their medical adviser for most of that time, is that not so?"

"It is."

"You must be in a position to have observed their characters, their relationships with one another."

Rathbone stiffened, but did not yet interrupt.

Lovat-Smith smiled, glanced at Rathbone, then back up at Hargrave.

"Please be careful to answer only from your own observation," he warned. "Nothing that you were told by someone else, unless it is to account for their own behavior; and please do not give us your personal judgment, only the grounds upon which you base it."

"I understand," Hargrave acknowledged with the bleakest of smiles. "I have given evidence before, Mr. Lovat-Smith. What is it you wish to know?"

With extreme care as to the rules of evidence, all morning and well into the afternoon Lovat-Smith drew from Hargrave a picture of Thaddeus Carlyon as honorable and upright, a military hero, a fine leader to his men, an example to that youth which looked to courage, discipline and honor as their goals. He had been an excellent husband who had never ill-used his wife with physical violence or cruelty, nor made excessive demands of her in the marriage bed, but on the other hand had given her three fine children, to whom he had been a father of devotion beyond the normal. His son adored him, and rightly so, since he had spent much time with the boy and taken great care in the determination of his future. There was no evidence whatsoever that he had ever been unfaithful to his wife, nor drunk to excess, gambled, kept her short of money, insulted her, slighted her in public, or in any other way treated her less than extremely well.

Had he ever exhibited any signs whatever of mental or emotional instability?

None at all; the idea would be laughable, were it not so offensive.

What about the accused, who was also his patient?

That, tragically, was different. She had, in the last year or so, become agitated without apparent cause, been subject to deep moods of melancholy, had fits of weeping for which she would give no reason, had absented herself from her home without telling anyone where she was going, and had quarreled violently with her husband.

The jury were looking at Alexandra, but with embarrassment now, as if she were someone it was vulgar to observe, like someone naked, or caught in an intimate act.

"And how do you know this, Dr. Hargrave?" Lovat-Smith enquired.

Still Rathbone sat silently.

"Of course I did not hear the quarrels," Hargrave said, biting his lip. "But the weeping and the melancholy I saw, and the absences were apparent to everyone. I called more than once and found unexplainably that she was not there. I am afraid the agitation, for which she would never give me a reason, was painfully obvious each time she saw me in consultation. She was so disturbed as to be hysterical—I use the word intentionally. But she never gave me any reason, only wild hints and accusations."

"Of what?" Lovat-Smith frowned. His voice rose dramatically with interest, as if he did not know what the answer would be, although Monk, sitting almost in the same seat as on the previous day, assumed he must. Surely he was far too skilled to have asked the question without first knowing the answer. Although it was just possible his case was so strong, and proceeding without challenge, that he might have thought he could take the risk.

The jury leaned forward a trifle; there was a tiny rustle of movement. Beside Monk on the bench Hester stiffened. The spectators near them felt no such restraints of delicacy as the jury. They stared at Alexandra quite openly, faces agog.

"Accusations of unfaithfulness on the general's part?" Lovat-Smith prompted.

The judge looked at Rathbone. Lovat-Smith was leading the witness. Rathbone said nothing. The judge's face tightened, but he did not interrupt.

"No," Hargrave said reluctantly. He drew in his breath. "At least, they were unspecific, I was not sure. I think she was merely speaking wildly, lashing out at anyone. She was hysterical; it made no sense."

"I see. Thank you." Lovat-Smith inclined his head. "That is all, Doctor. Please remain where you are, in case my learned friend wishes to question you."

"Oh indeed, I do." Rathbone rose to his feet, his voice purring, his movements tigerlike. "You spoke most frankly about the Carlyon family, and I accept that you have told us all you know, trivial as that is.'' He looked up at Hargrave in the high, pulpitlike witness stand. "Am I correct, Dr. Hargrave, in supposing that your friendship with them dates back some fifteen or sixteen years?''

"Yes, you are.'' Hargrave was puzzled; he had already said this to Lovat-Smith.

"In fact as a friendship with the family, rather than General Carlyon, it ceased some fourteen years ago, and you have seen little of them since then?''

"I—suppose so.'' Hargrave was reluctant, but not disturbed; his sandy face held no disquiet. It seemed a minor point.

"So in fact you cannot speak with any authority on the character of, for example, Mrs. Felicia Carlyon? Or Colonel Carlyon?''

Hargrave shrugged. It was an oddly graceful gesture. "If you like. It hardly seems to matter; they are not on trial.''

Rathbone smiled, showing all his teeth.

"But you mentioned your friendship with General Carlyon?''

"Yes. I was his physician, as well as that of his wife and family.''

"Indeed, I am coming to that. You say that Mrs. Carlyon, the accused, began to exhibit signs of extreme distress— indeed you used the word *hysteria*?''

"Yes—I regret to say she did,'' Hargrave agreed.

"What did she do, precisely, Doctor?''

Hargrave looked uncomfortable. He glanced at the judge, who met his eyes without response.

"The question disturbs you?'' Rathbone remarked.

"It seems unnecessarily—exposing—of a patient's vulnerability,'' Hargrave replied, but his eyes remained on Rathbone; Alexandra herself might have been absent for all the awareness he showed of her.

"You may leave Mrs. Carlyon's interest in my hands,'' Rathbone assured him. "I am here to represent her. Please answer my question. Describe her behavior. Did she scream?" He leaned back a little to stare up at Hargrave, his eyes very wide. "Did she faint, take a fit?" He spread his hands wide. "Throw herself about, have hallucinations? In what way was she hysterical?"

Hargrave sighed impatiently. "You exhibit a layman's idea of hysteria, if you pardon my saying so. Hysteria is a state of mind where control is lost, not necessarily a matter of uncontrolled physical behavior."

"How did you know her mind was out of control, Dr. Hargrave?" Rathbone was very polite. Watching him, Monk longed for him to be thoroughly rude, to tear Hargrave to pieces in front of the jury. But his better sense knew it would forfeit their sympathy, which in the end was what would win or lose them the case—and Alexandra's life.

Hargrave thought for a moment before beginning.

"She could not keep still," he said at length. "She kept moving from one position to another, at times unable even to remain seated. Her whole body shook and when she picked up something, I forget what, it slipped through her fingers. Her voice was trembling and she fumbled her words. She wept uncontrollably."

"But no deliriums, hallucinations, fainting, screaming?" Rathbone pressed.

"No. I have told you not." Hargrave was impatient and he glanced at the jury, knowing he had their sympathy.

"Tell us, Dr. Hargrave, how would this behavior differ from that of someone who had just received a severe shock and was extremely distressed, even agonized, by her experience?"

Hargrave thought for several seconds.

"I cannot think that it would," he said at last. "Except that she did not speak of any shock, or discovery."

Rathbone opened his eyes wide, as if mildly surprised. "She did not even hint that she had learned her husband had betrayed her with another woman?"

He leaned a little forward over the rail of the witness box. "No—no, she did not. I think I have already said, Mr. Rathbone, that she could have made no such dramatic discovery,

324

because it was not so. This affair, if you wish to call it that, was all in her imagination."

"Or yours, Doctor," Rathbone said, his voice suddenly gritted between his teeth.

Hargrave flushed, but with embarrassment and anger rather than guilt. His eyes remained fixed on Rathbone and there was no evasion in them.

"I answered your question, Mr. Rathbone," he said bitterly. "You are putting words into my mouth. I did not say there was an affair, indeed I said there was not!"

"Just so," Rathbone agreed, turning back to the body of the court again. "There was no affair, and Mrs. Carlyon at no time mentioned it to you, or suggested that it was the cause of her extreme distress."

"That is . . ." Hargrave hesitated, as if he would add something, then found no words and remained silent.

"But she was extremely distressed by something, you are positive about that?"

"Of course."

"Thank you. When did this occur, your first observation of her state of mind?"

"I have not a precise date, but it was in July of last year."

"Approximately nine months before the general's death?"

"That is right." Hargrave smiled. It was a trivial calculation.

"And you have no idea of any event at this time which could have precipitated it?"

"No idea at all."

"You were General Carlyon's physician?"

"I have already said so."

"Indeed. And you have recounted the few occasions on which you were called to treat him professionally. He seems to have been a man in excellent health, and those injuries he sustained in action were quite naturally treated by the army surgeons in the field."

"You are stating the obvious," Hargrave said with tight lips.

"Perhaps it is obvious to you why you did not mention the

one wound that you did treat, but it escapes me," Rathbone said with the smallest of smiles.

For the first time Hargrave was visibly discomfited. He opened his mouth, said nothing, and closed it again. His hands on the rail were white at the knuckles.

There was silence in the courtroom.

Rathbone walked across the floor a pace or two and turned back.

There was a sudden lifting of interest throughout the court. The jury shifted on their benches almost imperceptibly.

Hargrave's face tightened, but he could not avoid an answer, and he knew it.

"It was a domestic accident, and all rather foolish," he said, lifting his shoulder a little as if to dismiss it, and at the same time explain its omission. "He was cleaning an ornamental dagger and it slipped and cut him in the upper leg."

"You observed this happen?" Rathbone asked casually.

"Ah—no. I was called to the house because the wound was bleeding quite badly, and naturally I asked him what had happened. He told me."

"Then it is hearsay?" Rathbone raised his eyebrows. "Not satisfactory, Doctor. It may have been the truth—equally it may not."

Lovat-Smith came to his feet.

"Is any of this relevant, my lord? I can understand my learned friend's desire to distract the jury's minds from Dr. Hargrave's evidence, indeed to try and discredit him in some way, but this is wasting the court's time and serving no purpose at all."

The judge looked at Rathbone.

"Mr. Rathbone, do you have some object in view? If not, I shall have to order you to move on."

"Oh yes, my lord," Rathbone said with more confidence than Monk thought he could feel. "I believe the injury may be of crucial importance to the case."

Lovat-Smith swung around with an expressive gesture, raising his hands palm upwards.

Someone in the courtroom tittered with laughter, and it was instantly suppressed.

Hargrave sighed.

"Please describe the injury, Doctor," Rathbone continued.

"It was a deep gash to the thigh, in the front and slightly to the inside, precisely where a knife might have slipped from one's hand while cleaning it."

"Deep? An inch? Two inches? And how long, Doctor?"

"About an inch and a half at its deepest, and some five inches long," Hargrave replied with wry, obvious weariness.

"Quite a serious injury. And pointing in which direction?" Rathbone asked with elaborate innocence.

Hargrave stood silent, his face pale.

In the dock Alexandra leaned a fraction forward for the first time, as if at last something had been said which she had not expected.

"Please answer the question, Dr. Hargrave," the judge instructed.

"Ah—er—it was . . . upwards," Hargrave said awkwardly.

"Upwards?" Rathbone blinked and even from behind his elegant shoulders expressed incredulity, as if he could not have heard correctly. "You mean—from the knee up towards the groin, Dr. Hargrave?"

"Yes," Hargrave said almost inaudibly.

"I beg your pardon? Would you please repeat that so the jury can hear you?"

"Yes," Hargrave said grimly.

The jury was puzzled. Two leaned forward. One shifted in his seat, another frowned in deep concentration. They did not know what relevance it could possibly have, but they knew duress when they saw it, and felt Hargrave's reluctance and the sudden change in tension.

Even the crowd was silent.

A lesser man than Lovat-Smith would have interrupted again, but he knew it would only betray his own uncertainty.

"Tell us, Dr. Hargrave," Rathbone went on quietly, "how

327

a man cleaning a knife could have it slip from his hand so as to stab himself upwards, from knee to groin?" He turned on the spot, very slowly. "In fact, perhaps you would oblige us by showing us exactly what motion you had in mind when you—er—believed this account of his? I presume you know why a military man of his experience, a general indeed, should be clumsy enough to clean a knife so incompetently? I would have expected better from the rank and file." He frowned. "In fact, ordinary man as I am, I have no ornamental knives, but I do not clean my own silver, or my own boots."

"I have no idea why he cleaned it," Hargrave replied, leaning forward over the rail of the witness box, his hands gripping the edge. "But since it was he who had the accident with it, I was quite ready to believe him. Perhaps it was because he did not normally clean it that he was clumsy."

He had made a mistake, and he knew it immediately. He should not have tried to justify it.

"You cannot know it was he who had the accident, if indeed it was an accident," Rathbone said with excessive politeness. "Surely what you mean is that it was he who had the wound?"

"If you wish," Hargrave replied tersely. "It seems a quibble to me."

"And the manner in which he was holding it to sustain such a wound as you describe so clearly for us?" Rathbone raised his hand as if gripping a knife, and bent his body experimentally into various contortions to slip and gash himself upwards. It was perfectly impossible, and the court began to titter with nervous laughter. Rathbone looked up enquiringly at Hargrave.

"All right!" Hargrave snapped. "It cannot have happened as he said. What are you suggesting? That Alexandra tried to stab him? Surely you are supposed to be here defending her, not making doubly sure she is hanged!"

The judge leaned forward, his face angry, his voice sharp.

"Dr. Hargrave, your remarks are out of order, and grossly prejudicial. You will withdraw them immediately."

"Of course. I'm sorry. But I think it is Mr. Rathbone you should caution. He is incompetent in his defense of Mrs. Carlyon."

"I doubt it. I have known Mr. Rathbone for many years, but if he should prove to be so, then the accused may appeal on that ground." He looked towards Rathbone. "Please continue."

"Thank you, my lord." Rathbone bowed very slightly. "No, Dr. Hargrave, I was not suggesting that Mrs. Carlyon stabbed her husband, I was pointing out that he must have lied to you as to the cause of this wound, and that it seemed undeniable that someone stabbed him. I shall make my suggestions as to who, and why, at a later time."

There was another rustle of interest, and the first shadow of doubt across the faces of the jury. It was the only time they had been given any cause to question the case as Lovat-Smith had presented it. It was a very small shadow, no more than a flicker, but it was there.

Hargrave turned to step down.

"Just one more thing, Dr. Hargrave," Rathbone said quickly. "What was General Carlyon wearing when you were called to tend this most unpleasant wound?"

"I beg your pardon?" Hargrave looked incredulous.

"What was General Carlyon wearing?" Rathbone repeated. "In what was he dressed?"

"I have no idea. For God's sake! What does it matter?"

"Please answer my question," Rathbone insisted. "Surely you noticed, when you had to cut it away to reach the wound?"

Hargrave made as if to speak, then stopped, his face pale.

"Yes?" Rathbone said very softly.

"He wasn't." Hargrave seemed to regather himself. "It had already been removed. He had on simply his underwear."

"I see. No—no blood-soaked trousers?" Rathbone shrugged eloquently. "Someone had already at least partially treated him? Were these garments lying close to hand?"

"No—I don't think so. I didn't notice."

Rathbone frowned, a look of suddenly renewed interest crossing his face.

"Where did this—accident—take place, Dr. Hargrave?"

Hargrave hesitated. "I—I'm not sure."

Lovat-Smith rose from his seat and the judge looked at him and shook his head fractionally.

"If you are about to object that it is irrelevant, Mr. Lovat-Smith, I will save you the trouble. It is not. I myself wish to know the answer to this. Dr. Hargrave? You must have some idea. He cannot have moved far with a wound such as you describe. Where did you see him when you attended it?"

Hargrave was pale, his face drawn.

"In the home of Mr. and Mrs. Furnival, my lord."

There was a rustle of excitement around the room, a letting out of breath. At least half the jurors turned to look up at Alexandra, but her face registered only complete incomprehension.

"Did you say in the house of Mr. and Mrs. Furnival, Dr. Rathbone?" the judge said with undisguised surprise.

"Yes, my lord," Hargrave replied unhappily.

"Mr. Rathbone," the judge instructed, "please continue."

"Yes, my lord." Rathbone looked anything but shaken; indeed he appeared quite calm. He turned back to Hargrave. "So the general was cleaning this ornamental knife in the Furnivals' house?"

"I believe so. I was told he was showing it to young Valentine Furnival. It was something of a curio. I daresay he was demonstrating its use—or something of the sort . . ."

There was a nervous titter around the room. Rathbone's face registered a wild and fleeting humor, but he forbore from making the obvious remark. Indeed he turned to something utterly different, which took them all by surprise.

"Tell me, Dr. Hargrave, what was the general wearing when he left to go back to his own house?"

"The clothes in which he came, of course."

Rathbone's eyebrows shot up, and too late Hargrave realized his error.

"Indeed?" Rathbone said with amazement. "Including those torn and bloodstained trousers?"

Hargrave said nothing.

"Shall I recall Mrs. Sabella Pole, who remembers the incident quite clearly?"

"No—no." Hargrave was thoroughly annoyed, his lips in a thin line, his face pale and set. "The trousers were quite intact—and not stained. I cannot explain it, and did not seek to. It is not my affair. I simply treated the wound."

"Indeed," Rathbone agreed with a small, unreadable smile. "Thank you, Dr. Hargrave. I have no further questions for you."

The next witness was Evan, for the police. His testimony was exactly what most would have foreseen and presented no interest for Monk. He watched Evan's sensitive, unhappy face as he recounted being called to the Furnivals' house, seeing the body and drawing the inevitable conclusions, then the questioning of all the people concerned. It obviously pained him.

Monk found his attention wandering. Rathbone could not provide a defense out of what he had, no matter how brilliant his cross-examination. It would be ridiculous to hope he could trick or force from any one of the Carlyons the admission that they knew the general was abusing his son. He had seen them outside in the hallway, sitting upright, dressed in black, faces set in quiet, dignified grief, totally unified. Even Edith Sobell was with them and now and again looked with concern at her father. But Felicia was in the courtroom, since she had not been subpoenaed to give evidence, and therefore was permitted inside the court. She was very pale behind her veil, and rigid as a plastic figure.

It was imperative they had to find out who else was involved in the pederasty, apart from the general and his father. Cassian had said "others," not merely his grandfather. Who? Who had access to the boy in a place sufficiently private? That was important; it had to be utterly private. One would hardly undertake such an activity where there was the slightest risk of interruption.

The interrogations went on and Monk was almost unaware of them.

Family again? Peverell Erskine? Was that what Damaris had discovered that night which had driven her nearly frantic with distress, so much so that she had been unable to control herself? After seeing Valentine Furnival she had come downstairs in a state bordering on hysteria. Why? Had she learned that her husband was sodomizing his nephew? But what could possibly have taken place up there that would tell her such a thing? Peverell himself had remained downstairs. Everyone had sworn to that. So she could not have seen anything. And Cassian was not even in the Furnivals' house.

But she had seen or heard something. Surely it could not be a coincidence that it had been the night of the murder? But what? What had she discovered?

Fenton Pole had been present. Was he the other one who abused Cassian, and in some way the cause of Sabella's hatred?

Or was it Maxim Furnival? Was the relationship between the general and Maxim not only one of mutual business interest but the indulgence of a mutual vice as well? Was that the reason for his frequent visits to the Furnival house, and nothing to do with Louisa? That would be a nice irony. No wonder Alexandra found a bitter and terrible humor in it.

But she had not known there was anyone else. She had thought that in killing the general she had ended it, freed Cassian from the abuse. She knew of no one else, not even the old colonel.

Evan was still testifying, this time answering Rathbone, but the questions were superfluous, only clarifying points already made, that Evan had found nothing to prove the jealousy Alexandra had denied, and he found it hard to believe in himself.

Monk's thoughts wandered away again. That wound on the General's leg. Surely it had been Cassian who had inflicted that? From what Hester had said of her interview with the boy, and her observation of him, he was ambivalent about the abuse, uncertain whether it was right or wrong, afraid to

332

lose his mother's love, secretive, flattered, frightened, but not entirely hating it. There was a frisson of excitement in him even when he mentioned it, the thrill of inclusion in the adult world, knowing something that others did not.

Had he ever been taken to the Furnivals' house? They should have asked about that. It was an omission.

"Did the general ever take Cassian to the Furnivals' house?" he whispered to Hester next to him.

"Not that I know of," she replied. "Why?"

"The other pederast," he replied almost under his breath. "We have to know who it is."

"Maxim Furnival?" she said in amazement, raising her voice without realizing it.

"Be quiet," someone said angrily.

"Why not?" he answered, leaning forward so he could whisper. "It's got to be someone who saw the boy regularly, and privately—and where Alexandra didn't know about it."

"Maxim?" she repeated, frowning at him.

"Why not? It's someone. Who stabbed the general? Does Rathbone know, or is he just hoping we'll find out before he's finished?"

"Just hoping," she said unhappily.

"Ssh!" a man hissed behind them, tapping Monk on the shoulder with his forefinger.

The reprimand infuriated Monk, but he could think of no satisfactory rejoinder. His face blazed with temper, but he said nothing.

"Valentine," Hester said suddenly.

"Be quiet!" The man in front swung around, his face pinched with anger. "If you don't want to listen, then go outside!"

Monk disregarded him. Of course—Valentine. He was only a few years older than Cassian. He would be an ideal victim first. And everyone had said how fond he had been of the general, or at least how fond the general had been of him. He had visited the boy regularly. Perhaps Valentine, terrified, confused, revolted by the general and by himself, had finally fought back.

How to be certain? And how to prove it?

He turned to look at Hester, and saw the same thoughts reflected in her eyes.

Her lips formed the words *It is worth trying*. Then her eyes darkened with anxiety. "But be careful," she whispered urgently. "If you're clumsy you could ruin it forever."

It was on the tip of his tongue to retaliate, then the reality of its importance overtook all vanity and irritation.

"I will." He promised so softly it was barely audible even to her. "I'll be 'round about. I'll try to get proof first." And he stood up, much to the fury of the person on his other side, and wriggled past the whole row, stepping on toes, banging knees and nearly losing his footing as he found his way out. The first thing was to learn what was physically possible. If Fenton Pole had never been alone with Cassian or Valentine, then he was not worth pursuing as a suspect. Servants would know, particularly footmen; footmen knew where their masters went in the family carriage, and they usually knew who visited the house. If Pole had been careful enough to travel to some other place to meet there, and go by hansom, then it would be a far harder task to trace him, and perhaps pointless.

He must begin with the obvious. He hailed a cab and gave the driver the address of Fenton and Sabella Pole's house.

All the remainder of the afternoon he questioned the servants. At first they were somewhat reluctant to answer him, feeling that in the absence of knowledge, silence was the wisest and safest course. But one maid in particular had come with Sabella on her marriage, and her loyalties were to Alexandra, because that was where her mistress's loyalties were. She was more than willing to answer anything Monk wished to know, and she was quite capable of discovering from the footman, groom and parlormaid every detail he needed.

Certainly Mr. Pole had known the general before he met Miss Sabella. It was the general who had introduced them, that she knew herself; she had been there at the time. Yes, they had got along very well with each other, better than with Mrs. Carlyon, unfortunately. The reason? She had no idea, except that poor Miss Sabella had not wished to marry, but to go into the Church. There was nothing anyone could say against Mr. Pole. He was always a gentleman.

Did he know Mr. and Mrs. Furnival well?

Not very, the acquaintance seemed to be recent.

Did Mr. Pole often visit the general at his home?

No, hardly ever. The general came here.

Did he often bring young Master Cassian?

She had never known it to happen. When Master Cassian came it was with his mother, to visit Miss Sabella during the daytime, when Mr. Pole was out.

Monk thanked her and excused himself. It seemed Fenton Pole was not a suspect, on the grounds of physical impossibility. The opportunity was simply not there.

He walked in the clear evening back to Great Titchfield Street, passing open carriages as people took the air, fashionably dressed in bonnets with ribbons and gowns trimmed with flowers; couples out strolling arm in arm, gossiping, flirting; a man walking his dog. He arrived a few moments after Hester returned from the court. She looked tired and anxious, and Major Tiplady, sitting up on an ordinary chair now, appeared concerned for her.

"Come in, come in, Mr. Monk," he said quickly. "I fear the news is not encouraging, but please be seated and we shall hear it together. Molly will bring us a cup of tea. And perhaps you would like supper? Poor Hester looks in need of some refreshment. Please—be seated!" He waved his arm in invitation, but his eyes were still on Hester's face.

Monk sat down, primarily to encourage Hester to speak, but he accepted the invitation to supper.

"Excuse me." Tiplady rose to his feet and limped to the door. "I shall see about it with Molly and Cook."

"What is it?" Monk demanded. "What has happened?"

"Very little," Hester said wearily. "Only what we expected. Evan recounted how Alexandra had confessed."

"We knew that would come," Monk pointed out, angry that she was so discouraged. He needed her to have hope, because he too was afraid. It was a ridiculous task they had

335

set themselves, and they had no right to have given Alexandra hope. There was none, none at all of any sense.

"Of course," she said a little sharply, betraying her own fragile emotions. "But you asked me what had happened."

He looked at her and met her eyes. There was a moment of complete understanding, all the pity, the outrage, all the delicate shades of fear and self-doubt for their own part in it. They said nothing, because words were unnecessary, and too clumsy an instrument anyway.

"I started to look at physical possibilities," he said after a moment or two. "I don't think Fenton Pole can be the other abuser. There doesn't seem to have been enough opportunity for him to be alone with either Cassian or Valentine."

"So where are you going next?"

"The Furnivals', I think."

"To Louisa?" she said with a flash of bitter amusement.

"To the servants." He understood precisely what she meant, with all its undertones. "Of course she would protect Maxim, but since it hasn't been mentioned yet, she won't have any idea that we are looking for abuse of children. She'll be thinking of herself, and the old charge about the general."

Hester said nothing.

"Then I'll go to the Carlyons'."

"The Carlyons'?" Now she was surprised. "You'll not find anything there, but even if you did, what good would it do? They'll all lie to protect him, and we know about him anyway! It's the other person we need to find—with proof."

"Not the colonel—Peverell Erskine."

She was stunned, her face filled with amazement and disbelief. "Peverell! Oh no! You can't think it was him!"

"Why not? Because we like him?" He was hurting himself as well as her and they both understood it. "Do you think it has to be someone who looks like a monster? There was no violence used, no hate or greed—just a man who has never grown up enough to find an appropriate closeness with an adult woman, a man who only feels safe with a child who won't judge him or demand a commitment or the ability to give, who won't see the flaws in his character or the clumsiness or inadequacy of his acts.''

''You sound as if you want me to feel sorry for him,'' she said with tight, hard disgust, but he did not know whether that disgust was at him, at the abuses, or only at the situation—or even if it was so hard because underneath it was the wrench of real pity.

''I don't care what you feel,'' he lied back. ''Only what you think. Just because Peverell Erskine is an agreeable man and his wife loves him doesn't mean he can't have weaknesses that destroy him—and others.''

''I don't believe it of Peverell,'' she said stubbornly, but she gave no reason.

''That's just stupid,'' he snapped at her, aware of the anger inside himself to which he chose to give no name. ''You're hardly much use if you are working on that level of intelligence.''

''I said I don't believe it,'' she retorted equally violently. ''I didn't say I wouldn't investigate the possibility.''

''Oh yes?'' He raised his eyebrows sarcastically. ''How?''

''Through Damaris, of course,'' she said with stinging contempt. ''She discovered something that night—something that upset her beyond bearing. Had you forgotten that? Or did you just think I had?''

Monk stared at her, and was about to make an equally acid reply when the door opened again and Major Tiplady returned, immediately followed by the maid with a tray of tea, announcing that supper would be ready in a little over half an hour. It was the perfect opportunity to change his tone altogether, and be suddenly charming, to enquire after Major Tiplady's recovery, appreciate the tea, and even to speak courteously to Hester. They talked of other things: the news from India, the ugly rumors of opium war in China, the Persian War, and unrest in the government at home. All the subjects were distressing, but they were far away, and he found the brief half hour most agreeable, a relief from responsibility and the urgent present.

* * *

The following day Lovat-Smith called further witnesses as to the unblemished character of the general, his fine nature and heroic military record. Once again Hester went to court to watch and listen on Major Tiplady's behalf, and Monk went first to the house of Callandra Daviot, where he learned from her, to his chagrin, that she had been unable to find anything beyond the merest whisper to indicate that General Carlyon had ever formed any relationships that were anything but the most proper and correct. However, she did have extensive lists of names of all youths who had served with his regiment, both in England and in India, and she produced it with an apology.

"Don't worry," he said with sudden gentleness. "This may be all we need."

She looked at him with something close to a squint, disbelief plain in her face.

He scanned down the list rapidly to see if the name of the Furnivals' bootboy was there. It was on the second page, Robert Andrews, honorable discharge, owing to wounds received in action. He looked up, smiling at her.

"Well?" she demanded.

"Maybe," he answered. "I'm going to find out."

"Monk!"

"Yes." He looked at her with a sudden awareness of how much she had done for him. "I think this may be the Furnivals' bootboy," he explained with a lift of hope in his voice. "The one who dropped all the laundry when he came face-to-face with the general on the night of the murder. I'm going to the Furnivals' house now to find out. Thank you."

"Ah," she said with a touch of satisfaction creeping into her expression at last. "Ah—well . . . good."

He thanked her again and bade her good-bye with a graceful kiss to the air, then hurried out to find a hansom to take him back to the Furnivals' house.

He reached it at a quarter to ten, in time to see Maxim leave, presumably to go into the City. He waited almost an hour and a half, and was rewarded by seeing Louisa, glamorous and quite unmistakable in a richly flowered bonnet and skirts so wide it took very great skill for her to negotiate the carriage doors.

As soon as she was well out of sight, Monk went to the back door and knocked. It was opened by the bootboy, looking expectant. His expression changed utterly when he saw Monk; apparently he had been anticipating someone else.

"Yes?" he said with a not unfriendly frown. He was a smart lad and stood very straight, but there was a watchfulness in his eyes, a knowledge of hurt.

"I was here before, speaking to Mrs. Furnival," Monk began carefully, but already he felt a kind of excitement. "And she was kind enough to help me in enquiring into the tragedy of General Carlyon's death."

The boy's expression darkened, an almost imperceptible tightening of the skin around his eyes and mouth, a narrowing of the lips.

"If you want Mrs. Furnival, you should 'ave gone to the front door," he said warily.

"I don't, this time." Monk smiled at him. "There are just a few details about other people who have called at the house in the past, and perhaps Master Valentine could help me. But I need to speak with one of your footmen, perhaps John."

"Well you'd better come in," the bootboy said cautiously. "An' I'll ask Mr. Diggins, 'e's the butler. I can't let you do that meself."

"Of course not." Monk followed him in graciously.

"Wot's your name, then?" the boy asked.

"Monk—William Monk. What is yours?"

"Who, me?" The boy was startled.

"Yes—what is your name?" Monk made it casual.

"Robert Andrews, sir. You wait 'ere, an' I'll see Mr. Diggins for yer." And the boy straightened his shoulders again and walked out very uprightly, as if he were a soldier on parade. Monk was left in the scullery, pulse racing, thoughts teeming in his mind, longing to question the boy and knowing how infinitely delicate it was, and that a word or a look that was clumsy might make him keep silence forever.

"What is it this time, Mr. Monk?" the butler asked when he returned a few minutes later. "I'm sure we've all told you all we know about that night. Now we'd just like to forget it and get on with our work. I'll not 'ave you upsetting all our maids again!"

"I don't need to see the maids," Monk said placatingly. "Just a footman would be quite sufficient, and possibly the bootboy. It is only about who called here frequently."

"Robert said something about Master Valentine." The butler looked at Monk closely. "I can't let you see him, not without the master's or the mistress's permission, and they're both out at the present."

"I understand." Monk chose not to fight when he knew he could not win. That would have to wait for another time. "I daresay you know everything that goes on in the house anyway. If you can spare the time?"

The butler considered for a moment. He was not immune to flattery, if it were disguised well enough, and he certainly liked what was his due.

"What is it you wish to know, in particular, Mr. Monk?" He turned and led the way towards his own sitting room, where they could be private, in case the matter should be in any way delicate. And regardless of that, it created the right impression in front of the other staff. It did not do to stand around discussing presumably private business in full view of everyone.

"How often did General Carlyon come here to visit, either Mrs. Furnival or Master Valentine?"

"Well, Mr. Monk, he used to come more often in the past, before he had his accident, sir. After that he came a lot less."

"Accident?"

"Yes sir—when he injured his leg, sir."

"That would be when he was hurt with the knife. Cleaning the knife, and it slipped and gashed him in the thigh," Monk said as levelly as he could.

"Yes sir."

"Where did that happen? In what room?"

"I'm afraid I don't know, sir. Somewhere upstairs, I believe. Possibly in the schoolroom. There is an ornamental knife up there. At least there was. I haven't seen it since then. May I ask why you need to know, sir?"

"No reason in particular—just that it was a nasty thing to happen. Did anyone else visit Master Valentine regularly? Mr. Pole, for example?"

"No sir, never that I know of." The first question remained in the butler's face.

"Or Mr. Erskine?"

"No sir, not as far as I know of. What would that have to do with the general's death, Mr. Monk?"

"I'm not sure," Monk said candidly. "I think it's possible that someone may have . . . exerted certain . . . pressures on Master Valentine."

"Pressures, sir?"

"I don't want to say anything more until I know for certain. It could malign someone quite without foundation."

"I understand, sir." The butler nodded sagely.

"Did Master Valentine visit the Carlyon house, to your knowledge?"

"Not so far as I am aware, sir. I do not believe that either Mr. or Mrs. Furnival is acquainted with Colonel and Mrs. Carlyon, and their acquaintance with Mr. and Mrs. Erskine is not close."

"I see. Thank you." Monk was not sure whether he was relieved or disappointed. He did not want it to be Peverell Erskine. But he needed to find out who it was, and time was getting desperately short. Perhaps it was Maxim after all— the most obvious, when one thought about it. He was here all the time. Another father abusing his son. He found his stomach clenching and his teeth ached with the tightness of his jaw. It was the first time he had felt even the briefest moment of pity for Louisa.

"Is there anything else, sir?" the butler said helpfully.

"I don't think so." What was there to ask that could be addressed to this man and yield an answer leading to the identity of whoever had so used Valentine? But however slender the chance of hearing any admission of a secret so desperately painful, and he loathed the idea of forcing the boy or tricking him, still he must at least attempt to learn something. "Have you any idea what made your bootboy behave so badly the night the general was killed?" he asked, watching the man's face. "He looked like a smart and responsible sort of lad, not given to indiscipline."

"No sir, I don't, and that's a fact." Diggins shook his head. Monk could see no evasion or embarrassment in him. "He's been a very good boy, has young Robert," he went on. "Always on time, diligent, respectful, quick to learn. Nothing to explain except that one episode. You had it right there, sir, he's a fine lad. Used to be in the army, you know— a drummer boy. Got wounded somewhere out in India. Honorable discharge from the service. Come 'ere very highly recommended. Can't think what got into him. Not like him at all. Training to be a footman, 'e is, and very likely make a good one. Although 'e's been a bit odd since that night. But then so 'ave we all—can't 'old that against 'im."

"You don't think he saw something to do with the murder, do you?" Monk asked as casually as he could.

Diggins shook his head. "I can't think what that might be, sir, that he wouldn't have repeated it, like it would be his duty to. Anyway, it was long before the murder. It was early in the evening, before they even went in to dinner. Nothing untoward had happened then."

"Was it before Mrs. Erskine went upstairs?"

"Now that I wouldn't know, sir. I only know young Robert came out of the kitchen and was on his way up the back stairs on an errand for Mrs. Braithwaite, she's the housekeeper, when he crossed the passage and near bumped into General Carlyon, and stood there like a creature paralyzed and let all the linens he'd fetched fall in a heap on the floor, and turned on his heel and went back into the kitchen like the devil was after him. All the linens had to be sorted out and some o' them ironed again. The laundress wasn't best pleased, I can tell you." He shrugged. "And he wouldn't say a word to anyone, just went white and very quiet. Perhaps

342

he was took ill, or something. Young people can be very odd.''

"A drummer boy, you said?" Monk confirmed. "He'd be used to seeing some terrible things, no doubt . . .''

"I daresay. I never bin in the army myself, sir, but I should imagine so. But good training. Given him his obedience, and the respect for his elders. He's a good lad. He won't never do that again, I'm sure."

"No. No, 'course not.'' Thoughts raced through his mind as to how he could approach the boy—what he could say—the denials, the desperate embarrassment and the boy's shame. With sickening doubt as to the wisdom of it, where his duty or his honor lay, he made up his mind. "Thank you very much, Mr. Diggins. You have been most helpful, I appreciate it."

"No more than my duty, Mr. Monk."

Monk found himself outside in the street a few moments later, still torn with indecision. A drummer boy who had served with Carlyon, and then come face-to-face with him in the Furnivals' house on the night of the murder, and fled in—what? Terror, panic, shame? Or just clumsiness?

No—he had been a soldier, although then little more than a child. He would not have dropped his laundry and fled simply because he bumped into a guest.

Should Monk have pursued it? To what end? So Rathbone could get him on the stand and strip his shame bare before the court? What would it prove? Only that Carlyon was indeed an abuser of children. Could they not do that anyway, without destroying this child and making him relive the abuse in words—and in public? It was something Alexandra knew nothing of anyway, and could not have affected her actions.

It was the other abuser they needed to find, and to prove. Was it Maxim Furnival? Or Peverell Erskine? Both thoughts were repulsive to him.

He increased his pace, walking along Albany Street, and within moments was at Carlyon House. He had no excitement in the chase, only an empty, sick feeling in his stomach.

All the family were at the trial, either waiting to give evidence or in the gallery watching the proceedings. He went to the back door and asked if he might speak to Miss Buchan. It stuck in his throat to say it, but he sent a message that he was a friend of Miss Hester Latterly's and had come on an errand for her.

After only ten minutes kicking his heels in the laundry room he was finally admitted to the main house and conducted up three flights of stairs to Miss Buchan's small sitting room with its dormer windows over the roofs.

"Yes, Mr. Monk?" she said dubiously.

He looked at her with interest. She was nearer seventy than sixty, very thin, with a sharp, intelligent face, long nose, quick faded eyes, and the fine fresh complexion that goes with auburn hair, although it was now gray, almost white. She was a hot-tempered woman of great courage, and it showed in her face. He found it easy to believe she had acted as Hester had told him.

"I am a friend of Miss Latterly's," he said again, establishing himself before he launched into his difficult mission.

"So you told Agnes," she said skeptically, looking him up and down, from his polished leather boots and his long straight legs to his beautifully cut jacket and his smooth, hard-boned face with its gray eyes and sarcastic mouth. She did not try to impress him. She knew from his look, something in his bearing, that he had not had a governess himself. There was no nursery respect in him, no memories of another woman like her who had ruled his childhood.

He found himself coloring, knowing his ordinary roots were as visible to her as if he had never lost his provincial accent and his working-class manners. Ironically, his very lack of fear had betrayed him. His invulnerability had made him vulnerable. All his careful self-improvement hid nothing.

"Well?" she said impatiently. "What do you want? You haven't come this far just to stand here staring at me!"

"No." He collected himself rapidly. "No, Miss Buchan. I'm a detective. I'm trying to help Mrs. Alexandra Carlyon." He watched her face to see how she reacted.

"You're wasting your time," she said bleakly, sudden pain obliterating both her curiosity and her humor. "There's nothing anyone can do for her, poor soul."

"Or for Cassian?" he asked.

Her eyes narrowed; she looked at him in silence for several seconds. He did not turn away but met her gaze squarely.

"What would you be trying to do for him?" she said at last.

"See it doesn't happen to him anymore."

She stood still, her shoulders stiff, her eyes on his.

"You can't," she said at last. "He'll remain in this house, with his grandfather. He has no one else now."

"He has his sisters."

She pursed her lips slowly, a new thought turning over in her mind.

"He could go to Sabella," he suggested tentatively.

"You'd never prove it," she said almost under her breath, her eyes wide. They both knew what she was referring to; there was no need to speak the words. The old colonel was in their vision as powerfully as if some aura of him were there, like a pungent smoke after a man and his cigar or pipe have passed by.

"I might," he said slowly. "Can I speak to Cassian?"

"I don't know. Depends what you want to say. I'll not let you upset him—God knows the poor child has enough to bear, and worse to come."

"I won't do more than I have to," Monk pressed. "And you will be there all the time."

"I most certainly will," she said darkly. "Well, come on then, don't stand there wasting time. What has to be done had best be done quickly."

Cassian was alone in his own room. There were no schoolbooks visible, nor any other improving kind of occupation, and Monk judged Miss Buchan had weighed the relative merits of forced effort to occupy his mind and those of allowing him to think as he wished and permit the thoughts which had to lie below the surface to come through and claim the attention they would sooner or later have to have. Monk approved her decision.

Cassian looked around from the window where he was gazing. His face was pale but he looked perfectly composed. One could only guess what emotions were tearing at him beneath. Clutched in his fingers was a small gold watch fob. Monk could just see the yellow glint as he turned his hand.

"Mr. Monk would like to talk to you for a while," Miss Buchan said in a matter-of-fact voice. "I don't know what he has to say, but it might be important for your mother, so pay him attention and tell him all the truth you know."

"Yes, Miss Buchan," the boy said obediently, his eyes on Monk, solemn but not yet frightened. Perhaps all his fear was centered in the courtroom at the Old Bailey and the secrets and the pain which would be torn apart and exposed there, and the decisions that would be made. His voice was flat and he looked at Monk warily.

Monk was not used to children, except the occasional urchin or working child his normal routine brought him into contact with. He did not know how to treat Cassian, who had so much of childhood in his protected, privileged daily life, and nothing at all in his innermost person.

"Do you know Mr. Furnival?" he asked bluntly, and felt clumsy in asking, but small conversation was not his milieu or his skill, even with adults.

"No sir," Cassian answered straightaway.

"You have never met him?" Monk was surprised.

"No sir." Cassian swallowed. "I know Mrs. Furnival."

It seemed irrelevant. "Do you." Monk acknowledged it only as a courtesy. He looked at Miss Buchan. "Do you know Mr. Furnival?"

"No I do not."

Monk turned back to Cassian. "But you know your sister Sabella's husband, Mr. Pole?" he persisted, although he doubted Fenton Pole was the man he needed.

"Yes sir." There was no change in Cassian's expression except for a slight curiosity, perhaps because the questions seemed so pointless.

346

Monk looked at the boy's hands, still grasping the piece of gold.

"What is that?"

Cassian's fingers closed more tightly on it and there was a faint pink color fresh in his cheeks. Very slowly he held it out for Monk to take.

Monk picked it up. The watch fob opened up to be a tiny pair of scales, such as the blind figure of Justice carries. A chill touched him inside.

"That's very handsome," he said aloud. "A present?"

Cassian swallowed and said nothing.

"From your uncle Peverell?" Monk asked as casually as he could.

For a moment no one moved or spoke, then very slowly Cassian nodded.

"When did he give it to you?" Monk turned it over as if admiring it further.

"I don't remember," Cassian replied, and Monk knew he was lying.

Monk handed it back and Cassian took it quickly, closing his hand over it again and then putting it out of sight in his pocket.

Monk pretended to forget it, walking away from the window towards the small table where, from the ruler, block of paper, and jar of pencils, it was obvious Cassian did his schoolwork since coming to Carlyon House. He felt Miss Buchan watching him, waiting to intervene if he trespassed too far, and he also felt Cassian tense and his eyes follow him. A moment later he came over and stood at Monk's elbow, his face wary, eyes troubled.

Monk looked at the table again, at the other items. There was a pocket dictionary, a small book of mathematical tables, a French grammar and a neat folding knife. At first he thought it was for sharpening pencils, then he saw what an elegant thing it was, far too sophisticated for a child. He reached out for it, out of the corner of his eye saw Cassian tense, his hand jerk upward, as if to stop him, then freeze motionless.

Monk picked up the knife and opened it. It was fine-bladed, almost like a razor, the sort a man uses to cut a quill to repair the nib. The initials P.E. were engraved on the handle.

"Very nice," Monk said with a half smile, turning to Cassian. "Another gift from Mr. Erskine?"

"Yes—no!" Cassian stopped. "Yes." His chin tightened, his lower lip came forward, as if to defy argument.

"Very generous of him," Monk commented, feeling sick inside. "Anything else he gave you?"

"No." But his eyes swiveled for an instant to his jacket, hanging on the hook behind the door, and Monk could just see the end of a colored silk handkerchief poking out from an inside pocket.

"He must be very fond of you," he said, hating himself for the hypocrisy.

Cassian said nothing.

Monk turned back to Miss Buchan.

"Thank you," he said wearily. "There isn't a great deal more to ask."

She looked doubtful. It was plain she did not see any meaning to the questions about the gifts; it had not occurred to her to suspect Peverell Erskine. Perhaps it was just as well. He stayed a few moments longer, asking other things as they came to his mind, times and people, journeys, visitors, nothing that mattered, but it disguised the gifts and their meaning.

Then he said good-bye to the child, thanked Miss Buchan, and left Carlyon House, his knowledge giving him no pleasure. The sunlight and noise of the street seemed far away, the laughter of two women in pink-and-white frills, parasols twirling, sounding tinny in his ears, the horses' hooves loud, the hiss of carriage wheels sibilant, the cry of a peddler a faraway irritant, like the buzzing of a bluebottle fly.

Hester arrived home from the trial weary and with very little to tell Major Tiplady. The day's evidence had been largely what anyone might have foreseen, first Peverell Erskine saying, with something that looked vaguely like reluctance, what an excellent man Thaddeus Carlyon had been.

Rathbone had not tried to shake him, nor to question his veracity nor the accuracy of his observations.

Next Damaris Erskine had been asked about her brother, and had echoed her husband's sentiments and seconded his observations. Rathbone had not asked her anything else at all, but had reserved the right to recall her at a later time, should that prove to be in the interests of the defense.

There had been no revelations. The crowd was growing more intense in their anger towards Alexandra. The general was the kind of man they most liked to admire—heroic, upright, a man of action with no dangerous ideas or unnerving sense of humor, no opinions they would have to disapprove of or feel guilty about understanding, a good family man whose wife had most hideously turned on him for no sane reason. Such a woman should be hanged, to discourage all other women from such violence, and the sooner the better. It was murmured all through the day, and said aloud when finally the court rose for the weekend.

It was a discouraging day, and she came back to Great Titchfield Street tired and frightened by the inevitability of events, and the hatred and incomprehension in the air. By the time she had recounted it all to Major Tiplady she was close to tears. Even he could find no hope in the situation; the best he could offer was an exhortation to courage, the greatest of all courage, to continue to fight with all one has even when victory seems beyond possibility.

The following day a crisp wind blew from the east but the sky was sharp blue and flowers were fluttering in the wind. It was Saturday, and there was no court sitting, so there was brief respite. Hester woke with a sense not of ease but of greater tension because she would rather have continued with it now that it was begun. This was only prolonging the pain and the helplessness. It would have been a blessing were there anything more she could do, but although she had been awake, turning and twisting, thrashing it over and over in her mind, she could think of nothing. They knew the truth of what had happened to Alexandra, what she had done, and why—exactly, passionately and irrevocably why. She had not known there was another man, let alone two others, or who they were.

There was little point in trying to prove it was old Randolf Carlyon; he would never admit it, and his family would close around him like a wall of iron. To accuse him would only prejudice the crowd and the jury still more deeply against Alexandra. She would appear a wild and vicious woman with a vile mind, depraved and obsessed with perversions.

They must find the third man, with either irrefutable proof or sufficient accusations not to be denied. And that would mean the help of Cassian, Valentine Furnival, if he were also a victim, and anyone else who knew about it or suspected—Miss Buchan, for example.

And Miss Buchan would risk everything if she made such a charge. The Carlyons would throw her out and she would be destitute. And who else would take her in, a woman too old to work, who made charges of incest and sodomy against the employers who had fed and housed her in her old age?

No, there was little comfort in a long, useless weekend. She wished she could curl over and go back to sleep, but it was broad daylight; through a chink in the curtain the sun was bright, and she must get up and see how Major Tiplady was. Not that he was unable to care for himself now, but she might as well do her duty as fully as possible to the end.

Perhaps the morning could be usefully spent in beginning to look for a new post. This one could not last beyond the confusion of the trial. She could afford a couple of weeks without a position, but not more. And it would have to be one where she lived in the house of the patient. She had given up her lodgings, since the expense of keeping a room when she did not need one was foolish, and beyond her present resources. She pushed dreams of any other sort of employment firmly out of her mind. They were fanciful, and without foundation, the maunderings of a silly woman.

After breakfast she asked Major Tiplady if he would excuse her for the day so she might go out and begin to enquire at various establishments that catered to such needs if there were any people who required a nurse such as herself. Unfortunately midwifery was something about which she knew almost nothing, nor about the care of infant children. There was a much wider need for that type of nursing.

Reluctantly he agreed, not because he needed her help in anything, simply because he had grown used to her company and liked it. But he could see the reasoning, and accepted it.

She thanked him, and half an hour later was about to leave when the maid came in with a surprised look on her face to announce that Mrs. Sobell was at the door.

"Oh!" The major looked startled and a little pink. "To see Miss Latterly, no doubt? Please show her in, Molly! Don't leave the poor lady standing in the hall!"

"No sir. Yes sir." Molly's surprise deepened, but she did as she was bidden, and a moment later Edith came in, dressed in half-mourning of a rich shade of pink lilac. Hester thought privately she would have termed it quarter-mourning, if asked. It was actually very pretty, and the only indications it had anything to do with death were the black lace trimmings and black satin ribbons both on the shawl and on the bonnet. Nothing would change the individuality of her features, the aquiline nose that looked almost as if it had been broken, very slightly crooked, and far too flat, the heavy-lidded eyes and the soft mouth, but Edith looked remarkably gentle and feminine today, in spite of her obvious unhappiness.

The major climbed to his feet, utterly disregarding his leg, which was now almost healed but still capable of giving him pain. He stood almost to attention.

"Good morning, Mrs. Sobell. How very nice to see you. I hope you are well, in spite of . . ." He stopped, looking at her more closely. "I'm sorry, what a foolish thing to say. Of course you are distressed by all that is happening. What may we do to comfort you? Please come in and sit down; at least make yourself comfortable. No doubt you wish to speak to Miss Latterly. I shall find myself some occupation."

"No, no! Please," Edith said quickly and a little awkwardly.

351

"I should be most uncomfortable if you were to leave on my account. I have nothing in particular to say. I—I simply . . ." Now she too colored very pink. "I—I simply wished to be out of the house, away from my family—and . . ."

"Of course," he said quickly. "You wished to be able to speak your mind without fear of causing offense or distress to those you love."

Her face flooded with relief. "You are extraordinarily perceptive, Major Tiplady."

Now his cheeks were very red and he had no idea where to look.

"Oh please sit down," Hester interrupted, acting to stop the awkwardness, or at least to give it respite. "Edith."

"Thank you," Edith accepted, and for the first time in Hester's acquaintance with her, she arranged her skirts elegantly and sat upright on the edge of the seat, as a lady should. In spite of the grimness of the situation Hester was obliged to hide a smile.

Edith sighed. "Hester, what is happening? I have never been to a trial before, and I don't understand. Mr. Rathbone is supposed to be so brilliant, and yet from what I hear it seems he is doing nothing at all. I could do as much. So far all he has achieved is to persuade us all that Thaddeus was quite innocent of any affair, either with Louisa Furnival or anyone else. And to add that Alexandra knew it too. What possible good can that do?" Her face was screwed up with incomprehension, her eyes dark and urgent. "It makes Alexandra look even worse in a way, because it takes from her any possible reason that one could attempt to understand, if not forgive. Why? She has already confessed that she did do it, and it has been proved. He didn't challenge that. In fact if anything he reconfirmed it. Why, Hester? What is he doing?"

Hester had told Edith nothing of their appalling discoveries, and now she hesitated, wondering if she should, or if by so doing she might foil Rathbone's plans for examination in the witness box. Was it possible that in spite of the outrage she would undoubtedly feel, Edith's family loyalty would be powerful enough for her to conceal the shame of it? Might she even disbelieve it?

Hester dare not put it to the test. It was not her prerogative to decide, not her life in the balance, nor her child whose future lay in the judgment.

She sat down in the chair opposite Edith.

"I don't know," she lied, meeting her friend's eyes and hating the deceit. "At least I have only guesses, and it would be unfair to him and to you to give you those." She saw Edith's face tighten as if she had been struck, and the fear deepened in her eyes. "But I do know he has a strategy," she hurried on, leaning forward a little, only dimly aware of Major Tiplady looking anxiously from one to the other of them.

"Does he?" Edith said softly. "Please don't try to give me hope, Hester, if there really isn't any. It is not a kindness."

The major drew breath to speak, and both turned to look at him. Then he changed his mind and remained silent and unhappy, facing Hester.

"There is hope," Hester said firmly. "But I don't know how great it is. It all depends on convincing the jury that—"

"What?" Edith said quickly. "What can he convince them of? She did it! Even Rathbone himself has proved that! What else is there?"

Hester hesitated. She was glad Major Tiplady was there, although there was nothing he could do, but his mere presence was a kind of comfort.

Edith went on with a faint, bitter smile. "He can hardly persuade them she was justified. Thaddeus was painfully virtuous—all the things that count to other people." She frowned suddenly. "Actually we still don't know why she did it. Is he going to say she is mad? Is that it? I don't think she is." She glanced at the major. "And they have subpoenaed me to give evidence. What shall I do?"

"Give evidence," Hester answered. "There's nothing else you can do. Just answer the questions they ask and no more. But be honest. Don't try to guess what they want. It is up to

353

Rathbone to draw it from you. If you look as if you are trying to help it will show and the jury won't believe you. Just don't lie—about anything he asks you.''

''But what can he ask me? I don't know anything.''

''I don't know what he will ask you,'' Hester said exasperatedly. ''He wouldn't tell me, even if I were to ask him. I have no right to know. And far better I don't. But I do know he has a strategy—and it could win. Please believe me, and don't press me to give you answers I don't have.''

''I'm sorry.'' Edith was suddenly penitent. She rose to her feet quickly and walked over to the window, less graceful than usual because she was self-conscious. ''When this trial is over I am still going to look for a position of some sort. I know Mama will be furious, but I feel suffocated there. I spend all my life doing nothing whatsoever that matters at all. I stitch embroidery no one needs, and paint pictures even I don't like much. I play the piano badly and no one listens except out of politeness. I make duty calls on people and take them pots of conserve and give bowls of soup to the deserving poor, and feel like such a hypocrite because it does hardly any good, and we go with such an air of virtue, and come away as if we've solved all their problems, and we've hardly touched them.'' Her voice caught for an instant. ''I'm thirty-three, and I'm behaving like an old woman. Hester, I'm terrified that one day I'm going to wake up and I will be old—and I'll have done nothing at all that was worth doing. I'll never have accomplished anything, served any purpose, helped anyone more than was purely convenient, never felt anything really deeply once Oswald died—been no real use at all.'' She kept her back to them, and stood very straight and still.

''Then you must find work of some sort to do,'' Hester said firmly. ''Even if it is hard or dirty, paid or unpaid, even thankless—it would be better than waking up every morning to a wasted day and going to bed at night knowing you wasted it. I have heard it said that most of what we regret is not what we did but what we did not do. I think on the whole that is

354

correct. You have your health. It would be better to wait on others than do nothing at all.''

"You mean go into service?" Edith was incredulous and there was a frail, slightly hysterical giggle under the surface of her voice.

"No, nothing quite so demanding—it would really be more than your mother deserves. I meant helping some poor creature who is too ill or too mithered to help herself." She stopped. "Of course that would be unpaid, and that might not work . . .''

"It wouldn't. Mama would not permit it, so I would have to find lodgings of my own, and that requires money—which I don't have.''

Major Tiplady cleared his throat.

"Are you still interested in Africa, Mrs. Sobell?''

She turned around, her eyes wide.

"Go to Africa? How could I do that? I don't know anything about it. I hardly think I should be of any use to anyone. I wish I were!''

"No, not go there.'' His face was bright pink now. "I—er—well, I'm not sure, of course . . .''

Hester refused to help him, although with a sweet surge of pleasure she knew what he wanted to say.

He threw an agonized glance at her, and she smiled back charmingly.

Edith waited.

"Er . . .'' He cleared his throat again. "I thought—I thought I might . . . I mean if you are serious about people's interest? I thought I might write my memoirs of Mashona-land, and I—er . . .''

Edith's face flooded with understanding—and delight.

"Need a scribe. Oh yes, I should be delighted. I can think of nothing I should like better! *My Adventures in Mashona-land*, by Major—Major Tiplady. What is your given name?''

He blushed crimson and looked everywhere but at her.

Hester knew the initial was *H*, but no more. He had signed his letter employing her only with that initial and his surname.

"You have to have a name," Edith insisted. "I can see it, bound in morocco or calf—nice gold lettering. It will be marvelous! I shall count it such a privilege and enjoy every word. It will be almost as good as going there myself—and in such splendid company. What is your name, Major? How will it be styled?"

"Hercules," he said very quietly, and shot her a look of total pleading not to laugh.

"How very fine," she said gently. *"My Adventures in Mashonaland,* by Major Hercules Tiplady. May we begin as soon as this terrible business is over? It is the nicest thing that has happened to me in years."

"And to me," Major Tiplady said happily, his face still very pink.

Hester rose to her feet and went to the door to ask the maid to prepare luncheon for them, and so that she could give rein to her giggles where she could hurt no one—but it was laughter of relief and a sudden bright hope, at least for Edith and the major, whom she had grown to like remarkably. It was the only good thing at the moment, but it was totally good.

11

MONK BEGAN THE WEEKEND with an equal feeling of gloom, not because he had no hope of finding the third man but because the discovery was so painful. He had liked Peverell Erskine, and now it looked inevitable it was he. Why else would he have given a child such highly personal and useless gifts? Cassian had no use for a quill knife, except that it was pretty and belonged to Peverell—as for a silk handkerchief, children did not use or wear such things. It was a keepsake. The watch fob also was too precious for an eight-year-old to wear, and it was personal to Peverell's profession, nothing like the Carlyons', which would have been something military, a regimental crest, perhaps.

He had told Rathbone, and seen the same acceptance and unhappiness in him. He had mentioned the bootboy also, but told Rathbone that there was no proof Carlyon had abused him, and that that was the reason the boy had turned and fled in the Furnival house the night of the murder. He did not know if Rathbone had understood his own action, what were the reasons he accepted without demur, or if he felt his strategy did not require the boy.

Monk stood at the window and stared out at the pavement of Grafton Street, the sharp wind sending a loose sheet of newspaper bowling along the stones. On the corner a peddler was selling bootlaces. A couple crossed the street, arm in arm, the man walking elegantly, leaning over a little towards the woman, she laughing. They looked comfortable together, and it shot a pang of loneliness through him that took him by surprise, a feeling of exclusion, as if he saw the whole of life that mattered, the sweeter parts, through glass, and from a distance.

Evan's last case file lay on the desk unopened. In it might lie the answer to the mystery that teased him. Who was the woman that plucked at his thoughts with such insistence and such powerful emotion, stirring feelings of guilt, urgency, fear of loss, and over all, confusion? He was afraid to discover, and yet not to was worse. Part of him held back, simply because once he had uncovered it there would be nothing left to offer hope of finding something sweet, a better side of himself, a gentleness or a generosity he had failed in so far. It was foolish, and he knew it, even cowardly—and that was the one criticism strong enough to move him. He walked over to the table and opened the cover.

He read the first page still standing. The case was not especially complex. Hermione Ward had been married to a wealthy and neglectful husband, some years older than herself. She was his second wife and it seemed he had treated her with coolness, keeping her short of funds, giving her very little social life and expecting her to manage his house and care for the two children of his first wife.

The house had been broken into during the night, and Albert Ward had apparently heard the burglar and gone downstairs to confront him. There had been a struggle and he had been struck on the head and died of the wound.

Monk pulled around a chair and sat down. He continued with the second page.

The local police in Guildford had investigated, and found several circumstances which roused their suspicions. The glass from the broken window was outside, not in, where one might have expected it to fall. The widow could name nothing which had been stolen, nor did she ever amend her opinion in the cooler light of the following week. Nothing was found in pawnshops or sold to any of the usual dealers known to the police. The resident servants, of whom there were six, heard nothing in the night, no sound, no disturbance. No footprints or any other marks of intruders were seen.

The police arrested Hermione Ward and charged her with having murdered her husband. Scotland Yard was sent for. Runcorn dispatched Monk to Guildford. The rest of the record presumably lay with the Guildford police.

The only way he could find out would be to go there. It was a short journey and easily made by train. But this was Saturday. It might be awkward. Perhaps the officer he needed would not be there. And the Carlyon trial would be resumed on Monday, and he must be present. What could he do in two days? Maybe not enough.

They were excuses because he was afraid to find out.

He despised cowardice; it was the root of all the weaknesses he hated most. Anger he could understand, thoughtlessness, impatience, greed, even though they were ugly enough—but without courage what was there to fire or to preserve any virtue, honor or integrity? Without the courage to sustain it, not even love was safe.

He moved over to the window again and stared at the buildings opposite and the roofs shining in the sun. There was not even any point in evading it. It would hurt him until he found out what had happened, who she was and why he had felt so passionately, and yet walked away from it, and from her. Why were there no mementos in his room that reminded him of her, no pictures, no letters, nothing at all? Presumably the idea of her was one thing too painful to wish to remember. The reality was quite different. This would go on hurting. He would wake in the night with scalding disillusion—and terrible loneliness. For once he could easily, terribly easily, understand those who ran away.

And yet it was also too important to forget, because his mind would not let him bury it. Echoes kept tugging at him, half glimpses of her face, a gesture, a color she wore, the way she walked, the softness of her hair, her perfume, the rustle of silk. For heaven's sake, why not her name? Why not all her face?

There was nothing he could do here over the weekend. The trial was adjourned and he had nowhere else to search for the third man. It was up to Rathbone now.

He turned from the window and strode over to the coat stand, snatching a jacket and his hat and going out of the door, only just saving it from slamming behind him.

"I'm going to Guildford," he informed his landlady, Mrs. Worley. "I may not be back until tomorrow."

"But you'll be back then?" she said firmly, wiping her hands on her apron. She was an ample woman, friendly and businesslike. "You'll be at the trial of that woman again?"

He was surprised. He had not thought she knew.

"Yes—I will."

She shook her head. "I don't know what you want to be on cases like that for, I'm sure. You've come a long way down, Mr. Monk, since you was in the police. Then you'd 'a bin chasin' after people like that, not tryin' to 'elp them."

"You'd have killed him too, in her place, if you'd had the courage, Mrs. Worley," he said bitingly. "So would any woman who gave a damn."

"I would not," she retorted fiercely. "Love o' no man's ever goin' to make me into a murderess!"

"You know nothing about it. It wasn't love of a man."

"You watch your tongue, Mr. Monk," she said briskly. "I know what I read in the newspapers as comes 'round the vegetables, and they're plain enough."

"They know nothing, either," he replied. "And fancy you reading the newspapers, Mrs. Worley. What would Mr. Worley say to that? And sensational stories, too." He grinned at her, baring his teeth.

She straightened her skirts with a tweak and glared at him.

"That isn't your affair, Mr. Monk. What I read is between me and Mr. Worley."

"It's between you and your conscience, Mrs. Worley—it's no one else's concern at all. But they still know nothing. Wait till the end of the trial—then tell me what you think."

"Ha!" she said sharply, and turned on her heel to go back to the kitchen.

He caught the train and alighted at Guildford in the middle of the morning. It was a matter of another quarter of an hour before a hansom deposited him outside the police station and he went up the steps to the duty sergeant at the desk.

"Yes sir?" The man's face registered dawning recognition. "Mr. Monk? 'Ow are you, sir?" There was respect in his voice, even awe, but Monk did not catch any fear. Please God at least here he had not been unjust.

"I'm very well, thank you, Sergeant," he replied courteously. "And yourself?"

The sergeant was not used to being asked how he was, and his face showed his surprise, but he answered levelly enough.

"I'm well, thank you sir. What can I do for you? Mr. Markham's in, if it was 'im you was wanting to see? I ain't 'eard about another case as we're needin' you for; it must be very new." He was puzzled. It seemed impossible there could be a crime so complicated they needed to call in Scotland Yard and yet it had not crossed his desk. Only something highly sensitive and dangerous could be so classed, a political assassination, or a murder involving a member of the aristocracy.

"I'm not with the police anymore," Monk explained. There was little to be gained and everything to be risked by lying. "I've gone private." He saw the man's incredulity and smiled. "A difference of opinion over a case—a wrongful arrest, I thought."

The man's face lightened with intelligence. "That'd be the Moidore case," he said with triumph.

"That's right!" It was Monk's turn to be surprised. "How did you know about that?"

"Read it, sir. Know as you was right." He nodded with satisfaction, even if it was a trifle after the event. "What can we do for you now, Mr. Monk?"

Again honesty was the wisest. So far the man was a friend,

for whatever reason, but that could easily slip away if he lied to him and were caught.

"I've forgotten some of the details of the case I came here for, and I'd like to remind myself. I wondered if it would be possible to speak with someone. I realize it's Saturday, and those who worked with me might be off duty, but today was the only day I could leave the City. I'm on a big case."

"No difficulty, sir. Mr. Markham's right 'ere in the station, an' I expect as 'e'd be 'appy to tell you anything you wanted. It was 'is biggest case, an' 'e's always 'appy to talk about it again." He moved his head in the direction of the door leading off to the right. "If you go through there, sir, you'll find 'im at the back, like always. Tell 'im I sent you."

"Thank you, Sergeant," Monk accepted, and before it became obvious that he did not remember the man's name, he went through the door and through the passageway. Fortunately the direction was obvious, because he remembered none of it.

Sergeant Markham was standing with his back to Monk, and as soon as Monk saw him there was something in the angle of his shoulders and the shape of his head, the set of his arms, that woke a memory and suddenly he was back investigating the case, full of anxiety and hard, urgent fear.

Then Markham turned and looked at him, and the moment vanished. He was in the present again, standing in a strange police duty room facing a man who knew him, and yet about whom he knew nothing except that they had worked together in the past. His features were only vaguely familiar; his eyes were blue like a million Englishmen, his skin fair and pale so early in the season, his hair still thick, bleached by sun a little at the front.

"Yes sir?" he enquired, seeing first of all Monk's civilian clothes. Then he looked more closely at his face, and recognition came flooding back. "Why, it's Mr. Monk." The eagerness was tempered. There was admiration in his eyes, but caution as well. " 'Ow are you, sir? Got another case?" The interest was well modified with other emotions less sanguine.

362

"No, the same as before." Monk wondered whether to smile, or if it would be so uncharacteristic as to be ridiculous. The decision was quickly made; it was false and it would freeze on his face. "I've forgotten some of the details and for reasons I can't explain, I need to remind myself, or to be exact, I need your help to remind me. You still have the records?"

"Yes sir." Markham was obviously surprised, and there was acceptance in his expression as habit. He was used to obeying Monk and it was instinctive, but there was no comprehension.

"I'm not on the force anymore." He dared not deceive Markham.

Now Markham was totally incredulous.

"Not on the force." His whole being registered his amazement. "Not—not—on the force?" He looked as if he did not understand the words themselves.

"Gone private," Monk explained, meeting his eyes. "I've got to be back in the Old Bailey on Monday, for the Carlyon case, but I want to get these details today, if I can."

"What for, sir?" Markham had a great respect for Monk, but he had also learned from him, and knew enough to accept no one's word without substantiation, or to take an order from a man with no authority. Monk would have criticized him unmercifully for it in the past.

"My own private satisfaction," Monk replied as calmly as he could. "I want to be sure I did all I could, and that I was right. And I want to find the woman again, if I can." Too late he realized how he had betrayed himself. Markham would think him witless, or making an obscure joke. He felt hot all over, sweat breaking out on his body and then turning cold.

"Mrs. Ward?" Markham asked with surprise.

"Yes, Mrs. Ward!" Monk gulped hard. She must be alive, or Markham would not have phrased it that way. He could still find her!

"You didn't keep in touch, sir?" Markham frowned.

Monk was so overwhelmed with relief his voice caught in

his throat. "No." He swallowed and coughed. "No—did you expect me to?"

"Well, sir." Markham colored faintly. "I know you worked on the case so hard as a matter of justice, of course, but I couldn't help but see as you were very fond of the lady too—and she of you, it looked like. I 'alf thought, we all thought . . ." His color deepened. "Well, no matter. Beggin' your pardon, sir. It don't do to get ideas about people and what they feel or don't feel. Like as not you'll be wrong. I can't show you the files, sir; seein' as you're not on the force any longer. But I ain't forgot much. I can tell you just about all of it. I'm on duty right now. But I get an hour for luncheon, leastways I can take an hour, and I'm sure the duty sergeant'll come for me. An' if you like to meet me at the Three Feathers I'll tell you all I can remember."

"Thank you, Markham, that's very obliging of you. I hope you'll let me stand you to a meal?"

"Yes, sir, that's handsome of you."

And so midday saw Monk and Sergeant Markham sitting at a small round table in the clink and chatter of the Three Feathers, each with a plate piled full of hot boiled mutton and horseradish sauce, potatoes, spring cabbage, mashed turnips and butter; a glass of cider at the elbow; and steamed treacle pudding to follow.

Markham was as good as his word, meticulously so. He had brought no papers with him, but his memory was excellent. Perhaps he had refreshed it discreetly for the occasion, or maybe it was sufficiently sharp he had no need. He began as soon as he had taken the edge off his appetite with half a dozen mouthfuls.

"The first thing you did, after reading the evidence, was go back over the ground as we'd already done ourselves." He left out the "sir" he would have used last time and Monk noted it with harsh amusement.

"That was, go to the scene o' the crime and see the broken window," Markham went on. "O' course the glass was all cleaned up, like, but we showed you where it 'ad lain. Then we questioned the servants again, and Mrs. Ward 'erself. Do you want to know what I can remember o' that?''

"Only roughly," Monk replied. "If there was anything of note? Not otherwise."

Markham continued, outlining a very routine and thorough investigation, at the end of which any competent policeman would have been obliged to arrest Hermione Ward. The evidence was very heavy against her. The great difference between her and Alexandra Carlyon was that she had everything to gain from the crime: freedom from a domineering husband and the daughters of a previous wife, and the inheritance of at least half of his very considerable wealth. Whereas, on the surface at least, Alexandra had everything to lose: social position, a devoted father for her son, and all but a small interest in his money. And yet Alexandra had confessed very early on, and Hermione had never wavered in protesting her total innocence.

"Go on!" Monk urged.

Markham continued, after only a few more mouthfuls. Monk knew he was being unfair to the man in not allowing him to eat, and he did not stop himself.

"You wouldn't let it rest at that," Markham said with admiration still in his voice at the memory of it. "I don't know why, but you believed 'er. I suppose that's the difference between a good policeman and a really great one. The great ones 'ave an instinct for innocence and guilt that goes beyond what the eye can see. Anyway, you worked night and day; I never saw anyone work so 'ard. I don't know when you ever slept, an' that's the truth. An' you drove us till we didn't know whether we was comin' or goin'.''

"Was I unreasonable?" Monk asked, then instantly wished he had not. It was an idiotic question. What could this man answer? And yet he heard his own voice going on. "Was I . . . offensive?"

Markham hesitated, looking first at his plate, then up at Monk, trying to judge from his eyes whether he wanted a candid answer or flattery. Monk knew what the decision would have to be; he liked flattery, but he had never in his life sought it. His pride would not have permitted him. And Markham was a man of some courage. He liked him now. He hoped he had had the honesty and the good judgment to like him before, and to show it.

"Yes," Markham said at last. "Although I wouldn't 'ave said so much offensive. Offense depends on who takes it. I don't take it. Can't say as I always liked you—too 'ard on some people because they didn't meet your standards, when they couldn't 'elp it. Different men 'as different strengths, and you weren't always prepared to see that."

Monk smiled to himself, a trifle bitterly. Now that he was no longer on the force, Markham had shown a considerable temerity and put tongue to thoughts he would not have dared entertain even as ideas in his mind a year ago. But he was honest. That he would not have dared say such things before was no credit to Monk, rather the reverse.

"I'm sorry, Mr. Monk." Markham saw his face. "But you did drive us terrible 'ard, and tore strips off them as couldn't match your quickness." He took another mouthful and ate it before adding, "But then you was right. It took us a long time, and tore to shreds a few folk on the way, as was lying for one reason or another; but in the end you proved as it weren't Mrs. Ward at all. It was 'er ladies' maid and the butler together. They were 'avin' an affair, the two o' them, and 'ad planned to rob their master, but 'e came down in the night and found them, so they 'ad to kill 'im or face a life in gaol. And personally I'd rather 'ang than spend forty years in the Coldbath Fields or the like—an' so would most folk."

So it was he who had proved it—he had saved her from the gallows. Not circumstance, not inevitability.

Markham was watching him, his face pinched with curiosity and puzzlement. He must find him extraordinary. Monk was asking questions that would be odd from any policeman, and from a ruthless and totally assured man like himself, beyond comprehension.

Instinctively he bent his head to slice his mutton, and kept at least his eyes hidden. He felt ridiculously vulnerable. This was absurd. He had saved Hermione, her honor and her life.

366

Why did he no longer even know her? He might have been keen for justice, as he was for Alexandra Carlyon—even passionate for it—but the emotion that boiled up in him at the memory of Hermione was far more than a hunger for the right solution to a case. It was deep and wholly personal. She haunted him as she could have only if he loved her. The ache was boundless for a companionship that had been immeasurably sweet, a gentleness, a gateway to his better self, the softer, generous, tender part of him.

Why? Why had they parted? Why had he not married her? He had no idea what the reason was, and it frightened him. Perhaps he should leave the wound unopened. Let it heal.

But it was not healing. It still hurt, like a skin grown over a place that suppurated yet.

Markham was looking at him.

"You still want to find Mrs. Ward?" he asked.

"Yes—yes I do."

"Well she left The Grange. I suppose she had too many memories from there. And folk still talked, for all it was proved she 'ad nothing to do with it. But you know 'ow it is—in an investigation all sorts o' things come out, that maybe 'ave nothing to do with the crime but still are better not known. I reckon there's no one as 'asn't got something they'd sooner keep quiet."

"No, I shouldn't think so," Monk agreed. "Where did she go, do you know?"

"Yes—yes, she bought a little 'ouse over Milton way. Next to the vicarage, if I remember rightly. There's a train, if you've a mind to get there."

"Thank you." He ate the treacle pudding with a dry mouth, washed it down with the cider, and thanked Markham again.

It was Sunday just after midday when he stood on the step of the Georgian stone house next to the vicarage, immaculately kept, weedless graveled path, roses beginning to bloom in the sun. Finally he summoned courage to knock on the door. It was a mechanical action, done with a decision of the

367

mind, but almost without volition. If he permitted his emotions through he would never do it.

It seemed an age of waiting. There was a bird singing somewhere behind him in the garden, and the sound of wind in the young leaves in the apple trees beyond the wall around the vicarage. Somewhere in the distance a lamb bleated and a ewe answered it.

Then without warning the door opened. He had not heard the feet coming to the other side. A pert, pretty maid stood expectantly, her starched apron crisp, her hair half hidden by a lace cap.

His voice dried in his throat and he had to cough to force out the words.

"Good morning, er—good afternoon. I—I'm sorry to trouble you at this—this hour—but I have come from London—yesterday . . ." He was making an extraordinary mess of this. When had he ever been so inarticulate? "May I speak with Mrs. Ward, please? It is a matter of some importance." He handed her a card with his name, but no occupation printed.

She looked a little doubtful, but regarded him closely, his boots polished and very nearly new, his trousers with a little dust on the ankles from his walk up from the station, but why not on such a pleasant day? His coat was excellently cut and his shirt collar and cuffs very white. Lastly she looked at his face, normally with the confidence of a man of authority but now a facade, and a poor one. She made her decision.

"I'll ask." Something like amusement flickered in her smile and her eyes definitely had laughter in them. "If you'll come to the parlor and wait, please, sir."

He stepped inside and was shown to the front parlor. Apparently it was a room not frequently used; probably there was a less formal sitting room to the rear of the house.

The maid left him and he had time to look. There was a tall upright clock against the nearest wall, its case elaborately carved. The soft chairs were golden brown, a color he found vaguely oppressive, even in this predominantly gentle room with patterned carpet and curtains, all subdued and comfortable. Over the mantelpiece was a landscape, very traditional, probably somewhere in the Lake District—too many blues for his taste. He thought it would have been subtler and more beautiful with a limited palette of grays and muted browns.

Then his eyes went to the backs of the chairs and he felt a wild lurch of familiarity clutch at him and his muscles tightened convulsively. The antimacassars were embroidered with a design of white heather and purple ribbons. He knew every stitch of it, every bell of the flowers and curl of scroll.

It was absurd. He already knew that this was the woman. He knew it from what Markham had told him. He did not need this wrench of the emotional memory to confirm it. And yet this was knowledge of quite a different nature, not expectation but feeling. It was what he had come for—at last.

There was a quick, light step outside the door and the handle turned.

He almost choked on his own breath.

She came in. There was never any doubt it was her. From the crown of her head, with its softly curling fair hair; her honey-brown eyes, wide-set, long-lashed; her full, delicate lips; her slender figure; she was completely familiar.

When she saw him her recognition was instant also. The color drained out of her skin, leaving her ashen, then it flooded back in a rich blush.

"William!" She gasped, then collected her own wits and closed the door behind her. "William—what on earth are you doing here? I didn't think I should ever—I mean—that we should meet again." She came towards him very slowly, her eyes searching his face.

He wanted to speak, but suddenly he had no idea what to say. All sorts of emotions crowded inside him: relief because she was so exactly what all his memories told him, all the gentleness, the beauty, the intelligence were there; fear now that the moment of testing was here and there was no more time to prepare. What did she think of him, what were her feelings, why had he ever left her? Incredulity at himself.

369

How little he knew the man he used to be. Why had he gone? Selfishness, unwillingness to commit himself to a wife and possibly a family? Cowardice? Surely not that—selfishness, pride, he could believe. That was the man he was discovering.

"William?" Now she was even more deeply puzzled. She did not understand silence from him. "William, what has happened?"

He did not know how to explain. He could not say, I have found you again, but I cannot remember why I ever lost you!

"I—I wanted to see how you are," he said. It sounded weak, but he could think of nothing better.

"I—I am well. And you?" She was still confused. "What brings you to . . . ? Another case?"

"No—no." He swallowed. "I came to see you."

"Why?"

"Why!" The question seemed preposterous. Because he loved her. Because he should never have left. Because she was all the gentleness, the patience, the generosity, the peace that was the better side of him, and he longed for it as a drowning man for air. How did she not know that? "Hermione!" The need burst from him with the passion he had been trying to suppress, violent and explosive.

She backed away, her face pale again, her hands moving up to her bosom.

"William! Please . . ."

Suddenly he felt sick. Had he asked her before, told her his feelings, and she had rejected him? Had he forgotten that, because it was too painful—and only remembered that he loved her, not that she did not love him?

He stood motionless, overcome with misery and appalling, desolating loneliness.

"William, you promised," she said almost under her breath, looking not at him but at the floor. "I can't. I told you before—you frighten me. I don't feel that—I can't. I don't want to. I don't want to care so much about anything, or anyone. You work too hard, you get too angry, too involved in other people's tragedies or injustices. You fight too

370

hard for what you want, you are prepared to pay more than I—for anything. And you hurt too much if you lose.'' She gulped and looked up, her eyes full of pleading. ''I don't *want* to feel all that. It frightens me. I don't like it. You frighten me. I don't love that way—and I don't want you to love me like that—I can't live up to it—and I would hate trying to. I want . . .'' She bit her lip. ''I want peace—I want to be comfortable.''

Comfortable! God Almighty!

''William? Don't be angry—I can't help it—I told you all that before. I thought you understood. Why have you come back? You'll only upset things. I'm married to Gerald now, and he's good to me. But I don't think he would care for you coming back. He's grateful you proved my innocence, of course he is—'' She was speaking even more rapidly now, and he knew she was afraid. ''And of course I shall never cease to be grateful. You saved my life—and my reputation— I know that. But please—I just can't . . .'' She stopped, dismayed by his silence, not knowing what else to add.

For the sake of his own dignity, some salve to his self-respect, he must assure her he would go quietly, not cause her any embarrassment. There was no purpose whatever in staying anyway. It was all too obvious why he had left in the first place. She had no passion to match his. She was a beautiful vessel, gentle at least outwardly, but it was born from fear of unpleasantness, not of compassion, such as a deeper woman might have felt—but she was a shallower vessel than he, incapable of answering him. She wanted to be comfortable; there was something innately selfish in her.

''I am glad you are happy,'' he said, his voice dry, catching in his throat. ''There is no need to be frightened. I shall not stay. I came across from Guildford. I have to be in London tomorrow morning anyway—a big trial. She—the woman accused—made me think of you. I wanted to see you—know how you are. Now I do; it is enough.''

''Thank you.'' The relief flooded her face. ''I—I would rather Gerald did not know you were here. He—he wouldn't like it.''

"Then don't tell him," he said simply. "And if the maid mentions it, I was merely an old friend, calling by to enquire after your health, and to wish you happiness."

"I am well—and happy. Thank you, William." Now she was embarrassed. Perhaps she realized how shallow she sounded; but it was at least past, and she had no intention of apologizing for it or trying to ameliorate its truth.

Nor did she offer him refreshment. She wanted him to leave before her husband returned from wherever he was—perhaps church.

There was nothing of any dignity or worth to be gained by remaining—only a petty selfishness, a desire for a small revenge, and he would despise it afterwards.

"Then I shall walk to the station and catch the next train towards London." He went to the door, and she opened it for him hastily, thanking him once again.

He bade her good-bye and two minutes later was walking along the lane under the trees with the wind-swung leaves dancing across the sunlight, birds singing. Here and there was a splash of white hawthorn blossom in the hedges, its perfume so sweet in the air that quite suddenly it brought him close to unexpected tears, not of self-pity because he had lost a love, but because what he had truly hungered for with such terrible depth had never existed—not in her. He had painted on her lovely face and gentle manner a mask of what he longed for—which was every bit as unfair to her as it was to him.

He blinked, and quickened his pace. He was a hard man, often cruel, demanding, brilliant, unflinching from labor or truth—at least he had been—but by God he had courage. And with all the changes he meant to wreak in himself, that at least he would never change.

Hester spent Sunday, with Edith's unintentional help, visiting Damaris. This time she did not see Randolf or Felicia Carlyon, but went instead to the gate and the door of the wing where Damaris and Peverell lived and, when they chose, had a certain amount of privacy. She had nothing to say to

Felicia, and would be grateful not to be faced with the duty of having to try to find something civil and noncommittal to fill the silences there would inevitably be. And she also felt a trifle guilty for what she intended to do, and what she knew it would cost them.

She wished to see Damaris alone, absolutely alone, without fear of interruption from anyone (least of all Felicia), so she could confront her with the terrible facts that Monk had found, and perhaps wring from her the truth about the night of the murder.

Without knowing why, Edith had agreed to distract Peverell and keep him from home, on whatever pretext came to her mind. Hester had told her only that she needed to see Damaris, and that it was delicate and likely to be painful, but that it concerned a truth they had to learn. Hester felt abominably guilty that she had not told Edith what it was, but knowledge would also bring the obligation to choose, and that was a burden she dared not place on Edith in case she chose the wrong way, and love for her sister outweighed pursuit of truth. And if the truth were as ugly as they feared, it would be easier for Edith afterwards if she had had no conscious hand in exposing it.

She repeated this over to herself as she sat in Damaris's elegant, luxurious sitting room waiting for her to come, and finding sparse comfort in it.

She looked around the room. It was typical of Damaris, the conventional and the outrageous side by side, the comfort of wealth and exquisite taste, the safety of the established order—and next to it the wildly rebellious, the excitement of indiscipline. Idealistic landscapes hung on one side of the room, on the other were reproductions of two of William Blake's wilder, more passionate drawings of the human figure. Religion, philosophy and daring voyages into new politics sat on the same bookshelf. Artifacts were romantic or blasphemous, expensive or tawdry, practical or useless, personal taste side by side with the desire to shock. It was the room of two totally different people, or one person seeking to have the best of opposing worlds, to make daring voyages of exploration and at the same time keep hold of comfort and the safety of the long known.

When Damaris came in she was dressed in a gown which was obviously new, but so old in style it harked back to lines of the French Empire. It was startling, but as soon as Hester got over the surprise of it, she realized it was also extremely becoming, the line so much more natural than all the current layers of stiff petticoats and hooped skirts. It was also certainly far more comfortable to wear. Although she thought Damaris almost certainly chose it for effect, not comfort.

"How nice to see you," Damaris said warmly. Her face was pale and there were shadows of sleeplessness around her eyes. "Edith said you wanted to speak to me about the case. I don't know what I can tell you. It's a disaster, isn't it." She flopped down on the sofa and without thinking tucked her feet up to be comfortable. She smiled at Hester rather wanly. "I'm afraid your Mr. Rathbone is out of his depth—he isn't clever enough to get Alexandra out of this." She pulled a face. "But from what I have seen, he doesn't even appear to be trying. Anyone could do all that he has so far. What's that matter, Hester? Doesn't he believe it is worth it?"

"Oh yes," Hester said quickly, stung for Rathbone as well as for the truth. She sat down opposite Damaris. "It isn't time yet—his turn comes next."

"But it will be too late. The jury have already made up their minds. Couldn't you see that in their faces? I did."

"No it isn't. There are facts to come out that will change everything, believe me."

"Are there?" Damaris screwed up her face dubiously. "I can't imagine that."

"Can't you?"

Damaris squinted at her. "You say that with extra meaning—as if you thought I could. I can't think of anything at all that would alter what the jury think now."

There was no alternative, no matter how Hester hated it, and she did hate it. She felt brutal, worse than that, treacherous.

"You were at the Furnivals' house the night of the mur-

374

der," she began, although it was stating what they both knew and had never argued.

"I don't know anything," Damaris said with absolute candor. "For heaven's sake, if I did I would have said so before now."

"Would you? No matter how terrible it was?"

Damaris frowned. "Terrible? Alexandra pushed Thaddeus over the banister, then followed him down and picked up the halberd and drove it into his body as he lay unconscious at her feet! That's pretty terrible. What could be worse?"

Hester swallowed but did not look away from Damaris's eyes.

"Whatever you found out when you went upstairs to Valentine Furnival's room before dinner—long before Thaddeus was killed."

The blood fled from Damaris's face, leaving her looking ill and vulnerable, and suddenly far younger than she was.

"That has nothing to do with what happened to Thaddeus," she said very quietly. "Absolutely nothing. It was something else—something . . ." She hunched her shoulders and her voice trailed off. She pulled her feet a little higher.

"I think it has." Hester could not afford to be lenient.

The ghost of a smile crossed Damaris's mouth and vanished. It was self-mockery and there was no shred of happiness in it.

"You are wrong. You will have to accept my word of honor for that."

"I can't. I accept that you believe it. I don't accept you are right."

Damaris's face pinched. "You don't know what it was, and I shall not tell you. I'm sorry, but it won't help Alexandra, and it is my—my grief, not hers."

Hester felt knotted up inside with shame and pity.

"Do you know why Alexandra killed him?"

"No."

"I do."

Damaris's head jerked up, her eyes wide.

"Why?" she said huskily.

Hester took a deep breath.

"Because he was committing sodomy and incest with hi
own son," she said very quietly. Her voice sounded ob
scenely matter-of-fact in the silent room, as if she had made
some banal remark that would be forgotten in a few mo
ments, instead of something so dreadful they would both
remember it as long as they lived.

Damaris did not shriek or faint. She did not even look
away, but her skin was whiter than before, and her eyes hol
lower.

Hester realized with an increasing sickness inside that, fa
from disbelieving her, Damaris was not even surprised. I
was as if it were a long-expected blow, coming at last. So
Monk had been right. She had discovered that evening tha
Peverell was involved. Hester could have wept for her, fo
the pain. She longed to touch her, to take her in her arms a
she would a weeping child, but it was useless. Nothing could
reach or fold that wound.

"You knew, didn't you?" she said aloud. "You knew i
that night!"

"No I didn't." Damaris's voice was flat, almost without
expression, as if something in her were already destroyed.

"Yes you did. You knew Peverell was doing it too, and to
Valentine Furnival. That's why you came down almost be
side yourself with horror. You were close to hysterical. I
don't know how you kept any control at all. I wouldn't have—
I don't think—"

"Oh God—no!" Damaris was moved to utter horror a
last. "No!" She uncurled herself so violently she half-fel
off the settee, landing awkwardly on the ground. "No. No
I didn't. Not Pev. How could you even think such a thing?
It's—it's—wild—insane. Not Pev!"

"But you knew." For the first time Hester doubted.
"Wasn't that what you discovered when you went up to Val
entine's room?"

"No." Damaris was on the floor in front of her, splayed

out like a colt, her long legs at angles, and yet she was absolutely natural. "No! Hester—dear heaven, please believe me, it wasn't."

Hester struggled with herself. Could it be the truth?

"Then what was it?" She frowned, racking her mind. "You came down from Valentine's room looking as if you'd seen the wrath of heaven. Why? What else could you possibly have found out? It was nothing to do with Alexandra or Thaddeus—or Peverell, then what?"

"I can't tell you!"

"Then I can't believe you. Rathbone is going to call you to the stand. Cassian was abused by his father, his grandfather—I'm sorry—and someone else. We have to know who that other person was, and prove it. Or Alexandra will hang."

Damaris was so pale her skin looked gray, as if she had aged in moments.

"I can't. It—it would destroy Pev." She saw Hester's face. "No. No, it isn't that. I swear by God—it isn't."

"No one will believe you," Hester said very quietly, although even as she said it, she knew it was a lie—she believed it. "What else could it be?"

Damaris bowed her head in her hands and began to speak very quietly, her voice aching with unshed tears.

"When I was younger, before I met Pev, I fell in love with someone else. For a long time I did nothing. I loved him with . . . chastity. Then—I thought I was losing him. I—I loved him wildly . . . at least I thought I did. Then . . ."

"You made love," Hester said the obvious. She was not shocked. In the same circumstances she might have done the same, had she Damaris's beauty, and wild beliefs. Even without them had she loved enough . . .

"Yes." Damaris's voice choked. "I didn't keep his love . . . in fact I think in a way that ended it."

Hester waited. Obviously there was more. By itself it was hardly worth repeating.

Damaris went on, her voice catching as she strove to control it, and only just succeeding. "I learned I was with child. It was Thaddeus who helped me. That was what I was talking

377

about when I said he could be kind. I had no idea Mama knew anything about it. Thaddeus arranged for me to go away for a while, and for the child to be adopted. It was a boy. I held him once—he was beautiful.'' At last she could keep the tears back no longer and she bent her head and wept, sobs shaking her body and long despairing cries tearing her beyond her strength to conceal.

Hester slid down onto the floor and put both her arms around her, holding her close, stroking her head and letting the storm burn itself out and exhaust her, all the grief and guilt of years bursting its bounds at last.

It was many minutes later when Damaris was still, and Hester spoke again.

''And what did you learn that night?''

''I learned where he was.'' Damaris sniffed fiercely and sat up, reaching for a handkerchief, an idiotic piece of lace and cambric not large enough to do anything at all.

Hester stood up and went to the cloakroom and wrung out a hand towel in cold water and brought it back, and also a large piece of soft linen she found in the cupboard beside the basin. Without saying anything she handed them to Damaris.

''Well?'' she asked after another moment or two.

''Thank you.'' Damaris remained sitting on the floor. ''I learned where he was,'' she said, her composure back again. She was too worn out for any violent emotion anymore. ''I learned what Thaddeus had done. Who he had . . . given him to.''

Hester waited, resuming her seat.

''The Furnivals,'' Damaris said with a small, very sad smile. ''Valentine Furnival is my son. I knew that when I saw him. I hadn't seen Valentine for years, you see, not since he was a small child—about Cassian's age, or even less. Actually I so dislike Louisa, and I didn't go there very often, and when I did he was always away at school, or when he was younger, already in bed. That evening he was at home because he'd had measles. But this time, when I saw him, he'd changed so much—grown up—and . . .'' She took a

378

deep, rather shaky breath. "He was so like his father when he was younger, I knew . . ."

"Like his father?" Hester searched her brains, which was stupid. There was no reason in the world why it should be anyone she had even heard of, much less met; in fact, there was every reason why it should not. Yet there was something tugging at the corners of her mind, a gesture, something about the eyes, the color of hair, the heavy lids . . .

"Charles Hargrave," Damaris said very quietly, and instantly Hester knew it was the truth: the eyes, the height, the way of standing, the angle of the shoulders.

Then another, ugly thought pulled at the edge of her mind, insistent, refusing to be silenced.

"But why did that upset you so terribly? You were frantic when you came down again, not quiet shaken, but frantic. Why? Even if Peverell found out Valentine was Hargrave's son—and I assume he doesn't know—even if he saw the resemblance between Valentine and Dr. Hargrave, there is no reason why he should connect it with you."

Damaris shut her eyes and again her voice was sharp with pain.

"I didn't know Thaddeus abused Cassian, believe me, I really didn't. But I knew Papa abused him—when he was a child. I knew the look in his eyes, that mixture of fear and excitement, the pain, the confusion, and the kind of secret pleasure. I suppose if I'd ever really looked at Cass lately I'd have seen it there too—but I didn't look. And since the murder I just thought it was part of his grief. Not that I've spent much time with him anyway—I should have, but I haven't. I know about Thaddeus, because I saw it once . . . and ever after it was in my mind."

Hester drew breath to say something—and nothing seemed adequate.

Damaris closed her eyes.

"I saw the same look in Valentine's face." Her voice was tight, as if her throat were burned inside. "I knew he was being abused too. I thought it was Maxim—I hated him so much I would have killed him. It never occurred to me it was

Thaddeus. Oh God. Poor Alex." She gulped. "No wonder she killed him. I would have too—in her place. In fact if I'd known it was he who abused Valentine, I would have anyway. I just didn't know. I suppose I assumed it was always fathers." She laughed harshly, a tiny thread of hysteria creeping back into her voice. "You should have suspected me. I would have been just as guilty as Alexandra—in thought and intent, if not in deed. It was only inability that stopped me—nothing else."

"Many of us are innocent only through lack of chance—or of means," Hester said very softly. "Don't blame yourself. You'll never know whether you would have or not if the chance had been there."

"I would." There was no doubt in Damaris's voice, none at all. She looked up at Hester. "What can we do for Alex? It would be monstrous if she were hanged for that. Any mother worth a damn would have done the same!"

"Testify," Hester answered without hesitation. "Tell the truth. We've got to persuade the jury that she did the only thing she could to protect her child."

Damaris looked away, her eyes filling with tears.

"Do I have to tell about Valentine? Peverell doesn't know! Please . . ."

"Tell him yourself," Hester said very quietly. "He loves you—and he must know you love him."

"But men don't forgive easily—not things like that." The despair was back in Damaris's voice.

Hester felt wretched, still hoping against all likelihood that it was not Peverell.

"Peverell isn't 'men,' " she said chokingly. "Don't judge him by others. Give him the chance to be all—all that he could be." Did she sound as desperate and as hollow as she felt? "Give him a chance to forgive—and love you for what you really are, not what you think he wants you to be. It was a mistake, a sin if you like—but we all sin one way or another. What matters is that you become kinder and wiser because of it, that you become gentler with others, and that you have never repeated it!"

"Do you think he will see it like that? He might if it were anyone else—but it's different when it's your own wife."

"For heaven's sake—try him."

"But if he doesn't, I'll lose him!"

"And if you lie, Alexandra will lose her life. What would Peverell think of that?"

"I know." Damaris stood up slowly, suddenly all her grace returning. "I've got to tell him. God knows I wish I hadn't done it. And Charles Hargrave, of all people. I can hardly bear to look at him now. I know. Don't tell me again, I do know. I've got to tell Pev. There isn't any way out of it—lying would only make it worse."

"Yes it would." Hester put out her hand and touched Damaris's arm. "I'm sorry—but I had no choice either."

"I know." Damaris smiled with something of the old charm, although the effort it cost her was apparent. "Only if I do this, you'd better save Alex. I don't want to say all this for nothing."

"Everything I can. I'll leave nothing untried—I promise."

12

ALEXANDRA SAT ON THE WOODEN BENCH in the small cell, her face white and almost expressionless. She was exhausted, and the marks of sleeplessness were plain around her eyes. She was far thinner than when Rathbone had first seen her and her hair had lost its sheen.

"I can't go on," she said wearily. "There isn't any point. It will only damage Cassian—terribly." She took a deep breath. He could see the rise of her breast under the thin gray muslin of her blouse. "They won't believe me. Why should they? There's no proof, there never could be. How could you prove such a thing? People don't do it where they can be seen."

"You know," Rathbone said quietly, sitting opposite her and looking at her so intensely that in time she would have to raise her head and meet his eyes.

She smiled bitterly. "And who's going to believe me?"

"That wasn't my point," he said patiently. "If you could know, then it is possible others could also. Thaddeus himself was abused as a child."

She jerked her head up, her eyes full of pity and surprise.

"You didn't know?" He looked at her gently. "I thought not."

"I'm sorry," she whispered. "But if he was, how could

382

e, of all people, abuse his own son?'' Her incomprehension was full of confusion and pain. ''Surely if—why? I don't understand.''

''Neither do I,'' he answered frankly. ''But then I have never walked that path myself. I had quite another reason for telling you, one of very much more urgent relevance.'' He stopped, not fully sure if she was listening to him.

''Have you?'' she said dully.

''Yes. Can you imagine how he suffered? His lifelong shame, and the fear of being discovered? Even some dim sense of what he was committing upon his own child—and yet, the need was so overwhelming, so consuming it still drove him—''

''Stop it,'' she said furiously, jerking her head up. ''I'm sorry! Of course I'm sorry! Do you think I enjoyed it?'' Her voice was thick, choking with indescribable anguish. ''I racked my brain for any other way. I begged him to stop, to send Cassian away to boarding school—anything at all to put him beyond reach. I offered him myself, for any practice he wanted!'' She stared at him with helpless fury. ''I used to love him. Not passionately, but love just the same. He was the father of my children and I had covenanted to be loyal to him all my life. I don't think he ever loved me, not really, but he gave me all he was capable of.''

She sank lower on the bench and dropped her head forward, covering her face with her hands. ''Don't you think I see his body on that floor every time I lie in the dark? I dream about it—I've redone that deed in my nightmares, and woken up cold as ice, with the sweat standing out on my skin. I'm terrified God will judge me and condemn my soul forever.''

She huddled a little lower into herself. ''But I *couldn't* let that happen to my child and do nothing—just let it go on. You don't know how he changed. The laughter went out of him—all the innocence. He became sly. He was afraid of me—of me! He didn't trust me anymore, and he started telling lies—stupid lies—and he became frightened all the time, and suspicious of people. And always there was the sort of . . . secret glee in him . . . a—a—guilty pleasure. And yet

383

he cried at night—curled up like a baby, and crying in his sleep. I couldn't let it go on!''

Rathbone broke his own rules and reached out and took her thin shoulders in his hands and held her gently.

"Of course you couldn't! And you can't now! If the truth is not told, and this abuse is not stopped, then his grandfather—and the other man—will go on just as his father did, and it will all have been for nothing." Unconsciously his fingers tightened. "We think we know who the other man is, and believe me he will have the same chances as the general had: any day, any night, to go on exactly the same."

She began to weep softly, without sobbing, just the quiet tears of utter despair. He held her gently, leaning forward a little, his head close to hers. He could smell the faint odor of her hair, washed with prison soap, and feel the warmth of her skin.

"Thaddeus was abused as a child," he went on relentlessly, because it mattered. "His sister knew it. She saw it happen once, by his father—and she saw the reflection of the same emotion in the eyes again in Valentine Furnival. That was what drove her to distraction that evening. She will swear to it."

Alexandra said nothing, but he could feel her stiffen with surprise, and the weeping stopped. She was utterly still.

"And Miss Buchan knew about Thaddeus and his father—and about Cassian now."

Alexandra took a shaky breath, still hiding her face.

"She won't testify," she said with a long sniff. "She can't. If she does they'll dismiss her—and she has nowhere to go. You mustn't ask her. She'll have to deny it, and that will only make it worse."

He smiled bleakly. "Don't worry about that. I never ask questions unless I already know the answer—or, to be more precise, unless I know what the witness will say, true or untrue."

"You can't expect her to ruin herself."

"What she chooses to do is not your decision."

"But you can't," she protested, pulling away from him and lifting her head to face him. "She'd starve."

"And what will happen to Cassian? Not to mention you."

She said nothing.

"Cassian will grow up to repeat the pattern of his father," he said ruthlessly, because it was the only thing he knew which would be more than she could bear, regardless of Miss Buchan's fate. "Will you permit that? The shame and guilt all over again—and another wretched, humiliated child, another woman suffering as you do now?"

"I can't fight you," she said so quietly he could barely hear her. She sat huddled over herself, as if the pain were deep in the center of her and somehow she could fold herself around it.

"You are not fighting me," he said urgently. "You don't need to do anything now but sit in the dock, looking as you do, and remembering, as well as your guilt, the love of your child—and *why* you did it. I will tell the jury your feelings, trust me!"

"Do whatever you will, Mr. Rathbone. I don't think I have strength left to make judgments anymore."

"You don't need it, my dear." He stood up at last, exhausted himself, and it was only Monday, June 29. The second week of the trial had commenced. He must begin the defense.

The first witness for the defense was Edith Sobell. Lovat-Smith was sitting back in his chair, legs crossed over casually, head tilted, as if he were interested only as a matter of curiosity. He had made a case that seemed unarguable, and looking around the crowded courtroom, there was not a single face which registered doubt. They were there only to watch Alexandra and the Carlyon family sitting in their row at the front, the women dressed in black and Felicia veiled, rigid and square-shouldered, Randolf unhappy but entirely composed.

Edith took the stand and stumbled once or twice when swearing the oath, her tongue clumsy in her nervousness.

And yet there was a bloom to her skin, a color that belied the situation, and she stood erect with nothing of the defensiveness or the weight of grief which lay on her mother.

"Mrs. Sobell," Rathbone began courteously, "you are the sister of the victim of this crime, and the sister-in-law of the accused?"

"I am."

"Did you know your brother well, Mrs. Sobell?"

"Moderately. He was several years older than I, and he left home to go into the army when I was a child. But of course when he returned from service abroad and settled down I learned to know him again. He lived not far from Carlyon House, where I still live, since my husband's death."

"Would you tell me something of your brother's personality, as you observed it?"

Lovat-Smith shifted restlessly in his seat, and the crowd had already lost interest, all but a few who hoped there might be some completely new and shocking revelation. After all, this witness was for the defense.

Lovat-Smith rose to his feet.

"My lord, this appears to be quite irrelevant. We have already very fully established the nature of the dead man. He was honorable, hardworking, a military hero of considerable repute, faithful to his wife, financially prudent and generous. His only failings seem to have been that he was somewhat pompous and perhaps did not flatter or amuse his wife as much as he might." He smiled dryly, looking around so the jury could see his face. "A weakness we might all be guilty of, from time to time."

"I don't doubt it," Rathbone said acerbically. "And if Mrs. Sobell agrees with your estimation, I will be happy to save the court's time by avoiding having her repeat it. Mrs. Sobell?"

"I agree," Edith said with a look first at Rathbone, then at Lovat-Smith. "He also spent a great deal of time with his son, Cassian. He seemed to be an excellent and devoted father."

"Quite: he seemed to be an excellent and devoted father,"

he repeated her precise words. "And yet, Mrs. Sobell, when you became aware of the tragedy of his death, and that your sister-in-law had been charged with causing it, what did you do?"

"My lord, that too is surely quite irrelevant?" Lovat-Smith protested. "I appreciate that my learned friend is somewhat desperate, but this cannot be allowed!"

The judge looked at Rathbone.

"Mr. Rathbone, I will permit you some leniency, so that you may present the best defense you can, in extremely difficult circumstances, but I will not permit you to waste the court's time. See to it that the answers you draw are to some point!"

Rathbone looked again at Edith.

"Mrs. Sobell?"

"I . . ." Edith swallowed hard and lifted her chin, looking away from where her mother and father sat upright in their row in the front of the gallery, now no longer witnesses. For an instant her eyes met Alexandra's in the dock. Then she continued speaking. "I contacted a friend of mine, a Miss Hester Latterly, and asked her help to find a good lawyer to defend Alexandra—Mrs. Carlyon."

"Indeed?" Rathbone's eyebrows shot up as if he were surprised, although surely almost everyone in the room must know he had planned this most carefully. "Why? She was charged with murdering your brother, this model man."

"At first—at first I thought she could not be guilty." Edith's voice trembled a little but she gained control again. "Then when it was proved to me beyond question that she was . . . that she had committed the act . . . I still thought there must be some better reason than the one she gave."

Lovat-Smith rose again.

"My lord! I hope Mr. Rathbone is not going to ask the witness to draw some conclusion? Her faith in her sister-in-law is very touching, but it is not evidence of anything except her own gentle—and, forgive me, rather gullible—nature!"

"My learned friend is leaping to conclusions, as I am afraid he is prone to do," Rathbone said with a tiny smile.

"I do not wish Mrs. Sobell to draw any conclusions at all, simply to lay a foundation for her subsequent actions, so the court will understand what she did, and why."

"Proceed, Mr. Rathbone," the judge instructed.

"Thank you, my lord. Mrs. Sobell, have you spent much time with your nephew, Cassian Carlyon, since his father's death?"

"Yes of course. He is staying in our house."

"How has he taken his father's death?"

"Irrelevant!" Lovat-Smith interrupted again. "How can a child's grief possibly be pertinent to the accused's guilt or innocence? We cannot turn a blind eye to murder because if we hanged the guilty person then a child would be robbed of both his parents—tragic as that is. And we all pity him . . ."

"He does not need your pity, Mr. Lovat-Smith," Rathbone said irritably. "He needs you to hold your tongue and let me proceed with uncovering the truth."

"Mr. Rathbone," the judge said tartly. "We sympathize with your predicament, and your frustration, but your language is discourteous, and I will not allow it. Nevertheless, Mr. Lovat-Smith, it is good counsel, and you will please observe it until you have an objection of substance. If you interrupt as often as this, we shall not reach a verdict before Michaelmas."

Lovat-Smith sat down with a broad smile.

Rathbone bowed, then turned back to Edith.

"I think you are now permitted to continue, Mrs. Sobell. If you please. What was your observation of Cassian's manner?"

Edith frowned in concentration.

"It was very hard to understand," she replied, thinking carefully. "He grieved for his father, but it seemed to be very—very adult. He did not cry, and at times he seemed very composed, almost relieved."

Lovat-Smith rose to his feet, and the judge waved him to sit down again. Rathbone turned to Edith.

"Mrs. Sobell, will you please explain that curious word *relieved*. Try not to give us any conclusions you may have

388

come to in your own mind, simply your observations of fact. Not what he seemed, but what he said, or did. Do you understand the difference?''

''Yes, my lord. I'm sorry.'' Again her nervousness betrayed itself in clenched hands on the witness box rail, and a catch in her voice. ''I saw him alone on several occasions, through a window, or from a doorway when he did not know I was there. He was quite at ease, sitting smiling. I asked him if he was happy by himself, thinking he might be lonely, but he told me he liked it. Sometimes he went to my father— his grandfather—''

''Colonel Carlyon?'' Rathbone interrupted.

''Yes. Then other times he seemed to go out of his way to avoid him. He was afraid of my mother.'' As if involuntarily, she glanced at Felicia, then back to Rathbone again. ''He said so. And he was very upset about his own mother. He told me she did not love him—that his father had told him so.''

In the dock Alexandra closed her eyes and seemed to sway as if in physical pain. A gasp escaped her in spite of all her effort at self-control.

''Hearsay,'' Lovat-Smith said loudly, rising to his feet. ''My lord . . .''

''That is not permitted,'' the judge apologized to Edith. ''I think we have gathered from your testimony that the child was in a state of considerable confusion. Is that what you wished to establish, Mr. Rathbone?''

''More than that, my lord: the nature of his confusion. And that he developed close, and ambivalent, relationships with other people.''

Lovat-Smith let out a loud moan and raised his hands in the air.

''Then you had better proceed and do so, Mr. Rathbone,'' the judge said with a tight smile. ''If you can. Although you have not shown us yet why this has any relevance to the case, and I advise that you do that within a very short time.''

''I promise you that it will become apparent in later testimony, my lord,'' Rathbone said, his voice still calculatedly light. But he abandoned the course for the present, knowing he had left it imprinted on the jury's minds, and that was all that mattered. He could build on it later. He turned back to Edith.

"Mrs. Sobell, did you recently observe a very heated quarrel between Miss Buchan, an elderly member of your household staff, and your cook, Mrs. Emery?"

A ghost of amusement crossed Edith's face, curving her mouth momentarily.

"I have observed several, more than I can count," she conceded. "Cook and Miss Buchan have been enemies for years."

"Quite so. But the quarrel I am referring to happened within the last three weeks, on the back stairs of Carlyon House. You were called to assist."

"That's right. Cassian came to fetch me because he was afraid. Cook had a knife. I'm sure she did not intend to do anything with it but make an exhibition, but he didn't know that."

"What was the quarrel about, Mrs. Sobell?"

Lovat-Smith groaned audibly.

Rathbone ignored it.

"About?" Edith looked slightly puzzled. He had not told her he was going to pursue this. He wanted her obvious un-awareness to be seen by the jury. This case depended upon emotions as much as upon facts.

"Yes. What was the subject of the difference?"

Lovat-Smith groaned even more loudly. "Really, my lord," he protested.

Rathbone resumed facing the judge. "My learned friend seems to be in some distress," he said unctuously.

There was a loud titter of amusement, nervous, like a ripple of wind through a field before thunder.

"The case," Lovat-Smith said loudly. "Get on with the case, man!"

"Then bear your agony a little less vocally, old chap," Rathbone replied equally loudly, "and allow me to." He swung around. "Mrs. Sobell—to remind you, the question was, would you please tell the court the subject of the quarrel between the governess, Miss Buchan, and the cook?''

"Yes—yes, if you wish, although I cannot see—"

"We none of us can," Lovat-Smith interrupted again.

"Mr. Lovat-Smith," the judge said sharply. "Mrs. Sobell, answer the question. If it proves irrelevant I will control Mr. Rathbone's wanderings.''

"Yes, my lord. Cook accused Miss Buchan of being incompetent to care for Cassian. She said Miss Buchan was . . . there was a great deal of personal abuse, my lord. I would rather not repeat it.''

Rathbone thought of permitting her to do so. A jury liked to be amused, but they would lose respect for Miss Buchan, which might be what would win or lose the case. A little laughter now would be too dearly bought.

"Please spare us," he said aloud. "The subject of the difference will be sufficient—the fact that there was abuse may indicate the depth of their feelings.''

Again Edith smiled hurriedly, and then continued.

"Cook said that Miss Buchan was following him around everywhere and confusing him by telling him his mother loved him, and was not a wicked woman." She swallowed hard, her eyes troubled. That she did not understand what he wanted was painfully obvious. The jury were utterly silent, their faces staring at her. Suddenly the drama was back again, the concentration total. The crowd did not whisper or move. Even Alexandra herself seemed momentarily forgotten.

"And the cook?" Rathbone prompted.

"Cook said Alexandra should be hanged." Edith seemed to find the word difficult. "And of course she was wicked. Cassian had to know it and come to terms with it.''

"And Miss Buchan's reply?"

"That Cook didn't know anything about it, she was an ignorant woman and should stay in the kitchen where she belonged.''

"Did you know to what Miss Buchan referred?" Rathbone asked, his voice low and clear, without any theatrics.

"No."

"Was a Miss Hester Latterly present at this exchange?"

"Yes."

"When you had parted the two protagonists, did Miss Latterly go upstairs with Miss Buchan?"

"Yes."

"And afterwards leave in some haste, and without explanation to you as to why?"

"Yes, but we did not quarrel," Edith said quickly. "She seemed to have something most urgent to do."

"Indeed I know it, Mrs. Sobell. She came immediately to see me. Thank you. That is all. Please remain there, in case my learned friend has something to ask you."

There was a rustle and a sigh around the court. A dozen people nudged each other. The expected revelation had not come . . . not yet.

Lovat-Smith rose and sauntered over to Edith, hands in his pockets.

"Mrs. Sobell, tell me honestly, much as you may sympathize with your sister-in-law, has any of what you have said the slightest bearing on the tragedy of your brother's death?"

She hesitated, glancing at Rathbone.

"No, Mrs. Sobell," Lovat-Smith cautioned sharply. "Answer for yourself, please! Can you tell me any relation between what you have said about your nephew's very natural confusion and distress over his father's murder, and his mother's confession and arrest, and this diverting but totally irrelevant quarrel between two of your domestics?" He waved his hands airily, dismissing it, "And the cause at trial: namely whether Alexandra Carlyon is guilty or not guilty of murdering her husband, your brother? I remind you, in case after all this tarradiddle you, like the rest of us, are close to forgetting."

He had gone too far. He had trivialized the tragedy.

"I don't know, Mr. Lovat-Smith," she said with a sudden return of composure, her voice now grim and with a hard edge. "As you have just said, we are here to discover the truth, not to assess it beforehand. I don't know why Alexandra did what she did, and I wish to know. It has to matter."

"Indeed." Lovat-Smith gave in gracefully. He had sufficient instinct to recognize an error and cease it immediately. "It does not alter facts, but of course it matters, Mrs. Sobell. I have no further questions. Thank you."

"Mr. Rathbone?" the judge asked.

"I have no further questions, thank you, my lord."

"Thank you, Mrs. Sobell, you may go."

Rathbone stood in the center of the very small open space in front of the witness box.

"I call Miss Catriona Buchan."

Miss Buchan came to the witness box looking very pale, her face even more gaunt than before, her thin back stiff and her eyes straight forward, as if she were a French aristocrat passing through the old women knitting at the foot of the guillotine. She mounted the stairs unaided, holding her skirts in from the sides, and at the top turned and faced the court. She swore to tell the truth, and regarded Rathbone as though he were an executioner.

Rathbone found himself admiring her as much as anyone he had ever faced across that small space of floor.

"Miss Buchan, I realize what this is going to cost you, and I am not unmindful of your sacrifice, nevertheless I hope you understand that in the cause of justice I have no alternative?"

"Of course I do," she agreed with a crisp voice. The strain in it did not cause her to falter, only to sound a little more clipped than usual, a little higher in pitch, as if her throat were tight. "I would not answer did I not understand that!"

"Indeed. Do you remember quarreling with the cook at Carlyon House some three weeks ago?"

"I do. She is a good enough cook, but a stupid woman."

"In what way stupid, Miss Buchan?"

"She imagines all ills can be treated with good regular meals and that if you only eat right everything else will sort itself out."

"A shortsighted view. What did you quarrel about on that occasion, Miss Buchan?"

Her chin lifted a little higher.

"Master Cassian. She said I was confusing the child by telling him his mother was not a wicked woman, and that she still loved him."

In the dock Alexandra was so still it seemed she could not even be breathing. Her eyes never left Miss Buchan's face and she barely blinked.

"Is that all?" Rathbone asked.

Miss Buchan took a deep breath, her thin chest rising and falling. "No—she also said I followed the boy around too much, not leaving him alone."

"Did you follow the boy around, Miss Buchan?"

She hesitated only a moment. "Yes."

"Why?" He kept his voice level, as if the question were not especially important.

"To do what I could to prevent him being abused anymore."

"Abused? Was someone mistreating him? In what way?"

"I believe the word is sodomy, Mr. Rathbone," she said with only the slightest tremor.

There was a gasp in the court as hundreds of throats drew in breath.

Alexandra covered her face with her hands.

The jury froze in their seats, eyes wide, faces aghast.

In the front row of the gallery Randolf Carlyon sat immobile as stone. Felicia's veiled head jerked up and her knuckles were white on the rail in front of her. Edith, now sitting beside them, looked as if she had been struck.

Even the judge stiffened and turned to look up at Alexandra. Lovat-Smith stared at Rathbone, his face slack with amazement.

Rathbone waited several seconds before he spoke.

"Someone in the house was sodomizing the child?" He said it very quietly, but the peculiar quality of his voice and his exquisite diction made every word audible even at the very back of the gallery.

"Yes," Miss Buchan answered, looking at no one but him.

"How do you know that, Miss Buchan? Did you see it happen?"

"I did not see it this time—but I have in the past, when Thaddeus Carlyon himself was a child," she said. "And I knew the signs. I knew the look in a child's face, the sly pleasure, the fear mixed with exultancy, the flirting and the shame, the self-possession one minute, then the terror of losing his mother's love if she knew, the hatred of having to keep it a secret, and the pride of having a secret—and then crying in the night, and not being able to tell anyone why—and the total and overwhelming loneliness . . ."

Alexandra had lifted her face. She looked ashen, her body rigid with anguish.

The jury sat immobile, eyes horrified, skin suddenly pale.

The judge looked at Lovat-Smith, but for once he did not exercise his right to object to the vividness of her evidence, unsupported by any provable fact. His dark face looked blurred with shock.

"Miss Buchan," Rathbone continued softly. "You seem to have a vivid appreciation of what it is like. How is that?"

"Because I saw it in Thaddeus—General Carlyon—when he was a child. His father abused him."

There was such a gasp of horror around the room, a clamor of voices in amazement and protest, that she was obliged to stop.

In the gallery newspaper runners tripped over legs and caught their feet in onlookers' skirts as they scrambled to get out and seize a hansom to report the incredible news.

"Order!" the judge commanded, banging his gavel violently on his bench. "Order! Or I shall clear the court!"

Very slowly the room subsided. The jury had all turned to look at Randolf. Now again they faced Miss Buchan.

"That is a desperately serious thing to charge, Miss Buchan," Rathbone said quietly. "You must be very certain that what you say is true?"

"Of course I am." She answered him with the first and only trace of bitterness in her voice. "I have served the Carlyon family since I was twenty-four, when I came to look after Master Thaddeus. That is over forty years. There is nowhere else I can go now—and they will hardly give me a roof over my head in my old age after this. Does anyone imagine I do it lightly?"

Rathbone glanced for only a second at the jury's faces, and saw there the conflict of horror, disgust, anger, pity, and confusion that he had expected. She was a woman caught between betraying her employers, with its irreparable consequences to her, or betraying her conscience, and a child who had no one else to speak for him. The jurors were of a servant-keeping class, or they would not be jurors. Yet few of them were of position sufficient to have governesses. They were torn in loyalties, social ambition, and tearing pity.

"I know that, Miss Buchan," Rathbone said with a ghost of a smile. "I want to be sure that the court appreciates it also. Please continue. You were aware of the sodomy committed by Colonel Randolf Carlyon upon his son, Thaddeus. You saw the same signs of abuse in young Cassian Carlyon, and you were afraid for him. Is that correct?"

"Yes."

"And did you know who had been abusing him? Please be careful to be precise, Miss Buchan. I do mean *know*, supposition or deduction will not do."

"I am aware of that, sir," she said stiffly. "No, I did not know. But since he normally lived at his own home, not in Carlyon House, I supposed that it was his father, Thaddeus, perpetuating on his son what he himself endured as a child. And I assumed that that was what Alexandra Carlyon discovered, and why she did what she did. No one told me so."

"And that abuse ceased after the general's death? Then why did you think it necessary to protect him still?"

"I saw the relationship between him and his grandfather, the looks, the touching, the shame and the excitement. It was exactly the same as before—in the past. I was afraid it was happening again."

There was utter silence in the room. One could almost hear the creak of corsets as women breathed.

"I see," Rathbone said quietly. "So you did your best to protect the boy. Why did you not tell someone? That would seem to be a far more effective solution."

A smile of derision crossed her face and vanished.

"And who would believe me?" For an instant her eyes moved up to the gallery and the motionless forms of Felicia and Randolf, then she looked back at Rathbone. "I'm a domestic servant, accusing a famous and respected gentleman of one of the most vile of crimes. I would be thrown out, and then I wouldn't be able to do anything at all."

"What about Mrs. Felicia Carlyon, the boy's grandmother?" he pressed, but his voice was gentle. "Wouldn't she have to have some idea? Could you not have told her?"

"You are naive, Mr. Rathbone," she said wearily. "If she had no idea, she would be furious, and throw me out instantly—and see to it I starved. She couldn't afford to have me find employment ever again, in case I repeated the charge to her social equals, even to friends. And if she knew herself—then she had decided not to expose it and ruin the family with the shame of it. She'd not allow me to. If she had to live with that, then she'd do everything in her power to keep what she had paid such a price to preserve."

"I see." Rathbone glanced at the jury, many of them craning up at the gallery, faces dark with disgust, then at Lovat-Smith, now sitting upright and silent, deep in concentration. "So you stayed in Carlyon House," Rathbone continued, "saying nothing, but doing what you could for the child. I think we may all understand your position—and admire you for having the courage to come forward now. Thank you, Miss Buchan."

Lovat-Smith rose to his feet, looking profoundly unhappy.

"Miss Buchan, I regret this," he said with such sincerity it was palpable. "But I must press you a little more harshly than my learned friend has. The accusation you make is abominable. It cannot be allowed to stand without challenge. It will ruin the lives of an entire family." He inclined his head towards the gallery, where now there was the occasional murmur of anger. "A family known and admired in this city, a family which has dedicated itself to the service of the Queen and her subjects, not only here but in the farthest parts of the Empire as well."

Miss Buchan said nothing, but faced him, her thin body erect, hands folded. She looked fragile, and suddenly very old. Rathbone ached to be able to protect her, but he was impotent to do anything now, as he had known he would be, and she knew it too.

"Miss Buchan," Lovat-Smith went on, still courteously. "I assume you know what sodomy is, and you do not use the term loosely?"

She blushed, but did not evade his look.

"Yes sir, I know what it is. I will describe it for you, if you force me."

He shook his head. "No—I do not force you, Miss Buchan. How do you know this unspeakable act was committed on General Carlyon when he was a child? And I do mean knowledge, Miss Buchan, not supposition, no matter how well reasoned, in your opinion." He looked up at her, waiting.

"I am a servant, Mr. Lovat-Smith," she replied with dignity. "We have a peculiar position—not quite people, not quite furniture. We are often party to extraordinary scenes because we are ignored in the house, as if we had not eyes or brains. People do not mind us knowing things, seeing things they would be mortified to have their friends see."

One of the jurors looked startled, suddenly thoughtful.

"One day I had occasion to return to the nursery unexpectedly," Miss Buchan resumed. "Colonel Carlyon had neglected to lock the door, and I saw him in the act with his son. He did not know I saw. I was transfixed with horror—although I should not have been. I knew there was something very seriously wrong, but I did not understand what—until then. I stood there for several seconds, but I left as soundlessly as I had come. My knowledge is very real, sir."

"You witnessed this gross act, and yet you did nothing?" Lovat-Smith's voice rose in disbelief. "I find that hard to credit, Miss Buchan. Was not your first duty clearly towards your charge, the child, Thaddeus Carlyon?"

She did not flinch.

"I have already told you, there was nothing I could do."

"Not tell his mother?" He waved an arm up towards the

allery where Felicia sat like stone. "Would she not have
een horrified? Would she not have protected her child? You
eem, by implication, to be expecting us to believe that Al-
xandra Carlyon," he indicated her with another expansive
esture, "a generation later, was so violently distressed by
e same fact that she murdered her husband rather than al-
w it to continue! And yet you say that Mrs. Felicia Carlyon
ould have done nothing!"

Miss Buchan did not speak.

"You hesitate," Lovat-Smith challenged, his voice rising.
Why, Miss Buchan? Are you suddenly not so certain of
swers? Not so easy?"

Miss Buchan was strong. She had already risked, and no
oubt lost, everything. She had no stake left, nothing else
uld be taken from her but her self-esteem.

"You are too facile, young man," she said with all the
effable authority of a good governess. "Women may be as
nmeasurably different from each other as men. Their loy-
ties and values may be different also, as may be the times
d circumstances in which they live. What can a woman
, in such a position? Who will believe her, if she accused
publicly loved man of such a crime?" She did not once
tray that she even knew Felicia was there in the room with
em, much less that she cared what Felicia thought or felt.
People do not wish to believe it of their heroes, and both
andolf and Thaddeus Carlyon were heroes, in their own
ays. Society would have crucified her as a wicked woman
they did not believe her, as a venally indiscreet one if they
d. She would know that, and she chose to preserve what
e had. Miss Alexandra chose to save her child, or to try
. It remains to be seen whether or not she has sacrificed
erself in vain."

Lovat-Smith opened his mouth to argue, attack her again,
d then looked at the jury and decided better of it.

"You are a remarkable woman, Miss Buchan," he said
ith a minute bow. "It remains to be seen whether any fur-
er facts bear out your extraordinary vision of events, but

no doubt you believe you speak the truth. I have nothing further to ask you.''

Rathbone declined to reexamine. He knew better than to gild the lily.

The court rose for the luncheon adjournment in an uproar.

The first witness of the afternoon was Damaris Erskine. She too looked pale, with dark circles under her eyes as if she had wept herself into exhaustion but had found little sleep. All the time her eyes kept straying to Peverell. He was sitting very upright in his seat next to Felicia and Randolf in the front of the gallery, but as apart from them in spirit as if they were in different rooms. He ignored them totally and stared without movement at Damaris, his eyes puckered in concern, his lips undecided on a smile, as if he feared it might be taken for levity rather than encouragement.

Monk sat two rows behind Hester, in the body of the court behind the lawyers. He did not wish to sit beside her. His emotions were too raw from his confrontation with Hermione. He wanted a long time alone, but circumstances made that impossible; however, there was a certain aloneness in the crowd of a courtroom, and in centering his mind and all his feelings he could on the tragedy being played out in front of him.

Rathbone began very gently, with the softly cautious voice Monk knew he adopted when he was about to deliver a mortal blow and loathed doing it, but had weighed all the facts, and the decision was irrevocable.

''Mrs. Erskine, you were present at the home of Mr. and Mrs. Furnival on the night your brother was killed, and you have already told us of the order of events as you recall them.''

''Yes,'' she said almost inaudibly.

''But I think you have omitted what most undoubtedly was for you the most devastating part of the evening, that is until Dr. Hargrave said that your brother had not died by accident, but been murdered.''

Lovat-Smith leaned forward, frowning, but he did not interrupt.

"Several people have testified," Rathbone went on, "that when you came down the stairs from seeing young Valentine Furnival, you were in a state of distress bordering on hysteria. Would you please tell us what happened up there to cause this change in you?"

Damaris studiously avoided looking towards Felicia and Randolf, nor did she look at Alexandra, sitting pale-faced and rigid in the dock. She took one or two moments to steel herself, and Rathbone waited without prompting her.

"I recognized—Valentine . . ." she said at last, her voice husky.

"Recognized him?" Rathbone repeated the word. "What a curious expression, Mrs. Erskine. Was there ever any doubt in your mind as to who he was? I accept that you did not see him often, indeed had not seen him for some years while he was away at boarding school, since you infrequently visited the house. But surely there was only one boy present?"

She swallowed convulsively and shot him a look of pleading so profound there was a murmur of anger around the room and Felicia jerked forward, then sat up again as Randolf's hand closed over her arm.

Almost imperceptibly Peverell nodded.

Damaris raised her chin.

"He is not the Furnivals' natural child: he is adopted. Before my marriage fourteen years ago, I had a child. Now that he is—is of nearly adult height—a young man, not a boy, he . . ." For a moment more she had to fight to keep control.

Opposite her in the gallery, Charles Hargrave leaned forward a little, his face tense, sandy brows drawn down. Beside him, Sarah Hargrave looked puzzled and a flicker of anxiety touched her face.

"He resembles his father," Damaris said huskily. "So much, I knew he was my son. You see, at the time the only person I could trust to help me was my brother, Thaddeus. He took me away from London, and he saw to the child's being adopted. Suddenly, when I saw Valentine, it all made sense. I knew what Thaddeus had done with my child."

"Were you angry with your brother, Mrs. Erskine? Did

you resent it that he had given your son to the Furnivals to raise?''

"No! No—not at all. They had . . ." She shook her head, the tears running down her cheeks, and her voice cracking at last.

The judge leaned forward earnestly, his face full of concern.

Lovat-Smith rose, all the brilliant confidence drained away from him, only horror left.

"I hope my learned friend is not going to try to cloud the issue and cause this poor woman quite pointless distress?" He turned from Rathbone to Damaris. "The physical facts of the case place it beyond question that only Alexandra Carlyon had the opportunity to murder the general. Whatever Mrs. Erskine's motive, if indeed there were any, she did not commit the act." He turned around so that half his appeal was to the crowd. "Surely this exposure of a private grief is cruelly unnecessary?"

"I would not do it if it were," Rathbone said between his teeth, his eyes blazing. He swiveled around on his heel, presenting his back to Lovat-Smith. "Mrs. Erskine, you have just said you did not resent your brother's having given your son to the Furnivals. And yet when you came downstairs you were in a state of distress almost beyond your ability to control, and quite suddenly you exhibited a rage towards Maxim Furnival which was close to murderous in nature! You seem to be contradicting yourself!"

"I—I—saw . . ." Damaris closed her eyes so tightly it screwed up her face.

Peverell half rose in his seat.

Edith held both her hands to her face, knuckles clenched.

Alexandra was frozen.

Monk glanced up at the gallery and saw Maxim Furnival sitting rigid, his dark face puckered in puzzlement and ever-increasing apprehension. Beside him, Louisa was quite plainly furious.

Monk looked along at Hester, and saw the intense concentration in her as she turned sideways, her eyes fixed on

Damaris and her expression one of such wrenching pity that it jolted him at once with its familiarity and its strangeness. He tried to picture Hermione, and found the memory blurred. He found it hard to remember her eyes at all, and when he did, they were bland and bright, without capability of pain.

Rathbone moved a step closer to Damaris.

"I regret this profoundly, Mrs. Erskine, but too much depends upon it for me to allow any compassion for you to override my duty to Mrs. Carlyon—and to Cassian."

Damaris raised her head. "I understand. I knew that my brother Thaddeus was abused as a child. Like Buckie—Miss Buchan—I saw it once, by accident. I never forgot the look in his eyes, the way he behaved. I saw the same look in Valentine's face, and I knew he was abused too. I supposed at that time that it was his father—his adopted father—Maxim Furnival, who was doing it."

There was a gasp around the room and a rustle like leaves in the wind.

"Oh God! No!" Maxim shot to his feet, his face shock-white, his voice half strangled in his throat.

Louisa sat like stone.

Maxim swung around, staring at her, but she continued to look as if she had been transfixed.

"You have my utmost sympathy, Mr. Furnival," the judge said over the rising level of horror and anger from the crowd. "But you must refrain from interruption, nevertheless. But I would suggest to you that you consider obtaining legal counsel to deal with whatever may occur here. Now please sit down, or I shall be obliged to have the bailiff remove you."

Slowly, looking bemused and beaten, Maxim sat down again, turning helplessly to Louisa, who still sat immobile, as though too horrified to respond.

Up in the gallery Charles Hargrave grasped the rail as if he would break it with his hands.

Rathbone returned his attention to Damaris.

"You spoke in the past tense, Mrs. Erskine. You thought at the time it was Maxim Furnival. Has something happened to change your view?"

"Yes." A faint echo of the old flair returned, and the ghost of a smile touched her mouth and vanished. "My sister-in-law murdered my brother. And I believe it was because she discovered that he was abusing her son—and I believe mine also—although I have no reason to think she knew of that."

Lovat-Smith looked up at Alexandra, then rose to his feet as though reluctantly.

"That is a conclusion of the witness, my lord, and not a fact."

"That is true, Mr. Rathbone," the judge said gravely. "The jury will ignore that last statement of Mrs. Erskine's. It was her belief, and no more. She may conceivably have been mistaken; you cannot assume it is fact. And Mr. Rathbone, you deliberately led your witness into making that observation. You know better."

"I apologize, my lord."

"Proceed, Mr. Rathbone, and keep it relevant."

Rathbone inclined his head in acknowledgment, then with curious grace turned back to Damaris.

"Mrs. Erskine, do you *know* who abused Valentine Furnival?"

"No."

"You did not ask him?"

"No! No, of course not!"

"Did you speak of it to your brother?"

"No! No I didn't. I didn't speak of it to anyone."

"Not to your mother—or your father?"

"No—not to anyone."

"Were you aware that your nephew, Cassian Carlyon, was being abused?"

She flushed with shame and her voice was low and tight in her throat. "No. I should have been, but I thought it was just his grief at losing his father—and fear that his mother was responsible and he would lose her too." She looked up once at Alexandra with anguish. "I didn't spend as much time with him as I should have. I am ashamed of that. He seemed to prefer to be alone with his grandfather, or with my husband. I thought—I thought that was because it was his mother who killed his father, and he felt women . . ." She trailed off unhappily.

"Understandable," Rathbone said quietly. "But if you had spent time with him, you might have seen whether he too was abused—"

"Objection," Lovat-Smith said quickly. "All this speech of abuse is only conjecture: We do not know that it is anything beyond the sick imaginings of a spinster servant and a young girl in puberty, who both may have misunderstood things they saw, and whose fevered and ignorant minds leaped to hideous conclusions—quite erroneously."

The judge sighed. "Mr. Lovat-Smith's objection is literally correct, Mr. Rathbone." His heavy tone made it more than obvious he did not share the prosecutor's view for an instant. "Please be more careful in your use of words. You are quite capable of conducting your examination of Mrs. Erskine without such error."

Rathbone inclined his head in acceptance, and turned back to Damaris.

"Did your husband, Peverell Erskine, spend much time with Cassian after he came to stay at Carlyon House?"

"Yes—yes, he did." Her face was very white and her voice little more than a whisper.

"Thank you, Mrs. Erskine. I have no more questions for you, but please remain there. Mr. Lovat-Smith may have something to ask you."

Damaris turned to Lovat-Smith.

"Thank you," Lovat-Smith acknowledged. "Did you murder your brother, Mrs. Erskine?"

There was a ripple of shock around the room. The judge frowned sharply. A juror coughed. Someone in the gallery stood up.

Damaris was startled. "No—of course I didn't!"

"Did your sister-in-law mention this alleged fearful abuse to you, at any time, either before or after the death of your brother?"

"No."

"Have you any reason to suppose that such a thing had

405

ever entered her mind; other, of course, than the suggestion made to you by my learned friend, Mr. Rathbone?''

"Yes—Hester Latterly knew of it."

Lovat-Smith was taken by surprise.

There was a rustle and murmur of amazement around the court. Felicia Carlyon leaned forward over the gallery railing to stare down at where Hester was sitting upright, white-faced. Even Alexandra turned.

"I beg your pardon?" Lovat-Smith said, collecting his wits rapidly. "And who is Hester Latterly? Is that a name that has arisen once before in this case? Is she a relative—or a servant perhaps? Oh—I recall: she is the person to whom Mrs. Sobell enquired for a lawyer for the accused. Pray tell us, how did this Miss Latterly know of this deadly secret of your family, of which not even your mother was aware?"

Damaris stared straight back at him.

"I don't know. I did not ask her."

"But you accepted it as true?" Lovat-Smith was incredulous and he allowed his whole body to express his disbelief. "Is she an expert in the field, that you take her word, unsubstantiated by any fact at *all*, simply a blind statement, over your own knowledge and love and loyalty to your own family? That is truly remarkable, Mrs. Erskine."

There was a low rumble of anger from the court. Someone called out "Traitor!"

"Silence!" the judge ordered, his face hard. He leaned forward towards the witness stand. "Mrs. Erskine? It does call for some explanation. Who is this Miss Latterly that you take her unexplained word for such an abominable charge?"

Damaris was very pale and she looked across at Peverell before answering, and when she spoke it was to the jury, not to Lovat-Smith or the judge.

"Miss Latterly is a good friend who wishes to find the truth of this case, and she came to me with the knowledge, which has never been disputed, that I discovered something the evening of my brother's death which distressed me almost beyond bearing. She assumed it was something else, something which would have done a great injury to another person—so I was

406

obliged, in justice, to tell her the truth. Since she was correct in her assumption of abuse to Cassian, I did not argue with her, nor did I ask her how she knew. I was too concerned to allay her other suspicion even to think of it."

She straightened up a little more, for the first time perhaps, unconsciously looking heroic. "And as for loyalty to my family, are you suggesting I should lie, here, in this place, and under oath to God, in order to protect them from the law—and the consequence of their acts towards a desperately vulnerable child? And that I should conceal truths which may help you bring justice to Alexandra?" There was a ring of challenge in her voice and her eyes were bright. Not once had she looked towards the gallery.

There was nothing for Lovat-Smith to do but retreat, and he did it gracefully.

"Of course not, Mrs. Erskine. All we required was that you should explain, and you have done so. Thank you—I have no more questions to ask you."

Rathbone half rose. "Nor I, my lord."

The judge released her. "You are excused, Mrs. Erskine."

The entire courtroom watched as she stepped down from the witness box, walked across the tiny space to the body of the court and up the steps through the seated crowd and took her place beside Peverell, who quite automatically rose to his feet to greet her.

There was a long sigh right around the room as she sat down.

Felicia deliberately ignored her. Randolf seemed beyond reaction. Edith reached a hand across and clasped hers gently.

The judge looked at the clock.

"Have you many questions for your next witness, Mr. Rathbone?"

"Yes, my lord; it is evidence on which a great deal may turn."

"Then we shall adjourn until tomorrow."

Monk left the court, pushing his way through the jostling, excited crowds, journalists racing to find the first hansoms

407

to take them to their papers, those who had been unable to find room inside shouting questions, people standing around in huddles, everyone talking.

Then outside on the steps he was uncertain whether to search for Hester or to avoid her. He had nothing to say, and yet he would have found her company pleasing. Or perhaps he would not. She would be full of the trial, of Rathbone's brilliance. Of course that was right, he was brilliant. It was even conceivable he would win the case, whatever winning might be. She had become increasingly fond of Rathbone lately. He realized it now with some surprise. He had not even thought about it before; it was something he had seen without its touching the conscious part of his mind.

Now he was startled and angry that it hurt.

He walked down the steps into the street with a sudden burst of energy. Everywhere there were people, newsboys, costermongers, flower sellers, men with barrows of sandwiches, pies, sweets, peppermint water, and a dozen other kinds of food. People pushed and shouted, calling for cabs.

This was absurd. He liked both Hester and Rathbone—he should be happy for them.

Without realizing what he was doing he bumped into a smart man in black with an ivory-topped cane, and stepped into a hansom ahead of him. He did not even hear the man's bellow of fury.

"Grafton Street," he commanded.

Then why was there such a heaviness inside him, a sense of loss all over again?

It must be Hermione. The disillusion over her would surely hurt for a long time; that was only natural. He had thought he had found love, gentleness, sweetness— Damn! Don't be idiotic! He did not want sweetness. It stuck in his teeth and cloyed his tongue. God in heaven! How far he must have forgotten his own nature to have imagined Hermione was his happiness. And now he was further betraying himself by becoming maudlin over it.

But by the time the cab set him down in Grafton Street some better, more honest self admitted there was a place for tenderness, the love that overlooks error, that cherishes weakness and protects it, that thinks of self last, and gives even when the thanks are slow in coming or do not come at all, for generosity of spirit, laughter without cruelty or victory. And he still had little idea where to find it—even in himself.

The first witness of the next day was Valentine Furnival. For all his height, and already broadening shoulders, he looked very young and his high head could not hide his fear.

The crowd buzzed with excitement as he climbed the steps of the witness stand and turned to face the court. Hester felt a lurch almost like sickness as she saw his face and recognized in it exactly what Damaris must have seen—an echo of Charles Hargrave.

Instinctively she turned her head to see if Hargrave was in the gallery again, and if he had seen the same thing, knowing now that Damaris was the boy's mother. As soon as she saw him, his skin white, his eyes shocked, almost unfocused, she knew beyond question that he understood. Beside him, Sarah Hargrave sat a little apart, facing first Valentine on the stand, then her husband next to her. She did not even try to seek Damaris Erskine.

In spite of herself, Hester was moved to pity; for Sarah it was easy, but for Hargrave it twisted and hurt, because it was touched with anger.

The judge began by questioning Valentine for a few moments about his understanding of the oath, then turned to Rathbone and told him to commence.

"Did you know General Thaddeus Carlyon, Valentine?" he asked quite conversationally, as if they had been alone in some withdrawing room, not in the polished wood of a courtroom with hundreds of people listening, craning to catch every word and every inflexion.

Valentine swallowed on a dry throat.

"Yes."

"Did you know him well?"

A slight hesitation. "Yes."

"For a long time? Do you know how long?"

"Yes, since I was about six: seven years or more."

"So you must have known him when he sustained th[e] knife injury to his thigh? Which happened in your home."

Not one person in the entire court moved or spoke. Th[e] silence was total.

"Yes."

Rathbone took a step closer to him.

"How did it happen, Valentine? Or perhaps I should say why?"

Valentine stared at him, mute, his face so pale it occurre[d] to Monk, watching him, that he might faint.

In the gallery Damaris leaned over the rail, her eyes des[-] perate. Peverell put his hand over hers.

"If you tell the truth," Rathbone said gently, "there is n[o] need to be afraid. The court will protect you."

The judge drew a breath, as if to protest, then ap[-] parently changed his mind.

Lovat-Smith said nothing.

The jury were motionless to a man.

"I stabbed him," Valentine said almost in a whisper.

In the second row from the front Maxim Furnival covere[d] his face with his hands. Beside him Louisa bit her nails[.] Alexandra put her hands over her mouth as if to stifle a cry[.]

"You must have had a very profound reason for such a[n] act," Rathbone prompted. "It was a deep wound. He coul[d] have bled to death, if it had severed an artery."

"I—" Valentine gasped.

Rathbone had miscalculated. He had frightened him to[o] much. He saw it immediately.

"But of course you did not," he said quickly. "It wa[s] merely embarrassing—and I'm sure painful."

Valentine looked wretched.

"Why did you do it, Valentine?" Rathbone said ver[y] gently. "You must have had a compelling reason—somethin[g] that justified striking out in such a way."

Valentine was on the edge of tears and it took him som[e] moments to regain his composure.

Monk ached for him, remembering his own youth, th[e]

desperate dignity of thirteen, the manhood which was so close, and yet so far away.

"Mrs. Carlyon's life may depend upon what you say," Rathbone urged.

For once neither Lovat-Smith nor the judge reproved him for such a breach.

"I couldn't bear it any longer," Valentine replied in a husky voice, so low the jury had to strain to hear him. "I begged him, but he wouldn't stop!"

"So in desperation you defended yourself?" Rathbone asked. His clear, precise voice carried in the silence, even though it was as low as if they were alone in a small room.

"Yes."

"Stop doing what?"

Valentine said nothing. His face was suddenly painfully hot as the blood rushed up, suffusing his skin.

"If it hurts too much to say, may I say it for you?" Rathbone asked him. "Was the general sodomizing you?"

Valentine nodded very slightly, just a bare inch or two movement of the head.

Maxim Furnival let out a stifled cry.

The judge turned to Valentine.

"You must speak, so that there can be no error in our understanding," he said with great gentleness. "Simply yes or no will do. Is Mr. Rathbone correct?"

"Yes sir." It was a whisper.

"I see. Thank you. I assure you, there will be no action taken against you for the injury to General Carlyon. It was self-defense and no crime in any sense. A person is allowed to defend their lives, or their virtue, with no fault attached whatever. You have the sympathy of all present here. We are outraged on your behalf."

"How old were you when this began?" Rathbone went on, after a brief glance at the judge, and a nod from him.

"Six—I think," Valentine answered. There was a long sigh around the room, and an electric shiver of rage. Damaris sobbed and Peverell held her. There was a swelling rumble of fury around the gallery and a juror groaned.

Rathbone was silent for a moment; it seemed he was too appalled to continue immediately.

"Six years old," Rathbone repeated, in case anyone had failed to hear. "And did it continue after you stabbed the general?"

"No—no, he stopped."

"And at that time his own son would be . . . how old?"

"Cassian?" Valentine swayed and caught hold of the railing. He was ashen.

"About six?" Rathbone asked, his voice hoarse.

Valentine nodded.

This time no one asked him to speak. Even the judge was white-faced.

Rathbone turned away and walked a pace or two, his hands in his pockets, before swinging around and looking up at Valentine again.

"Tell me, Valentine, why did you not appeal to your parents over this appalling abuse? Why did you not tell your mother? Surely that is the most natural thing for a small child to do when he is hurt and frightened? Why did you not do that in the beginning, instead of suffering all those years?"

Valentine looked down, his eyes full of misery.

"Could your mother not have helped you?" Rathbone persisted. "After all, the general was not your father. It would have cost them his friendship, but what was that worth, compared with you, her son? She could have forbidden him the house. Surely your father would have horsewhipped a man for such a thing?"

Valentine looked up at the judge, his eyes brimming with tears.

"You must answer," the judge said gravely. "Did your father abuse you also?"

"No!" There was no mistaking the amazement and the honesty in his voice and his startled face. "No! Never!"

The judge took a deep breath and leaned back a little, the shadow of a smile over his mouth.

"Then why did you not tell him, appeal to him to protect

412

you? Or to your mother. Surely she would have protected you.''

The tears brimmed over and ran down Valentine's cheeks unchecked.

"She knew." He choked and struggled for breath. "She told me not to tell anyone, especially Papa. She said it would . . embarrass him—and cost him his position."

There was a roar of rage around the room and a cry of 'Hang her!''

The judge called for order, banging his gavel, and it was several minutes before he could continue. "His position?" He frowned at Rathbone, uncomprehending. "What position?"

"He earns a great deal of money from army contracts," Valentine explained.

"Supplied by General Carlyon?"

"Yes sir."

"That is what your mother said? Be very sure you speak accurately, Valentine."

"Yes—she told me."

"And you are quite sure that your mother knew exactly what the general was doing to you? You did not fail to tell her the truth?"

"No! I did tell her!" He gulped, but his tears were beyond his control anymore.

The anger in the room was now so ugly it was palpable in the air.

Maxim Furnival sat upright, his face like a dead man's. Beside him, Louisa was motionless, her eyes stone-hard and hot, her mouth a thin line of hate.

"Bailiff," the judge said in a low voice. "You will take Louisa Furnival in charge. Appropriate dispositions will be made to care for Valentine in the future. For the moment perhaps it would be best he remain to comfort his father."

Obediently a large bailiff appeared, buttons gleaming, and forced his way through the rows to where Louisa still sat, face blazing white. With no ceremony, no graciousness at all, he half pulled her to her feet and took her, stumbling and

413

catching her skirts, back along the row and up the passage way out of the court.

Maxim started to his feet, then realized the futility of doing anything at all. It was an empty gesture anyway. His whole body registered his horror of her and the destruction of everything he had thought he possessed. His only concern was for Valentine.

The judge sighed. "Mr. Rathbone, have you anything further you feel it imperative you ask this witness?"

"No, my lord."

"Mr. Lovat-Smith?"

"No, my lord."

"Thank you. Valentine, the court thanks you for your honesty and your courage, and regrets having to subject you to this ordeal. You are free to go back to your father, and be of whatever comfort to each other you may."

Silently Valentine stepped down amid rustles and murmurs of compassion, and made his way to the stricken figure of Maxim.

"Mr. Rathbone, have you further witnesses to call?" the judge asked.

"Yes, my lord. I can call the bootboy at the Furnival house, who was at one point a drummer in the Indian army. He will explain why he dropped his linen and fled when coming face-to-face with General Carlyon in the Furnival house on the evening of the murder . . . if you believe it is necessary? But I would prefer not to—I imagine the court will understand."

"We do, Mr. Rathbone," the judge assured him. "Do not call him. We may safely draw the conclusion that he was startled and distressed. Is that sufficient for your purpose?"

"Yes, thank you, my lord."

"Mr. Lovat-Smith, have you objection to that? Do you wish the boy called so that you may draw from him a precise explanation, other than that which will naturally occur to the jury?"

"No, my lord," Lovat-Smith said immediately. "If the defense will stipulate that the boy in question can be proved to have served with General Thaddeus Carlyon?"

414

"Mr. Rathbone?"

"Yes, my lord. The boy's military record has been traced, [a]nd he did serve in the same immediate unit with General [C]arlyon."

"Then you have no need to call him, and subject him to [w]hat must be acutely painful. Proceed with your next wit[n]ess."

"I crave the court's permission to call Cassian Carlyon. [H]e is eight years old, my lord, and I believe he is of consid[er]able intelligence and aware of the difference between truth [an]d falsehood."

Alexandra shot to her feet. "No," she cried out. "No—[yo]u can't!"

The judge looked at her with grim pity.

"Sit down, Mrs. Carlyon. As the accused you are entitled [to] be present, as long as you conduct yourself appropriately. [B]ut if you interrupt the proceedings I will have to order your [re]moval. I should regret that; please do not make it neces[sa]ry."

Gradually she sank back again, her body shaking. On [ei]ther side of her two gray-dressed wardresses took her arms, [bu]t to assist, not to restrain.

"Call him, Mr. Rathbone. I will decide whether he is [co]mpetent to testify, and the jury will put upon his testimony [w]hat value they deem appropriate."

An official of the court escorted Cassian as far as the edge [o]f the room, but he crossed the small open space alone. He [w]as about four feet tall, very frail and thin, his fair hair neatly [b]rushed, his face white. He climbed up to the witness box [an]d peered over the railing at Rathbone, then at the judge.

There was a low mutter and sigh of breath around the [c]ourt. Several of the jurors turned to look where Alexandra [sa]t in the dock, as if transfixed.

"What is your name?" the judge asked Cassian quietly.

"Cassian James Thaddeus Randolf Carlyon, sir."

"Do you know why we are here, Cassian?"

"Yes sir, to hang my mother."

415

Alexandra bit her knuckles and the tears ran down her cheeks.

A juror gasped.

In the crowd a woman sobbed aloud.

The judge caught his breath and paled.

"No, Cassian, we are not! We are here to discover what happened the night your father died, and why it happened— and then to do what the law requires of us to deal justly with it."

"Are you?" Cassian looked surprised. "Grandma said you were going to hang my mother, because she is wicked. My father was a very good man, and she killed him."

The judge's face tightened. "Well just for now you must forget what your grandmother says, or anyone else, and tell us only what you know for yourself to be true. Do you understand the difference between truth and lies, Cassian?"

"Yes of course I do. Lying is saying what is not true, and it is a dishonorable thing to do. Gentlemen don't lie, and officers never do."

"Even to protect someone they love?"

"No sir. It is an officer's duty to tell the truth, or remain silent, if it is the enemy who asks."

"Who told you that?"

"My father, sir."

"He was perfectly correct. Now when you have taken the oath and promised to God that you will tell us the truth, I wish you either to speak exactly what you know to be true, or to remain silent. Will you do that?"

"Yes sir."

"Very well, Mr. Rathbone, you may swear your witness."

It was duly done, and Rathbone began his questions, standing close to the witness box and looking up.

"Cassian, you were very close to your father, were you not?"

"Yes sir," he answered with complete composure.

"Is it true that about two years ago he began to show his love for you in a new and different way, a very private way?"

416

Cassian blinked. He looked only at Rathbone. Never once had he looked up, either at his mother in the dock opposite, or at his grandparents in the gallery above.

"It cannot hurt him now for you to tell the truth," Rathbone said quite casually, as if it were of no particular importance. "And it is most urgent for your mother that you should be honest with us."

"Yes sir."

"Did he show his love for you in a new and very physical way, about two years ago?"

"Yes sir."

"A very private way?"

A hesitation. "Yes sir."

A sound of weeping came from the gallery. A man blasphemed with passionate anger.

"Did it hurt?" Rathbone asked very gravely.

"Only at first."

"I see. Did your mother know about this?"

"No sir."

"Why not?"

"Papa told me it was something women didn't understand, and I should never tell her." He took a deep breath and suddenly his composure dissolved.

"Why not?"

He sniffed. "He said she would stop loving me if she knew. But Buckie said she still loved me."

"Oh, Buckie is quite right," Rathbone said quickly, his own voice husky. "No woman could love her child more; I know that myself."

"Do you?" Cassian kept his eyes fixed on Rathbone, as if to prevent himself from knowing his mother was there, in case he looked at her and saw what he dreaded.

"Oh yes. I know your mother quite well. She has told me she would rather die than have you hurt. Look at her, and you will know it yourself."

Lovat-Smith started up from his seat, then changed his mind and subsided into it again.

Very slowly Cassian turned for the first time and looked at Alexandra.

A ghost of a smile forced itself across her features, but the pain in her face was fearful.

Cassian looked back at Rathbone.

"Yes sir."

"Did your father go on doing this—this new thing, right up until just before he died?"

"Yes sir."

"Did anyone else, any other man, ever do this to you?"

There was total silence except for a low sigh from somewhere at the back of the gallery.

"We know from other people that this is so, Cassian," Rathbone said. "You have been very brave and very honest so far. Please do not lie to us now. Did anyone else do this to you?"

"Yes sir."

"Who else, Cassian?"

He glanced at the judge, then back at Rathbone.

"I can't say, sir. I was sworn to secrecy, and a gentleman doesn't betray."

"Indeed," Rathbone said with a note of temporary defeat in his voice. "Very well. We shall leave the subject for now. Thank you. Mr. Lovat-Smith?"

Lovat-Smith rose and took Rathbone's place in front of the witness stand. He spoke to Cassian candidly, quietly, man to man.

"You kept this secret from your mother, you said?"

"Yes sir."

"You never told her, not even a little bit?"

"No sir."

"Do you think she knew about it anyway?"

"No sir, I never told her. I promised not to!" He watched Lovat-Smith as he had watched Rathbone.

"I see. Was that difficult to do, keep this secret from her?"

"Yes sir—but I did."

"And she never said anything to you about it, you are quite sure?"

"No sir, never."

"Thank you. Now about this other man. Was it one, or more than one? I am not asking you to give me names, just a number. That would not betray anyone."

Hester glanced up at Peverell in the gallery, and saw guilt in his face, and a fearful pity. But was the guilt for complicity, or merely for not having known? She felt sick in case it were complicity.

Cassian thought for a moment or two before replying.

"Two, sir."

"Two others?"

"Yes sir."

"Thank you. That is all. Rathbone?"

"No more, thank you, for now. But I reserve the right to recall him, if it will help discover who these other men are."

"I will permit that," the judge said quickly. "Thank you, Cassian. For the moment you may go."

Carefully, his legs shaking, Cassian climbed down the steps, only stumbling a little once, and then walked across the floor and disappeared out of the door with the bailiff. There was a movement around the court, murmurs of outrage and compassion. Someone called out to him. The judge started forward, but it was already done, and the words had been of encouragement. It was pointless to call order or have the offender searched for.

"I call Felicia Carlyon," Rathbone said loudly.

Lovat-Smith made no objection, even though she had not been in Rathbone's original list of witnesses and hence had been in the court all through the other testimony.

There was a rustle of response and anticipation. But the mood of the crowd had changed entirely. It was no longer pity which moved them towards her, but pending judgment.

She took the stand head high, body stiff, eyes angry and proud. The judge required that she unveil her face, and she did so with disdainful obedience. She swore the oath in a clear, ringing voice.

"Mrs. Carlyon," Rathbone began, standing in front of

419

her, "you appear here on subpoena. You are aware of the testimony that has been given so far."

"I am. It is wicked and malicious lies. Miss Buchan is an old woman who has served in my family's house for forty years, and has become deranged in her old age. I cannot think where a spinster woman gets such vile fancies." She made a gesture of disgust. "All I can suppose is that her natural instincts for womanhood have been warped and she has turned on men, who rejected her, and this is the outcome."

"And Valentine Furnival?" Rathbone asked. "He is hardly an elderly and rejected spinster. Nor a servant, old and dependent, who dare not speak ill of an employer."

"A boy with a boy's carnal fantasies," she replied. "We all know that growing children have feverish imaginations. Presumably someone did use him as he says, for which I have the natural pity anyone would. But it is wicked and irresponsible of him to say it was my son. I daresay it was his own father, and he wishes to protect him, and so charges another man, a dead man, who cannot defend himself."

"And Cassian?" Rathbone enquired with a dangerous edge to his voice.

"Cassian," she said, full of contempt. "A harassed and frightened eight-year-old. Good God, man! The father he adored has been murdered, his mother is like to be hanged for it—you put him on the stand in court, and you expect him to be able to tell you the truth about his father's love for him. Are you half-witted, man? He will say anything you force out of him. I would not condemn a cat on that."

"Presumably your husband is equally innocent?" Rathbone said with sarcasm.

"It is unnecessary even to say such a thing!"

"But you do say it?"

"I do."

"Mrs. Carlyon, why do you suppose Valentine Furnival stabbed your son in the upper thigh?"

"God alone knows. The boy is deranged. If his father has abused him for years, he might well be so."

"Possibly," Rathbone agreed. "It would change many

420

people. Why was your son in the boy's bedroom without his trousers on?''

''I beg your pardon?'' Her face froze.

''Do you wish me to repeat the question?''

''No. It is preposterous. If Valentine says so, then he is lying. Why is not my concern.''

''But Mrs. Carlyon, the wound the general sustained in his upper inside leg bled copiously. It was a deep wound, and yet his trousers were neither torn nor marked with blood. They cannot have been on him at the time.''

She stared at him, her expression icy, her lips closed.

There was a murmur through the crowd, a movement, a whisper of anger suddenly suppressed, and then silence again.

Still she did not speak.

''Let us turn to the question of your husband, Colonel Randolf Carlyon,'' Rathbone continued. ''He was a fine soldier, was he not? A man to be proud of. And he had great ambitions for his son: he also should be a hero, if possible of even higher rank—a general, in fact. And he achieved that.''

''He did.'' She lifted her chin and stared down at him with wide, dark blue eyes. ''He was loved and admired by all who knew him. He would have achieved even greater things had he not been murdered in his prime. Murdered by a jealous woman.''

''Jealous of whom, her own son?''

''Don't be absurd—and vulgar,'' she spat.

''Yes it is vulgar, isn't it,'' he agreed. ''But true. Your daughter Damaris knew it. She accidentally found them one day . . .''

''Nonsense!''

''And recognized it again in her own son, Valentine. Is she lying also? And Miss Buchan? And Cassian? Or are they all suffering from the same frenzied and perverted delusion—each without knowing the other, and in their own private hell?''

She hesitated. It was manifestly ridiculous.

''And you did not know, Mrs. Carlyon? Your husband abused your son for all those years, presumably until you

421

sent him as a boy cadet into the army. Was that why you sent him so young, to escape your husband's appetite?''

The atmosphere in the court was electric. The jury had expressions like a row of hangmen. Charles Hargrave looked ill. Sarah Hargrave sat next to him in body, but her heart was obviously elsewhere. Edith and Damaris sat side by side with Peverell.

Felicia's face was hard, her eyes glittering.

''Boys do go into the army young, Mr. Rathbone. Perhaps you do not know that?''

''What did your husband do then, Mrs. Carlyon? Weren't you afraid he would do what your son did, abuse the child of some friend?''

She stared at him in frozen silence.

''Or did you procure some other child for him, some bootboy, perhaps,'' he went on ruthlessly, ''who would be unable to retaliate—safe. Safe from scandal—and—'' He stopped, staring at her. She had gone so white as to appear on the edge of collapse. She gripped the railing in front of her and her body swayed. There was a long hiss from the crowd, an ugly sound, full of hate.

Lovat-Smith rose to his feet.

Randolf Carlyon let out a cry which strangled in his throat, and his face went purple. He gasped for breath and people on either side of him moved away, horrified and without compassion. A bailiff moved forward to him and loosened his tie roughly.

Rathbone would not let the moment go by.

''That is what you did, isn't it, Mrs. Carlyon?'' he pressed. ''You procured another child for your husband. Perhaps a succession of children—until you judged him too old to be a danger anymore. But you didn't protect your own grandson. You allowed him to be used as well. Why, Mrs. Carlyon? Why? Was your reputation really worth all that sacrifice, so many children's terrified, shamed and pitiful lives?''

She leaned forward over the rail, hate blazing in her eyes.

''Yes! Yes, Mr. Rathbone, it was! What would you expect me to do? Betray him to public humiliation? Ruin a great career: a man who taught others bravery in the face of the enemy, who went to battle with head high, never counting the odds against him. A man who inspired others to greatness—for what? An appetite? Men have appetites, they always have had. What was I to do—tell people?'' Her voice was thick with passionate contempt. She utterly ignored the snarls and hisses behind her.

''Tell whom? Who would have believed me? Who could I go to? A woman has no rights to her children, Mr. Rathbone. And no money. We belong to our husbands. We cannot even leave their houses without their permission, and he would never have given me that. Still less would he have allowed me to take my son.''

The judge banged his gavel and called for order.

Felicia's voice was shrill with rage and bitterness. ''Or would you have had me murder him—like Alexandra? Is that what you approve of? Every woman who suffers a betrayal or an indignity at her husband's hands, or whose child is hurt, belittled or humiliated by his father, should murder him?''

She leaned over the rail towards him, her voice strident, her face twisted. ''Believe me, there are a lot of other cruelties. My husband was gentle with his son, spent time with him, never beat him or sent him to bed without food. He gave him a fine education and started him on a great career. He had the love and respect of the world. Would you have me forfeit all that by making a wild, vile accusation no one would have believed anyway? Or end up in the dock—and on the rope's end—like her?''

''Was there nothing in between, Mrs. Carlyon?'' Rathbone said very softly. ''No more moderate course—nothing between condoning the abuse and murder?''

She stood silent, gray-faced and suddenly very old.

''Thank you,'' he said with a bleak smile, a baring of the teeth. ''That was my own conclusion too. Mr. Lovat-Smith?''

There was a sigh around the room, a long expelling of breath. The jury looked exhausted.

Lovat-Smith stood up slowly, as if he were now too tired to have any purpose in continuing. He walked over to the witness box, regarding Felicia long and carefully, then lowered his eyes.

"I have nothing to ask this witness, my lord."

"You are excused, Mrs. Carlyon," the judge said coldly. He opened his mouth as if to add something, then changed his mind.

Felicia came down the steps clumsily, like an old woman, and walked away towards the doors, followed by a silent and total condemnation.

The judge looked at Rathbone.

"Have you any further evidence to call, Mr. Rathbone?"

"I would like to recall Cassian Carlyon, my lord, if you please?"

"Is it necessary, Mr. Rathbone? You have proved your point."

"Not all of it, my lord. This child was abused by his father, and his grandfather, and by one other. I believe we must know who that other man was as well."

"If you can discover that, Mr. Rathbone, please do so. But I shall prevent you the moment you cause the child unnecessary distress. Do I make myself plain?"

"Yes, my lord, quite plain."

Cassian was recalled, small and pale, but again entirely composed.

Rathbone stepped forward.

"Cassian—your grandmother has just given evidence which makes it quite clear that your grandfather also abused you in the same manner. We do not need to ask you to testify on that point. However there was one other man, and we need to know who he is."

"No sir, I cannot tell you."

"I understand your reasons." Rathbone fished in his pocket and brought out an elegant quill knife with a black-enameled handle. He held it up. "Do you have a quill knife, something like this?"

Cassian stared at it, a pink flush staining his cheeks.

Hester glanced up at the gallery and saw Peverell look puzzled, but no more.

"Remember the importance of the truth," Rathbone warned. "Do you have such a knife?"

"Yes sir," Cassian answered uncertainly.

"And perhaps a watch fob? A gold one, with the scales of justice on it?"

Cassian swallowed. "Yes sir."

Rathbone pulled out a silk handkerchief from his pocket also.

"And a silk handkerchief too?"

Cassian was very pale. "Yes sir."

"Where did you get them, Cassian?"

"I . . ." He shut his eyes, blinking hard.

"May I help you? Did your uncle Peverell Erskine give them to you?"

Peverell rose to his feet, and Damaris pulled him back so violently he lost his balance.

Cassian said nothing.

"He did—didn't he?" Rathbone insisted. "And did he make you promise not to tell anyone?"

Still Cassian said nothing, but the tears brimmed over his eyes and rolled down his cheeks.

"Cassian—is he the other man who made love to you?"

There was a gasp from the gallery.

"No!" Cassian's voice was high and desperate, shrill with pain. "No! No, he isn't. I took those things! I stole them—because—because I wanted them."

In the dock Alexandra sobbed, and the wardress beside her held her shoulder with sudden, awkward gentleness.

"Because they are pretty?" Rathbone said with disbelief.

"No. No." Cassian's voice was still hard with anguish. "Because he was kind to me," Cassian cried. "He was the only one—who—who didn't do that to me. He was just—just my friend! I . . ." He sobbed helplessly. "He was my friend."

"Oh?" Rathbone affected disbelief still, although his own voice was harsh with pain. "Then if it was not Peverell Erskine, who was it? Tell me and I will believe you!"

"Dr. Hargrave!" Cassian sobbed, crumpling up and sliding down into the box in uncontrolled weeping at last. "Dr.

Hargrave! He did! He did it! I hate him! He did it! Don't let him go on! Don't let him! Uncle Pev, make them stop!''

There was a bellow of rage from the gallery. Two men seized Hargrave and held him before the bailiff could even move.

Rathbone strode over to the witness box and up the steps to help the child to his feet and put his arms around him. He half carried him out, and met Peverell Erskine down from the gallery and forcing his way past the bailiff and marching over the space in front of the lawyers' benches.

"Take him, and for God's sake look after him," Rathbone said passionately.

Peverell lifted the boy up and carried him out past the bailiffs and the crowd, Damaris at his heels. The door closed behind them to a great sigh from the crowd. Then immediately utter stillness fell again.

Rathbone turned to the judge.

"That is my case, my lord."

The clock went unregarded. No one cared what time it was, morning, luncheon or afternoon. No one was moving from their seats.

"Of course people must not take the life of another human being," Rathbone said as he rose to make his last plea, "no matter what the injury or the injustice. And yet what else was this poor woman to do? She has seen the pattern perpetuate itself in her father-in-law, her husband—and now her son. She could not endure it. The law, society—we—have given her no alternative but to allow it to continue—down the generations in never-ending humiliation and suffering—or to take the law into her own hands." He spoke not only to the jury, but to the judge as well, his voice thick with the certainty of his plea.

"She pleaded with her husband to stop. She begged him—and he disregarded her. Perhaps he could not help himself. Who knows? But you have seen how many people's lives have been ruined by this—this abomination: an appetite exercised with utter disregard for others."

He stared in front of him, looking at their pale, intent faces.

"She did not do it lightly. She agonized—she has nightmares that border on the visions of hell. She will never cease

426

to pay within herself for her act. She fears the damnation of God for it, but she will suffer that to save her beloved child from the torment of his innocence now—and the shame and despair, the guilt and terror of an adulthood like his father's—destroying his own life, and that of his future children—down the generations till God knows when!

"Ask yourselves, gentlemen, what would you have her do? Take the easier course, like her mother-in-law? Is that what you admire? Let it go on, and on, and on? Protect herself, and live a comfortable life, because the man also had good qualities? God almighty . . ." He stopped, controlling himself with difficulty. "Let the next generation suffer as she does? Or find the courage and make the abominable sacrifice of herself, and end it now?

"I do not envy you your appalling task, gentlemen. It is a decision no man should be asked to make. But you are—and I cannot relieve you of it. Go and make it. Make it with prayer, with pity, and with honor!

"Thank you."

Lovat-Smith came forward and addressed the jury, quiet, stating the law. His voice was subdued, wrung with pity, but the law must be upheld, or there would be anarchy. People must not seek murder as a solution, no matter what the injury.

It was left only for the judge to sum up, which he did gravely, using few words, and dismissing them to deliberate.

The jury returned a little after five in the evening, haggard, spent of all emotion, white-faced.

Hester and Monk stood side by side at the back of the crowded courtroom. Almost without being aware of it, he reached out and held her hand, and felt her fingers curl around his.

"Have you reached a verdict upon which you are agreed?" the judge asked.

"We have," the foreman replied, his voice awed.

"And is it the verdict of you all?"

"It is, my lord."

"And what is your verdict?"

He stood absolutely upright, his chin high, his eyes direct. "We find the accused, Alexandra Carlyon, not guilty of

427

murder, my lord—but guilty of manslaughter. And we ask may it please you, my lord, that she serve the least sentence the law allows.''

The gallery erupted in cheers and cries of jubilation. Someone cheered for Rathbone, and a woman threw roses.

In the front row Edith and Damaris hugged each other and then as one turned to Miss Buchan beside them and flung their arms around her. For a moment she was too startled to react, then her face curved into a smile and she held them equally close.

The judge raised his eyebrows very slightly. It was a perverse verdict. She had quite plainly committed murder, in the heat of the moment, but legally murder.

But a jury cannot be denied. It was the verdict of them all and they each one faced forward and looked at him without blinking.

''Thank you,'' he said very quietly indeed. ''You are discharged of your duty.'' He turned to Alexandra.

''Alexandra Elizabeth Carlyon, a jury of your peers has found you not guilty of murder, but of manslaughter—and has appealed for mercy on your behalf. It is a perverse verdict, but one with which I have the utmost sympathy. I hereby sentence you to six months' imprisonment; and the forfeit of all your goods and properties, which the law requires. However, since the bulk of your husband's estate goes to your son, that is of little moment to you. May God have mercy on you, and may you one day find peace.''

Alexandra stood in the dock, her body thin, ravaged by emotion, and the tears at last spilled over and ran in sweet, hot release down her face.

Rathbone stood with his own eyes brimming over, unable to speak.

Lovat-Smith rose and shook him by the hand.

At the back of the courtroom Monk moved a little closer to Hester.

1

W<small>HEN SHE FIRST</small> came into the room, Monk
thought it would simply be another case of domestic petty
theft, or investigating the character prospects of some suitor.
Not that he would have refused such a task; he could not
afford to. Lady Callandra Daviot, his benefactress, would
provide sufficient means to see that he kept his lodgings and
ate at least two meals a day, but both honor and pride neces-
sitated that he take every opportunity that offered itself to
earn his own way.

This new client was well dressed, her bonnet neat and
pretty. Her wide crinoline skirts accentuated her waist and
slender shoulders, and made her look fragile and very young,
although she was close to thirty. Of course the current fashion tended to do that for all women, but the illusion was
powerful, and it still woke in most men a desire to protect
and a certain rather satisfying feeling of gallantry.

"Mr. Monk?" she inquired tentatively. "Mr. William
Monk?"

He was used to people's nervousness when first approaching him. It was not easy to engage an inquiry agent. Most
matters about which one would wish such steps taken were
of their very nature essentially private.

Monk rose to his feet and tried to compose his face into

an expression of friendliness without overfamiliarity. It wa
not easy for him; neither his features nor his personality ler
itself to it.

"Yes ma'am. Please be seated." He indicated one of th
two armchairs, a suggestion to the decor of his rooms mad
by Hester Latterly, his sometimes friend, sometimes antag
onist, and frequent assistant, whether he wished it or no
However, this particular idea, he was obliged to admit, ha
been a good one.

Still gripping her shawl about her shoulders, the woma
sat down on the very edge of the chair, her back ramro
straight, her fair face tense with anxiety. Her narrow, beau
tiful hazel eyes never left his.

"How may I help you?" He sat on the chair opposite he
leaning back and crossing his legs comfortably. He had bee
in the police force until a violent difference of opinion ha
precipitated his departure. Brilliant, acerbic and at time
ruthless, Monk was not used to setting people at their eas
or courting their custom. It was an art he was learning wit
great difficulty, and only necessity had made him attempt
at all.

She bit her lip and took a deep breath before plunging in

"My name is Julia Penrose, or I should say more co
rectly, Mrs. Audley Penrose. I live with my husband and m
younger sister just south of the Euston Road . . ." Sh
stopped, as if his knowledge of the area might matter an
she had to assure herself of it.

"A very pleasant neighborhood." He nodded. It mear
she probably had a house of moderate size, a garden of som
sort, and kept at least two or three servants. No doubt it wa
a domestic theft, or a suitor for the sister about whom sh
entertained doubts.

She looked down at her hands, small and strong in thei
neat gloves. For several seconds she struggled for words.

His patience broke.

"What is it that concerns you, Mrs. Penrose? Unless yo
tell me, I cannot help."

"Yes, yes I know that," she said very quietly. "It is no

easy for me, Mr. Monk. I realize I am wasting your time, and I apologize. . . ."

"Not at all," he said grudgingly.

She looked up, her face pale but a flash of humor in her eyes. She made a tremendous effort. "My sister has been . . . molested, Mr. Monk. I wish to know who was responsible."

So it was not a petty matter after all.

"I'm sorry," he said gently, and he meant it. He did not need to ask why she had not called the police. The thought of making such a thing public would crush most people beyond bearing. Society's judgment of a woman who had been sexually assaulted, to whatever degree, was anything from prurient curiosity to the conviction that in some way she must have warranted such a fate. Even the woman herself, regardless of the circumstances, frequently felt that in some unknown way she was to blame, and that such things did not happen to the inncoent. Perhaps it was people's way of coping with the horror it engendered, the fear that they might become similar victims. If it were in some way the woman's own fault, then it could be avoided by the just and the careful. The answer was simple.

"I wish you to find out who it was, Mr. Monk," she said again, looking at him earnestly.

"And if I do, Mrs. Penrose?" he asked. "Have you thought what you will do then? I assume from the fact that you have not called the police that you do not wish to prosecute?"

The fair skin of her face became even paler. "No, of course not," she said huskily. "You must be aware of what such a court case would be like. I think it might be even worse than the—the event, terrible as that must have been." She shook her head. "No—absolutely not! Have you any idea how people can be about. . . ."

"Yes," he said quickly. "And also the chances of a conviction are not very good, unless there is considerable injury. Was your sister injured, Mrs. Penrose?"

Her eyes dropped and a faint flush crept up her cheeks.

433

"No, no, she was not—not in any way that can now be proved." Her voice sank even lower. "If you understand me? I prefer not to . . . discuss—it would be indelicate . . ."

"I see." And indeed he did. He was not sure whether he believed the young woman in question had been assaulted, or if she had told her sister that she had in order to explain a lapse in her own standards of mortality. But already he felt a definite sympathy with the woman here in front of him. Whatever had happened, she now faced a budding tragedy.

She looked at him with hope and uncertainty. "Can you help us, Mr. Monk? 'Least—at least as long as my money lasts? I have saved a little from my dress allowance, and I can pay you up to twenty pounds in total." She did not wish to insult him, and embarrass herself, and she did not know how to avoid either.

He felt an uncharacteristic lurch of pity. It was not a feeling which came to him easily. He had seen so much suffering, almost all of it more violent and physical than Julia Penrose's, and he had long ago exhausted his emotions and built around himself a shell of anger which preserved his sanity. Anger drove him to action; it could be exorcised and leave him drained at the end of the day, and able to sleep.

"Yes, that will be quite sufficient," he said to her. "I should be able either to discover who it is or tell you that it is not possible. I assume you have asked your sister, and she has been unable to tell you?"

"Yes indeed," she responded. "And naturally she finds it difficult to recall the event—nature assists us in putting from our minds that which is too dreadful to bear."

"I know," he said with a harsh, biting humor she would never comprehend. It was barely a year ago, in the summer of 1856, just at the close of the war in the Crimea, that he had been involved in a coaching accident and woken in the narrow gray cot of a hospital, cold with terror that it might be the workhouse and knowing nothing of himself at all, not even his name. Certainly it was the crack to his head which had brought it on, but as fragments of memory had returned, snatches here and there, there was still a black horror which

434

held most of it from him, a dread of learning the unbearable. Piece by piece he had rediscovered something of himself. Still, most of it was unknown, guessed at, not remembered. Much of it had hurt him. The man who emerged was not easy to like and he still felt a dark fear about things he might yet discover: acts of ruthlessness, ambition, brilliance without mercy. Yes, he knew all about the need to forget what the mind or the heart could not cope with.

She was staring at him, her face creased with puzzlement and growing concern.

He recalled himself hastily. "Yes of course, Mrs. Penrose. It is quite natural that your sister should have blanked from her memory an event so distressing. Did you tell her you intended coming to see me?"

"Oh yes," she said quickly. "It would be quite pointless to attempt to do it behind her back, so to speak. She was not pleased, but she appreciates that it is by far the best way." She leaned a little farther forward. "To be frank, Mr. Monk, I believe she was so relieved I did not call the police that she accepted it without the slightest demur."

It was not entirely flattering, but catering to his self-esteem was something he had not been able to afford for some time.

"Then she will not refuse to see me?" he said aloud.

"Oh no, although I would ask you to be as considerate as possible." She colored faintly, raising her eyes to look at him very directly. There was a curiously firm set to her slender jaw. It was a very feminine face, very slight-boned, but by no means weak. "You see, Mr. Monk, that is the great difference between you and the police. Forgive my discourtesy in saying so, but the police are public servants and the law lays down what they must do about the investigation. You, on the other hand, are paid by me, and I can request you to stop at any time I feel it the best moral decision, or the least likely to cause profound hurt. I hope you are not angry that I should mark that distinction?"

Far from it. Inwardly he was smiling. It was the first time he felt a spark of quite genuine respect for Julia Penrose.

"I take your point very nicely, ma'am," he answered,

rising to his feet. "I have a duty both moral and legal to report a crime if I have proof of one, but in the case of rape—I apologize for such an ugly word, but I assume it is rape we are speaking of?"

"Yes," she said almost inaudibly, her discomfort only too apparent.

"For that crime it is necessary for the victim to make a complaint and to testify, so the matter will rest entirely with your sister. Whatever facts I learn will be at her disposal."

"Excellent." She stood up also and the hoops of her huge skirt settled into place, making her once more look fragile. "I assume you will begin immediately?"

"This afternoon, if it will be convenient to see your sister then? You did not tell me her name."

"Marianne—Marianne Gillespie. Yes, this afternoon will be convenient."

"You said that you had saved from your dress allowance what seems to be a considerable sum. Did this happen some time ago?"

"Ten days," she replied quickly. "My allowance is paid quarterly. I had been circumspect, as it happens, and most of it was left from the last due date."

"Thank you, but you do not owe me an accounting, Mrs. Penrose. I merely needed to know how recent was the offense."

"Of course I do not. But I wish you to know that I am telling you the absolute truth, Mr. Monk. Otherwise I cannot expect you to help me. I trust you, and I require that you should trust me."

He smiled suddenly, a gesture which lit his face with charm because it was so rare, and so totally genuine. He found himself liking Julia Penrose more than he had anticipated from her rather prim and exceedingly predictable appearance—the huge hooped skirts so awkward to move in and so unfunctional, the neat bonnet which he loathed, the white gloves and demure manner. It had been a hasty judgment, a practice which he despised in others and even more in himself.

"Your address?" he said quickly.

"Number fourteen, Hastings Street," she replied.

"One more question. Since you are making these arrangements yourself, am I to assume that your husband is unaware of them?"

She bit her lip and the color in her cheeks heightened. "You are. I should be obliged if you would be as discreet as possible."

"How shall I account for my presence, if he should ask?"

"Oh." For a moment she was disconcerted. "Will it not be possible to call when he is out? He attends his business every weekday from nine in the morning until, at the earliest, half past four. He is an architect. Sometimes he is out considerably later."

"It will be, I expect, but I would prefer to have a story ready in case we are caught out. We must at least agree on our explanations."

She closed her eyes for a moment. "You make it sound so . . . deceitful, Mr. Monk. I have no wish to lie to Mr. Penrose. It is simply that the matter is so distressing, it would be so much pleasanter for Marianne if he did not know. She has to continue living in his house, you see?" She stared up at him suddenly with fierce intensity. "She has already suffered the attack. Her only chance of recovering her emotions, her peace of mind, and any happiness at all, will lie in putting it all behind her. How can she do that if every time she sits down at the table she knows that the man opposite her is fully aware of her shame? It would be intolerable for her!"

"But you know, Mrs. Penrose," he pointed out, although even as he said it he knew that was entirely different.

A smile flickered across her mouth. "I am a woman, Mr. Monk. Need I explain to you that that brings us closer in a way you cannot know. Marianne will not mind me. With Audley it would be quite different, for all his gentleness. He is a man, and nothing can alter that."

There was no possible comment to make on such a statement.

"What would you like to tell him to explain my presence?" he asked.

"I—I am not sure." She was momentarily confused, but she gathered her wits rapidly. She looked him up and down: his lean, smooth-boned face with its penetrating eyes and wide mouth, his elegant and expensively dressed figure. He still had the fine clothes he had bought when he was a senior inspector in the Metropolitan Police with no one to support but himself, before his last and most dreadful quarrel with Runcorn.

He waited with a dry amusement.

Evidently she approved what she saw. "You may say we have a mutual friend and you are calling to pay your respects to us," she replied decisively.

"And the friend?" He raised his eyebrows. "We should be agreed upon that."

"My cousin Albert Finnister. He is short and fat and lives in Halifax where he owns a woolen mill. My husband has never met him, nor is ever likely to. That you may not know Yorkshire is beside the point. You may have met him anywhere you choose, except London. Audley would wonder why he had not visited us."

"I have some knowledge of Yorkshire," Monk replied, hiding his smile. "Halifax will do. I shall see you this afternoon, Mrs. Penrose."

"Thank you. Good day, Mr. Monk." And with a slight inflection of her head she waited while he opened the door for her, then took her leave, walking straight-backed, head high, out into Fitzroy Street and north towards the square, and in a hundred yards or so, the Euston Road.

Monk closed the door and went back to his office room. He had lately moved here from his old lodgings around the corner in Grafton Street. He had resented Hester's interference in suggesting the move in her usual high-handed manner, but when she had explained her reasons, he was obliged to agree. In Grafton Street his rooms were up a flight of stairs and to the back. His landlady had been a motherly soul, but not used to the idea of his being in private practice and un-

438

willing to show prospective clients up. Also they were obliged to pass the doors of other residents, and occasionally to meet them on the stairs or the hall or landing. This arrangement was much better. Here a maid answered the door without making her own inquiries as to people's business and simply showed them in to Monk's very agreeable ground-floor sitting room. Grudgingly at first, he conceded it was a marked improvement.

Now to prepare to investigate the rape of Miss Marianne Gillespie, a delicate and challenging matter, far more worthy of his mettle then petty theft or the reputation of an employee or suitor.

take them to their camps, those who had been unable to